CATHY KELLY

Always and Forever

HARPER

Harper
An Imprint of HarperCollins*Publishers*
77–85 Fulham Palace Road,
Hammersmith, London W6 8JB

www.harpercollins.co.uk

This edition produced exclusively for
Woman & Home 2008

A catalogue record for this book
is available from the British Library

ISBN 978-000-784088-5

Set in Sabon by Palimpsest Book Production Limited,
Grangemouth, Stirlingshire

Printed and bound in Great Britain by
Clays Ltd, St Ives plc

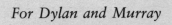

For Dylan and Murray

PROLOGUE

The woman stood as still as the mountains around her, taking in the view from Mount Carraig House – the windswept, overgrown gardens and the ragged path leading down to the small lake. Behind her towered Mount Carraig itself. Rob, the estate agent, had told her that 'Carraig' meant 'rock' in Irish, and that's exactly what Mount Carraig was: a spectacular rock dominating a smaller range of mountains known as the Four Sisters, which swelled to the southwest.

Spread out before her lay Carrickwell, the bustling market town that took its name from the mountain. It was bisected by the silver line of the River Tullow, and from here, high up, she could make out the gently winding main street, the sprawl of houses, shops, parks and schools, and the medieval cathedral at the centre.

A quarter of a century before, Carrickwell had been a sleepy backwater, within reach of Dublin but still very much a rural community. Time and the price of houses in the city had turned it into a busier town, but the air of tranquillity had remained.

Some said this was because of the ancient ley lines that crossed it. Druids, early Christians, religious refugees – all in their turn had come to Carrickwell and set up home in the benevolent shadow of Mount Carraig where they could seek refuge and thrive on the pure mountain spring water.

On a slope to the left of the mountain were the ruins of a Cistercian monastery, now a honey pot for tourists, watercolour painters and scholars. There was also the remains of a round tower where the monks had raced up rope ladders to safety when invaders came.

Across the town, near the pretty but slightly crumbling Willow Hotel, was a small stone circle that archaeologists believed to be the site of a druidic settlement. Mystical Fires, a small shop in the town that sold all manner of alternative artefacts, from crystals

1

and tarot cards to dream catchers and angel pins, did a roaring trade in books about the druids at midsummer.

At Christmas, visitors drifted unconsciously away from Mystical Fires to The Holy Land, a little Christian bookshop, where they could buy recordings of Gregorian chant, as well as prayer books, delicate Hummel Holy Water fonts, and the shop's speciality, mother-of-pearl rosary beads.

The respective owner of each shop, a pair of lovely septuagenarian ladies, each devout in her chosen creed, didn't mind in the slightest that their businesses waxed and waned in this manner.

'The wheel of fortune turns in its own way,' said Zara from Mystical Fires.

'God knows what's best for us,' agreed Una from The Holy Land.

With all the spiritual vibes, there was a great sense of peace hovering over Carrickwell and it drew people to the town.

It was certainly this aura that had drawn Leah Meyer to Mount Carraig House on a cold September morning.

Despite a thick woollen jumper under her old ski jacket, Leah could feel the chill sneaking into her body. She was used to the dry heat of California, where cold weather meant 68 degrees Fahrenheit, and the possibility of using less sunscreen. Here, the climate was so different and the unaccustomed cold made her feel achey. I'm beginning to feel my age, she thought, shivering, though she knew everyone marvelled at how young she looked.

She'd taken good care of herself over the years, but time had marched on and, eventually, no cream could keep away its mark. It had taken a discreet eye and brow lift a few years ago to give her back the finely sculpted face she'd been born with. Sixty really could be the new forty, Leah smiled to herself – as long as you had the right plastic surgeon.

And she could put up with the aching joints for a while because she'd finally found it, the place she had been looking for for years in which to build her spa. Carrickwell and Mount Carraig House were perfect. And in that state of mind, she didn't feel the air as cold, but as pure and cleansing.

'Calm,' she said finally, turning to the estate agent, who was standing a polite distance away. 'That's the word I was looking for. Don't you feel instantly calm when you stand here?'

Rob, the estate agent, studied the tumbling wreck that was Mount Carraig House and wondered whether it was he who needed his head examining or whether it was the elegant American visitor. All he saw was a ruin in a wilderness that had been on his agency's books for four years with ne'er a sniff of serious interest from anyone.

A few people had come to look, all right, drawn by the lyrical description written by a one-time employee who had a definite flair for making a silk purse out of the proverbial pig's ear.

This elegant eighteenth-century family house, once home to the famous Delaneys of Carrickwell, is designed in the grand classical style and boasts the fabulous high-ceilinged rooms of the period. The sweeping gravel drive and the great portico are reminiscent of a romantic era of horse-drawn carriages, while the abundant formal rose gardens, sheltered from the mountain breezes, need only a skilled gardener's hands to bring them back to their former glory. The views of the fierce beauty of Mount Carraig and the valley below are unrivalled, and a stately rhododendron walk, planted over a hundred years ago, leads down to the majestic Lough Enla.

The blarney had worked its magic on Mrs Meyer, for sure, because she'd seen the house on the firm's website and now, here she was, clearly captivated. Rob could tell when clients liked a place: they stopped noticing him and noticed only the property, imagining their furniture in the rooms and their family's laughter echoing in the garden. This woman showed all the signs of being besotted. He knew she had money too, because she'd arrived in a sleek black chauffeur-driven car from the airport. It had to be saidshe didn't dress like a millionaire – she wore jeans, a very ordinary blue padded coat, simple soft cream pumps and no jewellery.

It was hard to work out how old she was. Rob liked to put a date to property and people: eighteenth-century house; 'seventies bungalow; forty-something rich businessman buyer. But this woman's age eluded him. Elegantly slim, with silky chestnut hair and big dark eyes, she could have been anything from thirty to sixty. Her olive skin was unlined and glowing, and she looked so happy within herself. Early forties, perhaps ...

'I love the house,' Leah said, because there was no point beating around the bush. 'I'll take it.' She clasped Rob's hand and smiled. Now that she'd made the decision, she felt peace flooding through her.

She'd felt tired for so long, but already she was impatient to start work. Mount Carraig Spa? The Spa on the Rock? The name would come to her. A name suggestive of a haven, not a place where bored women would have their toes painted and men could do a few lengths in the pool and hope they were staving off the onslaught of Father Time.

No. Her spa would be about making people feel good from the inside out. It would be a place where people would come when

3

they were exhausted, drained and didn't know where else to go. They could swim in the pool and forget about everything, they could lie on the massage mat and feel their worries drain away along with their aches. With the refreshing water from the mountain running past the door, and the tranquil vibes of Carrickwell in the air, they would be revitalised and healed.

The magic of a similar place had once given her back some semblance of peace and serenity. Cloud's Hill had been its name, from the ancient American Indian name for the hill on which it had been built, and suddenly Leah realised that the same name would be perfect here.

The other Cloud's Hill, where she'd learned to enjoy life again, was a world away from here, but there was magic in this place too, she knew it. And with this spa she could do for other people what the original Cloud's Hill had done for her. Giving something back was her way of saying thanks, and setting up the spa was what she'd dreamed of for years, but had never found the perfect place to do so before. And, she calculated, if she started the work straightaway, the spa would be open within a year – or a year and a half at the latest.

'You . . . you mean you'll buy the house?' said Rob, shocked at the speed of the decision.

Leah's face was serene. 'I will,' she said softly.

'This calls for a drink,' said Rob, relief washing over him. 'On me.'

CHAPTER ONE

January, a year and a half later.

Mel Redmond dumped her fake Italian leather briefcase onto the cubicle floor, pushed the loo seat down with a loud clang, sat on it and began trying to rip the cellophane from the packet of ten-denier barely blacks. Haste made her clumsy. Damn packet. Was everything childproof?

Finally, the packet yielded and the tights unfolded in a long, expensively silky skein. The convenience store beside Lorimar Health Insurance was out of black and barely black sheers – ridiculous really, given that the store was bang in the centre of Dublin's office-land – so Mel had had to rush to the upmarket boutique beside the bank and shell out a whopping €16 for a pair. She would get a ladder in her tights on a day when the firm's chief executive was addressing the troops.

Years in public relations had taught Mel one of the central tenets of the working woman: look great and people notice you; look sloppy and they notice the sloppy part, whether it was smudged eyeliner, chipped nail polish or *omigod, look at her roots!*

Anyway, Hilary, head of Lorimar's publicity and marketing departments and Mel's boss, would probably turn chalk white under her Elizabeth Arden foundation if Mel committed the crime of turning up at the meeting with ripped tights.

Mel joked that Hilary was the person she wanted to be when she grew up: always organised, as opposed to doing her best to *look* organised, and with an emergency supply of headache tablets, tights and perfume in her briefcase, which was real Italian leather.

Mel's fake one contained her own emergency supplies of half a chocolate bar, a tampon with the plastic ripped off, one fluffy para-cetamol, several uncapped pens and a tiny toddler box of raisins so desiccated they now resembled something from Tutankhamen's tomb. Raisins were great for snacks, according to the toddler-feeding bibles, but Mel had discovered that chocolate buttons were far better for warding off tantrums in the supermarket at home in Carrickwell.

'Score another black mark for being a terrible mother,' Mel liked to joke to her colleague in marketing, Vanessa. They joked a lot about being bad mothers although they'd have killed anyone who'd actually called them such.

When you were a working mum, you had to joke about the very thing you were afraid of, Mel said. Her life was dedicated to making sure that two-and-a-half-year-old Carrie and four-year-old Sarah didn't suffer because she went out to work. If she could possibly help it, nobody would ever be able to describe Mel Redmond as lacking in anything she did.

She loved her job at Lorimar, was highly focused and had once vowed to be one of the company's publicity directors by the time she was forty.

Two children had changed all of that. Or perhaps Mel had changed as a result of having two children. Like the chicken and the egg, she was never quite sure which had come first.

The upshot was that she was now forty, the publicity directorship was a goal that had moved further away instead of closer, and she was struggling to keep all the balls in the air. As motherhood made her boobs drop, it made her ambition slide as well.

'When I grow up, I want to be a business lady with an office and a briefcase,' the eleven-year-old Mel had written in a school essay.

'Aren't you the clever girl?' her dad had said when she came home with the essay prize. 'Look at this,' he told the rest of his family proudly at the next big get-together, holding up the copy book filled with Mel's neat, sloping writing. 'She's a chip off the old block, our little Melanie. Brains to burn.'

Mel's dad would have gone to university except that there hadn't been enough money. It was a great joy to him to see his daughter's potential.

'Don't you want to get married at all?' asked Mel's grandmother in surprise. 'If you get married you can have a lovely home, with babies, and be very happy.'

Mel, who liked the parts of history lessons where girls got to fight instead of stay home and mind the house, simply asked: 'Why?'

Her father still thought it was hilarious, and regularly recounted the story of how his Melanie, even as a child, had her heart set on a career.

Mel loved him for being so proud of her, but she'd grown to hate that story. As a kid, she'd assumed that being smart meant you could have it all. She knew better now.

These days she had two jobs, motherhood and career, and even if everyone else thought she was coping, she felt as if she wasn't doing either of them right. Mel's standards – for herself – were staggeringly high.

The third part of the trinity, marriage, wasn't something she had time to work on. It was just freewheeling along with its own momentum.

'How does a working mother know when her partner has had an orgasm?' went a recent email from an old college pal. 'He phones home to tell her.'

It was the funniest thing Mel had heard for a long time, funny in an hysterical, life-raft-with-a-hole-in-it sort of way. But she couldn't share the joke with anyone, especially her husband, Adrian, in case he remarked how accurate it was.

In their household, lovemaking occupied the same level of importance as time spent with each other (nil) and long baths with aromatherapy products to reduce stress (also nil).

Mel's fervent hope was that if she kept quiet and jollied the house along, cheerily smiling at Adrian, Carrie and Sarah, then nobody would notice the places where her love and attention were spread thin.

'Delegate, have some me-time and don't let your family expect you to be superwoman,' cooed magazine articles about the stress of the working mother.

After her years working with journalists, Mel knew that these articles were written by one of two types: glamorous young women in offices for whom the notion of children was a distant one; or working mothers who were freelancing at the kitchen table in between picking up the children from school, having long since realised that you couldn't do it all, but were making a decent living telling people you could.

Me-time? What the hell was me-time? And how could you delegate the housework/weekly shop to a pair of under-fives and a man who didn't know how to check can labels for sodium content or benzoates?

She ripped her laddered tights off and stuffed them into her bag before struggling into the new ones. With one last tug at the tourniquet-tight bit cutting into her thigh, she smoothed down the fabric of her plum-coloured skirt – last season Zara, designed to look like Gucci – and raced out of the loo to the mirrors, where she hastily combed her short blonde hair with her fingers. Her roots had grown beyond the boundaries of good taste and were teetering on the line between funky and couldn't be bothered. Another task for her list.

At least she didn't look forty yet, which was handy, because she had neither the time nor the money for Botox. Looking younger than she was had been hell when she was eighteen, looked four years younger and had to produce her student card to get into grown-up films. Now, two children and endless sleepless nights later, it was a blessing.

Nature had given Mel a small face with a pointed chin, pale skin and arched brows above almond-shaped eyes the same clear blue as the sky after a storm, with hints of violet around the pupils. Maybelline New York had given her thick black lashes and kiss-proof cherry lipstain that would survive a nuclear attack. A sense of humour meant she had plenty of smile lines around her mouth and she didn't think she could stand the pain of doing anything about them. After her second labour, the one that had required the rubber ring for a week, she'd gone right off the idea of any sort of delicate stitching.

She looked at her watch. It was five past ten. Damn, damn, damn. Late. Too late for the lift. She galloped up the stairs, managing to find her lipgloss as she ran.

Edmund Moriarty, the chief executive of Lorimar Health Insurance, had just taken his seat at the top of the big conference room but there was still a mild hum of conversation, allowing Mel to slip in and make her way to a free seat on the left.

One of the biggest health insurance companies in the country, Lorimar had been a market leader for twenty years, but lots of new international firms were now on the scene and business was tough. Today's gathering was a strategy meeting about how Lorimar could face the increased threat of competition.

Normally, strategy meetings were for high-level executives, and someone like Mel, who was one of the company's four publicity managers, wouldn't have been invited. But this was a 'cheer up the team' meeting, 'to remind us that we're still tops,' as Hilary said, so lesser beings were there today with the firm's big-hitters. Privately, Mel thought that the only things that would cheer up the Lorimar team were a pay rise and bringing in that Calvin Klein underwear model as post boy. She just thanked God it was merely a meeting today instead of paintballing in the back of beyond, which had been last year's concept of team-building. Those paint balls bruised like hell.

Edmund Moriarty tapped his microphone to gain everybody's attention and all heads snapped round in his direction.

'How do we go forward? – that is the question,' he began, his voice gravelly. 'Lorimar is the market leader but stiff competition means we must keep striving.'

The seventy people in the room listened carefully. Mel took a pad of paper from her attaché case and uncapped the onyx and gold pen her parents had given her for her fortieth birthday. Although she dated the top piece of paper and kept her gaze on the boss, her mind was on the second sheet of paper. The top sheet was ready to be covered with gems of wisdom from the chief executive so that it looked as if she was paying attention. The other was the list of things Mel had to achieve that day – a day that was diminishing as Edmund pontificated to everyone about what they already knew. The list read:

Speech for Publicity Forum lunch.
Go over brochure photos with fine-tooth comb.
Phone *Sentinel* journalist *re* psychiatric case.
Pick up nappies, wipes and vegetables. Chicken, beans and
    kids' yogurts.
Talk to Adrian about Saturday. His mother? Can't ask mine.
Buy tights!!!
Fairy costume – where to buy?

Multitasking – a way of life, Mel knew, so that working mothers could hold on to their jobs and still keep the home fires burning.

She could see her female colleagues concentrating – or at least pretending to be – on what Edmund was saying. Hilary's face wore that serene expression that said she was listening intently, but Vanessa was staring glassy-eyed at where he was standing and simultaneously trying to text on her mobile phone. Vanessa had a thirteen-year-old son, Conal, and apparently, thirteen-year-old boys were even harder to control than two under-five girls.

Vanessa was divorced and was Mel's best friend in the company. They were nearly the same age, they had the same sense of humour and they'd both admitted privately to each other that balancing work and home life was ten times harder than doing the actual job at Lorimar.

'If management knew just how good we were at doing four things at once – like organising to get the washing machine fixed, sorting out after-school activities, remembering to pick up groceries, and fire-fighting in the office, then we'd both be promoted like a shot,' Mel had said the week before, when they were enjoying their once-a-month blow-out lunch at the Thai restaurant with the handsome young waiters.

'Yes, but if we were promoted, we'd have to stay even later in the office in the evening and be even guiltier about it. So why even try to break the glass ceiling? Sorry, the guilt ceiling!' Vanessa laughed, remembering their joke.

The promotion ceiling wasn't made of glass for working mothers, they'd decided – it was made of maternal guilt.

'Or possibly a gilt ceiling,' Mel added thoughtfully. 'Looks great but is fake close up. Like false boobs.' She looked down at her own now-modest 34B cup. 'I wish I had the money and the courage to get them done.'

'Oh, stop going on about your boobs,' Vanessa groaned. 'They're fine.'

'Yeah, if fine means they droop down to my knees, then they're perfectly fine,' Mel grinned. 'Anyway, we've got to stop using the word "fine". Do you know what it stands for? Fucked-up, Insecure, Neurotic and Emotional.'

'Sounds just like me,' said Vanessa. 'Next time anyone asks me, I'll say "I'm fine".' Hearing about struggles with Vanessa's son made Mel feel sorry about how easy she had it by comparison. She had left having children until she was that bit older, which meant she was ready to settle down into motherhood when she became pregnant at thirty-five. Vanessa had found the double blue line when she was twenty-four.

Plus, Mel had a husband to share it all with. Vanessa had an ex-husband who had a new wife, a new family and no real interest in the mistakes of his youth apart from trying to weasel out of his maintenance payments for Conal. Sure, the washer/dryer was a mystery to Adrian, and he still laboured under the impression that elves filled the fridge at night by magic. But despite all that, he was there, another grown-up to share the parenting burdens. Nobody who'd seen him painstakingly doing jigsaws with Carrie or making dinosaurs out of Plasticine with Sarah could deny that he was a brilliant, incredibly patient dad. Mel's own dinosaurs always looked like giant slugs.

She was lucky with childcare too. The Little Tigers Nursery beside Abraham Park on one of Carrickwell's prettiest tree-lined roads was a fantastic place for children. Mel had heard such horror stories about day care: babies who were allergic to dairy products being given milk; toddlers getting gigantic bites from other children . . . There had never been any such problems with Little Tigers. But what would it be like when Sarah went to school? Mel wisely decided that she'd worry about that later.

She counted her blessings. Look at all the people who'd kill for what she had – a great job, a great husband and wonderful kids. OK, so there was never much time for herself, but there was some. And she was working, something she'd sworn she'd never give up when she had her babies. She was living the modern woman's dream, wasn't she?

An hour later, Edmund Moriarty was still going strong. 'We care,' he intoned now. 'That's the message we have to deliver to each and every one of our customers: Lorimar cares.'

Mel nodded along with everyone else: We care – message received, O glorious leader.

When Edmund's laser gaze swept past her, like prison camp searchlights seeking out escapees, she went back to writing diligently on her notepad and sucked in her pelvic floor as she'd been shown in her one and only Pilates class. Might as well get something from the meeting.

Suck and hold for a count of ten. Pilates was the way forward and was even featured on the company's health website – which Mel was involved in – as a way for people to get into shape. Mel still wished she'd been able to manage more than one class after childbirth but she'd been back in work three months after Sarah was born, two after Carrie, and there just hadn't been the time to fit in Pilates. Her pelvic floor would have to stay as droopy as her boobs.

Finally, Edmund shut up and Mel was able to escape back to her desk. There were seventeen messages on her voice mail. They were all work-related except for the last one: 'Hi, Mel, this is Dawna from Little Tigers. Just to remind you that tomorrow's the zoo day for Sarah so she'll need extra warm clothes, and that Carrie can go if you'd like, but if it rains we won't take the little ones. I know it's a bad time of year but the Siberian tigers are only going to be there for another week and we've promised the children we'd go. It's fifty euro for both children – that covers the bus hire, entrance fee and lunch. Or twenty-five euro if it's just Sarah. See you tonight. Bye.'

Mel added another note to her list. 'Zoo day for girls. Leave money out for Adrian.'

Wednesday was Adrian's morning for taking the girls to Little Tigers. Mel did the nursery run the other four mornings before getting the train from Carrickwell into the Lorimar offices in Dublin, but on Wednesdays there was a breakfast meeting of the marketing and publicity departments, so Mel had to be in work early. She remembered when getting up earlier on Wednesdays had been a total pain because she had to set her alarm clock for seven instead of half-past. That was before the children had come along, and before they'd moved to Carrickwell. Seven was a lie-in these days, now that Carrie woke up bright and breezy at six every morning.

'Heyyo, Mummy,' she'd lisp when Mel hurried into the darkened, Winnie-the-Pooh-papered bedroom, showered but sleepy. It was hard to be grumpy when that little smiling face shone up at her, eyes bright with anticipation of the day ahead and small, fat hands outspread to be scooped from the cot. Although she was two and a half, she still didn't like to clamber out of the cot on her own, unlike her older sister, who'd been doing it from the age of two, but Mel knew it would happen any day now.

Early morning was one of Mel's favourite parts of the day. The pure unadulterated joy of being with her children, them kissing her hello, their childish pleasure at another day – it was what kept her going.

No perfume in the world was as beautiful as the morning scent of baby skin, a magical smell of toddler biscuits, baby shampoo and pure little person. Carrie loved being cuddled and wanted at least five minutes of snuggling before she'd consent to being dressed. Mel was usually torn between wanting just as much cuddling but knowing that the clock was ticking on.

Sarah was a morning person, all questions at breakfast.

'Why is Barney purple?' was her current favourite.

It was Mel's job to come up with funny reasons as she raced round the kitchen, sorting out breakfast for all of them.

'He fell into some purple custard and he liked it so much he didn't wash it off. Now he jumps into purple custard every day.'

'Mommy, that's silly!' Sarah had giggled that morning.

Carrie, slavishly adoring of her big sister, giggled too.

At her desk in the tiny cubicle on Lorimar's third floor, with its stunning views of Dublin's docklands, Mel reached over and touched the shell photo frame with Adrian, Sarah and Carrie's faces beaming at her. The three people she loved most in the whole world. The three people she did it all for.

Mel spent two hours working on the website with the help of two coffees and a Twix bar. Lunch was for people who had time to make sandwiches before they left the house in the morning, or the money to buy the overpriced ones from the guy who came round the office every lunchtime.

As she drank her second coffee, Mel looked at her list and idly circled the word 'zoo'. She and Adrian had taken Sarah to the zoo for the first time when she was two. Showing your child real tigers and elephants after so long looking at them in picture books was one of those parental milestones. How many parents never got to do things like that any more? she wondered. How many mothers missed the actual trip and instead got to read the nursery school diary: 'Carrie saw lions and seals, and piglets in the petting zoo. She had an ice cream and got upset when she saw the monkeys because of the noise. She was a good girl!'

Lunch over, Mel went through the most recent pages for the website, scanning every line and photo like a hawk. The previous month, a huge error had occurred when a paragraph on new procedures for hip replacements had slipped into an article about erectile dysfunction. There had been much giggling in the office at the idea that 'innovative keyhole surgery under local anaesthetic may do away with the need for painful replacement operations and would mean that patients will be back in action in just twenty-four hours'.

'I'd say a lot of male customers vowed to keep away from the doctor when they read that bit,' Otto from accounts had teased, as he'd delivered the expenses cheques. 'Willy replacement isn't exactly what every man wants to hear about when he's having trouble in that department.'

Mel's boss, Hilary, had been less amused, and completely uninterested in Mel's explanation that the error had surfaced mysteriously when the web designer was working on the page. Mel was responsible, end of story.

'This is an appalling mistake,' Hilary had said in that cold tone of disappointment that was far more scary than if she'd actually screamed at Mel. Hilary was Olympic standard at making people feel as if they'd failed. 'Maybe someone in design did it as a juvenile joke, but you should have spotted it. I'd bet my bonus it's going to be in all the Sunday papers' quote of the week sections.'

Hilary *hadn't* said that Edmund, who noticed everything, would undoubtedly blame Mel and that this would not look good on her file. Mel knew that herself. And mistakes on the file of a working mother were multiplied by a factor of ten. Being a working mother was like being a marked woman in Lorimar. Once a woman had children, no matter what sort of ambitious powerhouse she'd been beforehand, she was living on borrowed time afterwards. One child was seen to be careless, two was asking for trouble.

The fact that Hilary herself had three children was not a help. In all the years Mel had been working for Hilary, she'd never seen her boss either leave early over some child emergency or take a sick-baby day off.

'How does she do it?' Vanessa used to ask in September, when she was up to her eyeballs getting Conal sorted out with school books and uniform, desperately trying to take half-days here and there, while Hilary was at her desk at all times, mercilessly watching out for people skiving off.

'They can't be kids, they're robots,' Mel decided. 'That's the only answer.'

'Or is it having a husband who works from home and a nanny who gets paid more than the chairman of Microsoft?' asked Vanessa.

'You could have something there,' Mel agreed.

By five, Mel had returned all her phone calls and was finishing a batch of letters. There was still a report on the month's publicity activity to write for Hilary but she had to be out the door by five fifteen or she'd miss her train and be late to pick up the girls. She'd have to take the work and do it on the journey home.

Twenty minutes later, Mel swapped her heels for her commuting flats, filled her travel Thermos with coffee, and raced off into the cold. With luck, she'd be home by seven.

It was ten past seven before Mel parked the car in the drive and she helped Sarah and Carrie out and gathered up all their bags. It was a relief, as always, to be home.

'Carrickwell is such a gorgeous, mellow place,' their friends had all agreed when Mel and Adrian had given up their apartment in Christchurch to move to the country. Sarah was still a bump beneath Mel's 'Under Construction' maternity T-shirt then. 'Perfect for bringing up children. And the schools are great.'

Mel and Adrian had agreed and, catching each other's eye in the almost telepathic way of a couple who knew each other inside out, had said nothing about how they'd muddled their way to their decision.

Both of them were city people, born and bred, so the idea of this country idyll wasn't as appealing as everyone else seemed to think. There were other factors involved.

Mel's parents had moved out of the city ten years before to a small house halfway between Carrickwell and Dublin, which meant Mel's mum would be nearby to help take care of the bump.

In Dublin, they wouldn't have been able to afford a four-bedroomed semi in such a pretty road. And both of them felt it would be good for the children to have the countryside on the doorstep, perfect for family picnics. Or that was the theory. In reality, all Mel saw of the countryside now was from the confines of the train to and from work.

The clincher had been the local schools. However, they were now made to feel they had missed the boat there. Sarah and Carrie were down for all the best Carrickwell schools but the local Mummy Mafia had it that they should have had their names listed when they were embryos to guarantee a place in the very best, the Carnegie Junior School. Not to mention the fact that learning the recorder wasn't a part of the curriculum at Little Tigers. Serious mummies had their four-year-old poppets playing Bach on their recorders to impress the panel at the Carnegie. Sarah could play the television remote pretty well but Mel suspected this wasn't the same thing.

It was the large back garden at Number 2 Goldsmith Lawn that had really sold Carrickwell to them.

'We could have apple trees in it,' Adrian had said as they flicked through the auctioneer's brochure and saw the long, narrow swathe of lawn with a shabby green shed at the end.

'And we could put a swing on the cherry tree,' sighed Mel.

They'd smiled and she'd patted her burgeoning belly, conveniently forgetting that neither of them was able to so much as hammer in a nail without bringing down a shower of plaster.

Five years later, there were still no apple trees in the garden and the weeds had declared an independent state over by the shed, but there was a plastic swing under the cherry tree. Sarah loved it.

She ran happily ahead of her mother to the front door now, holding her pink and white spotted rucksack, while Mel struggled in behind with her briefcase, Carrie, and all Carrie's belongings.

The front door of Number 2 was a glossy green, flanked by two dwarf conifers in matching green wooden containers on the step. When they had moved in, Mel and Adrian had spent two months' worth of weekends sorting out the front garden so that it was maintenance-free and would fit in with their neighbours' beautifully cared-for gardens. The tiny sliver of grass had been replaced by beige gravel with various ornamental grasses and plants grouped in the two planting areas at either end. It all looked well cared for but this was a clever illusion.

Once Mel opened the front door, reality prevailed. The hall looked tired, the peeling paintwork and battered wooden floor badly in need of a month of DIY enthusiasm. Everything in their house needed work – don't we all? Mel thought grimly. There was never enough time. Adrian worked in IT in an industrial estate thirty minutes' drive from their home and since he'd been doing a Masters degree at night, he never had a moment for anything as mundane as Destroy It Yourself.

'Hi,' yelled Mel as she dumped her load onto the hall floor and kissed Carrie on the forehead before putting her gently down on her chubby little legs.

No reply, but the kitchen door was closed. With yells of delight, Sarah and Carrie erupted into their playroom. Mel felt that you needed somewhere to keep all the kids' stuff or it just took over the house, so the dining room was now the playroom, with the table shoved up against the wall and toys spilling out of all the big pink and purple plastic storage boxes. In the rigid tradition of children's colours, everything for little girls was lurid pink and purple. Mel longed for some subtle colours to take over.

'The dishwasher's broken,' announced Adrian as soon as she walked into the kitchen with the gym bags of dirty clothes from Little Tigers.

Sitting with his course books spread out over the kitchen table, he looked up at his wife and gave her a weary smile. Adrian had Scandinavian colouring, with short blond hair, pale blue eyes, and skin that reacted to a hint of sun so that he always looked golden, unlike Mel, with her Celtic complexion. Sarah and Carrie both had his fair hair and skin, but their mother's fine bones and lovely eyes. When Mel had first met Adrian, he'd had the build of a marathon runner, despite living off Chinese takeaways and pizzas. But over the years, lack of exercise and a fondness for the wrong sort of foods had made him more solid. Cuddly, she said.

'Needing to go to the gym,' Adrian would remark good-humouredly.

If they could afford the gym, that was.

Mel patted him affectionately on the arm on her way to the utility room to get a wash going.

'Are you sure the dishwasher's really broken?' she asked.

Broken appliances meant organising someone to come and fix them at a time when someone would be in, a task on a par with choreographing *Swan Lake* on ice.

'The dishes are dirtier now than when they went in,' Adrian said. He gestured to the worktop, where a white mug speckled with food particles sat.

'Sure there isn't a spoon stuck in the rotor?' asked Mel hopefully.

''Fraid not.'

She set the washing machine going, emptied out Carrie's juice cup and snack box, then tackled Sarah's spotty bag of equipment, her mind whizzing through all the tasks she had to complete before bed. Then she stuck the mushroom and pepper chicken for the girls' dinner in the microwave, put a pan of pasta on and got out a new wiping-up cloth, flinging the old one into the utility-room washing basket like a basketball pro.

'Will you keep an eye on the girls while I change?' Mel was halfway out the door as she spoke.

'Yeah,' replied Adrian absently.

Upstairs, Mel ripped off her work clothes and pulled on her grey sweatpants and red fleece. She removed her earrings quickly – Carrie loved pulling earrings and Mel had lost a really nice silver one already this week – and was back downstairs to finish the children's dinner within three minutes.

The girls were already on their father's lap, his college books shoved out of the way as they told him all about their day.

'I did a picture for you, Daddy,' said Sarah gravely. She was a daddy's girl and could cope with any childish trauma as long as her father's arms were around her.

'You're so clever,' said Adrian lovingly, and kissed her blonde head. 'Show me. Oh, that's wonderful. Is that me?'

Sarah nodded proudly. 'That's Carrie and that's Granny Karen and that's me.' From beside the cooker where she was stirring pasta, Mel looked over. Like all Sarah's pictures, it was in the crayon triad of pink, orange and purple, with Adrian, Mel's mother, Karen, and Sarah all big and smiling. Carrie, whom Sarah had never quite forgiven for being born, was a quarter the size, like a dwarf stickperson. There was no sign of Mel.

'Where's Mummy?' asked Adrian.

Mel, who'd read plenty on separation anxiety, wouldn't have asked, but her breathing stilled to listen to the answer.

'She's on another page. At work,' Sarah said, as if it were perfectly obvious. She produced another picture, this time of a bigger house with her mother outside with her briefcase in her hand. The briefcase was nearly as big as Mel herself, but she had to admit that Sarah had got her hair right: half brown, half blonde and frizzy.

'Oh,' Adrian said.

Mel could feel him looking at her sympathetically over Sarah's blonde head, and she flashed him a comforting look that said that she was fine. And she was, if the definition was Fucked-up, Insecure, Neurotic and Emotional.

'But Mummy is only at work sometimes. The rest of the time she's here, looking after all of us. She's a super mum,' Adrian insisted. 'She should be the star of the family picture, shouldn't she?'

Sarah nodded and snuggled up to her father, one delicate finger tracing her granny's lurid yellow hair. Granny was in the family picture but not Mummy. Mel felt another stab of bitterness, this time directed at her mother.

An energetic sixty-one-year-old, Karen Hogan was both Mel's secret weapon and the source of enormous resentment.

Karen was ready to leap into the breach if the girls were sick so Mel didn't have to take time off work, and unwittingly ready with remarks about how they'd sobbed for their mummy – or hadn't.

It wasn't that Karen didn't support her daughter's decision to work. She did. But without her, the whole show would have fallen apart, and somewhere in Mel's head was the notion that this wasn't quite the way it was supposed to be. *She* was supposed to be ultimately responsible for Carrie and Sarah – not their grandmother. Take Carrie's tonsillitis a month ago. Mel had taken her to the emergency surgery at the weekend, but when she hadn't improved by Monday, Granny Karen had taken her to their regular GP.

'The doctor says you might have to consider getting her tonsils out,' Mel's mother had reported on the phone that morning, as an anxious Mel stood outside the health forum conference that she just hadn't been able to miss. 'He says he needs to see you if you have the time.'

Mel bridled at the tone. *If she had the time*. Who'd sat up with Carrie all Friday night? Who'd driven to the emergency surgery and sat in anxiety, singing Bob the Builder tunes for two solid hours on Saturday until they saw a doctor?

'How dare he?' she snarled. 'I bet he never thinks how he can go out to work because he has a wife at home doing everything for him.'

'Mel, love, he didn't say it that way.' Her mother was defensive. 'You're a great mum; we all know it.'

Do we? thought Mel. And who's 'we'?

'He just meant that you should have a chat about the possibility of getting Carrie's tonsils out while she's still so young. Now that she's over two, they can do it and you wouldn't want to leave it too long. The older they are, the harder the recovery is.' Her mother knew everything. Where does this maternal wisdom come from? thought Mel. And when was she going to get it?

'That's a lovely picture, Sarah,' Mel said evenly. 'Will we pin it up on the fridge?'

Sarah nodded happily and Adrian smiled up at his wife.

Another difficult moment over, Mel thought. Everyone thought she was managing everything so well. What would they say if she revealed that sometimes she felt she barely coped?

The bathtime routine took for ever that evening. Carrie loved her bath and always played with her plastic duck as if she'd never set eyes on it before, gleefully pouring water into the head so that it poured out of the bottom, making the plastic wings flap.

'Mama!' she squealed delightedly as the wings worked faster and faster. 'Mama!'

Mel laughed too, feeling some of the tension of the day subside. How wonderful toddlers were – always excited, always ready to be happy. In contrast, Sarah was miserable and sat amid the lavender-scented bubbles looking like an abandoned child, her big blue eyes filled with sorrow.

'Will you come to the zoo tomorrow, Mummy?' she asked as Carrie splashed in frantic excitement.

Mel felt her heart constrict. Poor Sarah.

'You know I can't,' said Mel brightly. 'Mummy has to work but she wishes she could be at the zoo with you.'

'I want you to come.' Sarah aimed one of Carrie's floating fish at the duck and threw it. The fish missed the duck but landed on Sarah's foot, making her squeak with surprise and hurt. Her bottom lip wobbled precariously.

'Would you like to go to the farm with Mummy and Daddy at the weekend?' wheedled Mel, in desperation. The farm, complete with goats, sheep and a couple of Shetland ponies you could pet and feed, was a few miles away on the slopes of Mount Carraig, and both children loved it. Needless to say, going to the farm wasn't part of Mel's plan for the weekend, but they could manage it if she did the grocery shopping late on Friday instead of Saturday.

'Don't want the farm.' Sarah's damp head shook obstinately. 'Want Mummy and zoo.' She reverted to more babyish speech patterns when she was tired and fed up.

Mel knew she should have come up with some better explanation as to why she wouldn't be at the zoo but she just couldn't. Her energy had drained away.

'Sarah, I can't go with you. Dawna is going and you love Dawna.'

For a brief second, mother and daughter's eyes met, the same candid blue with glints of darkest violet near the irises giving them remarkable depth. In that moment, Mel thought her daughter looked old and knowing, as if she could see the exhaustion and guilt in her mother's eyes, and knew that Mel would have done anything to be in two places at the one time if it would make Sarah happy. Then it was gone, replaced by the childish incomprehension that Mummy was once again choosing work over Sarah's world. Mel wondered why Adrian told the children she was a super mum. She was a crap mum.

'You were a long time,' Adrian remarked when she finally arrived downstairs at ten past eight, carrying dirty clothes, wet towels and a half-eaten baby rusk that she'd found squashed into the landing carpet.

'Sarah didn't want to go to sleep,' muttered Mel. She dumped the laundry in the basket, which managed to look horribly full again, and headed for the fridge and a glass of wine. There was none. Hadn't that been last week's plan? No wine was to be opened during the week because then she had a glass every evening and surely it was bad for her. Bad, schmad. Where was the corkscrew?

The booze was locked in a cupboard in the dining room. Mel took out a bottle of the expensive Chablis that Adrian loved. She handed him a glass, which he took without looking up from his books. A plate of half-finished beans on toast lay beside him. His exams were in May and he was studying hard.

'Lovely wine,' he muttered, head back in his coursework.

'Mm,' she said, taking a deep gulp. Better than the old screwtop bottles they used to drink before they both had good jobs. There had to be some compensations for work. A thought drifted into Mel's mind: was that what her job was all about – making money? She went out to work and paid someone else to bring up her children so that she and Adrian could afford good wine?

Mel had eaten her beans on toast and was half reading the paper and half waiting for the washing machine to finish its cycle so she could put on another load, when Adrian said, 'Oh, forgot to tell you but Caroline phoned when you were doing the baths to remind you that you're all meeting up in Pedro's Wine Bar at half-eight on Thursday night, and if you're driving can you pick her up?'

'Oh, damn,' muttered Mel. 'It's the last thing I feel like this week. And she should know I don't drive to work.' Caroline was a very old friend who lived in Dublin's suburbia, and the party was their delayed Christmas get-together with a group of other old friends – cancelled so many times that they'd finally decided to have it in January. Once, Caroline and Mel had shared an apartment and worked in the same company, going on wild nights out, comparing notes on unsuitable men and planning how they'd run the world when their time came. Now Caroline was a full-time mother of three and dedicated herself to the job.

She was, as Mel and everyone else recognised, fabulous at it. Being a mother was her true vocation, and not drinking triple vodkas in shady clubs, as Mel loved to tease her.

Mel knew that her friend's three small sons had never eaten a single thing out of a jar when they were babies. If this had been anyone else but the tactful Caroline, Mel would have been made to feel hideously guilty. Her plans to mush up organic carrots had fallen by the wayside when she went back to work and discovered that huge organisation was involved in buying and mushing organic stuff, when it was easier to just buy cute baby jars with nice pictures on the outside. Anyway, the kids liked the jars more than they'd ever liked any of her painstakingly sieved mush.

It was all down to choice, Caroline said serenely. She liked being at home with her children making fairy cakes and having other rampaging toddlers round for tea, but that wasn't for everyone.

'You're out there talking the talk and walking the walk, Mel,' she said. 'One of us has to be a captain of industry, and since it isn't going to be me, I'd like it to be you. Just don't forget us humble old pals when you're getting the Nobel Prize for Services to the Business Sector or whatever.'

'Stop it,' begged Mel. 'You're making me cry.'

What she didn't quite understand was why Caroline hadn't gone back to work now that the boys were all in school. Not that she'd ever said that to Caroline, she thought as she tapped out her friend's number.

'Hi, Caroline, sorry I missed you. I was on bath duty.'

'Mel, I know, I phoned at the wrong time. It's just that I didn't want to bother you at work. So, how are you?'

Caroline sounded relaxed and happy, and for some reason this vexed Mel more than she could say. Caroline had given up her high-powered job to sit at home and watch the Disney Channel – she should be bored and irritable, not happy.

'We're all great,' Mel lied. 'Just great.' She paused, hoping that a sudden change of plan meant that the night out on Thursday had been cancelled. She daren't cancel again, although she longed to. How could she have agreed to a night out mid-week, such a horribly busy week at that? She'd have to go straight to the restaurant from

20

work, then get the late train home, and she'd miss seeing Sarah and Carrie.

'About Thursday night . . . ?'

'Val's coming, and Lorna's dying to get out,' Caroline said. 'You'd think she never left the house when I know for a fact that they were away for New Year. It'll be fabulous. I think I'm going to wear my new pink shirt – you know, the one I told you about. It's gorgeous, but it's a bit silky, so I probably should wear a camisole under it because if I wear a normal bra, you could see it through the shirt. I've tried it on twice already today and I'm still not sure. Although I tried on that cream printed one I told you about, and that might do. It's not as dressy but . . . I do love the pink one, though.'

Briefly, Mel imagined what it must be like actually to have time to decide what to wear on a night out instead of having the usual, last-minute panic in the morning where she ran upstairs and hastily dragged something sparkly from the wardrobe to take into work so she could brighten up her office clothes later.

'Would the pink be OK or will I be totally mutton dressed as lamb?' Caroline was asking.

Did other people ever want to kill their friends with their bare hands or was it just her? Mel thought. Had she turned into a fearsome old harpy now that she had all the things she'd said she'd ever wanted, like children and a good job?

'What do you think? Pink might be the navy blue of India or whatever, but baby-pink silk on a woman of thirty-nine, is it asking too much?'

'Pink sounds great,' Mel said evenly.

'OK, I'll wear it. I'm really looking forward to it, I can tell you. Sometimes you do need to get out of the house and realise there's a whole world out there, don't you?'

'Absolutely,' said Mel, 'absolutely.'

'Any wine left?' asked Adrian when she hung up.

'Yes, but we shouldn't have too much mid-week. We can finish the bottle tomorrow,' Mel said, and realised in a horrified moment that she was using the same placating voice she used for the children. Worse, Adrian didn't appear to notice.

Pedro's Wine Bar was the type of place where the people in Lorimar Health Insurance went on their lunch breaks when they wanted more than the usual half an hour for a snatched sandwich. It was a modern Italian establishment with shadowy candle-lit tables where plots were hatched, affairs were conducted, and people occasionally ordered too much wine because of their job/their home life/their credit card bill/all of the above.

21

Caroline, Lorna and Val loved it because it reminded them of their lives pre-children when they'd gone for long lunches in town and planned coups with their colleagues while handsome young waiters hovered in the background wielding bottles of Frascati and scenting large tips. All of which was exactly why Mel didn't like it.

'Ooh, cocktails,' squealed Lorna, as soon as they got through the door on Thursday evening. Grasping the laminated cocktail menu, she read out the list excitedly. Halfway down it, she began to laugh.

'Who wants a Slippery Nipple?' she said with glee.

Caroline and Val joined in the laughter.

'Wine for me,' said Val ruefully. 'Or I won't get up in the morning.'

'And me,' said Caroline, mindful of doing the school run.

'Oh, go on, let your hair down. Have a . . .' Lorna scanned the list, 'Vodkatini, Manhattan, no! a Pink Lady, to match your shirt. What about you, Mel? I'm sure you're out at events all week with your job. What's the fashionable drink now for us boring old mums?'

Mel found that she was still holding on to her handbag very tightly, the tendons in her hands standing out like vines. She was keyed up after the stress of the day with no numbingly familiar train journey to soothe it away. Gently, she put her bag on the seat beside her and tried to enter into the spirit of the night. She would not let Lorna get to her.

'Corporate events are few and far between these days,' she said evenly. 'And I never drink at them, so I'm the wrong person to ask advice about the hip new drinks. I'll have wine too, but only one glass. I've got an early meeting –'

'You executive types don't know how to let your hair down,' interrupted Lorna. 'Just one cocktail each and then we'll be sensible, OK?'

After the cocktails arrived, the conversation moved on to schools. Lorna was heavily involved in the parent/teacher association in her children's school and over their second cocktail, Mel was astonished to learn that Caroline had joined a national group who were lobbying for greater parental input in primary schools.

'You're so good to do that,' said Val guiltily, stirring her White Cranberry Ice, a lethal concoction that slipped down too easily. 'I should but . . .' she looked at Mel as if they were in this together, 'it's so hard to find the time, isn't it? I'm so busy with everything. I'm still going to WeightWatchers, and I've only half a stone to go.'

Everyone raised their glass to her and told her she looked wonderful.

'Thanks,' beamed Val. 'But I've got to fit in a long walk three times a week and what with all the extracurricular activities the kids are doing, like gymnastics – did I tell you Maureen's taken it up? Twice a week it is – there isn't the time for anything else.' She flashed another gaze of complicity at Mel.

Mel didn't return the look. She couldn't. There was no comparison between her and Val. Val was a twenty-four-hour mother and if she didn't manage to fit in the parents' association because she was busily baking additive-free carob cookies and keeping herself fit, then it was hardly a crime.

What was more, Mel was a non-mother during the hours of nine to five – or, more accurately, between half-seven in the morning and seven in the evening – and if Carrie or Sarah one day decided they wanted to do gymnastics, then how the hell would it be managed?

'How are Carrie and Sarah?' asked Lorna, turning her attention to Mel. 'Sarah must be going to school soon. It's such a milestone, isn't it?' She sighed. 'One minute they're babies, the next they're in school.'

Mel waited to see if Lorna would make the usual remark about how she was so glad she'd given up work when Alyssa was born because childhood went so quickly and you had to be there for it. She did it every single time they were out. Sometimes, to add insult to injury, she mentioned how hard it must be on Mel to have to miss all the important moments in her daughters' lives.

'I'm not getting at you, Mel, when I say this,' Lorna said with all the inevitability of thunder following lightning, 'but it must be so hard for anyone who has to go out to work. You do miss so much of their lives. I read something the other day in a magazine about a childcare worker who admitted that they lie to parents sometimes.'

'Lie about what?' asked Mel, ready to do battle.

'Lie about when the child has taken their first steps or whatever,' Lorna went on blithely. 'Apparently, they say the child has nearly done it, nearly walked, for example, so that when they do it at home, the parents think they're witnessing it for the first time. Sad.' She turned a fake smile on Mel. 'Honestly, women have to cope with so much, don't they?' she said. 'But it's worth it. Children make it all worthwhile.'

'Absolutely,' agreed Caroline.

'You said it,' added Val fervently.

Mel went through all the things she wanted to say to Lorna and thought she had better not.

The conversation whipped round to gossip about another friend of theirs who was about to get married for the second time and was having the wedding she'd always dreamed of on Australia's Gold Coast. As the others talked about how they'd love to go but couldn't, Mel felt herself sinking into the sort of self-berating misery that no amount of White Cranberry Ices could defeat.

Lorna's needling got to her every time for one simple reason: because Mel was so terribly scared that Lorna was right. If only Lorna could be more sensitive . . . After all, not everyone could afford to stay at home with their kids.

Adrian was half asleep when Mel slipped under the duvet beside him. It was after twelve and she felt sick at the thought that she had to be up again in just over five hours.

'Did you have a good time?' he murmured, turning to put one arm around her.

Mel snuggled into his embrace. The heating was off and she felt cold. Adrian was always warm and it was a long-running joke between them that he wanted just a sheet and the lightest duvet imaginable on the bed in winter, while she wanted an electric blanket, about four heavy blankets and a flannelette, instant-turn-off nightie.

'It was fine,' she said, settling herself into the comfiest position against him. But it hadn't been.

Lorna had been all set for going to a nightclub when Mel got up to leave, pleading exhaustion.

'You used to be a wild woman!' Lorna had said in the accusatory tone of the blind drunk as Mel pulled on her coat and checked that she had enough money for a taxi to the train station. 'What's happened to you? Are we such boring friends that you don't have time for us any more, is that really it?'

After an entire night of feeling guilty for the fact that she no longer had enough time to meet up with the girls more than a couple of times a year, Mel's patience snapped.

'I have a job, Lorna, a job where I have to produce results all day, and then, when I go home, I get to do all the work that you do but in about a quarter of the time. So forgive me if I'm not ready to party on all night but if I have a hangover, I can't go back to bed when the kids have gone to school. My job won't wait like the shopping or the washing. I'm not my own boss, you see.'

She was being unfair but she didn't care. Lorna had been unfair about Mel having to work: if she dished it, she should be able to take it.

'And since you find my company so boring,' Mel finished, 'don't bother to phone me next time you want a big night out where you get pissed and compare parent/teacher council stories. I don't have time for that. I'm too busy missing all the milestones in my children's lives.'

She'd left then, with Caroline, Val and Lorna staring open-mouthed after her. In the taxi to the train station, Mel had cursed herself for letting Lorna goad her. Why hadn't she held her tongue? It wasn't even that she'd been horrible to Lorna that mattered – Lorna was plastered and wouldn't remember any of it. And it was about time Lorna got some of her own medicine. Hurting Caroline, however, was different. Caroline was a true friend and now she'd think that Mel was one of those bitchy career women who looked down on stay-at-home mothers, when she wasn't. It was all such a mess.

'How's Caroline?' asked Adrian sleepily.

'She's OK,' Mel said. There was no point bothering him with any of this.

'We missed you,' Adrian said, his voice muffled against the silk of her hair.

'Missed you too,' she said truthfully. 'Go to sleep, love. Sorry for waking you up.'

'I couldn't sleep properly until you were in,' he said.

In the darkness, Mel smiled and curled her body closer into the curve of his. She was lucky to have a husband like Adrian. He told her he loved her and missed her. Not all men were able to be as honest. They made a good team and they'd get through the difficult times together, or so Adrian was always saying. It was just that the difficult times seemed to outweigh the good ones lately.

The next day, Mel didn't phone Caroline until just before lunch, when she knew her friend would be at home after the morning school run and the inevitable grocery shopping.

For the first time in their friendship, Caroline's tone was frosty. 'You didn't need to be so hard on Lorna,' she said sharply.

At her desk, Mel rubbed her tired face. Lack of sleep made her forget all the things she'd planned to say.

'Lorna made a difficult choice to stay at home with her children and give up her career for the moment; that doesn't mean she's a non-person,' Caroline continued. 'We're fed up with people asking, "What do you do?" and then tuning out when you say you stay at home with your kids. It's bad enough when men do it without another woman doing it too. I thought you understood why I gave up my job, Mel – that I couldn't bear to leave my babies for someone else to bring up. If I'd known that you really looked down on me, then I wouldn't have kept in touch with you.

I've got plenty of new friends who do what I do; I don't need to cling on to you for old times' sake just because we once sat at desks opposite each other and bitched about our boss.'

'Don't be like that, Caroline,' Mel begged. 'I didn't mean it like that, you know I didn't. I don't look down on you. In fact,' she laughed without mirth, 'I think the boot's on the other foot.' Why didn't Caroline understand that working mothers like Mel felt that the stay-at-home mothers like Lorna looked down on *them*? 'I wish I could stay at home and look after Carrie and Sarah too,' she began, and stopped in shock. There, she'd said it. She'd told someone her deepest secret, the secret she'd only just recognised in herself. She *did* wish she could stay at home. She was tired of her life, tired of running on a treadmill like a caffeined-up hamster and never getting anywhere.

'Of course, I know what you mean,' said Caroline, sarcasm glittering in her voice. 'You wish you could lounge around all day at home because that's what you think it's like, but it's not. It's not meandering round the shops and meeting other housewives for coffee and doing the odd bit of washing and ironing at home in between watching Oprah. It's damn hard and very boring.'

'I know, I realise that,' stammered Mel. 'You've got me wrong . . .'

'You think I don't remember what it was like to have an interesting job and have people look up to me? To earn my own money and use my talents to the full?' Caroline went on shakily. 'And now I'm just a stay-at-home mother, a housewife, a dependant, and nobody respects that. Graham jokes that I'm the CEO of the household but this is the only CEO job where nobody places the slightest value on what you do. I thought you understood all this, and that occasionally it was nice for me to touch the old world again with you and remember what it used to be like, but I can see I was wrong. You just look down on me.'

'No, Caroline,' begged Mel, 'I don't. It's just that Lorna really gets at me . . .'

'Mel, I don't have time to talk to you right now.' Caroline spoke crisply. 'I have things to do. Oprah's going to be on TV any minute and I'd *hate* to miss it. Goodbye.' And she hung up.

'Caroline, no . . .' How had they got themselves in this mess? Just when Mel suddenly understood why Caroline had given up her job in favour of taking care of her three little boys? Because now, finally, after years of trying to keep all the balls in the air, that's what Mel wanted too.

Hardly had Mel a chance to put the receiver back in the cradle, when the phone rang again.

'Mel, I'm sorry, I know it's lunchtime but I've got a journalist from the *Echo* on the line,' said Sue, the department assistant, 'a Peter Glennon and he's phoning about a statistic on the website about heart disease and how they aren't the right figures for Ireland.'

'Put him through,' said Mel pleasantly, as if she hadn't just got off the phone from a horrible conversation with one of her oldest friends. Lunch, like thinking about her row with Caroline, could wait. Everything had to wait for work, didn't it? Her life, her family, her friends. Work ruled.

CHAPTER TWO

The Willow Hotel had been a part of Carrickwell as long as anyone could remember. Other, grander establishments had come and gone, bringing variously nouvelle cuisine, Zen-like simplicity and chic modern style to the area, but only three hotels remained in the town: the Carrick Park, a motel on the main road to the city; the Townhouse, a small business establishment near the cathedral that did a roaring trade in office lunches, and the Willow, a big, rambling Georgian country house hotel that was crammed with shabby antiques, was hell to heat and had managed only to stay more or less solvent in the thirty years since Cleo's parents had taken it over.

Harry and Sheila Malin had been newly married then and thought the Willow would be a great place to rear a family, what with its enormous overgrown back garden and the big house for children to tear around in, and they'd thrown themselves into running the place with great gusto, even though they hadn't a smidgen of experience between the pair of them. Somehow they'd managed it, and thirty years and three children later, the Willow was still there: a landmark building on five valuable acres of land on the outskirts of the town.

It featured in guidebooks in the country house category, the sort of place where guests could feel they were visiting a friend's large, old-fashioned, comfortably down-at-heel home rather than a hotel.

There were sixteen bedrooms, each one different, two suites, and a tiny ballroom where small, intimate wedding receptions could be held.

The Willow Hotel was the same as it had always been. It was Carrickwell that had changed over the years. No longer a sleepy town, it had become a busy part of the commuter belt where property prices rocketed and where other hotel-owners were always trying to set up shop.

The most recent bit of competition had come from the large Victorian rectory on the Glenside Road, where all the bedrooms were done up like a Parisian brothel, complete with mirrors and an abundance of plum-coloured velvet and leopardskin. Cleo's father had surreptitiously checked it out and was able to report back that the breakfasts were bad – continental instead of the good solid fry-up that most people wanted, high cholesterol notwithstanding – and that the owner seemed more keen on having the place photographed in style magazines than attending to the daily routine of a hotel.

The leopardskin palace was a source of great amusement in the family quarters of the Willow, where the carpets were threadbare and the wallpaper hadn't been changed in aeons.

Harry Malin thought that its closure after only a year was reassurance that people liked solid home cooking and a cosy atmosphere instead of great style and expensive new furnishings.

Given that nothing at the Willow had been updated since she was a child, Cleo thought this was all just as well, but she didn't say so.

Sheila said it was proof that the Willow was part and parcel of Carrickwell, and didn't people drive out from the city just for Sunday lunch in the big dining room? People booked the Willow's Christmas Day lunch months in advance, and wasn't the waiting list for Christmas cancellations a mile long? Barney and Jason, Cleo's older brothers, said the Willow could be a little goldmine now they had cut a deal with the tour company taking people to see the Cistercian monastery and the round tower. And as it was all going so well, what was the point of shelling out lots of money to upgrade the heating system just because the plumber mentioned that the pipes were beyond their use-by date? That was plumbers for you – of course any plumber worth his salt was going to say the pipes were in need of work.

Sondra, Barney's wife, said that the family could always sell a bit of the land at the back of the hotel to developers, who'd whip up a couple of apartment blocks before you could whistle, and then, wouldn't everyone be in clover?

Cleo was the only one to sound a note of warning. Fresh from graduating in the top five per cent of her class in hotel management, she said they really ought to think about refurbishing because times were tough and it would be very easy for a hotel like the Willow to slide into the doldrums because of a lack of vision on the family's behalf. The big modern hotels were generally owned by corporations who could afford to invest with an eye to the long term, she said, while smaller establishments had to offer something special as boutique hotels, a concept that required high standards and lots of money spent.

Mrs O'Flaherty, who'd worked in the exquisite Victoria Jungfrau in Switzerland, had lectured Cleo's class on the future of the hotel industry, and she'd been passionate about the need of smaller hotels to do their best to keep up.

'If standards slip and the money isn't spent, then your thriving small hotel can go from having every bed occupied to being empty every night very quickly,' Mrs O'Flaherty had pointed out with great seriousness. 'That is the tragedy of the family-owned end of the business. There often isn't enough money for renovations but not investing is a recipe for disaster.'

The class, many of whom were from hotel-owning families, listened earnestly, making notes and wondering how they'd impart this information at home.

Cleo's friend and admirer, Nat, who came from a quaint twenty-bedroomed hotel in Galway that had been in his family for generations, used to say he had no hope of getting through to his widowed mother about the need for investment.

'She says there's a limit to how much money you can spend on a place and that if we doll it up too much, we'll have to charge miles more per room and all the old regulars won't come near us,' said Nat gloomily. 'I keep telling her we need to put thousands into the place or we'll go under, but she won't listen. So what can I do?'

Cleo shrugged her shoulders, which meant: don't ask me – you know my lot don't listen to what I say either.

Cleo was the youngest in the family and, at the age of twenty-three, she was still treated like a child at home.

Barney and Jason had no interest in the hotel except to discuss its finances. When they'd reached twenty-five, each brother had been given a ten per cent share in the business. Cleo was sure that her father had waited until her brothers had reached twenty-five because they were both reckless when it came to money. Her mother insisted it was because Harry wanted to make sure they were sensible enough to think of the hotel's future when they were finally part of the deal.

'Twenty-five is ridiculous. It's so far off it's almost Victorian,'

Cleo insisted at her twenty-first birthday, when she heard of this scheme for the first time and realised she wasn't old enough to be in it.

'It's the age of maturity,' her father said.

'In Jane Austen's time, perhaps,' Cleo said. She hated the fact that her father didn't realise she was already far more mature than her brothers would ever be – honestly, they were like children sometimes – and she was determined to change this. Dad *would* listen to her. It was crazy not to give her her share now so she could have a say in the running of the business. She had all the training, she knew what would work and she was so eager . . .

'Are you buying those magazines or are you practising to be in the wax museum?' demanded the man behind the counter in the newsagent's. Wrenching herself out of a daydream in which her family listened to her every utterance as if it was written on tablets of stone, Cleo realised she'd been staring blindly at the magazine rack for ages with two glossy magazines clutched to her chest.

'Sorry,' she said, going over to the counter and beaming at him. Cleo had a fabulous smile, everyone said, because it brought out her dimples and reached her eyes too. If Cleo had been the sort of girl who'd ever got into trouble – and she wasn't, as she moaned to her best friend, Trish – she'd have been able to wriggle out of it instantly, thanks to her hundred-watt beam.

The newsagent's face mellowed as he took the magazines to scan them. She was a grand girl and polite too, not like those hoydens who came in, flicked through every magazine in the place, read out the sex hints loudly, and went off without buying so much as a packet of crisps.

'Thank you.' Cleo took her change and her magazines, averting her eyes from the rows of chocolate at the till. Chocolate was evil, particularly the new white chocolate thing that just melted on your tongue and bypassed your stomach completely before resting on your backside. Cleo had never worried that much about her weight: she was tall with long legs and an athletic body. No matter what she ate, her stomach was enviably flat. Her breasts were the problem. A 38D was big in any language, and if she did put on any extra weight at least half went straight onto her chest.

Trish was waiting for her at the lights, huddled into her fake sheepskin coat because it was so cold, a knitted red hat flattened down on her head.

'Whatdidya get?' she demanded, poking at Cleo's purchases as they waited to cross the busy city centre street.

'Interior design magazines,' said Cleo, hoping it wasn't going to rain until she was on the bus home because she hadn't got either a hat or an umbrella. Her hair was bad enough as it was, all wild and mind-of-its-own, but if it got wet – then she turned into cave-woman.

'Why didn't you get nice gossip mags to cheer us up?' moaned Trish. 'I love those pictures of stars with no make-up, spots, cellulite and fags in their hands.'

Trish had recently given up smoking and there was nothing she loved better than to see other people looking unhealthy with cigarettes in their hands. It proved, she said with gritted teeth as she chewed another bit of nicotine gum, that she'd made the right decision.

'Because those mags are also full of diets and hints on how to look like J-Lo, and it always involves spending loads of money, which we don't have, and being a size six, which we aren't,' Cleo pointed out.

The green man flashed on the pedestrian lights and they hurried across the road to the Shepherd, the pub where they'd spent many an hour when they were both in college in the city. Five minutes on the bus was all that separated the two colleges, and plenty of Cleo's hotel management lecturers must have thought that Trish was enrolled there instead of on the business degree course across the River Liffey.

'We could be size six if we wanted to,' Trish said.

'If we didn't eat and had some of our important organs removed, then yes, it's a distinct possibility.' Cleo opened the swing door of the pub and felt the welcoming warmth of central heating on high.

'Why are you so grumpy?' demanded Trish, once they'd found a cosy nook and ordered two coffees.

'I turned down the Donegal job.'

'You didn't!'

'I did.' Cleo almost couldn't believe it herself. It wasn't the job she'd longed for – just assistant manager at the small Kilbeggan Castle Hotel in a ruggedly beautiful part of Donegal – but it was her first real job. And she'd said no. She must have been mad.

The man who owned the Kilbeggan Castle clearly thought so too.

'You were so keen and interested ...' he'd said in irritation when she'd phoned after getting the job offer in the post.

'I am so sorry,' Cleo said. 'I didn't mean to waste your time.'

'Well, you did.'

'Not intentionally,' she interrupted. 'It's just something's suddenly cropped up. You know I come from a hotel background? Well, there's a good reason for me to stay at home and work with my family right now.'

'I know tourism is down,' the man said. 'We're all feeling the pinch because people are too nervous to fly any more. I suppose your place is hit the same way. Enough said.' He sighed. 'I suppose I'll be reading your name in conjunction with all sorts of great ventures in the future. We were all very impressed with you, Miss Malin.'

'Thank you,' said Cleo with regret. Instinct told her Kilbeggan Castle would have been a lovely place to work. She *was* mad to turn it down. But in the end she just couldn't bring herself to give up on her heritage. She had to try to drag the Willow and her family kicking and screaming into the new century before the hotel went under.

'You're mad,' Trish said. 'Stone mad. Sorry, I know that's rude, but you are.' She glared across the small pub table at Cleo, the way she'd been glaring at Cleo since that first day in Miss Minton's class in Carrickwell Primary School, where they'd both decided they wanted to sit on the blue wooden chair and a fight had ensued with hair-pulling and lots of wild screaming.

Eighteen years later, there was no hair-pulling in the relationship, but occasionally there was a bit of screaming. Cleo had last roared at Trish when her friend shamefacedly admitted that she hadn't actually dumped her current boyfriend as planned, even though he'd been seen in a clinch with another woman at a New Year's party.

'He says he's sorry,' Trish protested.

'Until the next time,' Cleo said angrily. 'If he did that to me, he'd be on his way to casualty right now, whining for a morphine suppository to put him out of his misery.' She meant it. Cleo mightn't have had a long line of boyfriends but those she'd had had known not to mess her around. The guy who'd promised devotion after one evening, and that he'd phone but hadn't, would always remember having his drink poured over his head in the pub the next day while Cleo loudly, and to the amusement of the whole premises, told him not to make promises he didn't intend to keep.

'Honesty is the best policy,' she'd said as he sat with beer dripping down his astonished face. 'If you didn't want to see me again, all you had to do was say so. I'm not the sort of woman who likes waiting for the phone to ring.'

Today, Trish was the one trying to make her friend see sense.

'Why did you turn it down? Why? It was a perfectly good job. What is the point of saying no to a good job in Donegal when your family takes no notice of you? Your dad's not going to let you take over the place and show him how it should be done, is he? And neither are Barney or Jason. You said yourself Barney's secretly hoping everything has to be closed down so you can sell the land and he and Sondra can make a fortune out of their share and live in the lap of luxury. You can't save the Willow, Cleo, if they don't want it saved.'

It was a perfectly good point and one Trish had been making for the past month, ever since Cleo had become acutely aware just how badly her family's business was doing.

Terrorism meant tourism was down all around the world, but the Willow's problem could not be laid solely at this door. The first inkling of doom had struck Cleo when she'd come home for Christmas, having spent the seven months since she'd left college working nights on reception in a big hotel in Bristol. She found shift work hard to get used to but felt she'd learned a lot – both about the business and about a handsome French guy named Laurent with whom she'd had a brief but fun fling. Now she wanted to show them all at home just how much she'd learned, although she didn't plan on sharing Laurent's native kissing techniques.

The Willow had only been half full for Christmas, the first time this had ever happened. Even an expensive advert in a national newspaper had failed to bring in guests. For the big Christmas Day lunch, they'd had to close off part of the dining room to take the barren look off the place.

Jason, Barney, her mother and her father all acted as if this was some blip on the radar, a chance happening. But Cleo knew that it wasn't. It was the beginning of the decline. People wanted more from hotels than the faded grandeur they got in the Willow. They wanted silver tea services, elegant old furniture, the sense of gracious living that came from a beautiful old hotel – *and* hot water all day, a swimming pool and a beauty salon.

What could the much-loved Willow offer them?

'Mind you, Donegal wouldn't be hot enough,' Trish went on thoughtfully. 'If I were you, I'd get on the first plane out of here, go somewhere warm and gorgeous, and find a luxury hotel where I can come to stay and you can comp me a room. The Caribbean would be nice,' she added, 'sandy beaches, me on a lounger waving my hand in the air so some ebony god of a man with thighs like The Rock can smile at me and help move my sunshade.' Trish sighed at the thought of it all.

'Finished fantasising?' enquired Cleo. She opened one of her magazines. 'You see, this is my plan. If we did up the hotel ourselves, it wouldn't cost so much.' She found the page that had captivated her in the newsagent's: a home not unlike the Willow in décor, but with lots of fabulous paint effects on the walls and an incredible *trompe-l'œil* arched door in a wall leading into a tropical garden.

With something like that in their dining room, the hotel would look wonderful.

Trish sighed. 'Cleo, those houses look like that because they have a fleet of paint experts each with a Masters in fine art working round the clock to transform a dingy hallway into a Garden of Eden with just seventeen tins of paint. If normal people like us do it, it would look like those paintings done by chimpanzees.'

'It can't be that hard,' Cleo muttered.

Trish narrowed her eyes. 'Yeah, right, Leonardo. Get real. Your family think you're a kid who knows nothing. That's what being the youngest is all about. You should face facts and get out of there and get on with your life. Like I have,' she added defiantly.

Trish had moved to Dublin at the age of eighteen when she went to college. And she claimed that the secret to getting on with your family was not actually having to live with them. She'd lived away ever since. Cleo used to envy Trish for her independence in those days, but now she wasn't so sure. She'd been wildly keen to go to Bristol and experience a bit of the world, and yet, when she did, she found that she missed home.

'It was different for you, Trish,' Cleo pointed out. 'You needed to get out.' Trish's family were known for their volcanic arguments and door slamming. 'But I don't want to leave,' Cleo said sadly. 'I know if only I can make them see we're in trouble, that they'll do something, won't they?'

'OK, you have the family conference and tell them they're doing it all wrong and let's see what happens,' Trish said. 'And don't say I didn't warn you.'

As she walked to the bus, Cleo mulled it all over in her mind. She knew that staying in Carrickwell to revitalise her family business was unlikely to work for all the reasons Trish had mentioned: her father wouldn't listen to her, and her brothers probably hoped it would fail anyway. Neither Jason nor Barney had shown the slightest inclination to work as hoteliers. Jason worked in the travel business while Barney was a sales manager in a local car dealership. If the hotel and its land were sold, they could make a lot of money.

Cleo loved her brothers but the age difference between them meant she'd been excluded from their games as a child, and even now there was always a squabble between them when they met.

The bus was waiting, and Cleo got on board. As the bus doors shuddered to a close, she took her scarf off and wriggled lower into her seat to enjoy the ride.

'Cleo Malin, as I live and breathe. How *are* you?'

Mrs Irene Hanley, a friend of her mother's, deposited two huge bags of shopping onto the seat beside Cleo. 'Can I sit with you? I hate the journey home – drive you mad, wouldn't it, with boredom?' Without waiting for an answer, Mrs Hanley had removed her coat, rearranged her shopping on the floor so it fell onto Cleo's feet, and launched herself into the seat. Built along the same lines as the robust women of Tonga, Mrs Hanley took up all her own seat and a fair percentage of Cleo's too. Cleo was pushed nearer the window but all chance of staring happily out of it, in a world of her own, was now gone. Mrs Hanley was set for chat. First, she produced a box of chocolates from her shopping.

Cleo could feel hunger rising in her like a tidal wave as Mrs Hanley opened the box and dithered happily over her selection before choosing a succulent white chocolate and passing the whole box to Cleo.

'Have a chocolate – ah, go on,' she added, as Cleo shook her head. 'One won't hurt.'

Cursing herself for being so weak, Cleo took one. Chocolate caramel with a nut in the middle. She could feel the chocolate sensors in her body going on full alert. *We're back in business, boys!*

'Maybe I'll have another one,' she said.

Mrs Hanley's family, all girls and all with the same statuesque physiques, were apparently either married or nearly married to wildly eligible men.

'Now Loretta, her fellow, Lord, he's fabulous, calls me his second mummy, well, he's taking her to Lanzarote for Valentine's Day. Loretta, I said, Loretta, hold on to that man, I said.'

'Loretta, she was twenty-two last year?' asked Cleo suddenly, remembering Loretta from the vast Hanley clan. Loretta had worked briefly in the Willow as a chambermaid one summer and now ran the Carrickwell office of one of the bus tour companies.

'My baby.' Mrs Hanley got all misty and only a dark chocolate nougat could make her feel better.

Cleo sighed and took a cappuccino cream. Since the short-lived thing with Laurent, there was no sign of a man in her life – except Nat, who didn't count – never mind one with either the wit or the overdraft to take her to Lanzarote. How did Loretta do it?

Perhaps being less bolshie was the trick. Cleo knew she was tough with men, but you couldn't change that, could you? A firm hand was what was needed, whether it was throwing drunks out of the hotel at closing time or telling men that one date did not entitle them to stare glassily at her cleavage.

'Nearly there already. Lord, doesn't the time fly when you've got company?' Mrs Hanley said as the bus shuddered into the depot at the bottom of Mill Street. 'As I said, I'm counting on Loretta coming back from Lanzarote with an engagement ring, although keep that to yourself, but if she does, we'll have a bit of a bash. Nothing too fancy. They'll be saving for the wedding, I dare say. Loretta loves the Metropole in Dublin. Very classy. Or the Merlin Castle and Spa over in Kildare. Pity we've nothing like that here. There are builders working all hours of the day and night on the health farm in the old Delaney place. It's nearly finished, I believe, but it won't have a hotel with it, so Loretta will have to go out of town if she wants her posh wedding.'

The words were only out of Mrs Hanley's mouth when she realised what she'd said and clasped a beringed hand to her lips. 'Sorry, Cleo. Me and my big mouth. I didn't think. Don't tell your mother, please. You know I'm mad about her, it's just that young people, like Loretta, you know, they want different things at weddings these days and they like to make a weekend out of it. Say with the wedding on a Friday, then all sorts of treatments in the health centre on the Saturday, and a party that night. And you'd need a big ballroom too and at least fifty rooms to cater for all the people flying in from abroad. A small place with a few rooms wouldn't do . . .' She clamped a hand over her mouth again. 'I'm digging an even bigger hole for myself, Cleo, love. I didn't mean to offend you or your family.'

'Don't be silly, Mrs Hanley,' said Cleo briskly. She could hardly blame the woman for pointing out the truth as Cleo saw it herself. 'Anyway, you'll be hearing interesting things about the Willow soon. We have great plans for the future, you know,' she added. 'The work will be starting soon, in fact.'

Be positive about your hotel,' had been part of the advice in college. *'Don't be afraid to tell people the positive points and any future improvements, as long as you can back it up.'*

And they'd be able to do that soon, Cleo reasoned. If her family listened to her.

'I'm so glad,' Mrs Hanley said. 'I've been worried because the place has been a bit run down and your poor mother is worn out with it all. Myself and the girls from the book club talk about it all the time.'

'You do?'

Relief that Cleo hadn't taken offence made Mrs Hanley loquacious. 'She looks worn out, you know. Worn out. It can't be easy, although she keeps a brave face on her. But we have been worried, Cleo. I'm so fond of your mother, and your father too. I thought they might retire, to be honest, and head off for the sun. The heat's great for arthritis and your mother is a martyr to it. Stay off the tomatoes, Sheila, I tell her, they're ruinous for the old arthritis, but does she listen?'

Mrs Hanley pressed another chocolate upon Cleo before they parted company. 'You're only a slip of a thing,' Mrs Hanley said disapprovingly.

Cleo grinned and took the chocolate. Compared to the Hanley girls, she *was* a slip of a thing.

As she walked out of the bus depot, she chewed her chocolate slowly to make it last and thought of the truth in Mrs Hanley's words. Everybody could see that the hotel was in trouble. Except her family.

On her way up through Carrickwell to the Willow, Cleo passed The Holy Land, which looked a bit bare now Christmas had gone, and past the brightly painted façade of Little Tigers Nursery with its big tiger motif on the front door. It was half-six and parents were still rushing in to collect children, who emerged all wrapped up in warm clothes, running and skipping to their parents' cars, talking madly about what they'd been painting and what games they'd played. Cleo had never given much thought to it before, but it occurred to her that it must be hard to leave your child in a nursery all day, only picking him or her up when you were both worn out.

Cleo and her brothers had never been sent to a crèche or nursery. The hotel had been their nursery. There had always been someone around to keep an eye on them, and from when she was little Cleo had loved helping clean bedrooms as long as she had her own yellow duster and her own squirty bottle. She wondered if she'd have children some day and would they play in the hotel while she worked, learning how to make a bed properly and watching the chef rustling up twenty-four cooked breakfasts as easily as making a cup of tea.

It had been a fun way to grow up. Her children *would* play in the hotel, she decided. She'd want them to enjoy their birthright the way she had. Of course, that was years and years off, and she'd need a man first. That wasn't the sort of thing that could happen quickly. No way was she settling for any guy. She wanted *the* one. The right one. Perfect. Tall, naturally, so she wouldn't have to look down on him. Small men loved her for some reason, but she could never bear to go out with anyone shorter than herself.

Laurent had been tall and olive-skinned, with the most amazing grey eyes. And his accent ... when he said, 'You are so sexy, Clee-oh,' in that luscious Provençal drawl, Cleo had felt herself melt.

By the time she got home, Cleo's hair was woolly from the damp of the evening. Hat – she had to buy a new hat to replace the one she'd lost on a night out with Trish. A vibrant young business-woman needed decent hair. And she *was* a vibrant young busi-nesswoman, the sort of one who could have her pick of handsome tall men with fabulous accents. Who'd manage to drag their eyes from her bosom to actual eye-level.

With this cheering thought in mind, she walked in the front door and did what Mrs O'Flaherty, her favourite course lecturer, used to tell the students to do: imagine they were guests arriving at the hotel and see what it felt like. Cleo stood and tried to see the hotel with a dispassionate eye.

The flowers that had only one day left in them yesterday still stood on the big hall table and it was obvious that nobody had got round to changing the water. Murky and green like water from a gloomy pond, it gave the hall the aroma of bad eggs. The cush-ions on the two big armchairs in front of the fireplace still bore the imprints of whoever had last sat in them, and a newspaper was rolled up and squashed in a corner of one. Worse still, the door to the conservatory hallway was swinging open, admitting both a stiff breeze from the garden and the smell of eau-de-cabbage from the kitchens.

Cleo didn't have to exert her imagination to figure out what any self-respecting guest's reaction would be if they'd travelled in the cold evening to the Willow, hoping for warmth and welcome, to be greeted by all this. The place was only missing Bela Lugosi with extra sharp incisors to complete the atmosphere. Before she'd gone to college, before she'd spent work experience summers in other hotels, Cleo had thought that their hotel was the finest around. Creaking water pipes, quaint hot-water bottles for guests' bedrooms in winter and beautiful rugs with papery thin edges were part of an old hotel's attractions. Its charm had also come from the love and warmth her parents had put into it, charm that meant more than any new furnishings or thick carpets. Harry Malin's warmth was as much a part of the Willow's success as the sense of faded elegance in a world of monotone, identikit hotel chains. But the balance between her father's warmth and the state of the house had shifted.

Now she saw the Willow with new eyes. The hotel was tired, a dump. It badly needed a total revamp.

'Hello!' yelled Cleo into the empty hall.

Tamara, the hotel's part-time receptionist, poked her head out from behind a tiny gap in the office door, the door that was supposed never to be shut. Small and very blonde, like her elder sister, Sondra,

Cleo's sister-in-law, Tamara had the air of one who always had something better to do than talk to you.

She wasn't too keen on Cleo, mainly because Cleo was one of those people who never wanted to sit still. Tamara liked sitting still when there was nothing she felt inclined to do. Even better, she liked working on her nails. The acrylics had been too expensive, so she'd got rid of them and it was hard work getting her nails back into condition again. You really needed to rub nail conditioner in every hour religiously.

'Yeah, hi,' Tamara muttered, from where she sat, and went back to reading her magazine carefully so as not to dampen the pages with fingers slick with nail oil.

Cleo counted to ten. Then she went to twenty to be on the safe side. Screaming at staff was generally not encouraged in hotel management. But Tamara was not Cleo's idea of a proper hotel receptionist, even if she was 'almost family', as Barney put it.

In the grand tradition of keeping the business in the family, Barney's wife, Sondra, used to work as receptionist on a part-time basis, but now that she was pregnant, albeit only just, with the first grandchild of the Malin dynasty, she had given up work and her sister had been drafted in as her replacement.

Cleo had been all for hiring someone new but, no, family had to come first.

'Cleo, come on, charity begins at home and all that. Tamara's a bit low since she lost that job in the beauty salon,' Barney had said. 'And it's not as if you need much experience for reception.'

That, Cleo decided, was what was wrong with her brothers. They didn't understand the finer points of running a hotel. In Barney's view, any idiot who could do long multiplication and say 'Reception, how can I help you?' could operate a successful hotel.

'Barney, you do need experience for reception,' Cleo said in exasperation.

'Ah, Cleo, she'll be great,' wheedled Barney.

He had such an engaging smile, like Cleo's but with an added hint of rogue thrown in for good measure. It was hard to resist.

'Where is everyone, Tamara?' asked Cleo brightly now so that Tamara would hear her through the half-closed office door.

'Your mother's in the kitchen and your father's out.'

And there's nobody on reception in case a guest comes in, Cleo thought. The hotel didn't have a receptionist on all day; they couldn't afford to. Tamara was employed for times of the day when Harry or Sheila were busy elsewhere.

Cleo was heading for the door that separated the reception from the kitchen when the office phone rang sharply.

After five interminable rings, Tamara picked it up.

'Helloo, the Willow Hotel, how can I help yoou?' she intoned in the special voice she used only for the phone or talking to rich guests.

Tamara would have to go, Cleo decided. Family or no family. Because if she didn't go, Cleo would end up being arrested for hitting Tamara over the head with Tamara's cosmetic-filled Burberry handbag. Also not generally encouraged in hotel management.

Cleo's mother, Sheila, sat in the tiny alcove in the kitchen where an old church pew had been wedged in and covered with cushions so that people rushing around cooking and serving could take a rest and a cup of tea out of everyone's way. The pew was of worn oak and the cushions looked like a multi-coloured bric-a-brac display with two scruffy rose velvets lined up with a scratchy oatmeal barrel cushion, a few threadbare tapestry cushions and a toile de Jouy confection that was faded to nothing. All had once been somewhere else in the hotel and had ended up in the kitchen when they were too old and shabby to be in the public domain. A small card table covered with a floral oilcloth sat in front of the pew and it was there that Cleo had done much of her homework, working patiently away with sums and French verbs while her parents spun past as they cooked and cleaned.

'A good hotel-owner needs to be able to cook if the chef doesn't turn up,' Cleo's father always said. And Harry Malin could certainly cook. In the early days, it was from him that Cleo had learned her love of the business – and her skill with people. Dad just had that way with people that made them comfortable in his company. It was the perfect gift for an hotelier.

The kitchen was warming up for dinner time with Jacqui, the chef, surveying her empire with pride before she sloped off for a quick break before the rush. Jacqui had been with the hotel for a year now. The same age as Cleo and just as eager, she was always having arguments with Harry about innovative new menus. Harry liked substantial French cuisine with an Irish twist. Jacqui liked Pacific Rim food, worshipped lemongrass and longed to be allowed to create exotic recipes with coconut milk.

Cleo waved a greeting at Jacqui, filled a mug with coffee from the pot on the counter, then kissed her mother on the cheek. 'Where's Dad?'

'He and Bill are looking at the hot-water pump.' Bill was the hotel's part-time handyman and a genius with machines. He needed to be, given the age and decrepitude of most of the hotel's equipment. 'It's gone again and Bill has some new yoke to fix it.'

'Cardiac paddles are the only things that'll work on that pump,' Cleo joked. 'Or else a novena to St Jude.' It would take the patron saint of hopeless cases to perform a miracle.

Her mother nodded absently over her sewing. 'For sure.'

'Mum, look at these.' Cleo spread the interiors magazines in front of her mother.

Sheila moved her mug to make room. 'Those magazines are very expensive, love,' she muttered, peering through her glasses at the price stickers. Since she'd started wearing the spindly gilt bifocals, she looked so much older, Cleo thought sadly. For years, Mum had looked so young and lively, with her hair, same uncontrollable nut-brown curls as Cleo's, tied up in a bouncy bun with tendrils trailing around her neck. But suddenly her hair was almost all grey and the lines around her silvery blue eyes were so deep they looked as if they'd been carved with a compass. Her hands were misshapen with arthritis, the knuckles on both hands swollen, and where she'd once made an effort with pearly nail varnishes, now her nails were bare. Even her clothes looked aged. There was never any money in the Malin family for clothes. Every penny was ploughed back into the business. Cleo's school uniform had been patched so often it looked like a quilt, to her shame.

Mrs Hanley had been right: her mother was worn down by everything. Cleo felt a surge of remorse at not having noticed this herself before now.

'Bit of a waste of money, Cleo. If you're going to have enough money to buy a car for when you're working in Donegal, then you'll have to stop spending it on magazines.'

Cleo bit her lip. She still had to tell them she'd turned the job down. Everyone had been so pleased when she'd blurted out that she'd been offered it, particularly Mum and Dad. It had been almost upsetting. You'd think they were glad to get rid of her.

'Mum, I had this great idea. Well, I've been thinking about it for ages. We do need to upgrade the place a bit and then I saw this magazine and, what do you think of us doing some new paint effects? It wouldn't cost much,' she added hurriedly. She opened the magazine on the correct page for her mother. 'The dining room could do with a bit of work and just think if we had something like this paint effect on the far wall . . .' She got no further.

The back door opened, and Sondra and Barney arrived in a whirl of cold wind and Body Shop White Musk, a perfume Cleo had once liked and now hated because Sondra seemed to wear a pint of it every day.

'Hello, just thought we'd drop in to say hi,' Sondra said, newly pregnant and radiant in full make-up and a chic black dress.

'We've nothing in for dinner so we came up here to cadge a couple of free meals,' said Barney, who was nothing if not frank.

'Sit down, Sondra, love. Chef's got lovely sea bass and I can get her to rustle up some chips for you.'

Out of the corner of her eye, Cleo could see Jacqui smile as she came back from her break. She loved being called Chef.

'Great.' Sondra sighed as she sat down in the comfiest corner of the pew and flicked through Cleo's magazines while Barney scavenged in the main part of the hotel kitchen for a snack.

Jacqui knocked his hand away as it slid towards the chill drawer where the smoked salmon was ready. 'Don't touch.'

Barney got a fistful of almond cookies that had been made to accompany Sheila's homemade vanilla ice cream instead and squashed in beside his wife. She'd come to the *trompe-l'œil* page. The house really did have a look of the Willow about it – the same big windows, high ceilings and similar coving.

'That's nice,' said Barney, munching.

'Isn't it?' Sheila said. 'Cleo wonders if we could do something similar here.'

Sondra raised carefully painted eyes to Cleo. 'But impossible to copy,' she said. 'It'd cost a fortune.'

'You think?' Cleo said, wondering why Sondra complained about how she'd hated exams at school, since she was so scarily sharp about everything post-school.

'Lord, Cleo, don't they teach you anything in college? Paint effects cost a fortune. You weren't thinking of doing it yourself, were you?'

The first stirrings of anger roared through Cleo's veins. 'I was, actually,' she said. 'The whole place needs work and this is one option that wouldn't cost too much. We weren't full over Christmas and it's about time we all faced facts and did something about it. We don't want to lose the place, do we?'

She could sense rather than see her mother stiffen at these words.

'Cleo, the Willow will be going strong when we're all dead and buried,' came her father's voice.

Harry Malin stood in the kitchen unwrapping a scarf from his neck. 'The pump's fine. Bill has it working like a dream. How's my favourite daughter-in-law, then?' He smiled down at Sondra.

Cleo's inner fire roared a bit more. He was doing what they all did: deliberately avoiding any mention of the hotel's shortcomings. Like ostriches with their heads in the sand.

Cleo steeled herself. 'I wish I could agree with you about the hotel, Dad,' she said, 'but I can't. I love this place but we're on the slippery slope. We need to do something.'

'I think your father knows what he's doing,' Sondra shot in. 'He's been running this hotel for thirty years.'

Cleo's plans to be diplomatic took a dive. 'So a hotel management degree is a waste of time and money, is it, Sondra, and I know nothing about hotels?'

'You said it, not me,' smirked Sondra.

'Please don't argue,' said Sheila.

'All I'm saying is that the hotel is in trouble and nobody's even talking about it,' Cleo argued hotly. 'We might have managed in the past because people love the Willow but it's getting older; the whole hotel needs refurbishing. If you could see the money they spend in some of the hotels I've worked in ... Customers expect that now ...'

'The Willow doesn't stand up to the other places you've been then?' her father said evenly.

'No, Dad, that's not what I mean at all.' Cleo's eyes pleaded with him not to take offence. 'They were different sorts of hotels. We run a small, intimate house hotel where people feel welcomed into our world and that's what I love. That's what you created, Dad.' Her eyes were still pleading. 'But we need to improve the place somehow. Carrickwell's changing all the time and we've got to change with it, be ready for the future or else ...'

'Or else what?' asked Harry.

Cleo couldn't say it. She couldn't say they'd close down.

'Or else we'll see the profits dive,' she added lamely.

'Cleo, we've got twenty covers for dinner tonight,' Sheila Malin added. 'That's hardly bad for a week night.'

Everyone but Cleo smiled at this clear proof of the hotel's success.

'Make that twenty-two covers. Or even twenty-three.' Sondra patted her belly happily.

'You don't have any steak, Jacqui?' called Barney. 'I'm ravenous.'

'Chef does not have time to whip up private meals for you, Barney,' Cleo snapped at her brother. 'You've been up here four times in the past week for dinner. Can neither of you cook?'

'I'm pregnant,' Sondra said, looking daggers at her sister-in-law. 'Cooking makes me sick. I don't know why they call it morning sickness, when it's all-day sickness.'

'Lots of women have to work when they're pregnant and they can't afford to give up their jobs at the drop of a hat because their husband's family business will keep doling out money to support them,' Cleo said, taking the gloves off. She knew that her parents supplemented Barney's income with handouts. Handouts that Barney felt were entirely his due.

'It's a loan,' snarled Sondra.

'Four loans in the past two years?'

'It's none of your business.'

'It's my business when the hotel profits are being siphoned off into your pockets.'

'Cleo.' There was a warning in her father's tone but neither Cleo nor Sondra took heed.

'You could be contributing something if you were still working on reception, Sondra,' Cleo went on. 'We all know that Tamara is hopeless. She spends the whole time doing her nails.'

'How dare you talk about my sister like that?' shrieked Sondra.

'Don't, please,' Sheila begged her daughter.

'Yeah, who do you think you are, Cleo?' Barney said, remembering his husbandly duty. 'Apologise.'

Cleo was just about to say that she had no intention of apologising because every word she'd said was true, when Harry interrupted. 'Yes, apologise, Cleo.'

Stunned, she spun round to look at her father. 'For telling the truth?' she demanded.

'We don't have big rows in this family, Cleo,' Harry went on. 'That gets nobody anywhere. Please apologise to Sondra.'

Cleo felt betrayed. Her father rarely interfered in squabbles and it was hardly a family secret that she and Sondra didn't get on. They were grown-ups; they were entitled not to get on if they didn't want to. She loved and respected her father but he wasn't always right. All she'd done was tell the truth and she was being punished.

Although she knew why: her father hated rows and tried to avoid conflict at all costs. His mother had been what he euphemistically called 'fiery' and Harry had grown up watching his parents face each other like bullfighters, circling in rage, screaming insults several times a week. A person could have too much plate-throwing in their life, he used to say. Cleo knew she'd inherited her grandmother's passion – although not her harsh tongue. She would never hurt anyone with a rash word – she knew better than that, no matter how passionately she felt about something. Her grandmother's way was not the right way to do things.

'You're right, Dad,' she said calmly now. 'I went about it the wrong way. I'm sorry for talking about Tamara like that,' she said to Sondra. *But not sorry for the other parts.* 'That wasn't fair. I'm going out for a walk.' And she got up to go.

Her father muttered something about going into the office for a few moments, and he left too, by a different door.

Cleo went and sat where she'd always gone when she was wildly annoyed but trying to hide it. Down at the bottom of the garden, behind the orchard wall, on the cracked stone seat under the apple tree. The bark of the tree was coated with silver and there were no acid-green buds appearing. The tree was dying from neglect. Nobody in the Willow knew the first thing about trees and the men who worked on the garden had their hands full sorting out the front in the limited time available.

Some of the hotel's brides had found this secluded spot over the years and had been photographed there, just the bride and the groom, smiling under the apple tree. For that reason alone, the tree should have been taken care of but nobody had listened to Cleo when she said it. They never did. And they probably never would, Cleo realised with a jolt.

She knew she'd changed from a tomboyish kid, but to Mum, Dad, Jason and Barney, she was still the baby of the family.

Idly, she picked a bit of bark off the tree. Several beetles fell out, shocked at losing their home. Feeling like a murderer, Cleo tried to replace the bark but it wouldn't stick.

'Sorry, boys,' she said to the beetles who'd made a rapid exit on the stony ground at her feet.

They'd lost their home and the Malins would lose their home too.

She took the piece of newspaper from her jeans pocket and unfolded it for the nth time. Nat had seen it in a trade paper and had sent it to her. He'd understood what it meant.

'Roth Hotels Expansion Plans' ran the headline. The article reported how the vast international chain of Roth Hotels had decided to turn their attention to the Irish and UK markets. Not city hotels, the article went on to say, but some of their hugely successful country resorts complete with golf, health club and riding facilities. Locations mentioned included the eastern part of Ireland. Cleo felt sick to the pit of her stomach when she thought about it.

If a Roth Hotel opened up in Carrickwell, it would sound the death knell to the Willow.

CHAPTER THREE

Daisy Farrell had thought that tidying out her wardrobe was the perfect way to spend a rainy Sunday afternoon when Alex was away in London for the weekend working. But the task had palled somewhat as the day dragged on. Five o'clock and dusk arrived at the same gloomy moment, and every single item of clothing Daisy owned was still piled on the bedroom floor in their normally immaculate apartment, in so many tottering piles. All black, of course. Despite the fashion bibles screeching that red or pink or white were the new black, Daisy knew – like every fashionista worth her salt – that black would always be the new black.

Black made every lump and bump disappear and turned slender into skinny. Who needed bulimia when you had black?

She had so much stuff, she reflected, wishing she'd never started. How was it that a woman whose very job was picking clothes for other people – she was a buyer for Carrickwell's chicest designer shop, Georgia's Tiara – seemed to have so many fashion mistakes in her own wardrobe?

'This will have to go,' Daisy decided, holding up a tweedy skirt that had never quite suited her. 'And this.' Drapey chiffon shirts had never been her style, yet she loved them. They'd sold buckets of them in the shop, though. Daisy's style might waver when it came to dressing herself, but her instinct was spot on when it came to her job.

'How do you do it?' asked people, fascinated at how she knew the shop's customers would buy the clothes she bought at the fashion fairs six months in advance of stocking them.

'You pick clothes in January and then when summer comes, you hope they're in fashion and that women here buy them?' was the usual question when Daisy explained what being the fashion buyer for Georgia's Tiara meant. 'How do you know they'll like them?'

'I don't,' Daisy would say pleasantly. 'I've been doing it for years and it's a combination of experience, skill and, well . . . you've got to have an eye for it.'

'Ah.' That answer pleased most of the crowd because an eye was the same thing as luck: you either had it or you didn't. They could not be blamed for not having an eye, and therefore not having the apparent good fortune of Daisy Farrell. A nice apartment in the restored old mill in the centre of Carrickwell, a lovely red sporty car, two decent holidays a year, not to mention all that flying to fashion fairs in Germany and London, having champagne in club class, *and* a man like Alex Kenny. Some women had all the luck.

'Don't tell them that it's just down to having an eye for fashion. You make it sound too simple,' Alex chided. 'Tell them it's bloody hard work and there's no guarantee you'll sell a single thing you buy.'

Alex worked in investment banking in Dublin city, a job where it was mandatory to blow your own trumpet. Even after fourteen years with Daisy, Alex still couldn't understand her natural reticence. She was brilliant at what she did – what was wrong with telling people? And Daisy, safe in the love of the one person in the world who made her feel good about herself, laughed and said that being a fashion buyer was impossible to explain to the uninitiated. It was like wearing Prada and looking effortlessly cool, so effortlessly cool that nobody would ever guess all the hard work that went into the whole outfit.

Besides, Daisy, like all people who doubted their worth, had a horror of boring other people. She felt she'd bore everyone rigid if she told them about the years of following fashion from the side-lines and of how she'd tried to make clothes from odd scraps of fabric almost before she was old enough to sew. Daisy might have been blessed with an eye for fashion, but her lengthy apprenticeship had sharpened it.

'It's a female thing,' she added. 'Women don't like showing off.'

'It's a Daisy thing,' Alex replied. 'My office is full of women who have no qualms about telling people how talented they are.'

'Only because they're trying to impress you,' Daisy laughed. And it was true. At thirty-six, Alex still had the physique of the college rower he'd once been. Long and lean, he looked good in his office suits, even better out of them, and his glossy wolf's pelt hair and strong, intelligent face meant that women noticed him. One of the many, many things Daisy loved about him was that Alex didn't notice them back.

It never occurred to her that he might ever have to worry about men noticing her. Daisy had no illusions about her own beauty. A person didn't grow up overhearing their mother call them an ugly duckling, like Daisy's mother did, without drawing their own conclusions. But she had style, fabulous shoes, and Alex, the man she'd adored since their first meeting in a dingy college pub a lifetime ago.

Her beloved Alex was linked to the three questions that Daisy really hated. First up was, 'Are you and Alex ever going to get married, Daisy?'

Short answer: 'Perhaps,' delivered with a little smile that hinted at plans for something elegant on a far-flung beach where the party could pick exotic blooms to hang behind their ears as they stood, barefoot, in the sand. A Vera Wang dress, privately designed rings, and a select beachside party for their small group of friends, followed by a relaxed gathering in a restaurant when they got home from the honeymoon.

Daisy's real answer was: 'I'd love to but Alex's not interested. We've talked about it but he's not really into marriage. Why fix what's not broken, he says.'

She'd said it to Mary Dillon, her partner in the shop.

'That's such a man thing to say,' remarked Mary, who was just divorced and still inhabiting the all-men-are-pigs zone. Mary had started Georgia's Tiara ten years before, and Daisy had come on board shortly afterwards. Together, they made a great team.

'Getting married isn't about not fixing anything. It's a bigger commitment, that's all,' Mary went on. 'It's Alex saying he wants the world to know he's going to be with you for ever. Living with someone can't do that. Mind you,' she added gloomily, 'if I'd just lived with Bart instead of being stupid enough to marry him, we mightn't have ended up paying the lawyers so much. Every time I see my lawyer in his new Porsche, I feel like saying I own an eighth of that car, so when can I borrow it?'

'Yes . . .' said Daisy, wishing she hadn't started this. Mary was not the sort of woman to call a spade a metal digging implement and Daisy had just broken her own steadfast rule about couple loyalty. Never speak about your loved one in a negative way. Anything else was too like what she'd grown up with. 'I suppose I can see Alex's point,' Daisy went on untruthfully, backtracking out of guilt. It had been a private conversation with Alex. What on earth had made her spill it all out to Mary? 'We *are* happy as we are. I must be premenstrual, that's it. Ignore me.'

The only plus about not having plans to get married meant that Daisy didn't have to think about the dilemma of inviting both her parents to the wedding. It had been years since Daisy's mother had tolerated being in the same town as her father, much less the same room. Nan Farrell had insisted that her husband move out of

Carrickwell years ago so she could pretend – to herself, at least – that she was still a person of consequence in the town. Daisy's father had drifted in and out of her life for years. He lived in San Francisco now and seemed perfectly happy to send and receive nothing more than a Christmas card.

Whenever *Vogue* had a feature on beautiful brides, Daisy contented herself with the knowledge that she had commitment without the need for an intricate seating plan to keep all her family happy. Her family had been a bit of a non-family all her life. And surely, she reasoned, it was more modern to live with a loved one than rush up the aisle just for the sake of it?

Her second most hated question was even more personal.

'How did you lose all the weight?' interrogated all the people who hadn't seen her for years and who remembered Daisy as the rounded creature she would always remain in their heads.

Ignoring the rudeness of the question – weight was a terribly personal matter and yet so many recklessly demanded to know what you ate for breakfast if it would help them lose a few pounds – Daisy would say that she hadn't done a thing. Honestly.

For all his charming sociability, Alex was incredibly private and hated anyone knowing he'd been sick, so she couldn't say that the sheer worry she'd gone through over the two years of his mystery illness meant the weight, three stones of it, had just melted away.

'Not WeightWatchers, not the Atkins?' people would then say suspiciously, clearly convinced she was lying through her teeth, lived on nothing but cabbage soup and probably had terrible problems with bad breath.

'Not a thing,' Daisy replied, privately wondering was there an opening in the book world for the Epstein Barr Virus Diet.

Alex looked great now. Thanks to the last year as a patient of the fabulous Dr Verdan, he was glowing with health and brimming with his old energy. He was taking enough health supplements to open his own shop, but they all seemed to be working. She hoped the ones she'd begged him to ask Dr Verdan for were helping.

Which led on to the third question, the one that wasn't asked quite as often. Apparently, people were more aware of the delicacy of asking it these days, so that when a woman reached a certain age and no children had appeared, only the bumbling lumbered in and asked: 'What about kids? Don't you want them?'

Unfortunately, there were lots of bumblers out there, people who thought it was perfectly acceptable to ask a healthy thirty-five-year-old woman with a long-term partner if she'd ever considered the notion of children.

Hell, no, Daisy wanted to yell at them. 'We thought about it but we've heard that a child costs 30,000 euro in its first five years, so we're going to the Bahamas instead.' Only an answer so flippant could disguise the genuine physical pain she felt when asked such a question.

Because Daisy didn't want children. She craved them, yearned for them, cried for them in her sleep.

When she was thirty, she'd stopped taking the pill.

'It'll be fun making babies,' Alex had said at the time.

And it had been. Making love and hoping to get pregnant instead of the reverse was very sexy.

'The mother of my children,' Alex liked to murmur when he lay above her, his naked body moulded perfectly against her soft lush one.

Daisy had no particular love for her body. It was so defiantly different from what she'd have liked it to be, with rounded everything and fat that spilled out over her size fourteen waistbands, making her move miserably on to size sixteen. But when Alex was holding her gently, and her strawberry-blonde hair streamed around her, creamy skin pillowed out below him as they tried to conceive their child, that was the only time when she felt that she was almost beautiful.

Making babies didn't work out to be as straightforward as they'd thought, however. It was as if simply deciding to have one, instead of trying hard not to, had suddenly made pregnancy very difficult to achieve.

Magazines were full of miserable stories about declining fertility and how women were leaving it too late to conceive. Daisy hated those articles ever since the day she'd grasped the horrific news that women were born with all the eggs they were ever going to have and it was all downhill from then on.

'You mean, we don't make new eggs all the time?' she asked Paula, who worked in the shop and was addicted to health websites. 'I thought everything in the human body got replaced every seven years. I *read* that, I know I did,' Daisy added anxiously.

'No,' said Paula cheerily. 'You've got your lot, I'm afraid. When you're thirty, so are your eggs.'

Daisy blanched at the thought of her then thirty-year-old eggs and all the things her body had been through.

Could too much alcohol affect your eggs? Think of all those mad nights in her twenties when she'd had so much to drink that she'd almost drunk herself sober. Or drugs. Remember Werner, the Austrian student friend of Alex's who'd been very keen on smoking dope and who'd encouraged a disapproving Daisy to have a joint with the rest of them on that holiday. She'd never done drugs before, she disapproved of drugs, for heaven's sake, but she'd been stupid and said yes, and she *knew* that would come back to haunt her. Stupid cow, how could she not have known about her eggs?

Paula, who was younger than Daisy, didn't seem too worried about the state of her ovaries and the fact that she hadn't hatched anything, so to speak.

'Ah, sure, what'll be will be,' she said optimistically.

'Life is not a Doris Day song,' a little voice inside Daisy's head raged bitterly. Aloud she said: 'You're dead right, Paula. It's crazy to obsess over these things. We're only young, after all, and there's loads of things they can do now to help you have children.'

That thought, the thought of experiments at the cutting edge of science where people would be able to have babies without even being on the same continent as each other, kept her going.

Cutting back on caffeine didn't kickstart Daisy's reproductive system. Neither did eating all the so-called superfoods. The vegetable basket looked almost alive with all the green stuff in it, and Daisy did her best to cut down the glasses of wine at the weekend. But her periods came with a regularity she'd sworn wasn't there in the days when she hadn't wanted to get pregnant.

Still, there was time on their side, she counselled herself. They were young, healthy, successful in everything they touched.

Georgia's Tiara became more and more prosperous. Mary gave Daisy a share in the shop.

'I can sell ice to the Eskimos but I wouldn't be able to sell it unless you got the right ice,' Mary said firmly. 'You've put so much effort and energy into this business, you deserve to be a partner.'

Daisy had covered her mouth with her hands like a child. 'Mary, I can't believe it. You're so good to me.'

'Nonsense.' Brisk was Mary's middle name. 'You're so good to me, and for the shop. Running a business is second nature to me but I could spend a month of Sundays trying to learn what you do, and I'd still never manage it.'

Buoyed up by this – even her mother would have to say she was doing well – Daisy decided that she wasn't pregnant because the time wasn't right. It was like that old Buddhist saying: when the student is ready, the master will appear. She obviously wasn't ready. Career women had so much trouble balancing kids and work that it was probably easier at this point in her life not to have a child. Then, after a year of baby-making, Alex became sick. It seemed incredible that it had taken so long to get a diagnosis and they had gone through the seven valleys of hell before they'd found out what it was. Even now, Daisy quaked at the thought of what it could have been. She and Alex had suspected leukaemia. Now, she always put money in collection tins that had anything to do with cancer as if to ward off the evil.

But the bugbear had been Epstein Barr, an autoimmune disorder that turned normally energetic people into wrecks. Hard to detect and even harder to cure, the illness had taken its toll on both Alex and Daisy. Baby-making had not been on the agenda then, but it was at the back of Daisy's mind constantly, the sense of time passing slowly and of her elderly eggs getting even older. She also worried, although she would never say it, that Alex's illness was part of the problem.

And now they'd come out of the fire, together. For the past two years, Alex had been healthy and said he felt great. She felt great. She was going to get pregnant. It was her time, time to find out why she wasn't conceiving, if there was a problem with Alex's sperm due to the Epstein Barr, and to do something about it. The student was ready.

Standing in front of the mirror in their bedroom on a dark Sunday afternoon, Daisy said it out loud: 'I'm ready. I'm ready to get pregnant. Now.'

Nothing happened. No thunderbolt from on high to tell her that God was listening, no rustling of curtains to tell her that her guardian angel was hovering and would do his or her best.

There was no sign, just as there had never been any sign before.

'Alex, I want us to have tests to find out what's wrong. We can't afford to wait any longer. I'm getting older and . . .' Daisy's monologue to the mirror trailed off. She didn't want to tell the mirror – she wanted to tell Alex, and now.

She'd spent the weekend thinking of nothing else because, with Alex away, she had lots of time to reflect. He was in London with a group of investors on what he described as a 'bank hooley', where good food and expensive wine were laid on to help lubricate people's cheque books.

Although she hated being alone, his being away gave Daisy a chance to catch up on all the boring household chores, like cleaning the oven before it went up in flames. The oven now gleamed, thanks to much scrubbing on Saturday. But the wardrobe tidying had proved to be a bit of a marathon task.

She'd kept some of her 'fat' clothes for when she was pregnant. That silky sweater from Italy, the flowing Pucci shirt, they'd look lovely over a pregnant belly. Daisy had such plans for being a fashionable pregnant woman and now, faced with these clothes and no use for them in sight, her heart ached.

By five on Sunday afternoon, as she turned the bedroom lights on, Daisy realised she'd like nothing better than an early dinner in front of the box, but she still had to put away loads of clothes. At least fifty per cent of everything she owned was in heaps on the floor.

She was holding up a sweater – black, and expensive, so *how* could she get rid of it, even though it didn't really suit her? – when the phone rang.

'Alex, hello.' Daisy sank onto his side of the bed, cradling the phone into her shoulder, her voice softening with love. 'How are you? Miss you, you know.'

'I know, Daisy. But I'll be home tomorrow evening.' From his businesslike tone, it was clear that he wasn't alone.

'Can't talk, huh? No problem. How's it going?' she asked, suppressing the slightest tinge of irritation that he hadn't slipped away from the group for a moment to phone her privately. He was on his mobile, it seemed, and she hated those brusque 'All fine here, how are you?' conversations.

'All fine here,' said Alex, right on cue. 'And at your end?'

Daisy laughed and did her best to let the irritation slip away. She could hardly have said, 'Let's do something about why I'm not getting pregnant,' over the phone, could she? 'My end is great but it's lonely because it doesn't have your end to snuggle up against in bed. It was freezing here last night,' she added. 'I had to resort to my fleece pyjamas and my bedsocks as I didn't have you to warm me.' She couldn't resist the joke. He hated her bedsocks.

'Really?' said Alex blankly, but Daisy knew he must be grinning. Only someone who knew him well would hear the amusement over a crackly mobile and hundreds of miles.

'Really. So hurry home. Me and the bedsocks miss you.'

'You too. Better rush. We've got another meeting before dinner and it will probably be late, so I won't phone again. See you tomorrow.'

'Yes, can't wait.' She had so much to talk to him about. 'I know you can't talk, Alex,' Daisy said quickly, 'and you don't have to reply but I love you.'

There was silence in her ear. He'd hung up.

Daisy made herself put the receiver back without slamming it into the cradle. How was it that women invariably wondered what was wrong, even when there was nothing wrong, and men never divined anything out of the ordinary when emotional war was about to be declared? She'd like to see how pleased Alex would be if she'd hung up on him when she was working away and when he was burning to tell her something.

She dismally surveyed the piles of clothes on the beige carpet. Everything in the apartment was decorated in subtle shades of beige and caramel, with dark brown accents. Alex loved modern minimalism.

Daisy had once wondered how their flat would cope with a small child in it. She loved planning new floor coverings and washable paintwork, or working out how to lay out the baby's room. How sad was she?

That was it: her enthusiasm had vamoosed. She'd stack everything on her side of the room and do it during the week. There was a pepperoni pizza and oven chips in the freezer, a bottle of chilled wine in the fridge and probably some slushy romantic film on the movie channel. She could even give herself a manicure. And she'd put a conditioning treatment in her hair to bring it back to its glossy, strawberry-blonde glory. Her straightening irons and the colour played havoc with the split ends.

She'd look fabulous for when Alex saw her and he'd be flattened with both guilt and longing, and then she'd tell him what she'd really wanted to talk to him about.

Georgia's Tiara had two windows looking out onto Delaney Row, a street of grand, three-storey houses on the northern side of Carrickwell, and both windows had the words 'SALE' emblazoned across in giant, art deco lettering. Decorated in proprietress Mary Dillon's favourite lemon yellow, the shop was a clothes lover's paradise and included a tiny accessory department that sold shoes, bags and costume jewellery, three large changing rooms and, most important of all, sympathetic mirrors.

Mary had most of her warpaint on and was on her second cup of hot water and lemon – awful, but great for the insides, she'd read – by the time Daisy got into the shop on Monday morning.

'Sorry, traffic was brutal,' Daisy said, which was pretty much what she always said. The snooze button was just so seductive in the morning. She'd always been able to identify with the Chinese mandarin who insisted on being woken at four every morning just so he had the luxury of knowing he didn't have to get up yet. 'And the roadworks on the bridge . . . shocking.'

'Paula wanted fresh air so she went across to Mo's Diner to get the lattes,' Mary said, not even bothering to reply to the traffic story. The day Daisy arrived on time, Mary would know there was something seriously wrong. 'Take the weight off the floor and catch your breath,' Mary continued, handing over a bit of the newspaper.

Paula, who was now five and a half months pregnant with her first child, arrived with the lattes and three of Mo's famous blueberry muffins, and for a few moments, there was the weekend catch-up as Daisy asked how Paula felt, had the baby been kicking and how many bottles of Gaviscon had she gone through?

'Two,' admitted Paula, shamefacedly. She was torn between joy at being pregnant and misery at having heartburn like the eruption of Krakatoa.

'Only two?' said Daisy cheerily. 'You should have shares in the company.' Today she could joke with Paula. Up to now, she'd found it hard although she did her level best not to show it because she loved Paula and wouldn't have hurt her for the world. But today felt different. Now that Daisy had decided to take action, the pain had receded a little.

When everyone had their coffee – two lattes, and a decaf for the mother-to-be – blissful peace took over as the women flicked the pages of the tabloids, seeing who'd been wearing what at the weekend.

One of the shop's best customers, a ladies-who-lunch type who had loads of money and the fashion sense of a Doberman, was pictured at a movie premiere wearing a spaghetti-strapped embroidered dress in midnight blue, a French blue cashmere shrug and string of tourmalines – an outfit that Daisy had put together specifically for her. The only defect was the flash of nude tights visible between the dress and the skinny navy suede boots.

'You told her to wear black tights,' groaned Paula.

'The tights aren't too bad,' Daisy said. 'If she'd done them on purpose, we'd all be saying it was brilliant.'

'True,' muttered Mary. There was a fine line in the fashion world between the genius of doing something different and the stupidity of wearing the wrong tights. Likewise, blue eyeshadow could be spectacular on the right person, and a hideous mistake on the wrong one.

The morning was taken up with phone calls about the whereabouts of a shipment of Italian silk print scarves. In between, Daisy lent a hand to a trio who were looking for a mother-of-the-bride outfit that would go with a cream brocade wedding gown, and a bridesmaid's dress for the bride's sister.

'A dress that she can wear again, nothing with big flowers like a huge duvet cover,' insisted the bride, with the bride's sister nodding emphatically in the background. Once was quite enough to look like a refugee from the sofa factory – she was not wearing anything flowery and wildly frilly ever again.

Daisy quite liked the challenge of dressing bridal parties. Mary hated it because, in her current post-divorce state, she felt people weren't being advised of what they were letting themselves in for.

'There should be something more in the ceremony, something along the lines of a warning that it takes just one day to get married and five thousand days to work yourselves up to the divorce,' she said darkly, out of range of the happy trio. 'And bitterness . . . they never mention bitterness at weddings, do they? That's the bit that lasts longest. You might have long since forgotten where you've put the wedding album, and the Waterford stemware might be scattered all around the house, but by God, you can lay your hands on a bit of bitterness at any time of the day or night.'

Daisy didn't know what to say as they rummaged around at opposite ends of the storeroom, searching for a pale pink, beaded column dress with butterflies on the hem as well as a wool-silk mix dress with matching coat that would look good on a size sixteen at a winter wedding. It was odd that Mary could be so anti-marriage one minute, and pro-marriage the next. She'd raged at Daisy's story of how Alex didn't want to get married. Lately, Daisy had been censoring her conversation with Mary in case she rattled on too much about what she and Alex had done at the weekend, when she knew Mary was sitting at home on her own, worrying about cash flow or never having sex again.

'I blame Richard Gere,' Mary sniffed balefully. 'I thought life was going to be like in *An Officer and a Gentleman* and look where that's got me? Bloody nowhere. It's the uniform that did it for me.'

As Bart had never worn a uniform, Daisy wasn't quite sure what Mary was on about but she let her ramble.

'Triumph of hope over dumb bloody stupidity,' Mary said. 'Why do we all think we have to get married? What's wrong with women's brains that we feel we're not connected with the world unless we have a man to connect us with it? Men – who needs them?'

Mary's bedtime reading was currently of the women-who-love-bastards variety. She'd lent Daisy some of her books and Daisy had accepted them out of guilt, but they were still in the back of her car in their plastic bag, necessitating even more guilt. What if Mary saw them, patently unread, and realised that while *she* was unhappy, not everyone else was?

'Come on, Mary,' said Daisy now, feeling that some sort of cheering-up was in order. 'You're over Bart, you know you are.'

'Am I?' demanded Mary. 'Because I'm not, you know. I'm sad and depressed and I don't think I'll ever feel right again. That's what marriage does for you, Daisy, and don't you forget it.'

The lustre had gone out of dressing the wedding party for Daisy. She felt a bit headachey, so as soon as they had gone she nipped out for some painkillers and, on the spur of the moment, decided that a bottle of wine might cheer Mary up.

They closed at six and Daisy cracked open the bottle.

'Just one glass,' Mary warned. 'The kids have a friend over for dinner and I don't want to get a reputation as the divorced lush. That would give them something to talk about at the school gates. Alone and alcoholic isn't the sort of thing you want to advertise. Nearly as bad as lonely and desperate for sex.'

'None for me,' added Paula, holding up a hand in refusal. 'If I look at a drink, the baby will emerge phoning the child protection agency and my mother will be scandalised. She's never got over my sister-in-law having that glass of champagne at our wedding when she was pregnant. She *still* talks about the irresponsibility of it all.'

Daisy did a quick bottle/person calculation. She never drank more than one glass when she drove.

Mary edged off her shoes, put her feet up on the wicker bin behind the counter, and sighed. 'Don't know why I wear those blinking shoes,' she said, wiggling her toes luxuriously. 'They ruin my feet. I'll have bunions soon.'

'The girl today who was getting married was going to have the full works done in a beautician's just before the day,' Paula said. 'Manicure, pedicure, you name it.'

They all sighed at the thought.

'I've never had a professional pedicure,' Daisy said. 'I feel embarrassed enough about having a manicure, my nails are always such a mess, but my feet . . . ugh. That would be worse. I think they'd need industrial sanding equipment to get the hard skin off my feet and then the beautician would look at me and think I was a right old hick. No, I can't face it. I'd prefer to do it badly myself.'

'Ah, they don't care about the state of your feet,' Mary said. 'See enough feet and you can cope with anything. I've had everything done over the years. Feet, hands, that wrapped-up-like-a-mummy thing that makes you lose inches. Stinks, though; you feel smelly for the whole day with the mud. Can't afford any of it now, of course, thanks to Bart. Plus I don't have the time.'

'That's what we need,' Daisy said dreamily. 'A girls' day out at a fabulous beauty parlour where we can relax and be made beautiful, and I could have a pedicure and you'd be with me so I wouldn't feel inadequate because of my messy cuticles and hard heels!'

'That spa they were working on near the old Delaney place is opening up next week,' Paula said. 'I don't know who bought it but they've had builders working like madmen, according to my mother – she and her rambling club are there every week for their mountain walk. It's going to be all holistic, with yoga rooms, hot stone therapy and aromatherapy.'

'I wouldn't mind some of that hot stone thingy,' moaned Mary. 'I wish I had time for it . . .'

'Why not?' asked Paula. 'We could do it soon. If they're new, they'll have special offers, and they're bound to have pregnancy stuff. Special massages and treatments.'

'Right, I'll check it out,' said Daisy, fired up by this new idea.

Today was a day for plans. She'd phoned several fertility clinics today and she had news for Alex. Exciting news. She'd made an appointment for them both with one of the clinics. The only problem was that the appointment wasn't for several weeks. She'd go mad with anticipation until then. A spa day with the girls was just what she needed to look forward to in the meantime.

Daisy arrived home at seven, swinging the plastic bag of Mary's self-help books because she had to flick through them some time. The first thing she spotted was Alex's briefcase sitting on the walnut floor in the hall. What caught her eye was the flash of turquoise peeping out of the black leather folds. A Tiffany gift bag. She considered a quick peek to see what Alex had bought her and then thought better of it.

Imagine if he'd bought her a diamond as big as a marble for their engagement and she'd have to spend the rest of her life knowing that she'd looked before he'd produced it. How did you and Dad get engaged? the kids would ask, and she'd have either to lie or say, 'I stuck my big nose into his briefcase and found the ring, so I knew then . . .' Not the romantic story she'd like. Anyway, it couldn't be an engagement ring. They'd discussed that – they didn't need marriage to cement their relationship.

She yelled a cheery hello and Alex rushed from the bathroom, looking a bit pale. 'Dodgy stomach,' he said by way of greeting, then planted a speedy kiss on her cheek.

'Is that all the welcome I'm getting?' Daisy joked, following him into the bedroom where he began rapidly undressing, throwing his jacket and tie onto the silken caramel throw on their king-size bed. 'Oh-oh, *this* is the welcome . . .'

Halfway through pulling off his shirt, Alex grimaced. 'Honey, if you knew the weekend I've had . . . Those people wouldn't spend Christmas. I am so shattered. And the hotel wasn't as good as the last one.'

'Poor love.' She held out her arms to him, and for a minute he relaxed against her and laid his head on her shoulder.

Then, he moved away and finished undressing, before putting on jeans and a sweatshirt.

Daisy sat cross-legged on the end of the bed.

'I wanted to talk to you,' she began. 'It's OK,' she laughed, seeing his eyes widen, 'I haven't been fired and I haven't crashed the car! It's about the baby, our baby. Oh, Alex, we've waited so long – let's do something about it.' She smiled, having saved the best till last. 'I did some research today and phoned a couple of fertility clinics. With most of them, you've got to wait about a month for an appointment but the Avalon – I read about it in the paper and it's brilliant, although it's one of the more expensive – had literally just had a cancellation. They can see us on Friday three weeks at twelve fifteen.' Her eyes shone with excitement. 'Isn't that fantastic? Please say you can make it.'

Alex, frozen with one black sock on and one off, stared at her.

'We've been waiting for years, Alex. One before you got sick and two since.'

He flinched. She knew he hated being reminded about his illness.

'We've got to do something before I run out of time. I need to know why I'm not getting pregnant. I want a baby.' Even saying it made her feel emotional. 'And I know you do too. It's what we've wanted for so long, and now it's the right time.'

She held out a hand to him and, his expression unreadable, he took it, sitting down on the bed beside her.

'I don't know what to say.'

'You don't have to say anything,' Daisy rushed in, terrified that he'd say that he didn't want a baby that much after all. 'Alex, I think that's our problem: we think and plan and with some things in life, you can't think and plan. They should just happen. We've been waiting for the right time to have a baby and it's now.' Please agree with me, she pleaded silently.

'I don't know,' he repeated.

'Please, Alex. It's so important to me and I don't think we should wait any longer,' she added softly.

'I can't believe you've set up a meeting with a fertility clinic without asking me first, Daisy.'

Daisy breathed again. At least he hadn't said no. It was a start. Shock she was prepared for. Men didn't like asking for help with directions when they were driving: you'd need to multiply that behaviour by ten to recreate how most men would feel about having to produce sperm in a cup in some anonymous room to make their partner pregnant.

She tried again. 'I'm sorry. I know it's a big step and it can be hard on couples. I've read all the articles about fertility treatments.'

Going through the mill of fertility treatment had broken up many couples. But it wouldn't do that to them, Daisy vowed. All she had to do was convince him. 'We can do it, Alex. Please.'

There was doubt written all over Alex's face. But he hadn't said no.

'All we have to do is go this one time and see what they say,' she offered. 'And if you hate the idea, well, we can talk some more . . .' With this olive branch extended, he couldn't say no. 'OK, we'll stop talking about it. You need to think.'

Yes, stop haranguing him. Let him think about it. She changed the subject.

'Hey, want to tell me what else you were doing in London besides staying in a horrible hotel and ferrying rich, stingy people around?' she teased, thinking of the Tiffany bag. 'I can see you've been shopping. Anything you want to tell me?'

'Daisy . . .' he began and stopped.

'Sorry, I ruined the surprise, did I?' She was contrite. 'But it's not my birthday for ages. I thought it was some fun present, although nothing from Tiffany's could be strictly classed as purely fun. Serious fun!'

He looked blank.

'The Tiffany bag?'

Comprehension dawned.

'Was it for something else?' It couldn't be an engagement ring? No, of course not. 'Our anniversary's not just yet,' she said quickly.

Alex shook his head as he left the room. 'No.'

He returned with the bag in question and put it in front of her without any fanfare. What did she want an engagement ring for anyway? Daisy thought as she opened the bag and took out the Tiffany box. 'You buying this is a sign,' she said happily, taking the white ribbon off. 'A sign that this is a good time to change our lives.'

Inside the box was a silver necklace, not unlike the first present he'd bought her years ago, only this one was Tiffany silver and exquisitely pretty.

It was indeed a sign, Daisy realised. A sign that their love could endure no matter what. Alex needed time to think about fertility treatment and then he'd come round to her way of thinking. Having a family was the most natural thing in the world. It was a no-brainer, as Alex would say.

The first present he'd ever given her, a silvery necklace with a heart on it, was kept in her treasures box, along with the black satin trousers she'd been wearing the first time they'd met.

The necklace had tarnished black with age because it was only a cheap thing, but she loved it and wished she could still wear it, although it turned her neck an alarming shade of green. The matching bra and knickers she'd been wearing the first time they made love were there too. Daisy never told Alex she still had them; he'd have thought it was a bit silly, keeping such mementoes many years later.

The satin drainpipe trousers made her cringe now when she looked at them. In theory, satin trousers were sleek, narrow and made for people with hips like a greyhound's. At the time, an unbelievable fourteen years ago, Daisy was definitely not a greyhound sort of girl.

The others on the fashion design course wore edgy, frayed black things they'd customised themselves, and were instantly recognisable as design students on the sprawling campus. Daisy alone never wore her own stuff. This was partly because she'd realised, with much misery, that she wasn't much good at clothes designing. She lived for *Vogue*, understood bias cuts as if she'd learned at Schiaparelli's knee, and could draw like an angel. But she couldn't design for peanuts.

Besides, the sort of clothes she loved were garments made for tall, willowy brunettes with arrogant eyes and cheekbones like razor blades. Rounded girls with heavy legs and a bust straight out of the wench department in central casting looked better in all black, even black satin trousers topped with a long-line silk cardigan.

Of course, she hadn't thought she'd looked bad then. She'd thought the black satin disguised the fat bits and elongated her shape so she looked quite good, although hardly supermodel material. And Alex had thought so too, unlike some of the guys in college.

It was amazing the way being a big girl made you invisible. It should have been the other way round – if you were big, there was more of you and people couldn't avoid you. But they did. They averted their eyes like medieval peasants must have at the sight of lepers, yelling 'unclean'.

Alex Kenny, long, lean, dark-eyed and with biceps of steel from being uncrowned king of the rowing club, didn't avert his eyes.

'You don't wear mad stuff like the other design nuts,' he said in amusement that first time they'd met. 'You look normal.' And he'd reached out and lazily twirled a tassel of her rose-pink vintage silk scarf, making Daisy turn exactly the same shade of pink.

They'd been sitting in the Shaman's Armchair, the labyrinthine off-campus pub favoured by the rowing boys. Jules and Fay, classmates of Daisy's, were keen on some of the Lazer rowing team and an impromptu outing to the pub had been organised for one Saturday after a race. Well, it was supposed to be impromptu but Daisy had seen first-hand how long Jules and Fay had taken to get ready. The just-thrown-together look took an awful lot of time to achieve.

Daisy hadn't done much, make-up wise, but had gone to her usual enormous effort to look thin. Looking thin was her mission in life although she knew that she could never really manage it.

As Jules and Fay flirted happily in the pub, Daisy sat in a corner nursing her half-pint. She was stony-broke again. Her grant was almost gone and the pizza restaurant near the flat she shared with the girls didn't need her for late night shifts. She watched the flirting ritual, thinking how nice it would be to be like Jules and Fay, confident and good with men. She was good with men if she was asking them if they wanted their pizza with extra mozzarella, but otherwise, forget it. And then Alex arrived, took in the seating arrangements, and very definitely sat down beside her. Alex Kenny, a man so fine that even Jules and Fay had never thought of setting their cap at him.

'Did you make this?' Alex asked, gesturing at her poncho, also black but with tiny jet beads dotting the hem.

Daisy laughed. 'I'm as good at knitting as I am at rowing,' she said. 'But I sewed the beads on.'

'Did you?' He seemed astonished by this and pulled a chunk of poncho closer for further examination.

Daisy felt her heart flutter wildly at this intimacy.

'But there's millions of them,' Alex added. 'You'd be sewing for ever.'

'Sewing is a part of the whole designing clothes thing,' she informed him gravely.

Alex's eyes – coffee brown or melting chocolate, Daisy couldn't be sure – twinkled. 'Are you making fun of me, Madame Designer? Do you think I'm a big hick from the rowing team who's on a sports scholarship and has an IQ in double digits?'

'*Double* digits?' she asked in mock astonishment. And then ruined it by saying, 'Sorry, only joking . . .' in case she'd upset him.

But Alex only grinned more broadly and wanted to know how long it would take to sew on that many beads.

'I do it when I'm watching telly,' Daisy explained.

'How can you watch and sew? No,' he added, 'don't tell me. It's like how do you get to Carnegie Hall – practise.'

'Like rowing,' Daisy added, looking at his muscles, still very obvious despite the big porridgy sweater he was wearing.

'I'm out of shape,' Alex said ruefully. 'Need to get back in for the season.'

'And you practise a lot?' she asked hesitantly. 'I don't know anything about rowing.'

'Good. I hate rowing groupies. They discuss rowing with you like a pro but they've never put a foot in a scull in their life.'

And he rattled on, telling her about the hours of rowing and gym work, before weaving the conversation back to her and the sort of work it took to get into design college.

Daisy's shyness evaporated. Naturally, Alex wasn't interested in her in any romantic sense – nobody ever was – but he seemed to like talking to her, so that gave her an unaccustomed courage.

He wasn't just being kind talking to the shy, chubby girl because he really fancied one of her friends, kooky Fay, or elegant Jules, who had that Grace Kelly thing going. He was one of those beautiful people who liked talking to everyone. Daisy had decided that some students in college had a scale they worked whereby they wouldn't deign to talk to anyone below a certain rank. Daisy, no good at fashion design and pretty-ish but too big, was below the bar. The cool women ignored her and the cool men didn't see her. But life's gods, like Alex, were above rules and could bestow favour on any lesser mortal. Daisy was fairly sure that as soon as Fay and Jules drifted in Alex's direction, he'd stop talking to her and turn that charming gaze away. But for now, he was hers: the aquiline nose above the sculpted mouth, the faint tan that spoke of some sort of exotic Christmas holiday outside Ireland, the lazy smile of the man who knows he doesn't have to try too hard.

Saturday afternoon crept into Saturday evening and hunger hit. The pub did great traditional Irish potato crepes called boxty, so huge plates of boxty and more drink were ordered. The crowd swelled from the original three girls and four rowers to a big clatter of students. They took up a whole section of the Shaman's, laughing and joking and swapping stories on how unprepared they were for the new term. Still Alex sat beside Daisy.

Warmed up by the two hot whiskys Alex had bought her when she finished her half-pint, she told him that she loved clothes but had come to the painful conclusion that she wasn't much good at designing, something she'd only told Jules and Fay up to now.

'It's desperate,' she confided. 'When I think of how hard it was to get on the course, and now I'm here I can see that it's a mistake.' She could picture her mother's face when she heard. Her mother had pushed for Daisy to do a secretarial course in Carrickwell so she'd always have a steady income. In one of the few battles she'd attempted with her mother, Daisy had said no. She'd been the best in her class at school at art and had dreamed of design college since she knew such a thing existed. There weren't many of Daisy's dreams within reach – being beautiful, thin, adored by her mother – she couldn't let this vaguely achievable one escape.

'Really, Denise, you disappoint me,' her mother had said in deeply betrayed tones. Her mother tended to call her Denise, rarely Daisy. It was her father who'd called her 'my little Daisy', the nickname that had somehow stuck. 'After all we've been through surely you'd see the need for a sensible job, not a rackety one like your father had. I thought I'd taught you that at least. But do what you want. Don't think about what I want.'

Nan Farrell, as thin as the long cigarettes she chain-smoked, took out her cigarette case and flicked it open. It was silver and engraved, the one good thing she had left from her previous life as part of the Carrickwell élite. That life had ended when she'd got pregnant with Daisy – as she never ceased to remind her daughter – and had hit the real world with an almighty bang, married to a man who loved to enjoy himself and wasn't interested in either roots or hard work.

'It's not as if my opinion has ever mattered to you.'

If only, Daisy thought. Her mother's opinion was like the pyramids in relation to Cairo – huge, unyielding and no matter where you stood, you could still feel their presence, even if you couldn't see them.

The memory of the row and the glacier that still existed between herself and her mother took away the happy glow Daisy had been experiencing from talking to Alex. Forgetting for an instant that Alex was a gorgeous man and that she should have been puce with embarrassment just to be talking to him, Daisy leaned her head on her hands on the scratched pub table in the Shaman's. 'How can you have messed up your whole career when you're twenty?' she mumbled.

'All the best people do,' Alex said, patting her arm. He let his fingers roam to the back of her neck where he touched her gently, stroking the soft caramel curls that had escaped from her ponytail. It felt gorgeous, so sexy. Daisy gulped and sat up, forcing Alex to move his hand. She could have stayed there for ever but a man's attentions, the sort of thing that regularly happened to the likes of Jules and Fay, were not what she was equipped to deal with.

He didn't appear to notice her jitteriness.

'At least you know what you wanted to do. I didn't, still don't,' he said. 'A business degree was the obvious choice for me but it doesn't light my fire. It's not on kids' top-ten lists of brilliant jobs, is it? *What do you want to be when you grow up, son? Oh, Dad, I want to sit behind a desk and toil through spreadsheets for ever.*'

He told her that he often felt like giving up college if it weren't for the fact that his course guaranteed a good job at the end of it all. Money was important to him. Daisy got the impression, never voiced, that there hadn't been much spare cash in the Kenny household. She could empathise with that. There hadn't been much money in her house either. She and her mother lived in a small terraced house in the centre of Carrickwell, not physically far from the big house where her mother had grown up, but miles away socially. Daisy had been raised not to discuss money.

Nobody was to know that the gas heater was to be used sparingly, or that Sunday's meat could be made to last until Wednesday if enough imagination was involved.

'We've got our pride,' Nan insisted.

Despite this, Daisy didn't believe that money made you happy. Her mother had come from money and there was no proof anywhere that she'd *ever* had a happy family life, although she was probably more miserable without it than she had been with it.

Love, Daisy felt, was what mattered in life. Not money.

When Alex went to the bar in the Shaman's to get her a drink, Daisy watched him and knew she must look like a spaniel trailing sad eyes after a departing master. Being aware of how others saw her was Daisy's biggest failing. She couldn't walk into a room without wondering if people thought she looked like a whale in whatever she was wearing, and when she spoke during classes, she measured her words as carefully as she measured silk when she was cutting a pattern. Today, though, she wasn't measuring her words or angling her thighs on the seat so that she looked thinner. That was the effect Alex had upon her.

And so they began to go out. They appeared an unlikely couple: the handsome, popular Alex, who could have hooked up with any girl he wanted, and Daisy, who was sweet and pretty certainly, but why didn't she do something about her weight?

Other people didn't see that gentle loving Daisy gave Alex security. Steady, warm, like hot tea in front of a fire, Daisy made the dynamic Alex Kenny feel as if he'd come home.

Daisy tried the Tiffany necklace on. Silver suited her. Gold could make redheads look brassy, she knew. Her mother, who had genuine blonde hair, had warned her so often enough.

'It's beautiful,' breathed Daisy, turning to hug Alex again.

'I'm glad you like it,' he said woodenly, sitting down wearily on the end of the bed.

'Oh, love, don't be like that,' said Daisy. 'I know you're nervous, I am too, but this is so important to us.'

'Daisy –' he began.

'We can do it,' she interrupted. For so long she'd hidden just how important a child was to her; now she had to convince him. 'Alex, I want a baby so badly. I don't talk about it but it haunts me.' She sat down on the bed beside him and held his hands in hers. 'When I go into work and Paula's there, pregnant and so happy, it hurts me so much. Not that I begrudge her a moment of her happiness, but I want that for me, for us. There are babies everywhere you look, did you know that?' She squeezed his hand for support. 'In the shop, on the streets, in Mo's Diner sitting in highchairs staring around with big eyes. I never thought I'd feel this broodiness because it's not as if I was madly into babies or eager to babysit all the time when I was growing up.' Daisy's words were tumbling out now. 'If I'd had brothers or sisters, I'd maybe have had experience with younger children but I didn't, so I didn't think I was that maternal, but then whomp! It hit me.' She gave a nervous laugh. 'Alex, I think about having a baby all the time. Every month, I feel I've failed when my period comes. We've been trying to have a baby for five years now, that's over sixty times of feeling I've failed. I feel . . .' she searched for the right word, 'I feel empty, not quite a proper woman. Only half a person. It's so lonely and sad, and I look at pregnant women or women with children and I feel I'm from another planet. That they're part of this wonderful earth cycle of love and motherhood and I'm not. I'm different, excluded. They don't have a clue that I want my own baby, they probably think I hate kids! But I want my own child so much it hurts. God, it hurts.'

She stopped, aware that he had said nothing all this time. He was probably astonished at what she'd said. Daisy never quite told anybody everything, not even Alex. She thought it might be being an only child and not used to sharing confidences. She envied people who could tell their innermost feelings easily. But now that she'd done it, she'd found it was liberating and scary at the same time to reveal so much.

'I didn't know you felt like that,' he mumbled, not looking at her. 'Why didn't you tell me?'

'We were trying to get pregnant,' Daisy said lightly. 'I sort of thought you'd know how much I wanted a child.' All this time, Daisy had been crossing her fingers and praying every time her period was due, even during the years when Alex had been sick and their lovemaking had been curtailed. How could he not have known?

'I didn't.'

'It's only an appointment,' she begged. 'It can't hurt to go and see what they say. Please, Alex. For me. We've been through so much the past few years, with doctors and tests. I know you hate all that.' So had she. For every blood sample he'd given, Daisy wished she could have proffered her arm. And she'd been there with him through all of it. Couldn't it be her turn now?

Alex looked as if he was under enormous strain but he nodded tightly. 'We can go,' he said finally. 'If that's really what you want.'

CHAPTER FOUR

Mel wished she'd had more time to make an effort for the Lorimar charity ball at the end of February. A black-tie event which all senior staff were expected to turn up at upon pain of death, it had been the subject of much discussion in the office for the past month.

One Lorimar contingent – a Samantha from *Sex and the City* lookalike from marketing, three executive assistants and the head of telesales – planned to go all out for *Sex and the City* glamour, with perilous heels, just-left-the-Elizabeth-Arden-counter make-up and wildly contemporary outfits.

'Lots of red lippy is the key,' said the woman from marketing, who had spent hours on the party preparations, a mammoth task, which also involved ensuring that hundreds of red Lorimar balloons would fall from the ballroom ceiling when Edmund Moriarty announced a special Lorimar donation of €100,000 to the charity, a heart surgery research foundation. Edmund would go ballistic if his big moment was ruined, so most of marketing and a fair part of publicity were deployed on charity detail.

Another group of female staff were planning to get themselves fake-tanned to a decent colour, go to the hairdresser's, then dig out their reliable old black dresses, because nobody wanted to splash out on a new outfit for a mere office do. Vanessa had borrowed a red satin knock-out evening gown from her sister and said she was fully expecting Hilary to go into cardiac arrest when she saw it.

'Although there will be lots of cardiologists on hand if she does,' Vanessa said cheerfully.

And Mel . . . Mel had planned a bit of personal grooming time so she'd look her best on this important occasion. A new dress, perhaps. Or a trendy haircut. Something to show the world, and the top people at Lorimar, that Mel Redmond had her finger on the pulse.

Yet somehow, with fifteen minutes to go before she and Adrian had to leave the house on the Saturday night in question, Mel was upstairs frantically trying to revive her limp hair with a blast of hairspray. Her *maquillage* consisted of a faded bit of eyeliner that had originally been plastered on at nine that morning, and her skin tone was more Wet Weekend in Greenland than the delicious shade of Malibu Bronze most of the other Lorimar women were aiming for. Adrian was recovering from the flu and Mel realised miserably that even he looked better than she did. Feeling worn out after a hectic day and an even more hectic month, all she wanted to do was lie down on the bed and sleep.

Her diary had been black with dates for the whole of February. The second Friday of the month had been Adrian's younger brother, Eddie's, fortieth birthday and the landmark party had involved a big meal for the extended family in his favourite restaurant.

'My kid brother, forty . . .' Adrian kept remarking in an astonished way. 'It seems so old. I can remember us talking about what it would be like to be forty.'

'It was like being a million years old,' reflected Eddie. 'It seemed so far away. I sort of hoped I'd be forty before you because I was fed up with being two years younger and you got to do everything first.'

'For you to be forty first, Adrian would have had to have died,' said their mother, Lynda.

'Just as well it didn't happen then,' Eddie said gravely, 'although I came close to killing you often enough, big bro.'

The following weekend, Mel's aunt and uncle celebrated their fiftieth wedding anniversary and their children organised a big lunch party in a Dublin hotel, complete with a band playing Jim Reeves songs, and enlarged photos on the walls of the happy couple during their married life. Arrangements of pale pink roses decorated the tables, and to recreate the whole wedding effect, which had originally been low key because of a lack of funds, there was a blessing by the parish priest, champagne toasts and speeches.

'It's such an emotional event, isn't it?' said one of the guests dreamily to Mel after Uncle Dermot reduced the whole room to floods of tears by telling them how he didn't want to cope a single day without his Angela.

'Er, yes, very emotional,' replied Mel, sweat ruining her hair as she rushed off after Carrie, who'd run rampant as soon as she realised that the hotel was the perfect place for escaping her mother. So far, Carrie had hidden in a stall in the women's loos, under the draped tablecloth where the anniversary cake stood in state, and behind the swing door into the kitchen.

'Sit down and rest and I'll take care of Carrie,' said Mel's mum, as Mel sprinted past.

Mel stopped and thought of how her high-heeled party sandals were killing her and how the people who organised these events and invited children never seemed to plan anything specifically for them. 'Children welcome!' meant nothing when it didn't include a special child-friendly room where parents could alternate care while round-the-clock *Barney's Great Adventure/One Hundred and One Dalmatians* played on the video. Or else on-demand tranquillisers for the parents. Those glasses of red wine sitting invitingly at the edges of the tables were like a magnet for a child of Carrie's age.

'You're tired, Mel. Have a sit-down with Adrian. Get yourself a piece of the cake, go on. I'll keep an eye on her.' Karen got up from her seat and began to head off after the lilac-clad whirlwind that was Carrie.

'No, Mum, it's OK. You do enough,' Mel said firmly. If her feet hurt, she'd just take her shoes off. Who'd notice? 'Next thing, Carrie will think you're her mother and not me!' The brittle laugh that accompanied this comment didn't escape either of them.

'She wouldn't, don't be silly.' Karen's soft hand gripped her daughter's tightly.

'Course not. It was a joke!' Mel's face adopted its best PR executive smile. They both knew it was fake.

'See you later then, love,' said her mother. And although she'd never worked in PR, she managed a creditable imitation of her daughter's smile.

There was no respite at the office either. Mel was snowed under as the company's magazine, which was sent to all subscribers, was going quarterly instead of biannually, and everyone in the publicity department was being called upon to work overtime. To make matters more tense, there were ominous rumours of huge cutbacks. More work and less money – not a good combination, Mel felt.

Vanessa was under the same pressure and the only time they got to talk was in the morning in the ladies', where they compared notes on the dismal vibes that were circulating about how the company could Save Money.

'I was reading a bit in the paper the other day about how most working women do so much first thing in the morning that by the time they actually get into the office seventy-five per cent are knackered,' Vanessa said one day as she washed her hands and decided that she didn't have the energy for any other primping.

Mel, applying jet-black mascara to give her tired eyes some definition, almost laughed. 'Only seventy-five per cent? What sort of medication are the other twenty-five on?'

What had added most to Mel's sheer exhaustion was the fact that Sarah wasn't sleeping well. For several weeks, Sarah had refused to settle on week nights until she was falling with tiredness, and then she slept badly and woke up several times in the night crying. Mel had discussed this with Dawna, the nursery boss.

'I think I've got to the bottom of it,' Dawna said finally the Friday before the Lorimar charity ball, when Mel was at her wits' end. 'She doesn't want to miss being with you, Mel. When Mummy's out at work all day, we miss Mummy, don't we?'

Sarah nodded gravely.

'That's all it is. She doesn't want to go to bed and miss spending time when you're home in the evening,' Dawna went on blithely, not realising that she was injecting another hypodermic needleful of guilt into Mel's heart. 'I bet she goes down like a lamb at weekends when you're there all the time?'

Mel nodded. It was true: on Friday and Saturday nights, Sarah always slept well and Mel had tried to convince herself it was because the weekends were packed with activity and she was tired. She should have known it wasn't that.

Rather than ask for her mother's help again, Mel enlisted the aid of Adrian's mother, Lynda, to babysit on Saturday while she and Adrian went to the ball. Lynda was always thrilled to be asked, though that didn't happen often. This was partly because Mel didn't want to seem to take advantage of her but mostly because Mel felt that Lynda at some level disapproved of her.

Lynda had come from a generation who'd stayed at home with their children, and even though she never directly said a word to Mel about her job – Lynda wasn't the confrontational type – Mel felt the vibes anyway.

A youthful sixty-something with a trim figure from playing badminton and the same blonde colouring as her son, Lynda seemed the ideal mother-in-law. She lived far enough away not to be dropping round all the time and, although she'd been widowed for several years, she had her own social life and didn't cling to Adrian. But the odd comment Lynda made gave Mel to feel that she didn't want her beloved granddaughters brought up by strangers and was suspicious of her granny rival.

'Melanie, I can't get over how good the girls are with strangers. Carrie particularly. When my boys were that age, they just weren't used to people and they'd hide behind my skirt if they met new people,' Lynda remembered fondly. 'But the girls, why they're regular little grown-ups! It must be being at nursery all day.'

Mel had ground her teeth at that one.

'She didn't mean anything by it,' Adrian protested. 'She's only saying . . .'

'I know,' said Mel tightly. The memory of her mother-in-law's last comment: 'You career women! I don't know where you get the energy from. I wouldn't have been able to take care of my family and go out to earn a living, I can tell you!' was still fresh in her mind. If Lynda was *only saying*, why did it sting so bloody much?

By half-past six that evening, Mel had done all she could with her hair and would have to put her make-up on in the car. The day had been swallowed up with grocery shopping, taking the girls swimming and getting everything ready for Lynda that night.

Sarah had been upset that her parents were going out, and had been miserable with her mother all day. With her tiny heart-shaped face, huge blue and violet eyes and silvery blonde ringlets, she had the look of an enchanting little angel. But the angel-face hid fierce determination to have her own way in everything and, at the age of four and a quarter, she was well on the way to being empress of the Redmond household. Mel had read all the books on how to cope with strong-willed children and had finally come to the conclusion that none of the childcare experts had ever met anyone like her daughter.

At least swimming had tired her out, Mel thought, rapidly pulling on her long black evening dress, the one that could almost go to the ball by itself, it had been to so many work parties. Standing in the pool, holding Carrie up, had tired *her* out too. Downstairs, *Beauty and the Beast* was in the video, ready to go. Two chicken breasts in garlic and wild mushroom sauce sat in a dish on the kitchen counter with a bowl of baby potatoes beside them, waiting to be warmed up for Lynda's dinner. A joint of lamb was marinating in fresh rosemary and olive oil in the fridge for tomorrow, because Lynda stayed over till the following evening if she babysat and she was partial to a proper Sunday dinner. The spare bed was freshly made up with lilac sheets and Mel had even managed to iron the duvet cover, something she didn't do for herself and Adrian. The soft sheets on Sarah's bed and on Carrie's cot had been changed, and all their favourite cuddly toys were lined up in their correct places. Mel had left the thermometer and the children's paracetamol on top of the bathroom cabinet, too high for the children to reach but where Lynda could get them in an emergency, and the phone number of the local doctor and the venue for tonight's party were both written in big writing – Lynda was half blind without her glasses – beside the phone.

Surely Lynda would have no excuse to think that Mel's going out to work meant the family suffered.

'We're going to have a lovely time tonight,' Lynda cooed to her two grandchildren, who sat snuggled up beside her on the couch, cosy in their pyjamas and ready for fun with Granny Lynda.

Lynda had brought sweets with her, the sort of sugar-laden confections that were banned in the household because they made both children hyper. Mel knew she couldn't say anything.

Adrian, looking less pale, walked in finishing a biscuit. There was dinner tonight but what with the drinks reception first, who knew when they'd get a bite to eat. He was wearing a black fine wool suit with a silvery grey shirt that brought out the blue of his eyes. He looked great. 'Will you miss Daddy?' asked Adrian, quickly scooping Sarah up from the couch and turning her upside down, a game she'd loved since she was a baby.

'Yes,' giggled Sarah, trying to pull her long fair hair away from her face.

'No, really?' demanded Adrian, bouncing her up and down.

'Yes!!' she squealed with delight, loving being bounced. She had no fear of anything, Mel knew.

'Me, me!' yelled Carrie, her fat baby cheeks rosy with excitement. She looked like a mini version of her sister, without the stubborn chin.

More like our side of the family, Lynda said sometimes, and Mel took that to mean the stubborn streak in Sarah had come from her and was, therefore, not approved of.

'We should go,' Mel said automatically.

The fun seemed to stall for a moment. Sarah, still upside down, gazed at Mel with those knowing eyes as if to ask why her mother had to ruin it all.

Because there isn't enough time in the day, Mel wanted to scream. Somebody has to keep it all running on schedule. Imagine what would happen if she didn't keep them all to time.

Adrian put Sarah down and then quickly bounced Carrie a few times to keep the peace, before popping her back beside her grandmother.

'Be good for Granny,' Adrian told both his daughters, who smiled adoringly at him as if to imply that they didn't know the meaning of the word naughty.

'Bye, Carrie.' Mel bent to kiss her baby and was rewarded with two fat little hands clinging to her neck and a sloppy kiss planted on her cheek. She was growing so quickly, Mel thought with a pang. It seemed like only yesterday she was a tiny, fragile creature nestling in Mel's arms, tiny rosebud mouth sucking on her mother's nipple.

'Bye, Mummy,' Carrie cooed in her breathless voice.

Mel kissed her again. 'I love you,' she whispered gently.

On the other side of Lynda, Sarah now sat with a stash of forbidden sweets on her lap.

'Can I have a kiss goodbye?' Mel asked tremulously.

'Byee,' said Sarah, still engrossed in arranging her treasure, ignoring the request.

'Little scamp, you should kiss your mummy goodbye,' said Lynda fondly, ruffling Sarah's hair.

'Oh, they all get like that sometimes,' Mel said in a breezy voice. She would not let anyone know how she felt like breaking into betrayed, bitter tears. 'The new person is always more fun than boring old Mummy.'

'Give your mum a kiss,' urged Lynda.

Blissfully unaware of the pain it sent shooting into her mother's heart, Sarah kept her head down and ignored them all.

'Go on,' Lynda said, half-laughing. 'Isn't she a little rascal? She hates you going out, Mel.'

Suddenly, Sarah looked up, smiled her breathtaking smile, and blew her mother a speedy kiss with an idle wave of one hand.

'Good girl,' said Lynda. 'Now give me the television zapper and let's watch our film.'

'Have a great time.' Adrian was already making for the door.

'Yes, be good, darlings,' Mel added as she walked mechanically after her husband, feeling her disappointment like a physical ache. Sarah hadn't wanted to kiss her. Blowing a kiss didn't count, not as a proper kiss. Sarah always kissed her mother goodbye, always . . .

'Mel, your handbag,' reminded Adrian, handing it to her. 'How could you forget that?'

'Silly me,' said Mel, and went out of the door.

'You're exhausted, aren't you?' Adrian said, unlocking the car.

His wife sank into the front seat. As they sped down the road, she realised that her make-up bag was still on the hall table. All she had with her was a pale lipgloss and mascara. With limp hair and a nearly nude face, she'd look like she was the one with flu. But in her misery, for the first time in her perfectly groomed life, Mel Redmond didn't care.

The event was being held in the ballroom of a posh five-star city hotel called McArthur's, and the drinks reception in the foyer was already in full swing when Mel and Adrian arrived. Smiling grace-fully, aware she must look like a plague carrier, Mel held Adrian's hand as they progressed through the throng until they came upon one of Mel's good friends from work, Tony Steilman, and his wife, Bonnie. They were friends outside of work too, and Tony was a person Mel trusted entirely.

'Hey, great to see you,' said Tony, kissing her. 'You look terrible.'

Bonnie, hugging Adrian, gave her husband an exasperated look.

'Left my make-up at home in the rush to get out the door,' Mel shrugged.

'I don't have much with me,' Bonnie said, holding up a tiny evening bag, 'but you're welcome to use mine.'

Leaving the two men to talk, Mel and Bonnie made their way in the direction of the loos, but as they turned into the corridor, they almost literally bumped into Hilary and the chief executive, Edmund Moriarty – the very last people Mel wanted to see in her current state.

'Gosh, Mel, are you ill? A virus?' asked Hilary, moving a step away because whatever it was, she didn't want to catch it.

'No, it's being a working mum and always having to do every-thing at a rush,' laughed Bonnie brightly, the effects of her two glasses of pink champagne loosening her tongue. 'Honestly, Hilary, I don't know how she manages it. Our Mel is a regular heroine. I always say to Tony that he's lucky I'm there at home for him all day so he doesn't have to come home to the washing, like Mel. It's great that Lorimar are such supporters of working mums.' Bonnie's sweet round face shone with pride at her friend, thinking she'd said the right thing because Mel was *incredible*, really. Bonnie didn't know how *she*'d manage if she had to work as hard as Tony and Mel, and still be a mum.

There was silence.

Mel felt the smile straining on her face. She knew that it was absolutely the wrong thing for Bonnie to say. Edmund did not want to be reminded that Mel was a mother with any other responsi-bilities. He and Hilary wanted Lorimar to be her first priority and they genuinely didn't care what sort of hoops she had to jump through in order to do her job. A childless man, the only capri-cious, demanding and easily bored person Edmund wanted his employees interested in was himself.

Casting her mind about for some explanation that would satisfy everyone and keep her Super Career Woman image intact, Mel suddenly came up trumps. 'Actually, I was at the gym training and I had to rush home. You know how time flies when you're working out.'

Bonnie blinked.

'The mini marathon,' Mel went on. 'Lorimar have a group running and, obviously, I want to be there.'

The vision of a gang of his female workers wearing head-to-toe Lorimar merchandise as they ran past waiting photographers clearly appealed to Edmund Moriarty. Health, charity and good publicity – the perfect combination.

'Excellent,' he said. 'Didn't know we were sponsoring a team but excellent idea. Health is our aim and we are healthy. I like it.'

Hilary, who obviously didn't believe a word of it, gave Mel a bland stare. 'Great,' she said. 'We can talk about it on Monday.' And she led Edmund off to schmooze some more.

Mel managed to keep a stiff upper lip for the rest of the night and it was only when they were safely on their way home that she let her guard down.

'It looked so bad,' she groaned as they drove out of the hotel's underground car park. 'And for damage limitation, I said I was training for the mini marathon, which means I'll actually have to do it.'

'You're kidding, right?' Adrian was bemused by all of this. So what if Mel had looked tired? She hadn't been hired to look like a supermodel all the time; she was a normal person.

'No,' she snapped, angry at the world and, since the world wasn't there, Adrian would have to do.

'You can't have to run a mini marathon just because you looked tired at a party?' he went on.

'Yes I do because I said it in front of the boss and the boss's boss, so I have to, and it's all my bloody fault for looking a wreck. I can see why people have eyeliner tattooed on. At least you always look as if you've tried.'

Adrian laughed. 'Come on, love, it's not that important, really. You're great at your job, they know that. The rest is rubbish. Who cares about how you look?'

'It shouldn't matter but it does,' hissed Mel furiously. 'How I look does count because I'm a woman and I've got kids and I'm on borrowed time. You don't understand that. You're a man and nobody's watching you like a hawk for signs that your family are coming before your job, and that goes for your appearance too. Everything matters! You're not suspected of being the one who takes a sickie when Carrie has a temperature of a hundred and three. If *you* make the school Christmas play, everyone thinks you're in line for Dad of the Year. If I make it, I'm clearly shirking at work and if I don't make it, I'm clearly shirking as a mother. So yes, how I look *does* matter.'

'I've stayed home with the girls when they're sick,' Adrian pointed out.

'But with men it's seen as a one-off,' Mel said in exasperation. 'It never stops with women. It's like a bloody marathon. And not the mini marathon, either.'

'It can't be sexism in Lorimar, Mel, because Hilary's a woman too,' Adrian said doubtfully.

'Not so you'd notice,' Mel sighed. 'She's married to the job and you'd never think she has kids. In other words, the perfect female executive. Have your tubes tied or have someone else bring up your kids so you never see them and we'll give you a job at the very top.'

'But you love it,' Adrian insisted. 'You're a powerhouse, Mel. Everyone thinks you're great for all you do. *I* think you're great. The way you manage work and the kids, juggling it all . . .'

'I hate when they call it "juggling",' Mel said quietly. 'Juggling can't be that hard but this . . . this is like . . .' she searched blindly for the right words, 'this is juggling with hand grenades.'

'Is it that bad?'

Mel closed her eyes. 'Yes,' she said. 'It's a bloody nightmare, like a hamster wheel in a horror movie, and I can't get off.'

CHAPTER FIVE

Cleo was cleaning her favourite bedroom in the Willow, the Pirate Queen Suite. Named after the enigmatic Grace O'Malley, the beautiful, fiery pirate who sailed the seas around Ireland in the seventeenth century, the suite had a mahogany four-poster bed draped in once-opulent Prussian-blue velvets, an open fire with a tendency to smoke and a claw-footed bath that sat in state in the centre of the wooden floor in the adjoining bathroom.

Brides adored the Pirate Queen Suite, perhaps imagining themselves, as Cleo did, succumbing to their bridegroom in the four-poster like a seventeenth-century heroine romping with a handsome pirate captain amid crisp, white linens. Cleo had often thought that if she got married – and it was a big *if*, because, let's face it, she wasn't settling for *any* man, and would prefer to live her life alone rather than compromise – then she'd spend her wedding night in Grace O'Malley's room.

The only negative point about the room was that it was tough to chambermaid. The intricate carvings of the four-poster were fiddly to dust, and while Cleo could clean every room in the Willow in her sleep, the Pirate Queen Suite took the longest. It had to be perfect. Cleo was keen on perfection.

Since Cleo could walk, she'd toddled round after her mum, helping out until they could now whiz round each vacant room, dusting, polishing, tidying, vacuuming and changing sheets at high speed.

It was hard work, though, and since the advent of Trevor, super-cleaner extraordinaire, who'd come to work in the hotel when Cleo was in college, Sheila wasn't supposed to do it any more. Except that Trevor, and his crack team of cleaners – his two sisters and a first cousin – had suddenly all been struck down with a mysterious flu that kept them confined to bed. On raceweek in nearby Fairy-house too, Cleo noticed. And it was the second time in a month this had happened.

Trevor needed a few sharp words in his ear, but nobody appeared keen to do it. 'He's good really,' her mother had said that Friday morning when the phone call came to say Trevor was still weak but he was finally beating the flu.

Cleo, Sheila, and Doug, the breakfast shift chef, had been having an early morning cup of tea.

'I'd give him weak,' growled Cleo. 'Has he produced a sick note for all the times he's been off, or have any of the rest of them, for that matter?'

'No,' protested Sheila, 'but we don't really operate the sick note system here, love. I know you've been learning about all that, but running the Willow is not like running a big hotel. You've got to be careful of people's feelings, Cleo. If your father or I imply that Trevor isn't really ill, he might leave us.'

'And by taking two weeks off this month for a mythical flu, he's being careful of your feelings, is he, Mum?' Cleo was fired up with anger against Trevor, who was an admittedly nice man but so fond of the horses he deserved a steeplechase named in his honour. 'So what if he leaves? We're doing it ourselves anyway.'

'He's cheap,' her mother argued, getting to her feet.

'He's not cheap if we have to clean all the bedrooms ourselves *and* pay him sick money, without the proof of a sick note. If he's in bed sick and not heading off to the race course, then I'm Naomi Campbell!'

'You're getting way tough, lassie,' said Doug approvingly when Sheila had left the table. 'So they did teach you something in that course, after all.'

'Not so's anyone round here thinks,' Cleo sighed.

The local paper lay on the table and she pulled it towards her for something to take her mind off Trevor while she finished her tea. It was the usual local news: developers were looking for planning permission for a huge housing estate on the Kilkenny side of Carrickwell, and the girls at the Mercy Convent had raised €2000 for the local hospice by having a Valentine's Day production of *As You Like It* in the school hall. The bit that caught her eye was a large advert for Cloud's Hill Spa.

An American woman had been renovating the old Delaney mansion for the past year, Cleo knew, turning it into a state-of-the-art health farm-cum-spa. The Carrickwell spy network hadn't been able to throw up anything about the mysterious woman, although they'd done their best. And now it appeared that the spa was open.

'Cloud's Hill Spa: Life Refreshment.'

It sounded a bit corny, but the photo looked good. Expensive, elegant, and yet more competition for the Willow. Cleo had been planning to check it out, and now that it was open the time was right.

When breakfast was over, Cleo and Sheila headed off to do the bedrooms, Cleo still irritated with the missing Trevor. If *she* was running the Willow, she'd put an end to that sort of carry-on. She'd bet her bottom dollar that the woman who ran Cloud's Hill didn't have to scrub out her own sauna and launder the fluffy bathrobes.

Cleo didn't let her mother clean the baths any more: all that bending down wasn't good for Sheila's arthritis, so when they worked together Cleo insisted on doing the bathrooms. This morning, in the Pirate Queen Suite, Cleo could feel a film of sweat beading her forehead as she worked. Anger made her faster than usual. Scrub, scrub, scrub. She dug into the big old bath with her cloth as if intent on removing every last germ by force.

Ten minutes later, she went back into the bedroom to find her mother sitting on the four-poster bed, looking exhausted.

'Mum.' Cleo sank to her knees in front of Sheila. 'What's wrong? Are you OK?'

'Fine, fine.' Sheila waved Cleo's worry away. 'Just needed to catch my breath. Your father was having one of his snoring nights last night. No matter how much I nudged him, he wouldn't shut up, so I didn't get a wink.'

'Go downstairs now and have a rest,' Cleo ordered, relieved it was nothing more. Her father's snoring could waken the dead.

'I don't need a rest,' Sheila insisted. 'Who'll do the other rooms with you?'

'I don't need any help,' Cleo said firmly. 'Go on, rest. Shoo.'

'You're the best feather in my wing, Cleo,' Sheila Malin said fondly.

'Mum, don't be daft,' said Cleo, embarrassed but touched at the same time. 'You're an old softy.'

'I thought you were all set to turn into Ms Whiplash downstairs over Trevor phoning in sick,' her mother teased.

'To outsiders, I'm Ms Whiplash,' grinned Cleo. 'You lot all know I'm a pushover. I've been trained to sound managerial in college because that's how you get results from staff. And if you and Dad let me have a few words with Trevor, Mum, well . . . his work would improve,' she added earnestly. 'We've got to think of the Willow, and of you. Why employ a dog and bark yourself? Trevor has to knuckle down to work or he's fired. Don't you agree?'

Her mother forced a smile. 'I agree, love,' she said. 'You're right, I am exhausted. I'll just lie down on my bed for a while.'

When her mother was gone, Cleo cleaned with renewed vigour. Working out exactly what she'd say to the recalcitrant Trevor when she set eyes on him kept her going.

'You won't believe it, I was just going to text you. We must be psychic!' said Trish in delight when Cleo phoned her that afternoon.

'Psycho, perhaps,' Cleo agreed. 'I'm not so sure about psychic.'

'Well, I am,' Trish argued. 'I am full of wonderful vibes and mystic energy today, and I was going to text to ask you to come up to the city tomorrow because we're having a party in the house. With a DJ and everything.' Trish thought this was the last word in cool. The fact that the DJ was a friend of a friend of a friend was a minor point. He was bound to have more party CDs than her housemates had. Nobody would let her play her Beyoncé or Christina Aguilera stuff; she, in turn, refused to listen to any rap, and the only common ground was Barry's moody muso CD collection. No matter how much you loved REM, Trish pointed out, you couldn't dance to them.

'I can't, sorry.' Cleo would have loved a party on Saturday night but a busload of people from Finland were arriving that evening, and they were having dinner in the restaurant on both Friday and Saturday nights. It would be all hands on deck. 'We're booked up for the weekend and Mum's a bit wrecked. I can't go.'

'At least the place is full.'

'Yeah.' Cleo sounded dubious.

'Don't be old Moany Minnie,' Trish said in exasperation. 'You've been giving out stink about how the hotel is only ever half full and now when you're stuffed to the rafters, you're still moaning.'

'Thanks for that helpful advice, O person of wonderful vibes and mystic energy,' Cleo retorted sarcastically.

'Sorry.'

'Accepted. What I meant was that being full this weekend isn't as good as it sounds.'

'Why?'

'This booking is a year old and it will be the first time we'll have been full in roughly . . .' Cleo did the calculations in her head, 'eight months.'

'Point taken. A party would cheer you up,' Trish decided, irrepressible as ever. 'You might meet Mr Would-Do-For-A-While at it. While you're waiting for Mr Utterly Perfect, that is.'

'Nah, Mr Utterly Perfect doesn't exist, but thanks all the same,' Cleo said. 'The reason I was phoning was to ask you to come here tomorrow so we could check out the spa that's opened up at the old Delaney place. There was a piece in the paper about it and I'm dying to actually visit it because I could get some great ideas for the health centre we could develop here, but I don't want to ask anyone from home or else they'll say I've got more pie-in-the-sky ideas.'

'I can't come back to Carrickwell now,' Trish said apologetically, 'not with the party. What about Eileen?' Eileen was the third part of their schoolyard gang and worked in the local hospital as a nurse.

'Think this is one of her weekend shifts. I'll just have to go on my own.'

'And have treatments and stuff?'

'A full body massage by this holistic massage expert brought over from Australia, and he looks totally beautiful. Scuba diver, surfer, six-pack stomach, or is it an eight-pack . . . ?'

Trish fell for it. 'You cow . . . don't go this weekend, please. Wait until I can come.'

'Gotcha!!'

'Bitch.'

'Gobshite. How would I know what the staff are like, you idiot?'

'Well, if there turns out to be a gorgeous Aussie hunk there, phone me and I'll be down pronto,' Trish said. 'Knowing my luck, the talent at the party will belong to the OK-if-you're-really-desperate category.'

'I thought they were the only sort of guys you ever asked to your parties,' Cleo said innocently.

'You wait and see,' Trish promised. 'When I find a genuine Aussie scuba-diving surfer type with a ripped bod, then you'll be sorry.'

'I won't. I'll be asking for his brother's phone number,' Cleo said. 'Be hopeful: that's my motto.'

With limited funds at her disposal, Cleo had thought she might book something not too expensive, like a manicure, at Cloud's Hill Spa. But then she had hit on the better idea of just popping in that afternoon to pick up a brochure and look round.

She borrowed her mother's creaky old Austin, a car that had been in the family for fifteen years and still smelled vaguely of the sheepdogs the previous owner had bred. Spluttering along the countryside, the Austin finally creaked to a halt outside Cloud's Hill Spa. Cleo felt instantly dismayed. The photo in the local paper hadn't done it justice.

Without a ton of money, the Willow would never be able to compete with this. The house was elegant, beautifully restored and reeked of restrained luxury. The lovely gardens, studded with spring bulbs, were perfect. Even the big stone urns at the massive front door were just right, spilling over with stephanotis, the stone weathered enough to be old, but not so weathered as to look as if it might crack at the first sign of frost.

The urns outside the Willow were falling over and crumbly, and Cleo felt they were an insurance hazard.

She walked into the big reception and sighed with a combination of pleasure and envy. It was like entering a beautiful, but comfortable home. There were big creamy flagstones on the floor, lots of comfy low couches, books on one wall, and watercolours of botanical subjects and a big open fire on the other. The atmosphere was relaxed and opulent without being a bit showy. Money had been well spent here, and Cleo, with her hotelier's eye, could see how cleverly it had been done.

The receptionist made Cleo's heart sink further. An exquisite oriental girl with porcelain skin, she was dressed in the spa's signature colour of olive green, and was smiling warmly at Cleo in welcome. Smiling!

Cleo thought of sullen Tamara at the reception desk back home. Unless Tamara thought the entire cast of *Ocean's Twelve* were arriving for an orgy and were a woman short, she couldn't summon up a smile of any sort.

'Can I help you?' the receptionist said, warmth in every lightly accented syllable.

'I came for a brochure,' Cleo said firmly. She was here; she might as well do what she'd come for. This place was way out of their league but she could learn something.

'So many people have been here today, because of the piece in the paper, that we are out of brochures,' the girl said in delighted surprise. 'I will phone through for one for you.'

'It's a gorgeous place,' said Cleo, responding to such friendliness. 'I had no idea it was going to be so luxurious. And the uniform is lovely too. Well, you could wear a sack and look great,' she added genuinely.

'You think so? I think this colour is not suited to me,' the receptionist explained in her careful English. 'You think it is suited to me?'

'Fabulous,' enthused Cleo. 'But you're beautiful. Look at you! I'm sure half the clients will book treatments because they hope they're going to look like you at the end of it all.'

'No,' said the girl, going a subtle shade of peony. 'My sister, she is the pretty one. I am not. You are lovely with your hair. I very much like your curls.'

'The bane of my life, these curls,' sighed Cleo. 'I'd kill for silky straight hair like yours.' And then she laughed, because she would never have thought that anyone so glorious-looking as the girl in front of her could possibly have an ounce of self-criticism in her. Yet she did. 'Women! What are we like?' demanded Cleo. 'We all think we're ugly as sin.'

'I would hope neither of you two thinks so,' said a low voice as a woman emerged from a door beside the reception desk holding a sheaf of brochures.

'Mrs Meyer, thank you,' said the beauty.

Mrs Meyer handed one to Cleo, who felt as if the word 'imposter' was suddenly emblazoned on her forehead.

'Hi, I'm Leah Meyer.'

'Cleo Malin.' Cleo held out her hand. 'I dropped in to look round,' she said.

It would have been hard to lie under the friendly gaze of Leah Meyer. Tall and slender, there was something queenly about her and yet she looked the sort of person you could tell everything, rather than someone you kept things from.

'What do you think?'

'So far, it's fantastic.'

'I could give you a tour, if you'd like,' Leah said. 'What are you interested in? We have a lot of different treatments, although we're running an introductory one-day relax and revitalise package for the first month.'

Cleo's story began to seem even more feeble to her, so she improvised: 'My family own a hotel in the town and I wanted to see what this was like so I could advise guests to come here.'

'A partnership,' said Leah warmly. 'I should offer you a free treatment so you can see what we do here.'

'No, no, please,' said Cleo, embarrassed. 'Honestly, I couldn't.'

'You could and you will. Yazmin, may I see the appointments book?'

Leah flicked through a big diary quickly. 'Indian head massage for half an hour?' she suggested. 'And then you'll come into the hot tub with me? Ten minutes in the hot tub makes me feel human again, no matter what sort of day I've had, and I love company.'

It seemed churlish to refuse.

Cleo spent the first ten minutes of the head massage worrying about having not been truthful to Leah, then she gave in to the utter bliss of being able to think of absolutely nothing. Not the hotel and the family's money problems, not the lack of men in her life, simply nothing.

'I can't believe I've never had one of those before,' Cleo said three-quarters of an hour later when, wearing a cream robe and a borrowed swimming costume, she followed Leah down another mellowly lit corridor. She felt dizzy from the sheer relaxation of it all. 'Actually,' she corrected herself, 'I *can* believe I've never had that done before. I've never had even a quarter of the treatments you do here.'

'We'll have to change that,' Leah said, leading the way into a decked room that gave a spectacular view of the lake and Carrickwell below. Inside, taking up most of the space, was an enormous hot tub. The windows of the room could obviously slide back so you could hot tub practically al fresco if you wanted to.

'Wow,' was all Cleo could say.

'It is pretty wow,' smiled Leah. 'It's a bit extravagant but we had to have one. The hot tub is vital to the whole chilling-out experience. You need to look after yourself, Cleo. You're precious. You don't realise how stressed you are until you stop rushing around.' She shed her robe and sank into the tub, slim, olive-skinned limbs making Cleo feel more Amazonian than ever by comparison.

She followed Leah in quickly and let the hot water claim her.

'That's wonderful,' she murmured, sinking down until her head was the only bit visible.

They lay there in companionable silence for a while, with Cleo thinking how nice it was to be able to be silent with someone. If Trish had been there, she'd have been going on about the gorgeous ochre stone work or the view or where exactly did Leah come from in America, because her accent was so soft and mellow. But Cleo

83

gauged that Leah didn't need that – Leah just lay back with her eyes closed and a faint smile on her lips.

'Tell me about your hotel,' she said eventually.

So Cleo told her: the truthful version. How much she loved her home but how she was worried that the Willow wouldn't survive unless something radical happened. Leah was interested, asking questions in all the right places, and she didn't flinch when Cleo took a deep breath and admitted that she hadn't come to the spa to see if she could refer guests there.

'I hate lying,' she emphasised, 'and I didn't mean to deceive you by saying I was here just to see if we could send customers your way.'

'You didn't. You were checking out the competition, which is good business sense.'

'You're not upset?'

'I think I'd hire you. We could do with somebody with your smartness working here.'

Cleo felt ridiculously pleased. 'Thanks,' she said, 'but I'm committed to the Willow.'

'I understand,' Leah replied. 'Family comes first.'

Cleo nodded. 'Not everyone gets that,' she said.

'What will you do if the hotel closes down?'

The question threw Cleo. 'I don't know,' she said slowly. 'It would be awful, like losing your home only worse: other people would have it and you'd never be allowed in again. It would be horrible.' Although the water was warm, she shivered.

'You'd manage, though?'

Cleo thought of her family and how they'd got through lots of lean years. So many people were unlucky with their families. Trish's family deserved their own reality TV show so they could be mad and get paid for it. By comparison, the Malin family's squabbles were straight out of *The Waltons*.

'We'd manage,' she said easily. 'We always do.'

She drove home an hour later, exhausted yet mentally refreshed. And that night, she slept without the spectre of rival hotels once jumping into her dreams. Leah had been right about refreshing the body and the mind. If the Willow couldn't build their own health suite, they could certainly link up with Cloud's Hill Spa. That would be a clever plan.

Cleo couldn't help mentioning Leah Meyer to the family the next day. Barney had dropped into the hotel on his way to football, and he, Cleo and their parents had a rare sit-down in their own kitchen.

'She's beautiful, like something from a film, very serene and calm. And if you'd seen the whole place, Mum. It's like a temple to relaxation. It's fabulous,' she said, feeling gloomy at having to impart such news.

'Cleo, stop torturing yourself,' said Barney. 'That's my job!' he quipped.

The four of them laughed.

Barney was so much more like the brother she'd grown up with when Sondra wasn't around, Cleo thought fondly. She had to make more of an effort with him. It was stupid to let her and Sondra's animosity ruin Cleo's relationship with her brother.

'The spa's just so polished and perfect,' she added. 'I don't see how we can compete.'

'What do you mean?' asked her dad lightly. 'That we should sell up and emigrate because we're not like Cloud's Hill Spa?'

'Dad,' groaned Cleo. 'As if. They're just providing a different service from ours. Our hotel and their spa hit different markets.' She could almost believe it herself. It made sense, in fact.

On Monday morning, Cleo did the bank run for her father with all the cheques and cash from the weekend, and was back by eleven.

Her mother was sitting in the nook by the kitchen, petite and neat in her black jeans and soft angora sweater as she organised the post into neat piles.

'Cleo, love, would you ever put the kettle on, there's a good girl? Your father's got a visitor in the office with him and I don't want to send Doug in with the tea in case he overhears something.'

Cleo abandoned the notion of having a cup of coffee and rapidly assembled tea things on a silver tray, wondering who the mysterious visitor might be.

'Not that teapot,' her mother said, 'it's begun to leak. And don't forget the good spoons.'

'Oh, it's four cups, not two,' her mother added.

'Four?'

'For Barney and Jason.'

Cleo added two more cups. 'You mean the boys are in there with Dad too?' she asked. 'Who are they meeting?' Jason and Barney had almost nothing to do with the Willow.

'Oh, just the accountant, Mr Stavi.'

Cleo felt the familiar surge of temper but did her best to subdue it.

'Why didn't Dad ask me in too?' she enquired shakily. 'I told him I wanted to meet Mr Stavi.'

'Your father can handle it,' was all her mother said calmly.

Cleo clattered spoons onto the plate.

Her father smiled as she brought the tea tray in and Cleo instinctively smiled back. Ever the gentleman, he got to his feet, a tall, slender figure with silver hair brushed back from his high forehead and took the tray from his daughter. Cleo felt the anxiety kick in at the sight of his tired face.

'Thank you, my love,' Harry said, 'but Mr Stavi hasn't time for tea this morning. He has to go.'

The accountant was already on his feet, collecting papers quickly.

'Another appointment, I'm afraid,' he said, not meeting Cleo's gaze.

Barney and Jason fell on the homemade shortbread biscuits with delight. You'd swear they never got fed, Cleo thought crossly.

Mr Stavi shook hands with Harry Malin and moved towards the door.

Cleo held it open for him and looked him in the eye. 'Everything all right, Mr Stavi?' she asked brightly.

Mr Stavi looked at her sadly. Despite thirty years in the business, he was not a man skilled at hiding bad news. It was written all over his face.

'These are tough times,' Mr Stavi said gently and evasively. 'I must be off. Goodbye.'

'Talk about doom and gloom,' said Barney with his mouth full, when Mr Stavi had gone. 'Accountants are all the same – all misery guts and no good news. You'd swear the place was going to close down tomorrow.' He swiped another biscuit, took a final slurp of tea, grinned goodbye at everyone and was off. That was Barney for you, his sister thought: the original Speedy Gonzalez. Barney sold cars for a living and he said that people nowadays liked high-speed everything. Cleo disagreed. There should be time to relax and take it easy, that's what they liked in hotels: the illusion of calm, even if, below stairs, all was hectic.

Cleo felt her father's hand on her shoulder. 'It'll be all right, pet,' he said. 'We'll get by, we always do.' And he smiled at her with the same all-encompassing smile as her own.

Cleo took the plunge. 'That's not enough, Dad,' she said. 'We can't get by with hoping and praying for a miracle. We need to upgrade the hotel, borrow money from the bank, get someone else to invest in the place, *something*. We'll close down. Can't you see?'

Jason jumped in before their father could reply. 'Cleo, stop it, will you! We're all fed up to the back teeth with you complaining and telling us where we're going wrong. You should have gone off to Donegal and left us in peace. Why do you think me and Barney are at the meetings and you're not? 'Cos you drive us all mad with your questions. Everything's fine. You have Mum stressed out thinking otherwise. Leave it alone!'

'I won't,' retorted Cleo hotly, instantly matching Jason's school-yard tone.

'Cleo, Jason's right. Leave it alone,' her father said sharply. 'There's a time and a place for everything. This isn't it. I have plans up my sleeve.'

'Tell me,' Cleo said, face burning with frustration. 'Aren't I a part of this family too? Don't I deserve to know what's going on? I can help if you'll let me. Being first in my class in college counts for something.'

'A couple of years in college doesn't make you Bill Gates,' snapped Jason. 'You don't know everything, Cleo.'

'I'm not talking about this any more.' Her father's voice was final. He said it the way he used to say, 'Go to your room, Cleo,' when she'd had a fight with her brothers. 'I know that you think you're the only person around here with any experience of the hotel industry, but you're not. Leave the hotel to me.'

On Monday, Trish phoned to fill Cleo in on the party, the men, and how long it had taken to clean the place up the next day. Still weary because the celebrations hadn't ended until four on Sunday morning, Trish yawned as she explained that she hadn't met any nice men at the party but had found a fellow dance friend named Carol, who'd boogied wildly with her on the dance floor – the dining room with all the furniture pushed back – all night. Carol loved all Trish's favourite songs and the DJ had fancied Carol, so he'd played wall-to-wall girl dancing music all night.

'You'd love her, she's fantastic,' said Trish. 'Can that girl dance ... phew. And she loves all the same stuff as me. She's talking about going to Australia for a year to work – she's a physiotherapist – and she said would I like to go?'

Cleo felt a pang of left-outness. She and Trish had done everything together since Miss Minton's class nearly eighteen years before. She had no plans to travel any more until she'd sorted out problems at home, but she'd hoped that when she did, Trish might be keen to go with her.

'She knows all about work permits and stuff like that,' Trish went on blithely. 'Oh, Cleo, she's the best. When you first meet her, you think she's quiet, but whoa, baby, that girl is wild.'

'How did she come to be at the party?' asked Cleo, feeling like a maiden aunt enquiring after somebody else's beau's credentials.

'You know Sammy's friend Pat? Well, she's his sister's best friend and they were supposed to be going to a gig when the sister got sick and Pat said he'd bring her along to the party. I think he fancies her too,' Trish revealed.

'Really?'

Pat was on the periphery of Trish's Dublin circle of friends and had long been considered a fine thing by Trish and Cleo. Not that he'd ever looked at either of them. He was well known for dating models, which had to mean that Carol was model material.

Trish's phone beeped, signalling an incoming call.

'It's Carol,' she said. 'We're going to see a show at the comedy festival tonight. I don't suppose you can come up?'

'Can't, sorry,' said Cleo shortly.

'Better go. Call you tomorrow. Byee.'

It was partly because she was feeling like Billy No Mates, and partly because she was so upset about the row with her father, that Cleo said yes an hour later when Nat Sheridan phoned and asked her to come to Galway the following weekend for his mother's sixtieth birthday party in the family's hotel, the Railway Lodge, which Nat was learning to run. Normally, Nat texted on his mobile to keep in touch so Cleo knew it was a big deal if he was actually phoning. Texting was perfect for shy people and commitment phobes, Cleo had decided. You could keep in touch without ever speaking to a human being.

'I thought it would be nice if you came ... as a friend,' stammered Nat. 'Nothing more. And only if you wanted to. But it would be nice. I know it's short notice. I didn't want to bother you. I thought you'd have something else on ...'

Conversations with Nat were always like that. He got to the point slowly. He'd been Cleo's friend since the first day in college and the friendship had survived Nat asking Cleo out, and being turned down because Cleo said they'd be 'better as friends'.

Nat still hoped, and Cleo did her best not to encourage him.

It wasn't that he was unattractive. He had a quick, clever face, kind eyes that could be mournful at times, and his hobby was running, so he was fit and athletic. He simply wasn't her sort of man. He was '... *too nice?*' she'd said to Trish. 'Can a man be too nice?'

'Not the ones I meet,' Trish had grumbled. But she'd agreed. There was something infinitely good about Nat Sheridan, and to women waiting to be whisked off their feet by handsome bad boys, infinite goodness was a strangely uninviting quality.

'I'd really like to show you the hotel,' Nat offered. 'And the party's going to be a laugh.'

'Sure, I'd love to,' Cleo said, thinking of how non-existent her social life was. And it would get her out of home for a couple of days. Since the argument with her father, the atmosphere had been icy. Cleo and her dad never rowed, never, so it felt doubly strange and horrible.

* * *

Cleo drove up in her mother's car on Saturday morning. The Railway Lodge did lots of brisk business because of its location in scenic Oranmore, just outside Galway City, but this weekend it was full of Nat's family and their friends to celebrate his mother's birthday. Every room was pressed into service, with two of Nat's cousins sharing one of the attics that hadn't seen a vacuum cleaner in years.

When Cleo found herself in a large bedroom with a queen-sized bed piled with cushions and a large box of chocolates on the small table by the window, she knew she was in trouble. Despite Nat's protestations of it all being just about friendship, this had to be one of the best bedrooms in the place. To anyone who didn't know how hotels operated, this would mean nothing. But Cleo had a professional understanding of the language of bedrooms and by giving her this room, Nat was sending her a message with romantic intent.

Against her better wishes, they went into Galway for lunch alone together. Nat said he wanted to know what she thought about the Railway Lodge. In fact, he was happy simply to sit *à deux* in a bistro overlooking Eyre Square and to smile goofily at her.

'Any more news on Roth Hotels' plans?' Cleo asked finally, when she was fed up with the long silences. Roth Hotels were the people who could destroy the Willow if they set up in opposition to them in Carrickwell, and the big golden R symbol haunted many of Cleo's nightmares.

Nat shook his head. 'It could have been a mistake in the paper,' he said vaguely. 'They might not be interested in moving in here at all. They've hotels all over the world. What would they be interested in this country for?'

'Because Europe is opening up and Ireland is ripe for more development,' Cleo said, irritated. Honestly, Nat had no business awareness whatsoever. 'You don't build up a multibillion-dollar empire by not exploring other territories, Nat.'

'You're right, Cleo.' Nat looked suitably reproved. 'You're great for ideas; you should be lecturing in college. No, you should be running your own hotel,' he smiled.

Cleo did not smile back. She'd talked to Nat many times about her family's opinion of letting a feisty twenty-three-year-old with buckets of new ideas run the Willow and didn't want to be reminded once again that they had not changed their minds.

'You could turn this one around. The Railway Lodge, I mean.' Nat's puppy-dog eyes shone with a combination of devotion and excitement.

Cleo knew what he was offering her: him and the Railway Lodge on a platter. She could have her empire, an empire she could run without anyone telling her she wasn't able to, and he'd have her. Poor Nat. She felt very sorry for him.

'Let's not get into that now,' she said wisely, thinking that Mrs Sheridan would not have the party atmosphere she was hoping for if Nat was in the depths of romantic depression. In Cleo's opinion, it was easier to have the big arguments *after* the actual party.

'Let's get a move on, Nat. You said you hadn't bought your mother a present yet. We ought to go shopping and get back soon.'

Guests were still trickling in when Cleo and Nat returned with the pretty silver photo frame Nat had chosen, and he took over on reception whilst his mother retired to the office for some tea.

'Come on, Cleo, and join me,' she said. 'You must keep me away from the cream cakes if I'm to fit into my dress tonight.'

Mrs Sheridan was funny, forthright, and very easy to talk to. The Railway Lodge needed three times as much investment as the Willow did, but the positive side was that Nat's mother knew this.

'I'd love someone to be interested in buying us out of the business,' she said, pouring the tea.

'Would you really?' asked Cleo. 'My parents would hate that.'

'They set their place up themselves,' said Mrs Sheridan shrewdly. 'I married into ours. As an old relative of my mother's said, I walked up the aisle with a bouquet and walked down with a hotel.' She looked around at the cramped office, with its elderly grey filing cabinets and walls of black and white photos of the place in its former glory. 'I suppose that's why I don't have the same emotional stake in it. If I wasn't trying to keep the old place going for Nat, I'd have been off years ago. A hotel is a way of life, Cleo, and you've got to love it, because the Good Lord only knows, you don't make money at it.'

'I do love it,' Cleo said simply.

Mrs Sheridan looked astutely at her guest. 'You do, don't you? So does Nat. He's very fond of you, you know, Cleo. I don't suppose . . . no.'

Cleo's face made it utterly plain that no was indeed the answer.

'He was very excited about you coming here.'

Double torture in one day. Cleo knew it was time for bluntness all round.

'I'm incredibly fond of Nat, but not in that way. And I'd never lead him on.'

'I didn't think that for a moment,' Mrs Sheridan said. 'I can see you're not that kind of girl. You'd be great for him, though.'

Cleo shook her head. 'I wouldn't,' she said. 'He deserves someone who loves him the way he is. I'd be trying to change him.'

'Aisle, altar, hymn,' sighed Mrs Sheridan. 'Many's the marriage perishes on that rock. Don't leave him hanging, will you?'

The cake, decorated with only twenty-one candles – Mrs Sheridan said she didn't want the fire brigade being alerted at the blowing-out phase – had been cut and the party was well under way by the time Cleo got a chance to talk to Nat.

'Dance?' he said, holding out his hand with old-fashioned courtesy.

The band were playing Glenn Miller, which Cleo actually liked, but could never dance to. She was no good at waltzing.

'You've got to stop trying to lead,' her father always remarked whenever they took to the dance floor. 'The man leads.'

Says who? Cleo thought every time he said this.

'Sure, but I'm not good at this sort of dancing,' she warned Nat, taking his hand.

The Sheridan clan and friends were throwing themselves into the party spirit and there was much inexpert twirling to 'In the Mood'. Everyone was happy, especially Nat.

'You look lovely tonight,' he said, as they held hands and did a bit of twirling themselves.

Cleo's hair was pinioned into a loose knot, which suited her, with trails of nut-brown curls clustering around her face. She'd made an effort and was wearing the dress she had bought for last year's Christmas party at the Willow, a dusky grape chiffon thing with short fluted sleeves and a swirling hem that swung around her ankles as she moved. It was a delicate dress and Cleo felt delicate in it.

'Oh, Nat, you don't have to compliment me,' she said lightly.

'I do,' he said, not lightly at all.

The tempo switched in a flash down to the moody romance of 'Moonlight Serenade', a song made for lovers. Nat was too shy to grab Cleo and pull her close, but he moved in a bit tighter and laid a gentle hand on her waist. Her heart sank.

It was such a beautiful song and how glorious it would be to melt against an equally beautiful man and move with him to the music. She closed her eyes and dreamed of such a thing for a second.

When she opened them, Nat was closer to her, his face as near hers as it could be without actually touching. Instinctively, she pulled back and watched his kind face flood with disappointment.

'Nat, we've got to talk,' she said, pulling him away from the dance floor and out into the empty corridor.

He leaned against the wall miserably.

Cleo took a deep breath. 'I love you but not in that way,' she said, and it was one of the hardest things she'd ever done. Nat's expression was anxious, but she had to tell him the truth, the whole truth. It would be unfair to leave him in any doubt. 'You're my friend, Nat, but that's all I want from you. I can't let you think there will ever be anything more. I am so, so sorry.' She took his hands and they stood there in the corridor with the muffled sounds of music and laughter in the air.

If he was the sort of man she could love, Cleo realised irrationally, he wouldn't let her comfort him when she'd just turned him down: he'd have snatched his hands away and left, coat flying in the wind of his departure.

But Nat couldn't be that sort of guy, which was why she'd never fall in love with him.

'I shouldn't have come here,' she said, 'I never meant you to get the wrong idea.'

'I was hoping you'd feel differently if you saw me on my own ground,' he said. 'Here, I'm not as shy as I was in college. I can be whatever you want, Cleo. I can be dynamic and into business, and we can work together and . . .' he cast around anxiously, 'we make a good team, Cleo. I love you. That would be enough.'

'It wouldn't, Nat,' she said in exasperation. 'One person in love can't make a relationship. I don't want you to change and I can't see you differently. You're my friend, that's it. And that could be great but it's all it's going to be. Friendship.'

'I'm glad you're being honest with me,' Nat said quietly.

'Nat,' wailed Cleo, 'be angry with me, anything. Stop being so passive!'

'All right!' He jerked his hands away, his eyes brimming. 'Go away, Cleo. I can't cope with having you here. Go away.'

Though her eyes smarted with tears, his anger was almost a relief. 'I'm sorry,' she said. 'I never meant to hurt you.'

Nat said nothing, because his eyes said it all. He turned and went down the corridor, leaving Cleo alone, feeling miserable and cruel.

Life was unfair. She wanted a hotel to run but couldn't have one, while Nat wanted only her *and* he was offering her the chance to run his. Yet she craved passion and fire and a tempestuous relationship with a man who'd kill anyone if they looked crossways at her. She didn't want Nat, with his pleading puppy-dog eyes and his blind devotion, hotel or no hotel.

She left a note in the office for Nat's mother saying thanks but she'd had to go. She didn't mention what had gone on between her and Nat. Mrs Sheridan could work it out and Nat deserved the dignity of telling his mother in his own way.

Then she packed up her things, stripped the bed in her room so the chambermaid wouldn't have too much to do, and slipped out of the door to the car park. It would take her at least three hours to drive home, but she wanted the comfort of home tonight.

The midnight news bulletin was ending on the radio as she parked the car round the back of the Willow. It was good to be home, even if she felt as mean and horrible as she'd ever felt in her whole life. You couldn't force yourself to love someone, could you? That thought had tortured her for the entire trip.

In her bedroom, she got ready for bed and then turned to the best comfort she knew: her Rodriguez Sisters books. Bought in a church fête years ago, the five bodice-ripping novels were a series about three feisty sisters, Odelita, Graciela and Beilarosa, who lived in Spain in the eighteenth century. Their saucy exploits had thrilled Cleo since she'd first read them when she was a teenager. Dipping into them was like eating shortbread in bed but without the crumbs: delicious and comforting.

'Why do you read this muck?' asked Trish the first time she'd spotted her friend's well-thumbed collection. Trish was a fan of the slice-and-dice thriller herself.

'They're fun and I like historical fiction,' Cleo had said primly.

Trish grabbed one and read a few paragraphs from a page at random. Her mouth fell open. 'Historical fiction, be blowed,' she laughed delightedly. 'This is historical porn.'

'It's not porn,' objected Cleo defensively.

'"He dropped his sword to the floor and laid one calloused hand reverently upon her chemise, the silken nub of her breast springing to life underneath . . ."' read out Trish.

'OK, well, just a bit sexy. It was a romantic era – that doesn't make it porn. It's not dirty, right?'

'So a guy touching a woman's nipple is porn if it's happening in a lift in the meat-packing district of Manhattan but not if they're wearing period costume?' giggled Trish.

'There's no point trying to explain it to you,' Cleo said fiercely, hurt at the suggestion that there was anything sordid about her beloved historical sagas. Yes, there was some bodice-ripping, but it was utterly tasteful. People didn't jump into bed with other people just for the fun of it; in these books, they loved each other. There was morality, decency and honour. The only pity was that the modern world wasn't more like that.

Now, she curled up into the comfort of her bed with the first Rodriguez book: *The Graciela Conquests*.

There was something soothing and escapist in reading about a time when the men were men and the women loved it. Although it depressed Cleo beyond belief that such real men didn't seem to exist any more.

She opened the first page and sank into Graciela's world, where the arranged marriage with a steely-eyed duke was ready to take place, even though Graciela had vowed she'd die rather than submit to the ceremony.

As she lay imagining herself in Graciela's place, with her wedding gown laid out on the bed and her passionate heart with another man, Cleo was finally able to forget about poor Nat.

CHAPTER SIX

Mary stuck the sign up on the door of the shop: 'Closed for stock-taking', double-locked the door and walked to where Daisy was sitting in the car with the engine running.

'What are the odds,' Mary asked, settling herself into the passenger seat, 'that ten customers turn up this morning in a tizzy because they need something new *now*, only to discover that we're shut?'

'They won't,' laughed Daisy. 'Tuesday mornings are quiet as the grave. And we need girlie/bonding/relaxation time.' She edged out into the traffic.

'You're right.' Mary inspected her face in the sun visor's pull-out mirror and grimaced. 'Not to mention a total face overhaul.'

'Doubt if they do that in this spa,' joked Daisy. She was in a marvellous mood. She'd been eating healthily, as per her new bible, *The Smart Woman's Fertility Guide*, and she felt glowing with anticipation of the rewarding, baby-filled life that awaited her. Alex was a bit grumpy, sure, but there was an office audit going on and that always made him edgy. He was drinking Daisy's special morning fruit smoothies without a quibble, although Daisy hadn't mentioned that there were herbs in with the blueberries and yogurt. Herbs that did great things for male fertility.

'True.' Mary flicked through the brochure for Cloud's Hill Spa. It was beautifully printed in olive green and vanilla, with listings for treatments and massages, photos of the spa in the same colours as the brochure itself, and – source of great amusement to Mary – a mission statement. Proprietress Leah Meyer wrote that she hoped the spa would provide 'tranquillity, rest and beauty from within'.

'Does that mean they aren't too pushed about beauty on the outside?' fretted Mary. 'Beauty from within sounds like the concept of some supermodel type who eats all the right stuff, spends an hour standing on her head in the morning and looks like a goddess. People like that are always banging on about inner beauty. Some of us need help with the outside.'

'You look great,' said Daisy loyally. 'You're a wonderful woman at her sexual peak, looking for a new lover, preferably some modern young man who knows how to adore a more mature woman.'

Mary snorted. 'I wish. I don't have the energy to be at my sexual peak and the only young fellas I meet are the ones at the petrol station who ignore me and look lustfully at passing babes twenty years my junior.'

'Stop it. Faint heart never won fair nice young handsome boyfriend,' insisted Daisy.

'Oh, I don't want a man anyway.' Mary waved a hand dismissively in the air. 'Manless, I can sit up in bed with my facemask on and watch *Extreme Makeover* on satellite TV all night while getting chocolate slivers in the bed, and nobody can complain. You couldn't do that with a young lover, could you? No, you'd be waxing every inch of your body morning, noon and night; you'd be existing on nothing but grapefruit; and you'd have anti-cellulite cream coming out of your ears. No thank you. Who needs the hassle?'

At Paula's, they had to go in and admire the nursery. Newly decorated by Paula's husband, Enrico, in shades of yellow, with Beatrix Potter pictures on the wall, the former boxroom was baby heaven. There was a cot, a Moses basket, a zoo of soft cuddly toys, and a dresser full of fabric-conditioned baby garments folded with exquisite neatness as if by a team of crack Benetton staff.

'Oh,' sighed Daisy and Mary together, as the three of them squashed into the room and inhaled the scent of baby products.

'It's gorgeous.' Daisy hugged Paula. It was lovely to be able to feel really happy for Paula's good fortune, she thought. Until she'd made the appointment with the clinic, it would have been hard for her to stand in a nursery and admire it without feeling as if her heart would shatter like glass.

Back in the car, Paula turned out to be keen on the beauty-from-within concept, and thought the spa's mission statement was a wonderful idea.

'What we are is more important than how we look,' she said earnestly.

Mary, who'd moved into the back seat to let Paula have the expanse of the front, roared with laughter. 'So says the woman with a heated eyelash curler!'

'That was the old me,' said Paula loftily. 'The new me is going to be a better person and not be so concerned with stupid things like my hair or stretch marks.'

'You're afraid you're going to have a baby with Enrico's ears, aren't you?' Mary said suddenly.

They'd all heard how poor Enrico could still remember being called Dumbo at school.

Daisy smothered a grin. Trust Mary to get straight to the point.

'You're right. I'd love the baby to have Enrico's eyes, skin tones, hair, *anything* . . .'

'But not the ears.'

'Not the ears,' agreed Paula. 'It sounds so shallow to even talk about it.' She patted her bump to ask forgiveness.

'You can love someone and still not like their ears,' Mary said. 'And there's nothing shallow about wanting the best for your kids. The world is shallow because sticking-out ears matter and make kids tease other kids. You're just reacting to that. We're back to *Extreme Makeover*, I'm afraid. Nobody would want to lose fifty pounds, have their teeth straightened and have liposuction on their chin if how they looked didn't matter. The world sucks: we just go along with it.'

They were on their way out of Carrickwell now, past the road to the Willow Hotel, past Abraham Park, and on to what was known as Hill Road, a leafy, tree-lined lane that wound along for three miles before coming to a tiny hamlet and Cloud's Hill Spa.

Spring was pushing up enthusiastically everywhere, dotting the trees with acid-green buds and painting the hedgerows with baby shoots. Rain sparkled on the roadside grass, the air was filled with the smell of new growth, and the valley hummed with burgeoning life.

Daisy felt her spirits rise. She knew these roads well from her teenage years and had often peeped through the gates of the old Delaney place. 'My mother lives near here,' she said idly.

'Will we drop in?' said Paula, who didn't know much about Daisy's background.

'No,' said Daisy, shocked. 'I mean . . . she might not be there,' she finished limply.

Mary helped her out. 'My family are just like that too,' she said. 'They like a bit of a warning before anyone brings visitors in case they're all still faffing around in their pyjamas.'

'Yes, that's it,' added Daisy gratefully, as though the idea of her mother in any state of undress in the daytime was a possibility to be imagined. Control was Nan Farrell's favourite word and being in her nightclothes after seven in the morning would be very out of control. Daisy realised Mary was probably being tactful because she had met Daisy's mother on the very rare occasions she had crossed the threshold of Georgia's Tiara.

The first time, Nan Farrell had brushed her fingertips along rails of the shop's stock as if it was muck of the lowest order, instead of beautiful garments hand-picked by her talented daughter. Mary would not have needed psychiatric training to work out why Daisy was so hopelessly convinced she was useless at everything.

'Anyway, we'd be late if we dropped in to see your mum,' added Mary cheerily. 'We've got to be at Mount Carraig at ten and it's five to. Put your foot down, Daisy.'

'Isn't it lovely out here?' sighed Paula, as they raced along, the gleam of Lough Enla to the left, and a meadow dotted with sheep to the right.

'Gorgeous,' said Mary. 'I remember Bart and I looking at a house here years ago, but it was too far out of the town and it would have been hard for the kids to get to school. Lovely house too, much bigger than ours and on two acres. We could have had a pony for Emer. Mind you, it's as well we didn't. How could you split up a pony? One half for me and the other for Bart. Bet you I'd get the tail end.'

Mary and Paula started talking about schools and Daisy let the conversation slide over her as she drove along, thinking her own thoughts. She'd been sixteen when she and her mother had moved from the centre of Carrickwell to the cottage off Hill Road. It had been postcard pretty with a red-tiled roof, a herbaceous border and a moss-covered stone wall out front, but Daisy couldn't wait to move out of it. Her mother had seemed glad when Daisy left to go to college in Dublin too. With the hindsight of adulthood, Daisy could see that being a parent was not a role her mother had ever wanted.

It was odd that the great tragedy of her own life was not having children, while having a child – Daisy – at age seventeen, had proved to be the great tragedy of her mother's life. And sad too. If she and her mother had been close, she'd have been able to talk about how much she wanted a baby, and how happy she was now that she was finally going to do something about it. Instead, they spoke occasionally on the phone, restrained conversations when nothing that mattered was really discussed.

Mary was explaining how her thirteen-year-old daughter, Emer, was enjoying school. Daisy allowed herself the pleasure of imagining choosing a school for her baby. She and Alex would visit them all, of course, weigh up the options, make lists of pros and cons, and only then would they decide.

Alex had been so sporty when he was younger that he'd probably love a boy to follow in his footsteps and be a rower. St Cillian's School sounded good for that. But there was a part of Daisy that yearned for a little girl so she could right all the wrongs that had been done to her when she was a child. She would make sure nobody ever said things to her like, 'Keep out of the fridge, Daisy. You're turning into a proper piglet with your nose in the trough.' Although she knew it wasn't fair to have a child in order to relive your own childhood.

Suddenly, there was the sign for Cloud's Hill Spa and Daisy was pulled out of her thoughts.

'Would you look at this,' said Mary as they drove in the big iron gates and saw the old house. 'I have died and gone to heaven.'

Gone was the overgrown garden Daisy remembered as a teenager and in its place was one of the most beautiful landscaped gardens she'd ever seen. They were halfway up the mountain here, and from the drive they could all see the town, with the spires of St Canice's Cathedral reaching up to the heavens, and the ancient druidic settlement in the distance.

The house itself was no longer a crumbling Georgian wreck, but a graceful building beautifully restored, and behind the house they could just see the tastefully converted stables.

'I'm going to sell the shop and come to live here for ever,' Mary said in admiration.

'You wouldn't make enough money from selling the shop,' Paula pointed out.

'I'll sell the children too. I can just see myself here for the rest of my days.'

'Like living in a high-class nursing home?' teased Daisy.

'Yes, please.'

They parked on the gravel forecourt, with Mary remarking that they ought to be driving up in a carriage and four in order to fully fit in with the grand theme of the place.

'I think I'm underdressed,' murmured Daisy as they headed for the door. She'd gone for work-out chic in a grey marl tracksuit.

'This is the only thing that fits me any more,' Paula murmured back, gesturing to her enormous blue maternity T-shirt and marquee-sized skirt, 'so if I'm underdressed, they'll have to put up with me.'

Inside was an oasis of calm. The threesome were checked in and brought to a large changing room tiled with Italian stone. Then they were whisked off to a relaxation room that turned out to be a library overlooking the gardens. There were books, magazines, newspapers, a fridge full of juices, and a platter of fruit, as well as soft couches, easy chairs and some gentle background music that made Daisy instantly want to lie down and sleep.

'I could definitely live here,' Mary said again as they flopped on the couches with the latest magazines for a self-indulgent blob. 'Imagine when this place was some family's actual home?'

At that moment, the door opened and a tall woman with dark hair swept up into a knot walked into the room. 'I'm Leah Meyer. Welcome to Cloud's Hill Spa,' she said. Suddenly a mobile phone buzzed. 'Tranquillity ruined,' she said wryly, scooping the phone from her pocket. 'Staffing problems. I've got to take this.'

She was gone for a moment, then returned and apologised again. 'I don't usually carry my cellphone with me,' she said. 'It kind of ruins the atmosphere.'

'No, it's good,' insisted Mary. 'Otherwise it was all so perfect that we'd have been talking in hushed voices and would never have relaxed. Too much relaxing and whale music makes me nervous.'

Leah laughed. 'No whales, but we do have dolphin music, if you'd like it,' she said. 'We tend to keep it for special occasions. We rotate the music. Eight solid hours of dolphin sounds would drive everyone nuts. So we have an hour of everything. Jazz, classical, easy listening, Tom Jones.'

'No whale music?' said Daisy, instantly liking this tall, beautiful woman. 'I want my money back.'

'We did have a whale sound CD,' Leah said, 'but whenever I put it on, people kept sneaking up to the stereo, turning on Tom Jones and hiding the whales at the back of the file cabinet. I guess they were trying to tell me something, so it's stayed lost.'

Everyone laughed. Leah offered drinks and soon they were talking animatedly about everything from the shop to Paula's pregnancy to how utterly fabulous ten minutes in the hot tub could make you feel.

'And you get in every day?' Daisy was envious.

'Every day. Helps the aches and pains,' Leah revealed. 'You can't get to my age and not have a few aches.'

'Your age! Oh yes, right,' chortled Mary. 'Now when you're *my* age, you can talk about aching bones.'

'I'm pretty sure I'm older than you, Mary.' Leah's smile was broad.

'No way!' Mary retorted.

'What age do you think I am?'

They all regarded Leah carefully.

Forty-ish. Maybe forty-six or -seven, thought Daisy, but didn't say anything. What if she was horribly wrong and Leah was nearer forty than fifty?

'I'm forty-eight and you look younger, perhaps forty-three,' said Mary, eyes narrowed as she scrutinised Leah. 'No, no, forty.' She changed her mind.

'Close,' said Leah. 'To paraphrase my grandmom, I'm twenty-one with forty years' experience.'

Mary and Paula stared at her in mild confusion, but Daisy got it instantly. 'Sixty-one?' she gasped. 'Never.'

'Sixty-two in a few months,' Leah admitted.

The three women were silent in astonishment.

Leah looked incredible, Daisy thought. Some beautiful women had faces like blank canvases waiting for someone else to paint the expression on. But not Leah. Her shining brown eyes were bright with life, her cheekbones looked as if they'd grown so smooth and high from the very act of smiling, and the lines on her face had developed simply because her face was so expressive.

'You have to tell us your secret or we are leaving,' joked Mary.

'You were born beautiful and have young genes in your family,' suggested Daisy, because it really was the only suggestion she could come up with. How else could a person look so utterly fabulous and content?

'I'll tell you if you join me in the hot tub later,' Leah promised. 'Mom-to-be, you'll have to sit on the side and dangle your hands in the water,' she added to Paula.

A therapist dressed in white popped her head round the door to say hi and to check which treatments everyone was having.

'We'll have whatever Leah's had,' said Mary. 'And I want it all twice.'

They came together for lunch and then didn't meet up again until late afternoon, when Daisy and Mary found themselves alone in the hot tub, staring out at Carrickwell spread beneath them.

'This was an excellent idea,' Mary said with a contented sigh.

'Wasn't it? I feel so relaxed,' said Daisy, eyes closed.

'Good, I was a bit worried about you.'

Daisy sat up. 'About me?'

'You seemed stressed for a while . . .'

'Alex's been travelling so much, you know.'

'I thought you might be having problems,' Mary added, 'you know, since he said he didn't want to get married.' She was being uncharacteristically sensitive, which made Daisy realise she'd said far too much that day when she'd complained about Alex.

'We're over it,' said Daisy quickly. 'I was definitely PMT-ish.'

'Oh, OK.'

Daisy nodded. 'Hormones are a nightmare,' she said, hugging her hormone-related secret to herself. In two weeks – thirteen days to be exact – she and Alex would be at the fertility clinic. If that wasn't the ultimate commitment, what was? She'd love to be able to tell Mary about it but she and Alex had agreed: this was their secret.

'Leah's nice, isn't she?' Mary moved on to another topic. 'It's odd, but I feel as if I've seen her somewhere before.'

'Funny, I know what you mean.'

'Perhaps she's been on the cover of *Forbes* as a millionairess. She must have money if she's renovated this place, although those millionaire types normally don't do the hard grind themselves.'

Daisy grinned. 'I don't know enough millionaires to know if they do or they don't. She's beautiful, though, isn't she?'

'Great bone structure. I wonder would she come into the shop as a customer?'

'I'm sure she would,' Daisy said slowly, 'but I don't know if she's the sort of person who's into fashion. She doesn't look like she needs great clothes – it's as if she could dress in rags and nobody would notice the rags, they'd just notice her.'

'Style,' agreed Mary. 'She might put all her energies into decoration rather than clothes. This place is certainly stylish and there's no doubt that Carrickwell needs a bit of glamour. The Willow's fine but it's not exactly four-star luxury.'

'Don't say that; it's lovely,' argued Daisy, who'd found that the Christmas lunch at the Willow was about the only way to get through the day in the years she'd spent it with her mother. The warmth and friendliness of the Malins had made it bearable. 'Mr Malin is so kind and I think my mother rather fancies him, although she'd never say it.'

'Harry? He's a pet,' admitted Mary. 'His wife's nice, although, poor dear, she never has a bean to spend on clothes. The daughter's attractive too, very striking, tall girl. She'd pay for dressing. Legs up to her armpits.'

'Talking about me again,' said Paula, arriving slowly.

She was followed by Leah, who carried a tray laid with a jug of orange juice and four glasses.

While Paula sat in a lounger beside them, the other three relaxed in the tub and the Georgia's Tiara girls compared notes on their treatments.

Paula's mum-to-be massage had been heavenly because there was a special massage table with a cut-out bit made for pregnant women. 'Lying on your stomach is something you take for granted until you're pregnant,' Paula sighed. She'd had a manicure, pedicure and a gentle facial, and didn't think Enrico would recognise her when she got home.

Mary had gone for the fabled hot stone massage and liked it so much, she was thinking of getting one installed in her own house. 'Who'd have thought that boiled basalt could feel so good?' she said happily.

'Who'd have thought sitting in what's really a big bath could feel so good?' asked Daisy, who was in a state of blissful relaxation after an aromatherapy scrub followed by an aromatherapy wrap, and a paraffin manicure that made her hands feel softer than silk. 'I'd love to do all of this every day,' she said. 'Are you supposed to meditate or something, Leah, or just lie back in the water and relax?'

'I'm sure you can meditate if you're into that,' Leah said. 'I don't. I just lie back and think about the good parts and the bad parts of the day, and say thanks for it all.'

'So that's your secret?' asked Mary craftily. 'No special beauty treatments but saying thanks?'

Leah smiled enigmatically.

'No, seriously,' begged Paula. 'How do you look so fabulous?'

Leah appeared to relent. 'I was brought up in Los Angeles where how you look is of supreme importance. I've always looked after my skin and my figure. My mother aged really well, so it's in the genes as well. But I got caught up in the whole ageing thing. In LA, it's as if you don't matter as soon as you hit thirty. You become invisible.'

'You don't have to go to LA for that,' grumbled Mary.

'It happens later in the rest of the world, I guess,' Leah said. 'Fifty might be the watershed in most places, but in LA, it really is thirty. You have this vain hope that it will be different for you because you feel young, and hey, *a few lines don't matter*, baby, but one day you go out to the market and nobody looks at you. Nobody. You have become the invisible woman.'

'I can't believe that,' Daisy said. 'You're beautiful. You would be noticed anywhere.'

'Thank you for that,' smiled Leah. 'I was never insecure about myself because I looked just like my mother and she was a head turner. But in a city where the most beautiful people in the world congregate, beauty is commonplace. The guy who pumps gas for your car could be a model, the girl who serves you coffee could walk down the ramp for Victoria's Secret. Everybody is stunning. So, you panic.'

'And?' Mary asked breathlessly.

Leah laughed, a low husky laugh that wouldn't have been out of place in a hot bar at midnight. 'You go to the right cosmetic surgeon and you get him to freshen it all up a little.'

'I knew it!' Mary said.

'Only a little,' Leah argued. She tapped her forehead. 'Brow lift, lipo under the jawline and a bit of reshaping on the chin. The rest is me. No face lift. If you have it done too early, you need too many of them and start to look like you come from a planet where their ears grow on the tops of their heads.'

'You don't need a face lift,' Daisy said firmly.

'Good, because I'm never having anything done again. This face is going with me to the end. In LA, people are shocked when I say this – particularly my surgeon, who makes most of his money on repeat business. But if I had my time over again, I wouldn't have anything done.'

Everyone digested this information.

'Why not?' asked Daisy.

'Because I spent so long worrying about how I looked on the outside, I forgot about the inside, and that needed a lot more work.'

'Point taken,' Mary agreed.

Under normal circumstances, Daisy would have said nothing and nodded, as if she too got the point. She was always laughing at punchlines she hadn't heard, or jokes she didn't understand. But today, she wanted to understand. How did a person become comfortable with the way they looked? If the outside was good, then you had time and energy to work on the inside, surely?

'What do you mean exactly?' she said.

'I believed that everything I was, was what was on the surface,' Leah said simply. 'If my face was beautiful and men still turned to look at me as I passed, then God was in his heaven and all was right with my world. That's bogus, as my son might have said when he was going through his Bill and Ted days. Who you are is not about what you see in the mirror.'

'You're so right,' said Paula enthusiastically. 'She *is*,' she protested as Mary grinned at her.

'I know, but it's hard living it,' Mary shrugged.

'It does take a major life event to make you wake up and smell the coffee,' Leah admitted. 'But I'm happy with the way I am now. I like my age, I don't necessarily like creaking bones and waking in the night feeling as if my back has seized up, but I like the maturity.'

'You do?' said Daisy doubtfully. She'd identified what had made Leah happy: she was a mother, she had a child, was a member of the club. To Daisy, no amount of maturity could make up for not having that.

'I do. I don't want to go back to the person I was when I was twenty, even if it meant going back to looking and feeling as fit and beautiful as I did then.'

'It must be nice to be so content,' Daisy said wistfully.

Paula, Mary and Leah all looked at her.

'You have to work at it,' Leah explained. 'You have to think of what would make you happy and then stop telling yourself how it's impossible, but instead tell yourself it *is* possible. And go after it. Hopes and dreams aren't as far off as you think. What do you want, Daisy?' asked Leah. 'Remember, this is the hot tub of truth. You cannot cheat here. Or, if you do,' she amended, 'you develop a nasty rash.'

The other three laughed.

'Seriously. I got some stuff from that lady in the shop that sells tarot and crystals. Sprinkled on the water, it makes you tell the truth.'

'The shop's called Mystical Fires,' said Daisy. 'I didn't know they stocked truthful water, but they have nice angel cards. You get a pack and read one every day to see what messages the angels have for you. I think I might get some.' She hoped her angel card would say 'You shall have beautiful babies' every time, although she wasn't sure if there was a card for this.

'What message would you like most in the world? What would make you happy?' Leah asked.

Daisy bit her lip. Honesty was hard. She wasn't comfortable with telling people deeply personal things. Saying she wanted a baby, a family, would sound silly when Leah probably was asking if she'd like bigger lips or a flatter stomach or something.

'To be happy, and to eat as much chocolate as I want.'

'Get pregnant,' joked Paula, 'then you do both!'

Daisy's smile didn't falter. 'Great idea!'

'What about you then?' Leah turned to Paula.

'To have a healthy baby,' she said simply. 'Boy, girl, big ears,' she grinned at Mary and Daisy, 'whatever. As long as the baby is healthy, that's all Enrico and I want.'

'And you?' It was Mary's turn.

Daisy half waited for Mary to laugh and give some breezy riposte, which was her usual response to a conversation that was getting too deep.

'I don't want to be alone,' Mary said softly. 'It's not great passion I want, or someone buying me roses all the time and whisking me off to glamorous dinners. It's the company, the love. A hug in the morning, a person to smile at when one of the kids says something funny, a warm body to snuggle up against in bed when it's cold.'

Daisy was quiet.

'Companionship,' Leah suggested.

'That's the word.' Mary slid deeper into the bubbling hot water. 'I'm fed up with everyone talking about older women, sexy young men and being at it like knives morning, noon and night.'

'So overrated.' Leah nodded.

'Exactly. So what if you found a young stud who could go all night? He couldn't tickle you in that place at the base of your neck where your skin is sensitive, and make you remember the first time he did it years ago.'

'No, that's so true.'

Both Leah and Mary were staring off into the middle distance. Daisy felt a ripple of guilt. Clearly Leah was on her own now, like Mary. They shared a common thread, while Daisy and Paula were the lucky ones. Paula was happy with her lot, but Daisy needed to appreciate the good things in her life more. Maybe she wanted too much from life. Didn't she have enough already with her gorgeous Alex and a job she loved? Could you be too greedy for happiness?

CHAPTER SEVEN

Leah loved the tranquillity of Carraig Hill when the day was over and before it was time to oversee dinner for any guests. She liked being on her own, liked the peace of her own company and the chance to mull over the day in her head as she wandered through the peaceful old house. She didn't need to check that light switches and machines were off – whoever was on management duty that day did it. Leah just liked to walk through the house on her own and think. Sometimes she thought about the past, but not too often, because it was still painful. Time healed but there would always be a scar, the bone-deep scar of losing her beloved Jesse. It was easier to think about the day that had just gone instead of dwelling on the past. Time had taught her that, at least.

So she thought about that day and the many interesting people who'd come through the doors of Cloud's Hill Spa. Every day there was someone new, that lost look about them, the look that made Leah want to race over and enfold them in her arms.

Like Billy and Pearl, a lovely married couple who'd come to the spa for a three-day break when their holiday plans to Cyprus with another couple were dissolved without much explanation. Hurt and bewildered, Pearl and Billy told Leah that they'd always gone on holiday with Agnes and Ian.

'She was my bridesmaid; I was her matron of honour,' Pearl said over coffee in the relaxation room while they discussed what treatments she'd have. 'We've gone away together for twenty years. Malta, Cyprus and my favourite, Rhodes.'

'They said they didn't want to book this year,' Billy added. 'Just that. No real reason. They were going to Ian's sister, Marie, in Torquay instead.'

'Our daughter booked us in here as a treat, to make it up to us,' Pearl added. 'Fiona's got a great job and she's very good to us.'

Pearl liked the reflexology best. 'Agnes and myself tried a few things like this in the old days, but we don't now. Since we all retired, I thought we'd have more time but they don't want to be doing things now. I can't understand it.'

'Your friends are on a pension too?' Leah asked delicately.

Her guests nodded.

Leah thought of the kind daughter who had given her parents a health spa voucher and perhaps paid for their holiday to say thanks for what they'd given her over the years. She wondered aloud if Fiona was always so generous.

Billy nodded. 'She says we put her through university: it's our turn now.'

'Might the problem with Ian and Agnes be that they can't afford holidays on a pension?' Leah suggested. 'They don't have a grateful son or daughter who wants to say thanks?'

The couple were shocked that they'd never thought of that themselves. Money. That was the problem. How could they not have realised? Why had Ian and Agnes not just said so?

They phoned their friends that evening.

'We're all going to Torquay,' Pearl told Leah happily the next day. 'Agnes is thrilled we're coming because,' she lowered her voice, 'between you and me, she doesn't get on with Ian's sister, Marie, but you can't say, can you? We're all staying in Marie's house but it'll be easier if there's four of us. We can go off on our own to places and Marie needn't feel she has to entertain us.'

Pearl and Billy had gone on Tuesday, which was the day that Stephanie had arrived.

Stephanie was in her late twenties and was quite simply one of the most beautiful women Leah had ever seen. But she'd looked so pale and drawn when she'd arrived. Only now, two days later, had she been able to smile without the telltale twinkling of tears.

'You've made me realise that I don't need to feel stupid,' she'd confided to Leah that morning when they'd met doing laps in the pool. Stephanie's face was like that of a tranquil gazelle: huge eyes in an exquisite face, surrounded by a cloud of chestnut hair. 'You were right when you said that believing people when they're lying to you doesn't mean you're stupid.'

Her lover, Ralph, had made out that he was unhappy with his marriage. He was a good liar.

'The truth depends on where you're standing,' Leah had said wisely. 'He probably wanted to believe he had a bad marriage so he could be with you ... Why wouldn't he? You're warm, kind and beautiful.'

'You make it sound so plausible,' Stephanie sighed. 'I'd prefer to think he just couldn't help himself, not that he wanted to hurt me.'

'It doesn't sound like he wanted to hurt you,' Leah pointed out. 'He hurt himself too. And at least you can talk to friends about the pain of the affair and get on with life; Ralph has to hide how hurt he's feeling from everyone, especially now that his wife is having a baby. So you're doing better. You can share it and move on.'

'You're right,' said Stephanie, surprised.

People often couldn't see what was in front of them, Leah knew. Stephanie genuinely believed she was only reasonable-looking and couldn't see that her besotted, married lover would have sold his soul to the devil to be with her. The longer Leah lived, the more she realised that people were blind to so many things. The secret to surviving, as she had discovered for herself, was opening your eyes and seeing the world and yourself for what they both were.

Today, she had seen that Mary Dillon had done that. She was a survivor, Leah was sure. For all she was able to laugh about her ex-husband, she admitted that she had loved him dearly and it was clear that she was finding it hard bringing up their children on her own. But Leah knew that she would do it.

It was Daisy, sweet, trusting Daisy, who was in need of help.

Leah had good instincts and she was pretty sure that someone had once told Daisy not to wear her heart on her sleeve. When asked what she'd like most in the world, Daisy had been flip and had given only half the truth: 'To be happy and to eat as much chocolate as I want,' she'd said.

'Get pregnant, then you do both!' had been Paula's riposte.

Only Leah had seen the look of desolation that swept over Daisy's lovely face when Paula spoke. Was pregnancy what she really wanted above anything else? Perhaps.

Leah hoped she'd be able to help Daisy: she felt such warmth towards the younger woman. For all that she seemed to have it all – the partner, the career, the nice home – Daisy yearned for something else, and Leah was sure that a child was only part of it. Time would tell.

It was nearly time to get ready for dinner. Leah had one more room to walk through. She stepped into the hot tub room and stared out at the lights of Carrickwell, sparkling like rhinestones on a bed of velvet.

She loved this view of the town and the surrounding heartlands. High on her beautiful mountain, she felt as if she were watching over Carrickwell, ready for when she was needed to lend a hand.

Of course, solving other people's problems was always easier than solving her own.

It was nearly ten years since Leah had turned her own life around and dragged herself out of hell. What was it people said about hell? Religion was for people who were afraid of hell and spirituality was for people who'd already been there? She'd been there, but she'd learned so much on the journey there and back.

CHAPTER EIGHT

Mel sat propped up against the pillows on the spare room bed and rocked Carrie's small body rhythmically. The last coughing fit had been the worst and Mel would have gladly given a year of her life to be able to make the frightened look disappear from Carrie's eyes. She'd woken crying at just after two a.m. and had worked herself up into a frenzy of sobbing and a crowing cough for nearly three-quarters of an hour, and Mel was at her wits' end. Just when she thought she'd have to do something – phone the doctor, phone *somebody*, because warm sponging and the medicine hadn't taken down Carrie's temperature or calmed her – Carrie suddenly drifted off to sleep in her mother's arms.

That had been ten minutes ago, but Mel still rocked her gently, grateful that the toddler no longer felt so burning hot. But anxious that Carrie needed to rest, Mel wouldn't dare put her down on the cool sheets until she was truly in a deep sleep. So she rocked, ignoring the cramp in her shoulder and the tiredness that permeated every muscle of her body. Tiredness was nothing to the fear that something was seriously wrong.

Now they were back on safe ground, Mel allowed herself to relax just a fraction. She'd take Carrie to the doctor first thing in the morning, she promised. They'd be there at nine on the dot. No, earlier in fact. Everything else, including the Wednesday breakfast meeting, could go hang. Her baby was all that mattered. Her babies. Who'd said that children were like your heart running round on its own little legs? It was so accurate.

They were her heart and her soul, and yet she was always rushing to make time for them. What was the point of working all the hours so the girls could have a better future, when their present was a Mum-free zone? Since the row with Caroline, Mel hadn't been able to get the notion of giving up her job out of her head. She'd even mentioned it to Adrian, but instantly regretted it because he'd looked totally shocked at the idea.

'Well . . . financially, I mean, I suppose we'd save on the Little Tigers fees,' he'd said, doing his best to recover from his initial reaction, which was, 'You're not serious!'

'Forget I mentioned it,' Mel had said, angry with herself for raising the subject. If she gave up work, they'd find it difficult to manage. Mel's Christmas bonus had kept the family coffers afloat many a year. Adrian's salary would go up if he got his Masters degree, but the increase wouldn't be a lot. His augmented pay wouldn't support a family of four and the mortgage on Goldsmith Lawn, surely.

'It was a stupid idea,' she'd added quickly. 'I'm sorry I mentioned it. I'd go mad without the office, you know that.'

'No, *I'm* sorry for what I said,' Adrian had insisted. 'It was a shock, that's all. Seriously, if you want to give up work, Mel, we could just about manage.'

Mel had ruffled his hair then. 'I was just daydreaming. Can you see me giving up everything I've worked for at Lorimar? Not likely.'

The next morning, Sarah was fascinated to find her mother and baby sister asleep in the spare room.

'Why are you in Granny's bed?' she wanted to know, looking adorable in Winnie-the-Pooh pyjamas and one Tigger sock, her blonde hair tousled from sleep.

Mel stared at her blearily. It had been well after four when she had last noticed the small bedside alarm clock, and now it was after half-seven and they'd all overslept. Beside her, Carrie lay sleeping serenely.

'Carrie was sick in the night and I didn't want her crying to wake you, darling,' Mel said.

'I could have got into bed with you too.' Sarah objected to having been left out of this big late night treat, and clambered into the bed to set things right. She wriggled close to her mother and began to suck her thumb. Using one hand to hold Sarah, Mel stroked Carrie into wakefulness with the other. Carrie felt mercifully cool to the touch and her cheeks were no longer flushed. Yawning delicately, she opened her eyes and beamed up at her mother, long blonde lashes spiky around her huge blue eyes.

Despite her tiredness and her dread of the day ahead, a day where she'd have to juggle like mad to take time off work, Mel felt blissfully happy. This was where she should be. Not at work, where she'd worry about her babies, but here, hugging them and taking care of them. Mothering them. It was the most basic instinct, after all. Nobody could care for Sarah and Carrie quite like her. She was genuinely irreplaceable to her children.

The doctor's surgery was packed, even at ten to nine in the morning, and Mel, who had rushed there with Carrie after dropping Sarah off at Little Tigers, began to see her notion of making it in to work by twelve receding.

Her mother was coming to take care of Carrie at eleven, but Mel wondered if they'd be out of the surgery by then, never mind back home. She looked at the other patients, for the most part women with small children, and wondered if she stood at the top of the room and said she was a busy executive and had to be in work soon, would they let her go next? She'd probably be stoned to death with copies of *GolfPro* and *Hello!*

With Carrie balanced in her arms, clutching her purple and green fluffy sheep, and the rest of the waiting room listening, Mel began the delicate task of resetting her day.

First up was a call to Sue, the publicity department assistant who, unaccountably, hadn't taken her office phone off voice mail. 'If you're screening calls, Sue, please pick up. This is urgent. I've

110

had to miss the eight-thirty meeting to take Carrie to the doctor and although I phoned Vanessa in marketing and asked her to make my apologies, I only got her mobile voice mail and she hasn't phoned back, so can you check that she did and phone me to confirm? Then, you've got to cancel my eleven o'clock. I'd do it myself but the number's on my desk and I haven't got my Palm Pilot with me.'

Idiot . . . Mel could visualise it on the charger on her desk, left behind as she made her usual mad dash out the door the evening before.

'Mummy, want to go home,' whimpered Carrie. 'Doan like this place.'

After some cuddles and some juice, Mel attacked the phone again.

'Then could you beg Anthony to take over that briefing with the work experience students? I should be in by . . .' she faltered. Twelve? Half-twelve? Should she go for broke and say after lunch? 'One,' she said finally.

With nothing but magazines they'd read before to amuse themselves, the other patients must be listening to every detail of Mel's increasingly frantic attempts to track down Sue.

None of the mothers looked at her with any vestige of feminine sympathy. Mel thought of how, in their place, she'd send a smile of sympathy to another woman struggling, as a sign of sisterhood. But perhaps these women saw Mel, in her smart plum crêpe suit and contrasting amethyst-coloured necklace, as only a brittle power-broker, a creature from another planet who had no place in their world of sick, tired babies and everlasting waits in doctors' surgeries.

Well, she wanted to scream at them, they were wrong. She *was* from their world. Their no-sleep-with-crying-toddler world. Only they couldn't see beyond the suit.

Mel made it to the Lorimar building by nearly half-past twelve, in time to meet Hilary – power-suited in red with matching lips – walking out of the building with one of the finance directors. Those guys all looked the same to Mel: weight-of-the-world expressions and suits that tried too hard to be Michael Douglas in *Wall Street*.

Knowing she was unforgivably late, Mel gave a half-smile and was rewarded with a rather chilly look from her boss.

'I was looking for you earlier, Mel,' Hilary said in a way that demanded an explanation.

Mel took a deep breath. 'My younger daughter was sick and I had to take her to the doctor,' she said evenly.

'Oh.' Nobody could invest the word 'oh' with as much depth as Hilary. *Oh. You are in so much trouble, you wouldn't believe,* it said.

The sick feeling Mel had felt all the way in on thetrain because she was late jumped up a notch to stomach-churning.

'She was very bad during the night and I was worried,' Mel added.

The finance guy looked utterly unmoved. He probably had kids. Mel was sure she'd seen them wheeled out at the company barbecue, along with his long-suffering wife, a woman who didn't have to keep office hours but could iron pinstripe shirts expertly and knew how to put the kids to bed on her own when he went out for a team-building drink with the hotshots from Lorimar. But he cared nothing for sick kid stories. Neither, it seemed, did Hilary.

'You know how awful it is when small children are sick,' Mel tried again, hoping for some motherly bonding to kick in. 'They break your heart with those big, sad eyes and only Mummy will do.'

Hilary nodded. 'See you after lunch,' she snapped.

And so did something inside Mel. 'Carrie goes to a day nursery, you see, Hilary, and when she's sick, my mother usually steps in. But last night she was so ill, coughing so badly, I wanted to be at the doctor with her myself.' Mel was speaking more quickly than her usual calm office tone. Mr Finance Guy was suddenly finding his watch very interesting. 'In fact, it's a long time since I've taken her to the doctor myself because I've got to come to work here, in a health insurance company. *Lorimar cares* –' she chanted the company's new motto brightly – 'unless it's an employee's child who's sick, in which case Lorimar don't give a shit. It's funny that. Ethics around here are skin-deep but hard-nosed corporate nastiness cuts to the bone.

'The thing is, Hilary, Lorimar might not care but I do. Because one day I won't be working here any more and nobody will remember who I was because as employees we're all expendable. But,' she glared at Hilary, who stared back, unblinking, 'I'm not expendable as a mother. And when I finally crawl out of this workhouse for the last time, it will be too late for me to make it up to Sarah and Carrie for all the things I missed because I was chained to my desk. All I'm asking for is for you to understand that. I'm a better employee because I want to do the right thing by everybody, not a worse one.'

'This is neither the time nor the place for this conversation,' Hilary said, unmoved. 'I'll see you in my office at half-two.'

'Long lunch, then?' Mel said, unable to stop herself from being snide.

'We're planning redundancies,' Hilary said briskly.

'We'll guess who'll be top of the list, then,' Mel said, and marched into the building.

In the cool of the tiled lobby, she stopped and leaned against the wall for a moment, her heart racing, her breath coming in shallow gasps. What had she done? It might have been hugely satisfying to tell Hilary and Finance Guy the truth, but she'd have to pay for it.

During the lunch hour, Mel did none of the things she ought to do. Instead, she ignored the stack of emails in her in-box, left the pile of phone messages and reports on her desk and went out shopping. She bought a magazine and sat reading it over a sandwich and a piece of wildly rich cheesecake in the coffee shop of a nearby department store. Then she walked round the shop, her mind working overtime as she ran her hands over children's clothes, chic lingerie and prettily coloured duvet covers. Redundancy. She'd heard it on the grapevine that there were a few planned but the notion of taking a voluntary one had never occurred to her before now. Redundancies were for people fed up with their career, or people who wanted a change of job, or for women who couldn't hack being a working parent and needed the security blanket of a payoff. Not for her.

Except that, suddenly, maybe it was.

Her career had stalled, that was for sure. Becoming a mother had affected her chances of promotion.

But then she viewed her career differently too. Having children had changed her priorities. It wasn't that she did less work – in fact, she worked harder now than she'd ever done, taking care of Sarah and Carrie, *and* doing her job – but she was less prepared to deal with the rubbish that went with a career.

Office politicking, high drama over a negative story in the newspapers, pursed lips when she was late, even if she would make up the time twice over – all this bored her. She didn't know how, but being a parent had taught her that there was more to life. She was sure she had her priorities right. It was a pity that Hilary and Lorimar hadn't.

'Can I help you?' asked the beautiful young woman at the make-up counter in the cosmetics department.

'I need a whole new look,' Mel said, taking in the gleaming white and gold of the counter, with its delicious array of pots, jars and tubes of lipstick in every exquisite shade imaginable. 'I haven't changed my moisturiser for years and I think it's about time. Moisturiser, toner, cleanser, whatever you think I need. But what I'd like too, if you can do it in half an hour, is a make-up session. Glamorous, successful, a bit of a change from now,' she added ruefully. Make-up had been her last priority that morning.

The girl patted the chair beside her. 'No problem. Going anywhere special tonight?'

Mel swung herself onto the chair and leaned back against the padded headrest. 'I'm leaving my job,' she said.

'Oh, how long were you there?' The girl was asking out of politeness, Mel knew, her expert eyes already summing up Mel's skintone and flaws to see what magic she could work with her brushes and her pots.

'Fourteen years,' Mel said, 'but it's time to move on.'

'That's what I always say,' the girl smiled, wielding a moisturising wipe. 'Move onwards and upwards.'

Clothes might not maketh the man, but make-up sure as heck cheered up the woman. Mel walked back to the office with a swing in her step, a hefty department store bag of expensive creams by her side and a glowing, newly made-up face. After all, it might be a long time before she'd be able to afford anything but supermarket creams again. This was her redundancy present to herself.

Hilary looked a little surprised when Mel walked into her office at half-past two looking fresh and serene.

'Cheesecake and retail therapy,' Mel explained calmly, sitting down in one of Hilary's upright leather chairs without being asked. 'Nothing like it. So, redundancy. What's the story? I take it that after today, I'm on your list.'

'I was considering you for redundancy before today,' Hilary said crisply.

Mel felt the barb hit home but she didn't wince. She was leaving the company one way or the other, the only priority was to make sure she got as much money as possible. Giving Hilary a piece of her mind would be a bonus.

'Thanks for that vote of confidence, Hilary,' Mel said, just as crisply. 'I've always worked hard and it's not nice to see that my efforts haven't been appreciated.'

'They were appreciated until the past few years,' Hilary interrupted.

'Are you trying to imply that I wasn't working as hard?' asked Mel, still calm.

'You weren't as available, you had other things on your mind,

Mel, and that affected your job. When I first met you, you were very driven, very ambitious. That's changed.'

'When you met me I was twenty-seven, so of course I've changed. You've changed, I expect. Life changes a person. *Having children changes a person.*' Mel emphasised the last bit.

For the first time, Hilary lost her much-vaunted cool. 'You were my protégée, Mel,' she said. 'I backed you and I wanted you as my second in command. You could have been a publicity director if you'd managed to stick it out.'

'If I'd not had children, you mean. Or if I'd been like you, Hilary, and pretended I hadn't got them?' Mel said. 'I chose to have my daughters once I'd built up my career.' She didn't want to say their names, as if identifying them to Hilary would contaminate them. 'The funny thing is, I thought I wouldn't be affected by any working mother discrimination because I worked for you, a woman. And you have kids. I thought you'd understand it all much better. But you're not just as bad as a male boss, you're worse. You *should* understand but you make an issue out of not understanding.'

'Don't give me the children thing,' hissed Hilary. 'I've spent all my working life proving that having children doesn't mean that I'm any different to the men I work with. If you use your family as an excuse, it lets all of us down. They love to think we can't do it as well as they can just because we have ovaries.'

'But you *are* different,' said Mel in exasperation. 'You are and I am and Vanessa is. We have children and that makes us different from the guy who can phone home on a whim and say he'll be late. Do you ever do that without making five phone calls to set it all up? I certainly can't. Does that make us worse employees? I don't think so.'

'Yes it does,' Hilary shot back. 'If you can't give it all, you shouldn't be in the game in the first place.'

'Reverse feminism at work?' Mel asked. 'When I was young, I looked up to my mother and while I adored her, I didn't want to *be* her. She'd given up her job when she got married and she was dependent, really dependent, on my father all her life. I didn't want to be that person. I've told you that before, Hilary. The point is, I wanted to be able to work and be a mother, and I thought I could. But I can't if people like you don't understand that being a mother changes women and changes the way they work. A little bit of flexibility, that's all I needed, and I would have paid you and Lorimar back in full.' She stopped, she'd said it all. Who knew if Hilary had taken a word of it on board?

'I'm sorry you feel that way, Mel. Because of how long you've

115

worked here, there would be a package that we feel is quite generous for you.' Hilary opened a drawer and took out some papers.

Mel stared at the silver photo frame of Hilary's children on the polished clean desk. Three boys, laughing on a sun-dappled boat deck with palm trees in the background. They were quite young in the photo, the youngest six, the eldest perhaps ten. So it had to have been taken some years ago. She knew they were nearly grown up now, with the eldest boy at university. Yet this was the most recent photo Hilary had in her office. Why? wondered Mel. And then, in an instant, she knew.

Hilary took standard corporate holidays, worked many weekends, and never left the office before seven. Just how often would she have had the chance to persuade her growing boys to pose for the camera? She might think that she hadn't lost out by acting as a man in a man's world, but she had. She had missed seeing her children grow up, and in that moment, Mel pitied her from the bottom of her heart.

When Mel finally emerged from Hilary's office clutching the terms and conditions of her redundancy, Vanessa was there to meet her. The two of them slipped into the store cupboard to talk.

'What's going on?' Vanessa asked in concern.

'If only we could get the people in charge of the office grapevine to work in publicity,' Mel laughed, 'we'd never have any trouble spreading news. Not,' she added, 'that Lorimar's publicity is an issue I'm concerned about any more.'

Vanessa's hands flew to her chest in shock. 'Oh, Mel, I can't believe it. Stacey in accounts phoned me just after lunch and said Nylon Nigel was looking for your file. He's doing the redundancy packages.'

'Yes he is. Hilary's just offered me one.' She recounted her conversation with Hilary to a silent and stunned Vanessa.

'That old bitch,' Vanessa said at the end of the saga. 'She wants us all to be Stepford executives like herself. We work miles harder now than we ever did. Shit, I didn't know what work was until I had Conal but when I had to put food on the table for him, I became an absolute career woman. How dare she say things like that to you? You never stop, Mel. None of us knows how you manage it all. You stay on top of the work, you've got great kids and you even manage to look good.'

Mel hugged her friend. 'Thank you,' she said, a little tearful now the shock was wearing off.

'Where will you go?' asked Vanessa. 'Set up your own agency with the redundancy? I hear KBK are looking for a new partner.

They have a couple of big pharmaceutical accounts; they'd leap at the chance of hiring you with your experience in this sector.'

'I'm going to stay home and bring up my children myself,' Mel said lightly. 'No more nursery, no more getting my mother to stand in for emergencies, no more burning the candle at both ends.'

Vanessa was stunned for the second time in ten minutes. 'You, stay home?'

'Why not? I've tried the working mother thing; it might be nice to try the other option, go over to the other side.'

'The dark side,' joked Vanessa, 'where they don't approve of people like you and me and think we're heartless for using crêches and nurseries. Don't,' she begged. 'I need a friend who understands. My mother never stops telling me the damage I'm doing to Conal by working full time. As if I could work part time and still afford to pay the mortgage and for holidays, his new mountain bike, the ever-changing football kit. Doh! Only if I was working on the flat of my back the rest of the time. Oh, Mel, don't go. I need my bitching partner. Who else can I talk to like this?'

Mel laughed, but inside she felt the pull of the only life she'd ever known. Would she be able to leave it all behind? The drive, the excitement, the buzz of coping with it all, phones ringing, modems crackling . . .

Then she thought of the silver-framed photo on Hilary's desk and how sad that was. 'A woman's gotta do what a woman's gotta do, Vanessa.'

'We'll miss you,' said Vanessa gloomily. 'The Stepford executives will take over and they won't miss any time at work because of having babies. They'll just pop them out in their lunch hour in some posh clinic and be back at work by three. Baby: check that off the list. Nanny: check. Next meeting: check. Schedule in liposuction and a tummy tuck for the flabby bits: check.'

Mel laughed again. 'Keep this up and you too could be offered redundancy.'

'I hope not.' Vanessa shuddered. 'If I have to sleep with Nylon Nigel to stay at Lorimar, I will. I need this job. At least you've got Adrian to be the wage slave.'

'Yeah, at least I have him,' Mel agreed.

'What's he think about it all?'

'That's the funniest part of all. I haven't been able to tell him. He was doing a training session all afternoon, so he was unreachable.'

'He doesn't know?'

'He married me for richer or poorer,' quipped Mel, trying to sound flippant although her heart ached at dropping this news at Adrian's feet. 'This is the poorer section of the deal.'

She waited until the children were in bed before opening a bottle of wine – that would have to go when they were economising – sticking a couple of frozen Indian meals in the microwave, and sitting Adrian down with the statement, 'I've got some news for you.'

Adrian sat. 'Should I be worried?' he asked, not looking worried. Mel seemed so calm, in a good mood really, despite being up half the night before with Carrie, who, after an afternoon in the tender care of her grandmother, was in marvellous form. 'We've won a cruise in the Lorimar credit union draw?'

'No. Not even warm.'

'We've won a skiing holiday in the credit union draw?'

'Still cold.'

'You've been promoted?'

'Icy.'

Adrian stopped the game at this point. 'What's wrong, Mel?'

'Hilary is making me redundant,' she said quickly. 'She was furious today that I was so late and, well, I lost my temper with her.'

'Go on.'

Adrian was with her, she thought with relief. He wasn't the type of man to rage at her for stupidity.

'I went for the home truths conversation. Well,' she added, seeing him grimace, 'I was sleep-deprived and, anyway, what sort of company punishes a person for taking their sick toddler to the doctor? It's crazy.'

He put his arms around her. 'I agree, Mel, I agree.'

'So she said there were redundancies and it was clear that she wanted me to take one. I know I don't have to. If she wanted to just get rid of me, she could give me the usual written warnings, et cetera, but it would happen all the same. I'm tired of the game and she knows it.'

Adrian hugged her tightly.

'I thought I'd try being at home with the girls,' she said, 'for a few years, until we don't need the nursery any more. We could use some of the redundancy to pay off a chunk of the mortgage. We could manage, although we'd have to cut back . . .' She looked at her husband, knowing this was a life change for both of them. Adrian would be the breadwinner; their standard of living would certainly drop with only one salary.

'If we had gym membership, that could go for a start,' Adrian said, counting off on his fingers.

'Absolutely,' Mel added, getting into the spirit of it. 'I'm always hearing about people who have gym passes and never use them. It's a waste of money.'

'Exactly. I think it works out at thirty quid every time they go for a swim because they go a couple of times a month maximum. So that's one area we've already cut back on.'

'And food.'

'Who needs food?' Adrian asked. 'We can grow our own vegetables, surely? It can't be that hard to grow a can of beans?'

They both laughed.

'I love you,' Mel said, moving to sit on her husband's lap, her head resting on his shoulder.

'Love you too.'

'Realistically, we'd have to cut back a lot. Holidays.' She surveyed the table with its empty dishes and wine bottle. 'Even wine.'

'Dinners out.' Adrian looked mournful for a moment, then shook his head. 'No going back – onwards and upwards!'

'Funny, that's just what the woman in the cosmetics department said to me today,' Mel said.

'It's true. We can't look back, only forward. It'll be great for Carrie and Sarah.'

'That's what makes me sure this is the right thing to do, Adrian. I can't bear leaving them every day, and no matter what anyone says, it's hurting me and I feel so scared that it's hurting them. Now we've got this chance for me to stay at home – for a while, anyway. Most women don't get that chance. I want to be a mum like my mum.'

Adrian kissed her gently. 'You're a fabulous mum,' he said softly. 'Whether you're out working or home working. Hey,' he added with an impish grin, 'does this mean I'll be getting incredible home-cooked meals every evening and you'll be dolled up to the nines waiting for me with my slippers out, the paper ready for me to read and the bed warmed?'

Mel patted his cheek fondly. 'You wish. I want to be a mum like my mother, not turn into her.'

CHAPTER NINE

Two weeks of hard work helping her mother had enabled Cleo to push the Nat incident to the back of her mind. She had a hotel to renovate: there was no time for feeling sorry for herself over not loving someone.

She'd texted Nat a couple of times but he'd never responded, so she hadn't tried again.

'He'll get over it,' Trish had said breezily. 'Forget him.'

Trish could be very hard-headed, Cleo felt.

Trish was still going out a lot with her new friend, Carol, and every time Trish talked about her, Cleo was conscious of a child-like feeling of jealousy for the unknown interloper. She did her best to quell it, but sometimes it broke through. Just because she was stuck in Carrickwell trying to do her best for her family and the Willow, didn't mean she didn't want to be out enjoying herself with Trish in the city.

When Cleo felt upset, she threw herself into work, which was why she'd decided that the attic bedrooms needed to be tackled. Seeing the ones in Nat's place, unused except for ancient luggage and insect life, had made her realise that the Willow had similar unused space ripe for development.

After many hours spent sanding and painting and cleaning, the three attic bedrooms with their sloping ceilings looked totally different. Cleo's nails would never look the same again, mind, but she didn't care.

It had been a question of cleaning, painting everything white, and adding appropriate accessories. One room had been transformed with a nautical theme that had seen Cleo scour the hotel and the local junk shop for seafaring bits and bobs. Another she had designed in country garden style, with florals everywhere, and the third was a combination of white and pink toile de Jouy. She'd paid for the expensive toile bedspread and pillow cases herself, because she didn't want to ask her father for the money from the petty cash.

If only it were as easy to transform the atmosphere in the family's private quarters. Since the accountant's visit, Cleo's father had been subdued, although he still wouldn't talk about why to his daughter. He'd looked at her redecorated bedrooms with a sad smile and said it was very nice, but nothing more.

Cleo, after all her hard work, felt hard done by.

Her mother was still suffering from aches and pains, although, thankfully, Trevor and his team had returned to work, so she wasn't having to struggle so much with the cleaning. Cleo, with her mother's reluctant agreement, had had a private word with Trevor, praising him for his good points, as she had been taught to do on her course, but making sure that he understood absolutely that further absences without sick notes would lead to trouble. But this conversation and the work in the attics were as much as Cleo was allowed to interfere in the running of the hotel.

'You're still sulking, then?' asked Trish in the middle of another lengthy phone call about how depressing it all was.

'No,' insisted Cleo. 'This isn't sulking. I'm talking to everyone but I want them to know that I'm not a child any more and they should stop treating me like one.'

'Grown-up sulking, so?'

'It's lucky we have a history going way back, Trish, or I'd hang up right now,' Cleo said equably.

'I'm only trying to make you laugh. I don't know why you're so bothered, anyway. Why don't you leave them all to it and get a job in Dublin? I could move out of this hellhole and we could get a place together.'

Trish house-shared with six other people and the rows over who cleaned the bathroom and who should buy loo roll went postal on occasion.

'I don't want to leave Carrickwell,' Cleo said stubbornly, feeling even more irritated at this on the grounds that she hadn't seen Trish in three weeks and had heard nothing but 'Carol this . . .' and 'Carol that . . .'. 'I want to stay here and work. It's the principle of the thing,' she said crossly as she heard her friend sigh theatrically. 'I did a hotel management degree because we had a hotel and I wanted to run it. Why would I have bothered if Mum and Dad were going to let the place stagnate? All because they won't try any new ideas and I know all the new ideas,' she added in frustration. 'That's the worst thing, Trish. Dad could have asked for my advice but he won't. Instead he cabals with Jason and

Barney, and between them they haven't a clue. Even Sondra has more say in the hotel than me. I mentioned that awful Tamara should do fewer shifts because she's so hopeless on reception, and Mum said that actually, Tamara was going to be doing more. But, hey, what do I know?'

'Then leave.'

'I'm going to Bristol for two weeks,' Cleo informed her. 'The hotel I worked in there last year is stuck for staff and they're going to pay my flights if I do the graveyard shift for a fortnight. I need the money too – I spent loads on that blooming toilet for the third bedroom and nobody seems in the slightest bit impressed with my hard work.'

'Things might be different when you get back,' Trish said in cheering-up mode.

'Only if Sondra has a head transplant and my parents win the lottery.'

Cleo enjoyed her two-week break, even though she didn't see Laurent again. It was just nice being part of a young team in a busy, well-run establishment. When she walked in after the long journey home, it was a wet and gloomy evening, not, she thought, the best time to appreciate the Willow. It needed summer daylight to show up the elegance of the honey-coloured stone and the charming way an off-white climbing rose hung prettily over the hall door.

Cleo felt sorry for the couple who walked into the hall just ahead of her, staring around, trying to orient themselves.

There didn't appear to be anybody on duty, so even though she was tired after her trip from Bristol, she took immediate action. She shoved her own small bag into a corner, wriggled out of her damp coat, and went to greet them.

'Good evening. My name is Cleo, and welcome to the Willow Hotel. Are you checking in?'

It took ten minutes to sort out Mr and Mrs Barker from Somerset and they seemed pleased with the Rose Garden Room at the back of the house. Cleo was less pleased because she got a definite whiff of disinfectant from their en suite bathroom and she hated that. Clean-smelling rather than chemical-smelling was the hotel motto.

With the Barkers installed, she danced down the stairs, feeling pleased that she was home. It was altogether more satisfying to welcome people into a hotel you felt a part of as distinct to welcoming them into a giant hotel where you felt like nothing more than a tiny cog in the wheel.

The two weeks away had done her good and she'd begun to

think that perhaps she was being too impatient with her family. They needed to stand together in this time of difficulty and she had to be more diplomatic about it all.

Downstairs, the reception was still empty and she wondered where everyone was. It was just before six on a Friday evening, and normally there would have been a buzz of activity. Instead, there was ghostly calm and no smell of dinner cooking.

Cleo walked into the kitchen to find out if the ovens had finally packed in and discovered her family and Sondra sharing champagne round the table. Everyone was quite dressed up, with her mother in her best navy suit and daisy brooch, and Jason and Barney in their Sunday best, albeit with their ties loosened. Her father, also besuited, had his yellow silk tie still perfectly knotted.

'Hi, Cleo,' smiled Sondra, this time in a pink maternity tunic that made her look angelic in the manner of an MTV starlet trying to look sweet for the camera.

'Great, we hoped you'd be here soon,' said her mother, getting up to hug Cleo in a warm embrace.

'Hi, Mum. What's going on?'

'We're celebrating,' Sondra said cheerfully.

Cleo looked at her father but he was busy opening another bottle, determinedly not glancing in her direction. 'Celebrating what?'

'We're selling the Willow,' Jason said. 'And it's a fabulous offer. Twenty per cent more than the estate agent thought we'd get. *Twenty per cent,*' he repeated gleefully.

Cleo heard her brother say the words but they sounded as if they were coming from some dark bad dream in her mind.

'What? Why?' Cleo asked the first questions that popped into her head.

'Your dad and I are thinking of buying a house abroad. France maybe, or Greece, somewhere hot,' said Sheila Malin apologetically, although she was stroking one arthritic elbow as if she were already basking in the sun. 'Not to retire, really. We might open it up as a bed and breakfast,' she added. 'We don't know yet. There's still so much to be decided. I know it seems sudden, Cleo, but –'

'The big decision's made and it's final,' Jason interrupted, lest his sister think it hadn't been. 'There's a local property developer who's been sniffing around and as soon as he heard we might be putting the place on the market, he jumped. We closed the deal in the solicitor's office this afternoon.'

Cleo ignored him and looked at her father, who was still busy with the other champagne bottle. It was as if he was waiting to see how Cleo would react before he spoke.

Cleo willed him to tell her it was all a mistake, that they hadn't really made the decision to sell her home. But he kept silent.

'There's not quite as much money as we hoped there might be,' Barney said quickly, 'not as much as if the place wasn't mortgaged to the hilt, but it's a good move financially. For all of us.' He sneaked a pleased smile at Sondra, who looked as if she might pass out with joy, dreaming no doubt of what she could buy with her share of the money.

'Dad?' Cleo turned to her father again.

For the first time, he looked into her eyes. 'It's true, Cleo,' he said quietly. 'We've been losing so much money that we can't keep the hotel in business. It was going to bankrupt us. This was the only option and we didn't really have a choice. Beggars can't be choosers.'

'There's always a choice,' Cleo whispered.

'I'm tired,' he said, speaking to her as if they were the only two people in the room. 'Your mother and I are tired and we want a bit of peace for ourselves.'

'You didn't have to sell the hotel for that,' Cleo said. 'I could have run it for you.' She didn't add: if only you'd have faith in me, but that's what she meant.

'You run it?' demanded Jason, blustering the way he did when there was conflict. 'Get real, Cleo. You're only out of college. What hope would you have had to turn this place around? Anyway, the deal's done. This is the best move for all of us. The developer wants to build ten big houses here. It was always going to happen. I reckon this land is too valuable to keep a hotel on. We did the right thing.'

'We could all see the writing on the wall, Cleo,' Barney said. 'Except you with your pie-in-the-sky ideas. We're realists. It's better that you were away from it all. We all knew you'd never understand. You can't be emotional about these things, sis.'

Cleo realised her brothers were speaking the truth. It was a done deal. The Willow had been sold. Just like that.

The only way she could cope with the moment was to remove herself from it mentally. Think of another place, she told herself, a happy place, or a simple word and say it over and over again. But she'd never been the meditating type and her mind was too full, too chaotic. It was horrible to sit there in silence with the family watching her anguish.

Her happy place was under the apple tree and her simple word was *home*. All these would now be taken away so that Barney and

Sondra could drive an even bigger car and impress the neighbours, and so that Jason could admit to the world at large that he didn't really enjoy working and would far rather sit at home with the satellite remote in one fist and a beer in the other.

Bitterness welled up in her like bile. 'Why did you decide all of this while I was away?' she asked, so harshly that everyone except Sondra, who was staring into the distance smiling smugly, looked at her in surprise. 'I said I'd be back this evening; we could have talked about it.'

'We've been talking about it for a long time,' Harry Malin said slowly. 'That's all we do – talk. While the bank are never off the phone to me and I lurch from week to week trying to pay the staff.'

'Dad, what do you mean, *we've* been talking about it for a long time? Where was I when all this "we" stuff was going on?' Cleo demanded, her face red. 'Where was I when you were unilaterally making decisions that affect me? Did nobody think to ask me what I think or why I spent years slaving away at hotel management college so you could sell the hotel out from under me? You could have told me when the accountant was here. That must have been what you were talking about!'

'Calm down, little sis,' attempted Barney.

Cleo rounded on him like a tigress, eyes blazing. 'Don't "little sis" me, you slacker.'

'How dare you call him that?' Sondra's mind wrenched itself away from the purchase of shiny expensive things and she tried to stare down her sister-in-law. 'He's a hard worker and he has the sense to see that this place is like a millstone that never made any money till now.'

'Money!' Cleo spat the word out. 'That's all you think about, Sondra. Money and more money. You'd throw away a lifetime's work so you can shop till you drop and never have to work for it. That's all you're good for and that's all Barney's any good for either. Parasites, the pair of you.'

She was frightening in her rage and her father looked aghast.

'Don't talk to your brother like that,' begged Sheila. 'Please, love. It's not worth fighting over. It's only a business. We can't let it destroy us. And it would have killed us all if we'd had to close because the bank called the mortgage in. Can you see us coping if everyone knew it had been repossessed? It would be a nightmare. This way is better, surely?'

'You don't understand, do you, Mum?' Cleo said. 'Dad does, although he won't say it. This is more than a hotel to me – it's something else, it's in my blood.'

'Don't be so dramatic,' snapped Sondra. 'You only chose hotel management because you knew there was an easy job here for you when you left college. If you'd really wanted to work you wouldn't have turned down that perfectly good job in Donegal so you could stay here in the lap of luxury and be the boss's daughter. Don't think I don't know what you're like, madam. My poor sister Tamara sees what you're like too. Lording it over us because we don't have degrees.' All the pent-up bitterness was coming out now.

'I turned that job down so I could be here and change things,' Cleo said, not even bothering to reply to Sondra's ridiculous claims. 'I wanted to make a difference. Do you honestly think I couldn't see how the place was being run into the ground, Dad?' She faced her father and the fire had gone out of her face, to be replaced by defeat. 'It killed me to love you and look up to you and yet see you do it wrong.'

Harry could only look at her sadly.

'I love you,' she said, now speaking only to him. 'I respect you and I wanted you to respect me but you haven't. If you had, you'd have had faith in me to bring this place round but you didn't. I'm just the kid in the family,' she added bitterly.

'And you're acting like one now,' Jason snapped.

'If being childish is telling the truth as you see it, then yes, I'm childish,' Cleo said.

'Listen, Cleo, if you don't like it, get the hell out of here,' yelled Barney.

Cleo ignored him and looked at her parents. 'Is that what you want?' she asked quietly.

Her father merely looked jittery, as he always did during family rows.

'We want you to cop onto yourself,' Barney said, obviously feeling braver now that his father didn't appear to be kowtowing to his bloody sister.

Cleo could feel the balance of her life lying like a tiny bead on the palm of her hand. Tilting gently in one direction, she knew that her parents needed to get away and to let go. They'd worked hard and it would have been lovely if their three children could have taken over the hotel. If she tilted the other way, she could see Barney and Jason were to blame for so much of what had gone wrong. If they'd joined with Cleo and made it work, together they could have saved the hotel. But she was afraid that her brothers were too lazy, too stupid, too keen for the quick fix without any of the hard work. It was time to restore the balance. Her dream was shattered but the deed was done and they had to move on. Cleo might have had the fire of her grandmother but she had something else that Evelyn Malin had always lacked: she had enormous loyalty. She had to support Mum and Dad. *I hate what you've done but I'll support you.* The words were in her head, en route to her mouth, when Sondra jumped in to fan the flames.

'Are you going to stay, Cleo, and get your share of the money, or stand by your convictions and walk off?' she demanded.

The entire Malin family looked at her and then at Cleo, who waited for someone to tell Sondra to back off, that this wasn't the way they did things and that Cleo had just had a huge shock. Loyalty had to work two ways.

'We'll work it out,' she thought her mother might say, before ordering someone to put on the kettle and find Jacqui's secret stash of shortbread biscuits. And Dad would hug her and say he was sorry, but how did she feel about helping him set up his B & B? And at least they'd sold to a local developer, instead of people like Roth Hotels. Cleo could never have coped with that. Even her brothers would mutter that there was no need for it to come to this and the Malin temper was a terrible thing, and would she just have a glass of champagne and calm down?

But nobody said a word.

Up to that point, there had been hope. The awful silence of her family saying nothing to comfort or support her dashed that hope. Nobody wanted to comfort or support Cleo. They were all looking after number one.

'Stand by my convictions, of course,' Cleo said firmly, determined that nobody would know how terribly hurt she felt. 'I never thought you'd all do something so awful behind my back. I thought I was a part of this family but I can see that I'm not. So the only thing I can do is leave.' She was shaking with emotion although she tried to hide it. 'I'd hate to stay here and watch them tear our home apart. I couldn't face it. You're all making a big mistake.'

When Trish got the phone call five minutes after the big row, she was dumbfounded. Her own family had always fought like cats and dogs, but Cleo's family were different. Her parents genuinely seemed to like peace and serenity and did their best to quell any minor wars. If there was any rift, it had to be because Sondra, Barney or Jason had run amok and upset Cleo.

'No,' said Cleo sadly. 'It wasn't them.' Yes, they'd added to it, but it wasn't just them. She couldn't bring herself to tell her best friend that the person who'd really betrayed her was her dad. The person she'd watched and idolised and admired all her life, the person she'd wanted to impress by graduating at the top of her class. The person who'd decided to sell the family hotel, sell her birthright. The person who hadn't stood up for her when he knew she was hurting.

That was too painful to tell even her closest friend.

'And you're not going back on what you said?' asked Trish, still unable to believe all this. 'You're not going back?'

'No, I'm not,' said Cleo.

'Imagine, thrown out of the family home like some eighteenth-century heiress who shamed her family by having a passionate fling with a gorgeous farmer's son who's promised to another and beneath her station,' joked Trish, trying to make light of the situation.

'Nobody's throwing me out. I'm leaving – or I will as soon as that taxi gets here,' Cleo said, sounding like her old self for a minute.

'There isn't another room in our house but you could kip on my bedroom floor,' Trish said, trying to be practical.

'Thanks, but no. I would not be able to face another bus today. Could you phone Eileen for me and ask if I can stay with her for a few days?' Cleo said. 'I can't explain it again or I'll cry.' Eileen lived in a small apartment complex in Carrickwell and it boasted a cupboard that the estate agent described as a second bedroom but that she had never managed to let out to anybody.

'Well, it's only Wednesday, so I can't bunk off work but I'll be down on Friday night and we'll go out and go wild,' Trish promised. 'It won't solve anything but it'll be fun.'

'Sounds good to me,' said Cleo mechanically.

'Come on, Cleo,' Trish tried to cheer her up. 'It'll all blow over. They'll come round.'

Cleo's voice was steady. 'They might but I won't.'

The taxi driver had dropped off and picked up at the Willow many times in his career in Carrickwell, but it was the first time he'd had to shove bin bags stuffed full of clothes into the cab. The girl he was picking up, one of the Malin family, he knew, was a tall, long-legged Amazonian creature who could have dragged all seven bags into the car herself, but she looked so woebegone that he wanted to help her.

When the last bag was squashed in the car, he asked 'Is that it?' with an attempt at levity, having decided that he wouldn't try the time-honoured 'cheer up, it may never happen' approach. Clearly, it had happened.

'That's it.' She got into the passenger seat. 'Drive. Please,' she added.

'You moving out?' he said as they rattled off down the drive. Potholes galore, he thought. They'd need to do something about the drive or it'd take the bottom out of somebody's car.

'Yes,' said Cleo, concentrating on not looking back, like Lot's wife.

It was a funny way to be moving out, the taxi man thought and he said as much. 'No suitcase in your house, then, eh, seeing as you're already in a hotel?'

The old Cleo would have smiled her beaming smile at him and perhaps laughed, saying, 'Yes, they had loads but I was in a rush, you know ...'

The new improved Cleo, the hardened version whom she hoped would never, ever trust anyone as long as she lived, said: 'I'm allergic to suitcases, actually. That's why I'm getting out of the business. It's hard to work in hotels when you can't handle a suitcase.'

'Well, no,' said the taxi man, 'undoubtedly that would be a hard one. Although I knew a girl once worked in a hairdresser's and couldn't be within fifty foot of perming solution. Allergic to work, she was.'

'That's me too,' Cleo agreed. 'Allergic to work.'

Eileen took the arrival of Cleo and seven bin bags full of belongings quite well.

'Trish said it was a row,' Eileen said, opening the white door to her small flat wide to allow the bin bags to come in.

Cleo, who suddenly found she couldn't be trusted to speak now she was in the company of a friend, nodded.

'Double mocha chocolate-chip ice cream or Mo's chocolate and vanilla pudding?' Eileen asked.

Cleo's bottom lip trembled.

'Both, I think,' Eileen said. 'Right so.'

In a town like Carrickwell, the news didn't take long to spread.

By lunchtime the next day, the story of Cleo's departure had mysteriously linked up with the news of the big developer who wanted to buy the Willow. By half-four, the latest story was that Cleo Malin had run off into the night after telling her family she was pregnant and the family were selling up to dodgy people from abroad who wanted to set up a lap-dancing club ...

'And the father of the child has abandoned her?' asked Mrs Maguire in shock when she heard the gossip in the newsagent's as she queued for the evening paper. She liked Cleo, she was a nice girl. But still, she must have had no luck at all to get herself entangled with a man who'd dump her as soon as she was pregnant. In this day and age too ... scandalous it was.

'I don't know,' said Mrs O'Gorman, sucking in her cheeks in a way that suggested she was trying to extract a bit of juice from a recalcitrant lemon. 'She was crying in the taxi, they say, which is never a good sign. Although I'm shocked at Harry and Sheila Malin to throw her out. That doesn't sound like them at all.'

'I don't believe that for a second,' said Mrs Hanley, who'd heard it all and was disgusted at the gossipmongers. 'They're the closest family I know. There's got to be more to it.'

By Friday, Cleo had eaten Mo's chocolate and vanilla pudding for the third day in a row, and knew it would be hard to fit into her going-out jeans and the sparkly top that Eileen said was suitable for town-painting.

'I don't want to go out,' Cleo said dolefully as they waited for Trish to turn up. 'I want to stay here and watch TV and mope.'

'Moping's bad for your health,' Eileen said.

'So's bucketloads of Mo's pudding,' Cleo sighed.

'Medicinal. So it doesn't count.'

'Why don't you and Trish go out and let me stay here?' begged Cleo. 'I'll be no fun. I'm not in the mood for partying.'

And she wasn't. Neither Trish nor Eileen seemed to realise just how hurt Cleo was. They both brushed the whole incident off as a family tiff. But the Malins didn't have tiffs. And this was much more. The Willow had been sold – Cleo's home. That was no tiff. It was like her childhood and her family being destroyed in a single move. And her father hadn't tried to make her stay, that was the worst thing.

'You need some chilling-out time.' Eileen was sanguine about it all. 'An hour out with us and you'll feel better.'

At half-eight that evening, Cleo, Trish and Eileen congregated in Eileen's small but very warm bathroom and made themselves beautiful. The high cost of using the storage heaters meant that the rest of the flat was usually cold, but the bathroom was tiny so that, once heated up, it stayed toasty.

Eileen had pride of place on the loo seat where she could see herself in the huge mirror that covered half of one wall and gave any person showering a frightening glimpse of their naked self when they pulled the shower curtain back.

'That mirror could not stay if I was living here,' said Trish firmly from her position on the floor where she was surveying an empire of bronzing products to tan up her freckled skin. 'Who wants to see themselves getting in and out of the bath?'

'Cameron Diaz?' suggested Cleo, who was perched on the edge of the bath with her make-up on her knees and a lip pencil in her hand. 'Halle Berry?' Since Eileen's pep talk, she was trying to be more cheerful but it was just a façade.

'I don't mind seeing myself,' said Eileen in surprise.

Cleo and Trish were struck momentarily dumb. Cleo thought of the very definite love handles on her hips and the way her boobs took over unless they were restrained in an industrial-strength bra. Trish thought of her freckles and how, in some places, they seemed to join up to give her a green tinge rather than the tanned caramel colour a person might expect.

'But seriously . . . without your killer knickers and your uplift bra and all the rest?' Trish said.

'Naked is natural,' shrugged Eileen. 'The human body is beautiful.'

'You have to stop doing yoga,' Trish said, shaking her head. 'It's changing you from the neurotic person we all know and love. I don't know about you girls, but after the week I've had, I need a whole lot of slap.'

Hammerhead Jack's, the town's trendiest nightclub, was throbbing with activity by nine o'clock when the girls arrived. Trish and Eileen were both out to have a great time, but in different ways. For a start, neither Cleo nor Eileen was a big drinker. Cleo had helped her father calm down too many drink-fuelled arguments in the Willow to be interested in being a party animal. But Trish considered no night a success unless she'd had a couple of beers and at least one cocktail so she felt all swanky and cosmopolitan.

Eileen's idea of a good time was to meet up with lots of her friends from the hospital and throw a few shapes on the dance floor when the DJ in Hammerhead Jack's stopped playing ambient music and put on a few decent chart hits. Eileen was not a gifted dancer. She was a great one for throwing her arms wildly out to the sides and twirling like a dervish, but she enjoyed herself too much to care.

Trish liked to hunt for gorgeous men and flirt like a woman possessed. To this end, she was wearing belly-skimming trousers and a teeny little cotton T-shirt that looked as though she'd picked it up in Oxfam's children's section. The outfit was proving to be successful.

In the midst of such party spirit, Cleo knew she was being unusually quiet but dancing and chatting up men all seemed so futile in comparison with what had just happened. She didn't even feel in the mood for a glass of wine, because she knew it would make her feel even more miserable. And it was hard to get worked up about either the music or the talent.

Trish, on the other hand, was definitely excited about the male talent. 'I can't believe I haven't been in Hammerhead's for this long,' she kept saying in surprise. 'I'd taken Carrickwell off the radar and I was wrong. There are decent men in this town. I mean, the TH count is quite high. Where are they coming from? Are they shipping men in or growing them like baby aliens in a warehouse somewhere? Oh, look,' she swivelled on her seat, her eyes fixing on a guy like a seagull's beady gaze locked on a trawler. 'As I live and breathe, TH8, no less.'

Trish had a great line of abbreviations that helped their search for Mr Right. Nobody wanted to be heard saying, 'Oh, he's gorgeous!!!!' out loud and having the object of their desire notice this and smirk, thereby ruining the whole thing, so her friends from business college had decided that it was easier to say TH6 or 7 or even, rarely, TH10. That meant Total Hunk with a score of ten out of ten. The ideal was a TH10 who promised to phone you the next day and actually did. Unfortunately, these were few and far between, as Trish and Cleo had discovered. TH10s with nice manners went for other girls, while Cleo and Trish had a magnetic pull for W, MWNDCI or VD/SMWPWYH otherwise known as Weirdos, Men With Next Day Commitment Issues and Very Drunk/Stoned Men Who Play With Your Hair.

Eileen, who had never wanted to play the game, eventually began to flounder with this shorthand.

'Wow, TH8 at seven o'clock,' murmured Trish out of the corner of her mouth. 'Very high on the SO and definitely not an MNO. No ring mark, see?'

'Wha?' Eileen asked Cleo in bewilderment.

'Total Hunk, scoring eight, standing at the bar to Trish's left. She rates him very high on the Shag-ometer and says he's probably not married as she can't see a mark where he took his wedding ring off, so he's OK and won't be one of those guys who give you their Mobile Number Only.'

'You're sick,' snarled a guy at the bar beside them. 'No wonder you're all on your own.'

Trish flipped him the bird and sauntered off to the loo. 'The mystery bus has been,' she said dreamily when she got back. 'I feel so much better.'

'The mystery bus,' Cleo explained to Eileen, 'is what Trish says happens when you have a few drinks, go to the loo so that the drink can go to your head, and come back to find that all the ugly men have magically been whisked away on the mystery bus and all you're left with is gorgeous ones.'

'The mystery taxi is what happens when you wake up next morning with an ugly guy instead of the gorgeous guy you went home with,' giggled Trish. 'The mystery taxi has taken the gorgeous guy away and left some neanderthal who needs to shave his back.'

By eleven, Cleo could take no more and was fed up with Diet Coke. She wanted to be at home in her makeshift bed in Eileen's broom cupboard so she could mull over everything in privacy.

'Come on, Trish, let's go. You'll thank me in the morning,' she said to her friend, who was busy formulating a plan to go on to another nightclub where even finer men might be lining the walls.

'Meanie pig person,' protested Trish, who, despite liking a drink, had no tolerance for it. 'I want to stay out. Don't be a spoilsport.'

'Trish, I'm not in the mood, sorry. Come on, let's go home.'

Trish threw her arms around her friend. 'Sorry, sorry,' she muttered. 'I am so sorry about everything, so sorry.' And she burst into tears.

'Home,' said Eileen, who was as sober as Cleo.

'Definitely home,' replied Cleo.

Handbags, coats and big woolly scarves were collected for the journey home, although Trish had been hit by the Vodka Jacket Syndrome, which meant she was both mentally and physically warm and felt that wearing a coat over her skimpy halterneck was utterly unnecessary, despite the cold.

'She'll catch pneumonia,' groaned Cleo as she and Eileen linked Trish out of the club.

'Pneumonia isn't that easy to get,' Eileen said prosaically as they reached the taxi rank. 'And there's nothing wrong with Trish's chest.'

'There's nothing wrong with your chest either, that's for sure, love,' roared someone from the head of the queue at Cleo, who blushed puce and clutched her coat closer. 'You'll make some man very happy one day. Bags it be me, pleeeease . . . !'

'Ah, feck off,' roared Trish back.

A group of people emerging from the elegant restaurant beside the taxi rank turned to stare and Cleo felt a surge of embarrassment. There were four men and a woman, all dressed up sedately and obviously not part of the usual Carrickwell night-time scene. Cleo locked eyes with the tallest of the group, a crop-haired man in a dark coat with a face like stone, supercilious eyes over a hooked nose and a chin that said 'I want it NOW'. He was good-looking, if you liked that type of Alpha Male, but his expression was anything but friendly.

'Feck off yourself,' yelled the voice from the top of the queue. 'I was only telling her she's a lovely girl.'

'She doesn't want to know, so *you* feck off . . .' began Trish, with Cleo tugging at her to be quiet. She didn't want a scene. It was bad enough having an audience, without it including some posh disapproving tourists.

'Lovely town, pity about the locals,' said a male voice. 'Probably a hen party.' It was the tall man. Alpha Male. He stared at Cleo, Trish and Eileen with disgust in his eyes.

Enraged by this, Cleo glared back. How dare he assume she was part of some awful boozing party?

'We are not a hen party,' she snapped, with a shake of her curls and a flare of her nostrils. The cheek of him.

'You're not married? None of you girls are married?' slurred the drunk who'd started it all. 'There's hope for us all yet.'

The sole woman in the restaurant party clutched a camel-haired coat closer about herself. The tall guy put a hand on her arm.

'I must apologise,' he said.

Cleo raised her chin regally and prepared for his apology.

'I apologise for the behaviour around here,' he added to the people he was with. 'It's the laddish culture that makes women go out and get drunk. Not the ideal picture of Carrickwell, but otherwise it's a lovely town, I assure you. I suppose every beautiful place has its downside.'

Sheer temper made Cleo feel momentarily weak. The arm holding Trish up flopped and so did Trish. She collapsed onto the pavement in a heap, making a mad clutch at Cleo's legs for support. Unfortunately, Cleo was wearing her highest heels. ('You must wear them,' Eileen had insisted earlier. 'High heels are empowering!') On a damp pavement, with a drunken friend pulling at her, Cleo's heels ceased to be empowering and became toppling. She fell clumsily and grazed her hand on a paving stone.

'Ouch!' she said, half in pain, half in shock.

Ever-practical, Eileen went in with a fireman's lift to raise Trish, who was a bit unsteady on her feet after the fall.

A stranger's hand reached out and pulled Cleo to her feet, not unkindly, but not gently either. With shocked tears in her eyes, she had an impression of a soft dark coat against her face as she was righted. It was Mr Alpha Male, up close and personal. He was taller than she was, and physically very strong, from the way he held her as if she were a dainty little thing. And he was so very masculine, with that close-cropped haircut showing off a face that was all hard angles, dominated by a Medici nose and hooded, dark eyes.

'I think,' he murmured, his breath thrillingly close to her face, 'that you shouldn't drink so much.'

'Party time!' giggled Trish, weaving over to Cleo to hug her.

The man released Cleo, so she reached out and got a good grip of Trish again, then swivelled her head to her prey, who was going to get the dressing-down of his life. His nose would bleed with the shock of the words she would deliver . . .

But he was gone. All she could see was his sleek black head

disappearing into an equally sleek black car, and then the door clunked shut.

'How dare you?' she shrieked at the top of her voice at the departing car. 'We are not a hen party; I am not drunk. I haven't had a single bloody drink, not one, you, you . . . meanie pig person!'

'Oh, my head,' moaned Trish, feebly reaching for her ears. 'I feel funny all of a sudden. Please don't shout, Cleo.'

'Yeah,' slurred a familiar voice: the drunk. 'Don't shout. If the police come, we'll all be in trouble.'

'There is chocolate in the flat,' Eileen said diplomatically. 'Those new Nestlé things and Magnum ice creams in the freezer. Oh, and chocolate muffins from Mo's Diner but they're a few days old and they might be gone hard, so you wouldn't like them.'

Cleo began to haul her half of Trish towards home. 'Never say never when it comes to Mo's muffins,' was all she was able to trust herself to say. She would see that man again and have her say if it was the last thing she did.

CHAPTER TEN

Daisy sat with her handbag – a pink boiled wool, handmade work of art, because she wanted to look her best today – on her black-clad knees and tried not to look at the huge clock on the beige waiting-room wall.

It was ten past ten in the morning and their appointment with the doctor in the Avalon Fertility Clinic had been for half-nine. There were lots of other couples waiting, some looking relaxed, most tense, and all trying to pull their eyes away from the clock. Nobody had gone up to the fresh-faced receptionist behind the desk and complained about how long they'd been waiting. It wasn't that sort of place. Instead, everyone looked as if the Holy Grail was buried somewhere in the building and they were anxiously waiting to be called into its presence. The air was twenty-five per cent nitrogen, twenty-five per cent oxygen and fifty per cent hope.

Everyone looked up eagerly each time a white-coated person appeared and called out names, and everyone sank back onto their hard banquettes when it wasn't their name.

Alex was not good at waiting, and Daisy could see that he was very nervous. He lounged back in his seat with one leg casually crossed over the other, the very picture of nonchalance, but he was rotating one ankle as if modelling for an airline video on how to avoid deep vein thrombosis. His eyes were cast down too, as if he was terrified of meeting anyone he knew.

Daisy glanced at him. 'You all right?' she asked, for what had to be the tenth time since breakfast.

'Fine,' he said brusquely, as he had each time.

Nerves, it was just nerves. Daisy reached over and took his hand. His fingers gripped hers tightly, comfortingly, and she closed her eyes and tried to think happy, calm thoughts. In two days, she was due to fly to Düsseldorf for a clothes fair, and normally she would have been at home putting the finishing touches to her packing so that her fashion fair wardrobe was perfect. Today, she didn't care what she wore to Düsseldorf. This was more important than anything else.

She got up from her seat yet again to riffle through the papers on the low coffee table. There were lots of old women's magazines, a couple about yachting and a single *National Geographic* with a picture of Peru on the cover. She picked it up.

'Look, Alex,' she said brightly. 'Peru. We always said we'd go.' Offering it to him like an Inca priest offering up a heart, she smiled hopefully.

Alex had just taken the magazine from her when a tall dark woman in a white coat opened the waiting-room door and said, 'Daisy Farrell and Alex Kenny, please.'

Daisy sprang to her feet like a jack-in-the-box. 'That's us,' she said breathlessly.

It was like a normal visit to a normal doctor, Daisy thought, except that the tall woman, Dr Makim, was filling in a history of their fertility, asking about brothers and sisters, previous children if any, previous pregnancies, if any, operations, illnesses.

It took quite a while, and Daisy had relaxed into feeling that this was all perfectly ordinary after all and she hadn't needed to have been so nervous, when Dr Makim put down her pen and began to talk about what the clinic did. She gave them sheaves of paper as she spoke.

'You're thirty-five, which is when we do notice a decline in the fertility of women,' she told Daisy, who felt the usual pang of guilt that this was all her fault. 'But fertility is a complex issue and can affect either partner.'

If the problem was the quality of the sperm, there were various methods of helping, from washing the sperm to advanced IVF techniques, right up to using donor sperm.

Daisy hardly dared to look at Alex at this point. He was staring stonily at the doctor. Men could find their infertility an emasculating experience, according to Daisy's bible, *The Smart Woman's Fertility Guide*. Daisy honestly didn't mind if the problem was hers, just to save him the pain of thinking it was his fault. She'd go through it all without a word for the sake of their baby. Who cared who was to blame once she could get pregnant? She laid a comforting hand on his knee but he was too engrossed in what the doctor was saying to respond.

Next, Dr Makim wanted them to understand what they were letting themselves in for. Lengthy hormonal treatments that were, in rare cases, fatal, enormous emotional strain and, often, failure.

'The success rates vary from clinic to clinic but the general success rate, what we call the take-home baby rate in the Avalon,' she said, her face sympathetic as Daisy winced at the bluntness of this description, 'is around twenty per cent.'

'And people think you have for ever to have babies, thanks to science,' Daisy said jokily, to hide her nerves, while praying to be one of those twenty per cent.

'Science is science, not God.' Dr Makim shrugged wryly with the air of one who'd seen evidence of this at first hand. 'There are no guarantees. Understanding that is the biggest step. Despite what you read, this is not an easy route to take.'

Daisy and Alex were silent as they digested this information.

'First, we test you both,' went on the doctor. 'Sperm tests for the man, blood tests for you both, a post-coital test, then finally a laparoscopy for the woman. That's a procedure where we insert a micro camera through an incision in your navel to see if you have endometriosis or any other problems with your ovaries, uterus or tubes. It's an overnight stay with a general anaesthetic. You haven't had a reaction to an anaesthetic, have you?' She was writing as she asked.

'No,' said Daisy. With or without an anaesthetic, she was up for it.

'An operation?' interrupted Alex. 'With an anaesthetic? I didn't know the tests would involve surgery.'

It was Daisy's turn to feel a flicker of irritation. She'd given him *The Smart Woman's Fertility Guide* to read the week before and the options were all there. Hadn't he read it?

'Infertility clinics are often accused of handing out treatment to people who don't really need it,' Dr Makim said, steel in her voice.

'That is not the case at the Avalon Clinic. We will not treat any couple unless we have done all we can to determine the reason, if we can find one, for their infertility. Without the full battery of tests, we will do nothing.'

If they decided to enter the programme, they would have to attend a lecture on infertility treatments given by the clinic's director, and they'd have to come to two counselling sessions with one of the Avalon's team of psychologists.

'We're not telling you that you don't know your own mind and haven't decided properly that you want to enter our programme,' Dr Makim added, 'but we want you to know all the facts and have thought it all over before you do.'

Daisy nodded agreement, inwardly wishing they could bypass all that stuff and start now. She and Alex wanted a baby – why wait?

They left with a sheaf of literature about the clinic, consent forms and an IVF diary of a couple's trip through the process that the doctor said people often found helpful.

Daisy sat in the passenger seat of Alex's car, hugging the literature to her chest. She felt almost too excited to breathe. It was happening, finally.

It could just be fluke and she was madly fertile and all it would take would be some drugs before she'd be pregnant. Wasn't she always hearing those sort of stories?

'It's nearly twelve thirty,' she said, glancing at her watch. 'Why don't we get a sandwich for lunch, then you can drop me at my car and head back to the office?'

As the clinic was in Dublin, they'd both driven into the city that morning, so Daisy could head back to Carrickwell afterwards.

'Yeah, sure,' said Alex distractedly.

He drove to a restaurant, and left Daisy sitting at the table while he went to the bathroom. 'Order me soup, a chicken sandwich, and a latte,' he said.

Daisy placed their orders and then allowed herself the thrill of opening the IVF diary. A real person's description of the whole process would make more sense to Daisy than any dry medical text.

The diary was by a woman named only as F. There was no mention in the introduction if she and her partner, T, had actually had a baby.

Can't believe this is real. We've been saving for a long time for this and T is almost as excited as me. We'd stopped talking about kids for the past four years and now we are letting ourselves mention them again. In our home, we had what we called the nursery right up until I was diagnosed with polycystic ovary syndrome. We called it the spare bedroom from then on.

Last night, T said we should redecorate the nursery. Those were his words. I loved him so much when he said that. He believes we can do it.

Daisy flicked further on, eager to read more, to see what happened next.

The injections are horrible. It's like a pen you stick into your stomach. The one diabetics use. T has to do it for me because I'm terrible with needles, even when they're disguised as pens. My stomach feels bloated and I've read that some people can really feel all the extra eggs you emit because of the hormones. They call them follicles. That sounds silly – follicles are on the end of your hair. T says I'm daft. I prefer to feel full of eggs to make our baby instead of follicles!

She flicked a few pages again.

Waiting is the worst part. The doctor said that but I didn't believe him. And he's right. It's hell on earth. Do normal people wait to see if they're pregnant like this?

Daisy felt a bond of sympathy with the unknown F. Please let it have worked for her. Alex came back at the same time as the waitress with their food. Daisy's appetite, absent at breakfast, returned with a vengeance and she tucked into her sandwich and juice with gusto. Alex didn't touch his sandwich, just stirred his latte, staring into it as if the secret to the universe lay therein.

'We can do it!' Daisy whispered across the table at him, eyes shining with happiness. 'We're going to have a baby!'

'Daisy, I think we should take a break,' he said quickly. 'This is all too intense, this clinic stuff.'

Daisy blinked. The piece of cucumber in her salad sandwich suddenly tasted like rubber. 'What . . . what do you mean? A break from what? We've only just got started.'

'I don't mean the clinic. I mean us, a break from us. A trial separation.' Now that he'd started, the words rushed out. 'I'm not comfortable with this *treatment* . . .' He said it with distaste, as if the word itself was distasteful. 'It's stressing me out and you too.

Look at how obsessed you are. You never talk about anything else.'

'Well, it's so important,' Daisy said anxiously, 'but I can cope with it, I promise. We can cope with it, Alex. This morning was tough but it's better to know all the facts straight up, isn't it? We can deal with it.'

He shook his head. 'We can't; I can't. It's taking over,' he said. 'There's got to be more to life than this babymania. Babies, babies, babies, that's all I hear.'

'That's not fair.' Daisy knew she didn't talk about babies all the time. Hell, if she'd talked about it as often as she felt like, then they would have no other conversation at all. But she didn't. She held herself in check, constantly censoring her conversation.

'I'm sorry, Daisy, I can't deal with this. I'm sorry, really sorry.'

He kept staring anxiously, dark eyes fixed on hers, the handsome face she knew so well looking more strained than she could remember.

'You can't mean that,' she said, and as she said the words, she realised that he did. He actually wanted a break from their relationship. It was too enormous for her to take in. Alex and Daisy not together. The world was turning upside down.

'I do,' he said helplessly. 'We need some time apart.'

'You can't mean that,' she said, more urgently this time. 'I love you, we've been together for ever, we should be getting married and having a baby . . . not *this*.'

'We just need some time apart.' He repeated the words like a mantra. 'It's for the best, Daisy. Please, do this for me. It makes sense.'

'How can it make sense?'

'It does, trust me.'

An old joke sprang inappropriately into her mind. What does a liar say when he wants to say, 'Screw you'? He says, 'Trust me.'

'I don't want to hurt you, Daisy.' He was staring into his latte again and that was very unsettling. 'We've been through so much together –'

'We can get through it,' interrupted Daisy fiercely. 'Don't do this, Alex, please. I love you. You can't leave me, you can't . . .'

'I have to,' he snapped, and shoved his cup away with such force that coffee spilled in a milky puddle.

'Oh shit.' She began to cry and shake at the same time, great globs of tears running down her face. She couldn't stop the shaking and when she looked down at her hands in disbelief, she could see the tremor. They looked like somebody else's hands on top of the table.

'Please don't go.' She didn't care if it sounded pathetic – every fibre of her being wanted him to stay. Longing for something so much could make it happen, couldn't it? 'Please stay.' It was a whisper now. 'I can't go on without you, Alex. Whatever's wrong, we can sort it out.'

'Stop saying that.' He wasn't begging. He was sharp, annoyed with her for being so weak, so craven. 'Come on, Daisy, it'll be fine. Lots of couples split up for a bit, to work things out.'

Yes, lots of couples did. She leaped at this evidence that this was a relationship hiccup, some awful rite of passage and they'd be back together again soon. 'It'll be all right again?' She didn't care that she sounded like a small child stammering for her mummy.

His reply was a friendly pat on the arm. 'I'll go stay with David tonight. It's better that way. I'll pick up a few things while you're at work and we can talk when you get back from Germany, OK?'

'OK,' repeated Daisy. Then something occurred to her. 'Alex, is there another woman?'

For a millisecond, she thought he was going to say yes. 'Of course not,' he said easily. 'I'll order a taxi for you back to your car.' He got to his feet. 'I have to fly back to the office. I've been gone too long already this morning.'

He was all business, signalling to the waitress for the bill, asking her to call a taxi. Daisy sat in her seat weakly and he pressed a fifty-euro note into her hand. 'For the taxi,' he said, and kissed her kindly on the forehead.

Some still-functioning part of Daisy's brain told her that fifty was far too much money for a taxi. Her car was only a mile away. He could have dropped her to it as easily.

'We'll talk when you get back from Germany. Have a good trip and take care of yourself. Don't shop too much!'

It was what he always said. Daisy's credit card burned in her purse when she was let loose and it burned with even more intensity when she was abroad. Today, his warning sounded shallow.

'You'll be fine, Daisy. You love the shows and Düsseldorf's the best, isn't it? We'll talk, right?'

Alex mimed holding a phone to his ear, the way he'd do to a fleeting acquaintance glimpsed across a crowded room to say he'd phone. 'Awful gobshite,' he'd mutter to Daisy, who'd giggle, 'but he's a useful contact. Got a finger in a lot of pies.'

She felt like the awful gobshite today: someone to be waved at and avoided.

'Bye,' he said, and strode off before she could reply.

She sat numbly, busy lunchtime noise all around her, and hoped nobody would appear to say her taxi had come. She didn't know if she'd be able to get to her feet and physically walk out with everybody looking at her. Fear, like a giant lump, was back.

When she'd been a teenager, at her heaviest, Daisy had gone through a period where she hadn't wanted to meet anyone. It had been the summer they'd moved to the cottage, so she didn't see her old friends from town so much and it had been easy to slip into a type of agoraphobia.

She hid from the postman, who drove his van up to the cottage, keen to talk to the new inhabitants. She ducked into gateways of fields when cars passed as she walked to the local shop on errands for her mother, and when she got there, she crept into the shop, trying to take up as little space as possible, hoping people wouldn't see her.

She hadn't felt like that for years, since she'd met Alex, and now it came crashing into her head. Fear, loathing, self-hatred. The big girl's best friends.

'Taxi for Farrell!' roared a voice.

Feeling as if every eye in the place was upon her, Daisy made it to the door and into the taxi. Every movement was like walking against a hurricane. Was this how it had felt for Alex when he'd had Epstein Barr, exhausted, unable to move without enormous effort?

The taxi dropped her in a speedy five minutes and Daisy got into her own car and sat staring at the dashboard as if she'd never seen it before. Her world had shifted from joy to horror in a matter of moments, and she felt utterly lost. Who *was* she without Alex? Nobody, that was who. He was her compass and her strength. She couldn't cope without him.

Three days later, in a chic cream and teak hotel room in Düsseldorf, Daisy looked at the clothes neatly hung in the wardrobe and sighed. She didn't speak Italian or Japanese, but she felt as if she did because everything she owned was Fendi, Miu Miu, Missoni, Yamamoto, Matsui, all rolling off the tongue. She had the language of fashion down pat and was wildly inarticulate in the real world.

She had a choice of two suits for the day, both the inevitable black. Daisy chose the Comme des Garçons suit with supple suede boots in charcoal and the silvery grey pearls she'd picked up for a song in a market in Paris. In the mirror, a tall, elegant woman with a shock of strawberry-blonde hair stared back at her; the picture of urban sophistication. Daisy looked just right, but why, she wondered, did she feel so wrong? Was it the four mini-bar vodkas she'd consumed the night before after her flight got in, the Valium she'd poached from Mary's supposedly secret stash at work, or was it merely because her life was crashing round her?

The people who wanted to know how Daisy bought clothes for the shop six months ahead of time would also ask if the shows were awash with champagne, cocaine and scary fashion editors with glued-on nails and glued-on sunglasses. Daisy would usually laugh and say she'd never encountered cocaine but perhaps she simply didn't know the right people. There occasionally was some champagne but the scary magazine editors only turned up at the international fashion weeks at London and Paris instead of the prêt-à-porter shows where Daisy bought most of her stock. The London, Paris and Milan shows were fashion's zenith, awash with fashion journalists from every sort of publication and models who normally only stared down at the world from the covers of *Vogue*. Daisy loved the London and Paris fashion weeks but she didn't go every year because it was expensive and if there was a designer she loved, she could buy their clothes from one of their agents.

She thought back to her first couture designer show years ago when her mentor, a fellow redhead who had been one of Daisy's guest lecturers at college and who always took the gingers under her wing just to annoy the blondes, told her that the number one rule was not to look impressed.

'Even if the models are divine, the clothes exhibit the hand of God and you want to grab the designer and bang his brains out, don't look impressed,' said Diana. 'Look as you do when you think you might have broken a nail minutes after you've shelled out for a manicure – seriously underwhelmed. Only novices look impressed, sweetie.' Diana's words, available these days for $5.99 to readers of the celebrated fashion bible *Et Tu, Beauté*, were worth their weight in gold, and Daisy did her best. But it was hard. She loved clothes and got such a thrill from the whole thing that it was hard not to look bowled over.

Today's prêt show in Düsseldorf was vastly different from the theatrical perfection of a Galliano fashion show.

For a start, it was very hard work rushing round trying to see everything and to order the right things. Buyers like Daisy trawled the huge conference halls and looked at beautiful merchandise from round the world. Clothes, accessories, shoes, hats, belts were all set out at hundreds of stands. Several times a day, there were fashion shows, where exquisite girls with concave stomachs and spines with sticking-out knobs like an abacus displayed the clothes for real. The difficulty was that an outfit you'd adored on the hanger or on a model might look hopeless on a less than perfectly proportioned human being and vice versa, meaning lots of chopping and changing of orders.

Daisy's job was to go to her regulars and buy what she felt would sell well in Georgia's Tiara. But she was also constantly searching out new labels that would appeal to her customers. There were buyers from every sort of outlet in the world and, with each show lasting a mere three to four days, there was no time to relax.

At couture shows, there were fabulous parties held by designers but there was no point going unless you had the very best passes to the VIP areas – otherwise, you were just mingling with the minging and were sure to spot someone you hated swanning ostentatiously past with a VIP pass.

The prêt shows were more low key. Daisy knew a group of other buyers who went to the same shows every year, and together they went out each evening to gossip and compare notes.

This year, the Jazzy label was throwing a huge tenth anniversary party in a five-star hotel and it seemed like the best option for the evening. Jazzy had four lines: a glamorous plus-size label, a working woman range, pregnancy clothes and a trendy teen line.

In the back of a cab on the way to the party, Daisy sat squashed up against an exquisite doll-like buyer from Poland called Beata.

Beata always looked as if she should be on the catwalk instead of in the buyers' seats, and today she was wearing black accented with azure blue, which was fabulous against her blue-black hair. The bucket seats were occupied by two Scottish buyers who looked as though Coco Chanel herself had just dressed them two minutes ago, and on Daisy's other side was a glamorous redhead from Cork who wore the most eccentric clothes – lime green, anybody? – and managed to make them look utterly incredible.

'Daisy, you are so slim,' announced Beata, taking Daisy's hand to admire the bracelet that matched her necklace. 'Dieting, yes? I put on two kilos last week. I am not eating a thing today.'

The cab's inhabitants all laughed. All-or-nothing diets were a daily part of their world.

'You do look great, Daisy,' added the Cork buyer, a slip of a woman called Sorcha, warmly. 'How are you?'

Daisy thought about telling the truth. My boyfriend wants time out from our relationship, and last night I slept only thanks to a Double Vee cocktail of Valium and vodka after eating all the chocolate in the mini-bar. She pictured the shock at such unvarnished truthfulness. Everybody would be stunned, although they'd hide it. She'd be the watchword for *how not to do it.*

'Fantastic,' she said, summoning up a smile. 'The shop's doing so well and it's just rush, rush, rush.'

Everyone smiled. Rush, rush, rush was something they were familiar with. It was business as usual. If Daisy kept her eyes open and focused on something familiar, like the pale blue Marc Jacobs handbag that sat expensively on the seat beside her, then she could almost believe the world was still normal. Only when she closed her eyes, the nightmare returned. There was no Alex in her world. It was as if she was seventeen again, elephantine, scared to go out, scared to stay in. Scared and alone.

On her last morning in Düsseldorf, Daisy had breakfast early and got a cab to the airport. She marched resolutely past the duty free and sat in the lounge waiting for her flight. Alex would be proud of her for not succumbing to the temptation of buying something. *Alex*. As she waited alone in her hard seat, she closed her eyes and allowed herself the luxury of thinking about him. During the past few days, she'd tried to blot out thoughts of him with alcohol, trying, and failing miserably, to convince herself that everything was normal, and if she kept believing that, it would be. On her way back to her real life, she had to face facts.

Alex wanted a separation and Daisy had come to the conclusion that it could only be over the whole infertility issue. The question was: what should she do?

During the wakeful nights in Düsseldorf, she'd done nothing else but think about this. They *could* put the whole infertility business off for a while. Time was on their side, sort of. Perhaps that was what he'd hoped for all along – that Daisy would say, 'Forget about the clinic and the tests,' and then, they would be back where they'd started. Together. Together but without a baby.

That was what scared her. That she'd have to make that choice. If Alex was scared of having a baby *ever*, could she live with him knowing what she'd given up for his love? Could she live with herself? Daisy searched around inside herself for the answer.

In the distance, she could see an elderly man walking slowly to his departure gate. His bearing was upright but he needed to use a cane and he was having some difficulty pulling his little suitcase on wheels. There was nobody helping him, nobody holding his arm. How horrible to be alone and lonely. Unloved. Daisy shuddered. It was the worst way to live.

Away from home, in the lonely limbo of the airport, Daisy made a decision. It would be better to have her darling Alex and no children than children and no Alex. He was her touchstone, her talisman, the one who made her life worthwhile. Not many people had such love. Not having kids wasn't such a sacrifice in the face of such love.

The solution was simple, then. She *would* say, 'Forget about the clinic.'

All she had to do was tell him and this horrible separation would be over.

The Dublin airport customs people must have thought Daisy was transporting something wildly toxic or illegal from the speed with which she ran through baggage and out past customs into the arrivals hall. Eagerness to see Alex, to talk to him and make up, was coursing through her veins. If she explained it to him the way it had hit her – that they were *meant* to be together and that she understood how scared he was about having a baby – everything could be all right again. She loved him, that was all that mattered. She couldn't live without him, and if it was just going to be him and no baby, then that would be enough for her.

Thrilled that she had solved the problem, Daisy jumped into her car and sped along the motorway towards the city, singing her head off to the radio.

Daisy spotted Alex outside the bank's imposing glass offices. He was walking across the road with Louise, his assistant, and they were talking animatedly, the way people did when they knew each other well. Louise, a single mother with a ten-year-old son, was someone Daisy had enormous admiration for. Nobody had ever handed Louise anything on a plate. She'd worked hard for what she had. As Alex said, she was the exact opposite of the typical bank assistant, as she answered back and had a finely tuned bullshit-ometer. But she got away with it, partly because she was so witty and sharp, and partly, Daisy reckoned, because she was so good-looking. There was definitely more leeway in life if you had a perfectly oval face, a full-lipped smile, and long dark hair that looked like it had been washed in liquid silk. She didn't seem interested in men, though. 'I've got my son, I don't need anyone else,' she'd once said when Daisy was toying with the idea of setting Louise up with someone.

'Yeah, Louise isn't interested,' Alex had said sharply.

He was probably right, Daisy had decided: there was nothing worse than well-meaning pals setting you up with people *they* thought were fabulous but you thought were deranged lunatics. Knowing someone for years meant you stopped noticing the halitosis, the paunch and the predilection to talk non-stop about how much they earned. Sometimes, people were single for a good reason.

'Hi,' called Daisy, finally catching up with the pair of them outside the Coffee Bank Restaurant, which was where half the bank went at lunchtime.

Louise gasped and Daisy touched her on the sleeve, smiling apologetically. 'Sorry, didn't mean to creep up on you both. I just needed to see Alex.' She beamed up at him, thinking that despite all the trial separation thing, he'd be pleased to see her. But he just looked as shocked as Louise.

'Are you going to lunch?' Daisy asked, unworried. She'd surprised him, that was all.

'Yes,' stammered Alex, as the three of them stood awkwardly on the pavement.

'Is this lunch some high-level business meeting or can anyone join in?' Daisy joked.

'I have to go actually,' said Louise quickly, and she fled off down the street, without saying goodbye.

Daisy watched her go in astonishment.

'Listen, Daisy –' began Alex.

'I'm sorry,' she said automatically. Why did so many of her conversations start with 'I'm sorry'? 'I should have phoned but I thought I'd come and see you as soon as my plane landed. I wanted to say let's get married, Alex. Let's do it. And stop worrying about having a baby. I know how scary that is for you and we don't have to. Even if we never have children, we still have each other, right?'

She faltered. Suddenly all this didn't seem like such a good idea after all. Alex looked positively uncomfortable. So had Louise just now.

'I should have phoned on my way here,' Daisy said again, wondering exactly what she had said wrong. 'Sorry. I arrived at a bad time. Me and my Mr Spocks.' It was a private joke between them, the theory that *Star Trek*'s Mr Spock had to have big, pointy feet to go with his big, pointy ears. Today, Alex's face didn't crease up in amused recognition of the joke. Daisy felt the slightest shiver of strangeness. Something was wrong. 'What is it?' she asked.

'We can't really talk here,' Alex said.

'The Coffee Bank, then?'

'Christ no,' he muttered. 'You can't have a private conversation in there.'

Daisy's unease grew into full-blown goose bump infestation. They'd talked privately in the restaurant before. Once, they'd sat in the small alcove near the kitchen and Alex had kissed her so intensely that her stomach flipped with excitement.

'We'll go to the Rio Lounge, come on.'

Situated on a small alley, the Rio Lounge was as far removed from the sunlit beaches of Rio de Janeiro as it was possible to be: dark, dingy and the pub of choice for people toying with the idea of investing in another lump of hash. This was because it was so badly lit that drug deals could be done without anybody else being any the wiser. Tourists also liked it because it was decorated in olde Oirish style and appealed to anyone who liked dingy nooks, genuine sawdust and strange farming implements bought as a job lot by the pub interior decorator.

Daisy followed Alex obediently inside.

Despite its aura of grubbiness, the Rio Lounge clearly did a roaring lunchtime trade and was packed, so Alex and Daisy couldn't locate stools and had to stand at one end of the counter. Alex ordered drinks without asking Daisy what she wanted, and he kept his face turned expectantly towards the barman until the drinks had arrived and he'd paid for them.

Daisy took her quarter bottle of white wine silently and watched Alex pour most of his small bottle of red into his glass and take a huge gulp. Whatever he was about to tell her, it was serious.

Like a man about to step off the platform for a two-hundred-foot bungee jump, Alex looked at her and plunged right in. 'Louise is pregnant.'

Then why had Louise looked so miserable? Maybe she was in shock and had just found out. Or maybe she didn't want the baby. 'She doesn't want it, then?' For one crazy moment, Daisy almost added, 'We'll take it!' A baby nobody wanted; a baby she and Alex could love . . .

'Of course she wants it.'

'Oh.' A pause. 'Well, what's the problem?' She thought for a beat, her mind still flooded with the picture of her and Alex with this darling baby. 'The father doesn't want to know? Is that it? Oh, poor Louise.'

'That's not it.' Alex no longer looked as if he was about to bungee jump. He looked as if he already had and the rope had sheared in two.

'He's married, right?' Daisy stopped feeling sorry for herself and felt sudden sympathy for Louise. 'The father's married.' Men had it both ways, she thought darkly. They could have the fling and none of the consequences.

'Not exactly.'

'What then?'

Alex looked down into his wine and then, reluctantly, up into Daisy's wide-open, innocent eyes. He'd looked at her in many ways over the years they'd been together but never like this; never with naked pity. Not even when she'd had her wisdom teeth out and her jaw was swollen to twice its normal size, making her look like a hamster after a day in the cream bun factory. The pity had been mingled with love then. Now, it was just naked pity.

'Daisy, do you not see . . . ?'

And in that instant, she saw. There could only be one reason for the frozen look on Alex's face.

The baby was his. Alex had been having an affair with Louise, which was why he'd wanted the trial separation. And Louise was pregnant with his baby. Presumably she'd been pregnant all along and the separation had been almost a mercy thing, a case of let's-not-give-Daisy-all-the-details-yet-or-she'll-have-a-breakdown. The news was to be drip-fed to her. First the separation, then the news about Louise. Finally, the baby. Except that she had upset the whole plan by rushing home from the airport with *her* plan.

'It's your baby.'

'Yes, it's mine.'

'You didn't want babies,' Daisy said, almost disbelieving.

'No, but it happened this way and there's no turning back.'

'I thought you didn't want babies at all! That's what I thought. I was going to sacrifice having children for being with you. It would have killed me but I was going to do it and now this. How can you do this to me?' she said.

Her innocent plans for their new life together, their wedding even, their rose-tinted future – it was disintegrating before her eyes.

'When were you going to tell me?' Daisy was proud of that sentence. She didn't know how she'd conjured up the energy to say it without great gulping sobs.

'I don't know. Louise wanted us to be truthful from the start. We never meant it to happen, I promise.'

Us, there was an us and it was no longer Daisy and Alex.

'I didn't want to hurt you,' he said.

That was almost funny.

'But you have,' Daisy said in a lost voice.

'I know. If there was any way I could have avoided it, I would.' He was earnest. 'If there was any way, Daisy, believe me . . .'

She was still too stunned to cry. 'Believe you? That's what I have been doing and look where it's got me, Alex,' she said, knowing she was close to cracking now. 'Just answer one thing: how long has it been going on with you and her?'

The bungee jump rope miraculously repaired itself and Alex's confidence reappeared. 'A couple of months,' he said easily, too easily . . .

Daisy thought of the last year where she'd sunk deeper and deeper into anxiety over her childlessness. And she thought of Alex moving coolly away from her so that she'd somehow felt she couldn't tell him what she was feeling. She'd been worried that it had been her fault for obsessing over babies, and all the time it had been this. 'You're lying,' she said flatly.

'No,' he protested.

'Don't lie,' she snapped back. 'Tell me the truth.'

The fight went out of his eyes. 'Since the conference in Kerry last year.'

April, she remembered, a big finance conference involving lots of advance dry-cleaning trips for her as she got his clothes ready. She'd developed a horrible flu while he'd been away and he'd been so sweet when he came back, making her cups of hot water and lemon to soothe her cough, buying her favourite fashion mags and cooking dinner each night until she recovered. It had been during a bad time for poor Mary, and Daisy could remember that guilty feeling of having a loving partnership while her friend and colleague didn't. And all the time, her loving relationship had been a sham.

'When is the baby due?'

'Five months' time.'

Daisy felt barren then. Not just childless, but like some great desert plain where no seed would ever grow, no matter what rain pelted into the ground. She was empty and flat-stomached, while Louise was swollen with life. Life with teeny little starfish fingers and huge dark pools of eyes and a curled-up body nestling in the womb until it wriggled into the world like a miracle.

Without really giving a damn, Louise had taken the two most important things in Daisy's life. Alex and his baby. Louise didn't even need them. She'd had a child, a boy to nurture and love, and she would always be a mother. Always.

And Daisy wouldn't.

She didn't even realise she was crying until she saw the pained expression on Alex's face. He hated her to cry, hated that outpouring of emotion. He had an expression he wore when she cried: tense around the mouth, pleading around the eyes. *Please stop*.

'I am sorry, so sorry,' he said. 'If there was any way I could turn the clock back and make it not happen –' he broke off helplessly. 'I would never want to hurt you, Daisy. We've been through so much together.'

Daisy barely heard him. 'Was the Tiffany necklace for me?' she asked, suddenly fingering the exquisite heart that had given her such comfort.

He exhaled, the puff gone out of him. 'Yes,' he said bluntly. 'I was going to tell you that night when I came home from London. I thought the necklace might help, show you that I loved you and had never meant to hurt you.'

'Why didn't you?'

He buried his face in his hands. 'I don't know. You were so excited about the fertility clinic and you wanted to go . . . I didn't know what to say. How could I tell you it was over when you were so happy?'

The tears kept flowing. Daisy brushed them away with her hand. 'But you let me hope and dream,' she whispered. 'That was so cruel; that was beyond cruel.'

'How could I tell you?' he repeated, frustration making him angry. 'You were so caught up in it. It was impossible to tell you that it was over. You just didn't see, Daisy, did you?'

'See what?'

'That we'd find the right people one day. We both knew we were biding our time. Who ends up with the person they dated in college? We're all looking over our shoulder, aren't we? I was looking for a special someone. Go on, be honest, you were too . . .'

'No,' she wailed, deeply shocked to think he could have looked at their love that way. 'Don't try and make it all right by lying about me. I was never waiting for anyone else, you were the one. You are the one for me.'

'You must have known. When I said there was no point in getting married, didn't you work it out?' he said helplessly.

'No.' The word was so soft it was almost inaudible.

'I tried to let you know, Daisy. I did,' he insisted.

'We were as good as married,' she said. 'We owned a flat together, we had plans, we spent Christmas and New Year and every single holiday of our lives together. What's not permanent about that? How could I know?'

Alex didn't seem to have an answer for that. Finally, he spoke again. 'I thought you understood when we talked about marriage. That's why I couldn't tell you it was over when you said you'd made the appointment with the clinic. Shit, Daisy, why are you so trusting, so bloody naïve?'

'Because I love you.'

'I'm sorry,' he said, getting to his feet. 'I'm sorry you love me but it's over, Daisy. Over. There's no nice way to say it. OK?'

She shook her head blindly. 'It's not OK. How will I cope without you?'

'That's not my problem. You're going to have to deal with it,' he said simply, and left.

Standing beside the bar in the jam-packed Rio Lounge, Daisy had never felt lonelier in her life.

The high-heeled boots didn't make her feel better, nor did the char-coal cashmere cardigan with the seductive V-neck and the clinging fit, but she bought them anyway. The sexy Damaris silk knickers with the flirty bow on the back – ludicrously expensive – were a total indulgence, but Daisy bought two pairs, one pair in oyster and one pair in damson with cream spots. Then she bought a tub of ice cream and drove home to Carrickwell, eating the ice cream with a plastic spoon as she sat in traffic.

Her shopping lay on the seat beside her, and she touched it sometimes, as if the sight of comforting, expensive things would block out the black hole inside.

Like a busy computer with a full hard drive and slow reactions, her head refused to open the new file: the one labelled Alex and Louise. If she stopped herself from thinking about it, perhaps it wouldn't be true.

In Carrickwell, she drove over the familiar bridge and saw the old man who occasionally played his accordion on her side of the river. He was frail and bundled up in a big coat, with a hat on the ground beside him for coins. Daisy hated the sad tunes he played but she always threw money into his hat when she passed.

Was he happy? she thought wildly now. Was his life better than hers? Probably. In the apartment, she mechanically put her new clothes away, unpacked her suitcase and sorted it into two piles – laundry and dry-cleaning. Neat, methodical. She took off the clothes she'd put on with such zest that morning in Düsseldorf and dressed in an old shirt and the brown slouchy velvet trousers she liked to wear at home.

When all was as it should be, Daisy got a bottle of wine from the fridge, and sat cross-legged on the couch, staring at the television for comfort. This could not be happening to her. Alex could not have left her. Could he?

Then she cried until her face was raw and the bottle was empty.

CHAPTER ELEVEN

The first Monday morning of Mel's new life, the alarm clock she'd forgotten to switch off rang lustily at six fifteen as usual and she lay for a moment the way she always did, savouring that moment of calm before the storm. Adrian did what he always did too: groaned in his sleep and rolled over for another few minutes' oblivion.

She started to race mentally through the day: what she had to do, what she should have done yesterday, what she might manage to put off until tomorrow. And then, with a delicious feeling like sinking into cool sheets with tired feet, she remembered. She wasn't going to work today. She no longer had a job outside the home. Being a mother was her job.

'Housewife.' She considered the word. Housewife. Stay-at-home mother. Was she different? In the half-light of morning seen through cream curtains, she stretched out one arm and looked at it. Exactly the same. Her hand was the same, with slightly ragged cuticles and no polish on the nails. Perhaps she could do things like get manicures now. No, they wouldn't be able to afford that. She could do them herself. She'd have time. And bake – yes, she'd bake. Muffins from that toddler cookbook, the one she'd had for years but had never used. Her own bread. Or perhaps that was a bit ambitious. There were clever ready-made bread mixes in the shops now; she could try them.

Indulging in her plans for the future, Mel rolled over in the bed, snuggled up against the warm shape that was Adrian, and slipped off into a half-doze. Was there an apron anywhere in the house? she wondered. Probably only the one that had come free with cans of beans years ago. She'd love a rosy, floral thing with a fifties feel. Proper mothers had proper aprons.

An hour later, she was in the kitchen bouncing twelve golden muffins out of the tin.

Carrie hadn't grasped the fact that they weren't going to the nursery this morning, or any other morning. It couldn't be the weekend because Daddy had gone to work as usual.

'I get my coat?' she kept saying hopefully.

'No, Carrie. Mummy's going to look after you today. We'll have lots of fun.' Carrie stuck a spoon in her mini fromage frais and then levered it out at high speed, splattering pink gunge everywhere. She giggled irrepressibly and her mother giggled back. No use crying over spilt fromage frais.

Sarah sat at the table and stared at the back of the cereal packet, lost in a fantasy world. She did this every morning, and normally Mel had to hold on to her temper because daydreaming made Sarah slower and then they weren't out of the house in time, and then Mel was in danger of missing the train. Not a problem today. Giddy with the sense of time stretching out in front of her with no deadlines and meetings, Mel sat down beside Sarah and stroked her hair.

'What will we do today?' Mel asked, luxuriating at those words. Not: 'Eat your breakfast, Sarah, *please*, or we'll be late.'

'Can Lily come over and play?' asked Sarah. Lily had recently superseded Tabitha as Sarah's best friend in nursery, although Mel didn't know her mother very well. Lily's mum was something high-powered in business and picked up Lily even later than Mel used to pick up Carrie and Sarah. Mel felt a passionate surge of relief that those days were over. Only now that she didn't do it any more, could she honestly admit how horrifically stressed and guilt-inducing it had all been.

'Lily's in Little Tigers all day,' Mel said. 'Now that Mummy isn't going out to work in the office, you aren't going there,' she reminded Sarah. 'We're going to meet new friends, although we can ask Lily here in the evening perhaps, or at weekends.'

'Want to see Lily now.' Sarah's bottom lip trembled.

'Let's phone her mummy later and talk about it,' Mel said. Luckily she had a note of the number from an old party invitation.

'Not later, now,' said Sarah sadly. 'She's my special friend.'

It was the one thing Mel stupidly hadn't envisaged: that the children would miss their friends. The nursery wouldn't take the girls on a morning-only basis and, anyway, they couldn't afford the nursery now, and there were no places at any of the Montessori in the town. They all got booked up so quickly and Mel had never needed them because of Little Tigers. She'd have to build in lots of play time with other kids.

'But I thought you wanted to have Mummy at home with you

all the time? Won't that be nice? I won't be going to the office any more. I'll be here to take you to the zoo and the park and the farm.'

'Today and the next day and the next day?' Sarah asked suspiciously.

'Yes, like I told you,' Mel said gently.

'OK.' With one word, the matter was settled. 'Can I have a muffin for breakfast, Mummy?' Sarah added. 'I don't like Weetabix any more.'

Breakfast over, Mel began to use her professional skills to find out where the local mother and toddler groups were. It took five phone calls to discover that on Monday mornings, there was one in St Simeon's school hall.

'We're going on an adventure,' she told the girls when she got off the phone. 'Somewhere new and exciting where you'll meet lots of new friends! Let's go upstairs to wash our hands and brush our hair.'

As Carrie and Sarah rushed to the stairs, Mel wondered why she hadn't thought of giving up work years ago. Compared to the pressure she'd have been feeling at this time on a normal Monday morning in work, this was so relaxed. She picked up one of her muffins and began to eat it on the way upstairs. Not bad for a first try.

There were two other women on Mel's road who went to the mother and toddler group beside the church. Mel recognised them as the buggies pulled up outside. One was tall, obviously pregnant and had a lot of rippling dark hair she wore loose. In a flowing purple pregnancy overshirt and trousers, and with a jewelled choker to distract from her huge bump, she looked very exotic. Mel had seen her driving in and out of the road. They'd never spoken before. Or even nodded. The other woman was smaller, slight and looked older, or maybe it was because she had five children, from what Mel had seen. She lived several houses away and Mel had noticed her in the past, loudly telling children to get into the people carrier and *no slapping*! The two women greeted each other at the door of the hall as though they were good friends.

It was like being fifteen and moving to a new school, Mel decided as she followed them. She knew nobody and everyone was looking at her with interest. There was a small group of women already sitting in the hall where chairs and a selection of toys and plastic cars were spread around the wooden floor. A high, toddler-proof table was set up with cups and unopened packets of biscuits. A homemade cake sat at the back. I could make a cake, Mel decided. Now that she'd conquered muffins, a cake wouldn't be beyond her.

She smiled hello at the group in general, and put her bulging mummy handbag onto a chair near the door, a gesture that she hoped showed that she was an outsider but knew it. Sarah and Carrie had no such qualms of shyness and were into the centre of the action instantly.

'Your first time here?' asked another heavily pregnant woman with a toddler clinging to her, koala-style.

Mel sat down beside the woman and nodded. 'You too?'

'No, we've been here loads of times but Cormac is still very shy.' The woman looked at Carrie and Sarah, who were happily playing. 'Your girls are great at fitting in. They're very sociable.'

'They've been at nursery since they were small,' Mel said, then found herself apologising for this fact by saying, 'I've just given up work to be with them.'

'Nursery makes them much more outgoing,' the woman sighed. 'We live a few miles out in the country and Cormac has never really mixed with other children. I've recently realised that he needs to – well, particularly when the new baby comes along.'

'I'm Mel.' Mel waved hello as the woman clearly had no hands left to shake with. 'When are you due?'

'Six weeks. I can't wait. I'm Elaine.'

'Astrid.'

'Sylvia.'

'Bernie.'

'Lizanna.' The woman in the flowing purple with the long rippling hair.

'Claire.'

'Ria.' The woman with five kids who lived nearby.

The women introduced themselves rapidly, and Mel smiled back, suddenly feeling that this wasn't first-day-of-school after all. They were welcoming her. Some were very chic, glamorous even, although Mel had never managed that look at the weekends. She had a work look (suits and high heels) and a home look, which was characterised by old jeans, sweatshirts, no lipstick and hair whatever way it felt like.

Astrid, or at least Mel thought it was Astrid, was the glossy magazine illustration of a busy young mum picking kids up from school with her blonde ponytail, cream cords and caramel suede shirt.

Elaine was in final stage of pregnancy sartorial hell, wearing black jogging pants, and what was probably her husband's striped shirt. She looked hot, tired and sweaty.

'I overheard you saying you've just given up work,' an attract-ive brunette with a baby on her lap said to Mel. Claire was her name, Mel thought. 'What did you do?'

'I worked in Lorimar Health Insurance,' Mel said hesitantly, not wanting to sound like Ms Career Babe who felt she'd been short-changed by giving it all up. That would not win friends and influ-ence people here.

'Did you?' asked someone else. Sylvia? 'I worked in BUPA for a while.'

They were trading health insurance industry stories in minutes and discovered they had both once worked with a sweetheart of a computer boffin who'd gone on to be something big in IT.

Sylvia's little boy screamed to be given some juice. 'Shane, ask nicely,' his mother said without missing a beat. 'Do you miss it? The office, work, the buzz?'

Mel hesitated. 'This is my first day,' she said. 'I'm still finding my feet. I don't miss getting the early train or having to wear heels all day.'

'But the free time . . .' sighed someone else. It was Bernie, a woman in worn jeans with a small boy playing at her feet. 'I was an accountant – *am* an accountant,' she corrected herself. 'There's no time for yourself when you're at home.'

'You said it,' groaned Sylvia. 'When you're not earning, you feel guilty if you want me-time. I haven't had my hair cut for two years in my old salon because it's too hard to take Shane and the buggy there. I go to the tiny place in the shopping centre now just because they've got wide doors.'

'And if you spend money on yourself, it is like taking it out of someone else's bank account,' added Claire.

'But it shouldn't be like that,' Mel said, startled. 'You're doing an important job, taking care of the kids. If your partner or husband paid you for all the things you do, you'd be earning more than he does. Wouldn't you?'

The other women exchanged knowing smiles.

'Leave it a month and then see how you feel,' Sylvia said. 'It's not that easy. You'll never run into the chemist's and buy an expen-sive lipstick just for the hell of it again.'

'You might, but you'll hide it,' Claire pointed out.

'Or say it came free in a magazine,' laughed someone else.

'Oh, come on,' said Mel, laughing too. 'My husband wouldn't notice an expensive lipstick if it jumped up and bit him.'

'Nor mine,' said Sylvia. 'It's the personal guilt. He doesn't care but you do, because you're not earning money so you feel bad about spending any, and that fifteen euro could have gone on another batch of baby vests or new shoes or something that you feel guilty about depriving your children of.'

Carrie scampered back to her mother for reassurance and Mel picked her up for a cuddle. 'I thought working mothers were the ones who felt guilty.'

'All mothers feel guilty,' Claire said. 'It comes with the stretch marks and,' she lowered her voice, 'the no sex life.'

Everyone laughed.

'Speak for yourself!' said Sylvia.

'I'd take a healthy dose of guilt any day over office politics,' added Bernie. 'I was in the bank,' she added to Mel. 'I wouldn't mind working again but never in the bank.'

'Well, this is the best Monday morning I've had for a long time,' Mel said, 'so I don't want to go back.' And it was true: Monday was normally the toughest day of her week, when she was tired after rushing round with the kids all weekend, and she was used to the constant feel of them with her. Monday was like that first day back in work after maternity leave all over again.

'I'd love to go back to work,' said Lizanna, the woman in purple, suddenly. 'If I could work and be with the kids, but have some of the status I had before, I'd love it.'

'What did you do?' asked Mel curiously.

'Finance director in a publishing company,' Lizanna said. 'We published *Style* magazine, *HousePerfect*, every magazine you can think of. It was a great job. I loved it, but when I had Theo,' she looked at the small boy making vroom noises as he pushed a battered toy car along the floor, 'I gave it up. Thought I'd done it all, scaled the heights and now I could sit back and be Mummy. It didn't quite work out that way.'

'But, Lizanna, you love being at home,' insisted Sylvia. 'I don't know how you managed it all before. Now you've got time to enjoy your child.'

'Time with Theo is incredible. I'm not disagreeing with that,' Lizanna said carefully, 'but it doesn't always make up for the change of life. I was proud of what I did and what I'd achieved. People admired me. Nobody really admires you when you're an at-home mother,' she added ruefully. 'Your status is less than zero. I used to be wined and dined at corporate functions; get taken on freebies; the *Style* editor and I were first in line to get the newest designer handbags; you name it. Yes, I know it all sounds shallow, but it was fun and I'd worked hard to get to that place. Now . . .' she paused, 'I don't know, perhaps I'm at that eight-and-a-half-months'-pregnant-get-the-baby-OUT stage, but I feel a bit scared. Another baby means my whole career seems further away. I'm dying to have this baby,' she added, 'don't get me wrong, but I feel I'm disappearing. Does anyone know what I mean?'

'We know,' said Elaine earnestly. 'We understand. God, we certainly understand. You can love your children and still realise they've taken over your life. You're Mummy, instead of whoever you were before.'

Lizanna nodded and looked as if she was sorry she'd opened her mouth. 'It sounds terrible when you put it like that . . . I love my babies.' She splayed an elegant hand over her belly. 'Both of them.'

'You could go back when they're in school,' volunteered Ria.

'That's a long way away,' Sylvia pointed out. 'I'd be nervous of going back then. Everybody would think I was past it. And what would you wear? How do mothers leave the house early looking ready for work? It takes me two hours if we're going out to a formal do because I don't know how to get all dressed up any more.'

'It's hard,' Mel agreed. 'I went back to work when Sarah was three months old. It felt like I was always on the hamster wheel, running, running, but never getting anywhere.'

'But I bet people didn't tune out at parties when they asked, "What do you do?"' said Bernie.

Mel realised she wasn't being funny.

'Oh, yeah, you'll love that,' Lizanna said to Mel. 'Their eyes literally glaze over. Men can be bad but career women are the worst.'

'No,' said Mel, feeling remorse because she might have been guilty of that crime herself. 'They're only guilty because they aren't with their kids in the way you are with yours. It's guilt.'

'It's pity,' Lizanna insisted. 'They think you had your brain sucked out as soon as you walked out the office door. And they pray to the God of Fabulous Shoes never to let them get pregnant.'

One hour rolled into two as the children played – sometimes even with each other – and the women talked. Subjects changed rapidly, as someone got up to tend to a wailing toddler or change a nappy. What fascinated Mel was how open they were about their lives. She'd never had such open conversations with the people she worked with, apart from Vanessa. But these women were perfectly happy to talk about anything.

Nobody pretended her life was perfect, which was what many of the working mothers Mel knew did. *She* knew their lives were the same hectic rush as hers, and *they* knew it, but admitting it was some sort of defeat.

By contrast, the women in St Simeon's laughed about their lives, flaws and all. The group ended at twelve, and Mel left with two happy children and lots of phone numbers programmed into her mobile. It had been refreshing talking about being a mother without feeling like a fraud.

And just as refreshing to find that the women who stayed at home with their kids had issues too. So it wasn't just me and Vanessa who worried, Mel thought. All mothers did it, even the ones who appeared to have it all under control. It was a comforting thought.

After lunch, when Carrie was having her nap and Sarah was watching a video, Mel decided to tackle some of the household jobs that had been annoying her for months. First, she scrubbed the kitchen floor, then she started on the utility room. There were corners where the tiled floor was filthy, so she got out her trusty bottle of Domestos bleach and scrubbed until the smell of ammonia was almost overpowering.

There was an enormous sense of satisfaction in cleaning, she decided.

'How's it going?' asked Adrian when he phoned.

'Wonderful,' answered Mel. 'Although I've spent so much time cleaning out the utility room with bleach that I'm definitely a Domestos goddess, not a domestic one.'

'Is it better being home than being in Lorimar?' Adrian said a bit anxiously.

'Miles better,' said Mel, surveying her kingdom with pride.

On Friday, Mel's mum was taking care of the girls for the morning to give Mel a break. Determined not to lose touch with her old life, Mel organised meeting Vanessa for lunch.

'I miss my girls,' Karen admitted, when she arrived at Mel's mid-morning.

'I know, Mum,' Mel said, feeling guilt from yet another source. For so long, her mother had been such a big part of Carrie and Sarah's weekly routine. It must be hard for her to be relegated to the second division now that Mel had given up her job. 'I'm sorry . . .' she began, but her mother stopped her.

'Don't say a word, Mel,' Karen said firmly. 'I miss the girls but I have never been happier for you since you gave up Lorimar. It was killing you, keeping all the balls in the air. Your dad and I were worried about you, but I could never have said it in case you thought I was getting at you.'

'I probably would have,' admitted Mel. She'd never have been able to admit it before. Being at home was definitely good for her: she was more relaxed, more open.

'Office jobs aren't made for mothers and that's the truth,' Karen went on. 'Until someone comes up with a plan to help women to work around their families, then women are going to be doing what you did: rushing, racing and feeling torn every day of their lives.'

'I can always go back to work when Carrie's finally at school,' Mel added.

'Exactly,' her mother said. 'I'm sure they'll be dying to have you back in Lorimar. The old witch Hilary is probably cursing for letting you go in the first place!'

Vanessa was five minutes late.

'Sorry, sorry,' she apologised as she rushed into the Oriental Palace in a flurry of perfume. 'We're working on more bloody focus groups for the nurse-call service to see what people really want, and they start tonight. Sorry,' she stopped herself, 'you don't want to hear all this stuff.'

'Yes, I do,' said Mel. 'I haven't had Lorimar surgically removed yet. I'm still family, God help me!'

'Great. I was afraid you'd have been mummy-fied. You wouldn't believe what's been going on.' Vanessa scanned the menu at high speed, raised an eyebrow at a waiter to summon him and he arrived, order pad at the ready. More than he'd done since Mel had been sitting there. She'd had to get the menus herself from the table next door, clearly having lost her invisible waiter-attention button.

'Beef and oyster mushroom special with pak choi,' Vanessa said, 'with a half bottle of number twelve. OK with you, Mel?'

'Er, yes. I'll have the cashew nut chicken. And water, still.'

'Yes, well, there was war over a problem in subscriptions where people were being charged twelve per cent extra for paying with credit cards. Processing error, although not our fault, the computer bods say. But Hilary's been putting fires out all week trying to keep it quiet. Oh, and you won't believe who Shaznay, that tall girl in subscriptions, has been seen out with . . .'

It was strange hearing about it all from a distance. Mel had thought she'd wanted to know all the news but it was hard to feel as excited over Shaznay from subscriptions having a romance with Peter from claims as it would have been. In-house gossip used to be the lifeblood of Lorimar. From outside, it all seemed a bit banal.

Mel realised that she wanted to hear that the place was falling apart without her and that Hilary had been seen wringing her hands in misery in the women's loos twice a day, saying, 'We didn't appreciate Mel Redmond until now. Get her back – I don't care what it costs.' That would make her day.

Except that nobody appeared to be wringing their hands over

Mel's absence at all. Her replacement, a twenty-five-year-old graduate from China, called Kami, had charmed everyone in the place and she and Vanessa were going out at lunchtimes.

'She knows how to handle Hilary, that's for sure,' Vanessa said approvingly as she wolfed down her meal. 'When Hilary's about to go postal, Kami's face loses all expression and she stares her down. Hilary can't handle it at all. You can't lose your cool with someone who never loses theirs.'

'Suppose not,' agreed Mel, who found that she was ravenous, despite having finished off Carrie's Shreddies in addition to her own breakfast that morning. It was hard not to eat when you were home all day: the kids needed endless healthy snacks, but when she opened the fridge to get them juice or fromage frais, she found herself nibbling bits of cheese or popping another garlic-and-oil-drenched olive into her mouth.

'How's it going, anyway? Gone to any coffee mornings yet?'

'Er ... well, there is one tomorrow,' Mel admitted, feeling instantly like every cliché of the pampered stay-at-home wife, even though the reality was very different. 'But we all have kids in the mother and toddler group: it'll be like having the group in someone's house really.'

'You're getting to know people then?'

In the midst of a mouthful of chicken – that sauce was delicious – Mel nodded. 'We've been invited to dinner next Saturday night. Astrid. They live near us but in these big posh houses.'

'See? You're in with the Carrickwell Mummy Mafia already,' joked Vanessa. 'What about your spa vouchers – have you used those yet?' Mel's farewell present from Lorimar had been a pair of vouchers for the new Cloud's Hill Spa.

'Not yet, I'm saving them for a special occasion,' said Mel.

'Wish I had the time to come, but it's just crazy at the moment,' said Vanessa, polishing off her wine. It was only ten to two. 'Better fly, Mel. I've got to rush into the supermarket and grab something for Conal's dinner.'

Mel still felt hungry so when she'd waved Vanessa goodbye, she meandered along and took a trip into the shopping centre where she had an after-lunch latte and a cream bun. There was some lovely stuff in the shops. She fell in love with a pair of cinnamon-coloured suede sandals that would really suit her. But they were expensive and with her not working, they didn't have the money for such luxuries.

The following Saturday, Mel wished she'd bought some of the fabulous clothes she'd seen after her lunch with Vanessa. Astrid's dinner

162

party was taking place that night and Mel realised that her evening wear consisted of corporate wear (sedate black and navy dresses), two sparkly tops that were donkey's years old and hadn't been fashionable since Abba were hot, a see-through black shirt that needed careful choice of underwear and a couple of dresses from her younger clubbing years. With the inevitable black trousers, they made up her evening out ensembles.

Her weekend clothes were all very casual and none of it was suitable for any dinner other than in Ronald McDonald's restaurant. The only other options were her dressed-for-success suits. Mel wasn't into clothes much but she began to see that she was badly equipped sartorially for her new life.

Then, at the back of the wardrobe, she found the old violet halterneck dress she'd bought on holiday in Italy when she and Adrian were first dating. It was vaguely 'thirties but timeless, and amazingly it still fitted. Tonight, when she didn't have to be Ms Redmond from publicity, it would be perfect.

Astrid's home was on one of Carrickwell's leafier, more expensive roads and turned out to be a detached redbrick pile beside a row of other, all slightly different, redbrick piles. It was five minutes' walk from Goldsmith Lawn but worlds apart in terms of price.

'We are moving in posh circles,' Adrian said as they walked up the curving, conifer-lined drive.

'Yeah,' agreed Mel. 'Do you think they'll be on for spag bol in the playroom-cum-dining room in our house? I'd even move some of the kids' toys so people's legs could actually fit under the table.'

'There's no need to go that far. Standing on a squeaky toy can be a great way to break the ice.'

Despite the grand façade, Astrid and Mike's home wasn't grand on the inside and had a lived-in, kid-friendly look. Astrid didn't go in for formal dinner parties either, Mel saw with relief, because there was no sign of expensive silver and cut-glass goblets at the big wooden table. It all looked casual.

Mike stood at the top and directed people to seats so couples wouldn't be together. Mel found herself between a youngish guy in chinos and a denim-blue sweater, and an older man in a snow-white shirt with monogrammed cuffs. His name was Colin and he lived next door to Astrid.

'What do you do?' he asked when they were all settled with wine and bread.

'I'm in publicity . . .' Mel began, then laughed at herself. 'I *used* to be in publicity. For Lorimar?'

Colin's eyes were keen with interest and Mel decided that he was cute for an older guy. Sexy in a charismatic way.

'Sounds interesting.' He moved his elbow a teeny bit closer to her on the table.

'I was part of a team that handled the website. The web is such an important part of our business now. Well, it was when I was there.'

'What do you do now?'

'I've just given up work to stay at home with the children.'

Like a lightbulb switching off, the gleam of interest went out of Colin's eyes.

Mel knew she hadn't imagined it. 'I've got two little girls. One's two and a half and the other is nearly five,' she went on.

He sat back in his seat, breaking the cosy intimacy between them.

'Have you got children?' she asked, because she had to be utterly sure that her lack of a job was what had made him switch off and not the reference to children.

'Yeah, they're nearly grown up now. Costing me a fortune. I've got to work all hours to keep them in pocket money.' And the subject was closed. Colin took a sip from his wine and looked around the table as if he was suddenly ravenous and wondered where the food was.

Children were not the taboo, Mel realised. Being a stay-at-home mother was. Lizanna had been on the money. Colin's eyes had glazed over.

Astrid and Mike were good hosts. They kept the table lively, making sure that nobody was left out. Watching Adrian deep in conversation with his neighbour, while Colin studiously avoided her, Mel was grateful for Astrid occasionally dragging her into the discussion.

Football, house prices, local schools, the roadworks on the bridge in Carrickwell, the wisdom of giving children mobile phones and the new Bond film: all were discussed and laughed over.

Her other neighbour, Mr Denim-Blue Sweater, wasn't paying her any attention, but Mel didn't mind because it was clear that he'd been invited for one of the female guests, who was sitting on his other side. Astrid had got her matchmaking right, that was for sure. The pair talked incessantly, which meant Mel saw a lot of both her neighbours' shoulders.

But finally, with the aid of several glasses of wine and some brandy, Colin found Mel interesting to talk to again.

She listened for a while to him talking about his job (telemarketing company), his sport of choice (he had a power boat), and what he felt about the Formula One season (wouldn't it be great to see some new blood come into the pit?).

Mel didn't want to be rude at someone else's party, so she kept on smiling and watched her hands on her watch creep round to eleven. That was a suitable time to leave, surely? All the while, Colin's eyes – which were no longer even vaguely attractive – kept dipping below Mel's face to linger on the mounds of her breasts under the violet dress. She hadn't been able to find her halterneck bra that evening, so had gone braless. Vanessa would have laughed, Mel thought with an inner grin, to see a slightly drunken man admiring the boobs that Mel insisted were beyond saving.

But eventually, it began to get to her. Colin didn't know or care that she had been an ambitious career woman for all her adult life. All he saw was a woman with kids, a tight dress, no job and no bra.

Sexism wasn't new to Mel, but she'd always been able to deal with it because she knew she was so much more than the sum of her physical parts. If a guy whistled at her legs, Mel didn't care. She was far brighter than he was, and confident in her abilities. Let him whistle. So what? If a co-worker made a smart remark about women, Mel was perfectly capable of cutting him down to size. She knew she was more than any man's equal in the workplace.

Except her workplace had changed. The confidence of her career had been whipped out from under her, like a magician whisking a tablecloth out from under the teacups. And Colin's rheumy drunken eyes annoyed her.

She folded her arms across her chest where his eyes had been resting for several seconds. 'Why don't you take a photo? It'll last longer,' she said.

Colin's mind might have been on more primal things, but he got the hint. 'Sorry, well, just . . .' he mumbled, gaze suddenly up but too embarrassed to look her in the eye.

Mel caught Adrian's eye across the table and pushed back her chair with vigour. 'Astrid, Mike, wonderful party,' she said brightly. 'The food was fantastic, but it's eleven and we've got to go. Babysitters, you know!'

'Oh, yes,' agreed Adrian, who could read Mel's face like a book 'Thanks. The beef was lovely.'

After a flurry of thank yous, they were out on the street again and Mel recounted the whole sorry tale.

'I don't know why I didn't hit him,' she raged as they walked home.

'You should have,' agreed Adrian, holding her hand.

'He was so rude. As soon as he heard that I stayed at home with the girls, badda-bing! I was a boring housewife and he had nothing to say to me.'

'Probably has a small willy,' Adrian added.

'Don't try and distract me! He was just plain rude and he deserved to be humiliated in front of the whole party. And I don't know why I didn't do it!' Mel was walking at high speed, as she did when she was angry, despite her heels. 'And if I'd lied and said I still worked at Lorimar, he'd have been flirting with me all night. I know the type. Turned on by women in business.'

'I wouldn't have liked it if he'd flirted with you all night,' Adrian pointed out. 'Not that I'm the jealous type, but I prefer men not to flirt with you under my nose. It goes back to the cavemen, I think,' he said thoughtfully. '*Man no like other man messing with his woman* sort of thing. I'd have had to bash him over the head with my club or challenge him to a duel out on the plain with the dinosaurs ready to charge.'

'Dinosaurs and men were not around at the same time,' Mel interrupted.

'Really?' said Adrian, faking surprise.

She put an arm round his waist. 'You know well there weren't but it was the right answer. At times like this, I know why I married you.'

'Thank you for that vote of confidence, Mrs Redmond. And I love you too.'

CHAPTER TWELVE

The problem with big weddings, Cleo decided as she stood, still smiling, behind the vast ormolu reception desk of McArthur's Hotel in Dublin's wealthy embassy belt at nearly two o'clock in the morning, was that there was always a row. Always. Even in a top-class hotel where bottles of Château Petrus flew out of the cellar and where the room rate was 300 euro for a bog-standard double with no frills. She supposed families all had the same things to

argue about, no matter how grand or how modest the arrangements were.

'When's the fight starting?' asked Jean-Paul, the doorman, one
of the few people awake with Cleo. It often amazed Cleo how great
big hotels were so empty at night – upstairs, the guests slept, while
downstairs, a skeleton staff kept things going and the cleaning staff
drifted through the sweaty bowels of the hotel like ghosts.

'Fists will fly any minute now,' said Cleo brightly, as if she
wasn't half dead with exhaustion. 'Luigi's just phoned from the bar
to say there's a big argument going on between the bride's father
and the groom's uncle, and he can't manage on his own because
Vincent is in the cellar again. They want Napoleon Brandy, he says.
One for everyone in the audience.'

At four in the afternoon, the stylish nuptials of the Smiths and
the O'Haras had been perfect for the society magazines – lots of
gleaming happy faces, held-in stomachs, exquisite outfits in bright
flower colours and gold Rolexes rattling on Riviera-tanned wrists.
Ten hours later, the hard core of partygoers still at it in the bar
were looking the worse for wear. Faces, stomachs and outfits were
all somewhat creased, and although everybody kept looking at their
Rolexes to check the time and show people how carelessly wealthy
they were because they *had* one, nobody wanted to admit defeat
and go to bed.

The bride's parents had paid a fortune to have the wedding of
the season in McArthur's, and they were damned if they weren't
going to get their money's worth. Throwing them out of the bar
would be a bit difficult, especially since the bar bill had yet to be
settled.

'Two-hundred-year-old brandy?' Jean-Paul snorted. 'We could
serve them homebrew at this point and they wouldn't know the
difference.'

Three wealthy Arab businessmen walked into the lobby, suave
in Western suits, perfectly alert even at this hour of the morning.
They'd breakfasted at noon, had a light lunch at four, followed by
dinner at a private club at ten. Now they were going to wind down
their evening with some cards and business in the bar.

Jean-Paul, who knew which side his bread was buttered – those
guys were big tippers – stepped out from behind his desk and
urbanely steered the gentlemen in the direction of the Library Bar,
an ante room to the main bar, where they wouldn't be disturbed
by the high jinks of the wedding party.

Cleo was alone in the huge reception again, which she hated
because it gave her time to think. In the month since she'd swept
out of home with all her belongings, there had been too much time

for thinking: wondering whether the sale of the hotel had been completed, where would her family go now, how were her parents, and didn't any of the family miss her?

Trish's mother was able to fill her in on most of the news. Via the Interpol-style information service that was operating in Carrickwell, Trish's mother had found out that the hotel was indeed sold, but that the Malins hadn't moved out yet. There was talk of Harry and Sheila buying a small place in Brittany. Nobody volunteered if the Malins missed Cleo or not, and Cleo was too proud to ask.

She still passionately believed she hadn't done anything wrong: everyone else had. This fact she'd made plain to her mother a week after she left home when Sheila phoned to ask Cleo when she was coming to her senses.

'This silly row has gone on long enough, Cleo,' her mother had said firmly. 'You're not a child any more. Get back here and apologise, so we can put it behind us.'

'Me! Apologise!' Cleo had been thrilled to see her home number flash up on her mobile phone screen, but she'd been sure her mother was going to apologise to her on behalf of the rest of the family. 'I've done nothing wrong, Mum,' she said, feeling hot tears prickling at her eyes. 'Everyone said awful things to me and I feel so left out, so hurt . . .' Her father had hurt her most of all. He knew she idolised him. How come he hadn't bothered to phone her? Why didn't he want to talk to her?

'Oh, Cleo, for heaven's sake . . .'

It was the impatience in her usually gentle mother's voice that did it: Cleo felt her temper snap again. 'You're my family and I love you all,' Cleo said fiercely, 'but I am not a child any more and I won't be treated like one. I deserved to be involved in the future of my home. Until somebody apologises to me for not involving me, I don't see how I can come home.'

'Have it your own way,' her mother had said wearily. 'Bye.'

Cleo was sure she was right, that it was up to her dad, mum and the boys to come to her and say sorry. Until that happened, she was a Malin in name only.

Her name hadn't got her the sought-after temping job in the prestigious McArthur's. The reference from the French château and her college results had. McArthur's was the last word in hotel chic and prided itself on combining boutique hotel charm with grand hotel style, which meant that a club sandwich could be sold in the restaurant for the same price as a room in a cheap airport motel. The place ran like a fine Swiss watch and the privacy of the guests was assured in the style of Switzerland's other great industry, banking. Which was why it was the hotel of choice for rock stars, movie stars and the fabulously wealthy.

'Isn't it better to be working in Dublin than in the sticks?' Trish kept saying, knowing how upset Cleo still was and trying to console her. 'Think of the men you'll meet, film stars, bands, telly people. It'll be amazing.'

'You don't meet the great and the good at two o'clock in the morning,' Cleo pointed out. 'Well, you might, but if they're rolling up then, they're not looking at me: they're longing for their bed.'

'Temping is a step to a full-time job,' Trish said encouragingly.

'True,' said Cleo, trying to sound enthusiastic. Temping meant night shifts again, and she'd decided that she just hated shift work. There was a brain-numbing monotony to it, watching the clock crawl round. At three in the morning, she always felt shattered and only a couple of cans of Diet Coke could pep her up. By seven, when she clocked off and could go home to sleep, she'd inevitably passed the exhaustion stage and knew that she'd toss and turn for half the morning before managing a few fractured, nightmare-filled hours of sleep. She was staying at Trish's place now, which was not the ideal spot for sleeping in the daytime, either. It was situated bang on the train line, and Cleo's nightmares were often punctuated by the thunderous roll of the Belfast express hurtling past.

She didn't mind not sleeping for its own sake, although it was hard setting off to work every night on a couple of hours' sleep, but when she lay there awake, her head was as wired up as MTV with constant reruns of the row and how everyone *could* have behaved. If only Dad had said this or done that, went the non-stop soundtrack.

'Forget it. They'll forget it too and in a few years, you'll all wonder what the argument was about,' advised Trish. 'People let you down, Cleo. You've got to accept it. Move on.'

Except that Cleo wasn't like Trish and didn't think she could move on. Her family were important to her. Reaching out and exploring the world was possible when the Willow and all the Malins had been there in the background, her security blanket. Without them, the world was scarier. Feeling that they'd all let her down was worse. No matter what Trish said, your family were supposed to be there for you. Men might let you down, but not your mum and dad. Cleo just couldn't get away from that thought.

Paige, an attractive ponytailed girl from Mississippi who was pulling a split shift to cope with early morning check-outs, arrived at reception at five, yawning and carrying two takeaway lattes and a couple of early newspapers swiped from Jean-Paul's delivery.

'No sugar for you, right?'

'Thank you.' Gratefully, Cleo took the coffee.

Paige, who looked box-fresh despite the early hour, sat down and flicked through her paper. 'What's happening?'

Cleo recalled the night: '. . . so Luigi just managed to get the Smith O'Hara guests off to bed before blood was spilled. Oh, and Vincent is a happy bunny because he got tipped five hundred by the South American guys on the top floor,' she finished.

'Anyone bumped?' asked Paige.

All hotels overbooked. Traditionally, the reservations manager's job involved a delicate and continual balancing act to make sure the whole hotel was filled every night. Due to the inevitable cancellations, there were often spare rooms, hence overbooking to cover this. When 1004 guests turned up for 1000 rooms, someone got bumped. Usually the late night single male business traveller. 'Yeah, a couple of late night arrivals.' Cleo tapped her screen. 'We sent them to the BeauRegard. Greg Junior was still here and he was really sweet and helped me out when this guy who'd just flown in from London began to get really angry.' Greg Jun., along with his father, Greg Sen., the two concierges, were the men who really ran McArthur's, according to those in the know. The hotel manager might not be aware of which important businessman had hookers in his room overnight or which wealthy lady had tried to wrap her dressing-gowned self round the astonished room service waiter who'd delivered her midnight feast of champagne and Beluga. But the Gregs knew. From their misleadingly small desk to the left of the great revolving doors in the lobby, they had their fingers on the pulse of the entire hotel.

'Greg Junior is cute, isn't he?' Paige remarked.

Cleo considered Greg, who was athletic and clean cut. 'He's nice but he's not my type.' Cleo's type was tall, dark and with bad-boy tendencies. Strangely enough, disturbing memories of a tall, dark guy with close-cropped hair popped into her head at that moment.

Paige drank her coffee and yawned again. 'Five more minutes and I'll start,' she said, handing the first paper over to Cleo and picking up the second one. She flicked through it quickly.

'Now he is *my* type,' she said dreamily when she'd flicked to the boring business pages. 'Tyler Roth.' Paige twirled her blonde ponytail. 'Gorgeous face and gorgeous body.'

'Gimme a look.' Cleo leaned over to see for herself. Smiling out of the page, looking like he'd just been put second in line to the throne of Brunei, was the man who'd haunted her nightmares since that evening in Carrickwell. Mr Alpha Male, who'd picked her up from the pavement, insulted her and disappeared.

'As I live and breathe . . .' she said.

'What?'

'Nothing.' Cleo stared for a second more. Tyler Roth had been photographed outside a building site for some enormous new hotel. His hair was cropped very close to his skull, giving him a faintly dangerous air. Despite the beautiful suit, silk tie and veneer of sophistication, this man was a wolf at heart.

'He's a walking bank account,' Paige said. 'His father runs Roth Hotels and he's taken over the new acquisitions.' She ran a pink-tipped finger down the print. 'Hot business exec, they call him here. "Tough, uncompromising, ambitious and reportedly ruthless, he's a regular chip off the old Roth block." Says he's looking for hotels or hotel sites over here.'

Tyler Roth of Roth Hotels. How ironic, Cleo thought. And now she knew his name, she could find him because there was still a piece of her mind with his face on it and he was going to get it, one way or another.

Paige closed the paper, tidied up and moved to her screen. 'I'd work for him anytime. If you hooked a guy like him, you'd never have to work a day in your life again.'

Cleo felt a momentary sense of annoyance. Why would a clever, good-looking woman like Paige consider marrying a rich guy as a career option? Why didn't she see that making her own fortune from her own career was far more satisfying? That's what Cleo was going to do. If she built up her own empire, nobody could take it away from her. Nobody.

Everybody knew something about Tyler Roth.

Greg Sen. had worked in the first Roth Hotel over twenty years ago. 'The Manhattan Roth,' he sighed, when Cleo idly pumped him for information. 'Now *that* was a hotel. All the big stars stayed there. Lunch in the Roth Grill was the hottest ticket in town. Tyler was only a kid then – he was the youngest. From Levi's second marriage. There were a couple of older sisters, real beauties, little princesses, if you know what I mean.'

Cleo nodded.

'Daddy gave them everything. One of them made an album and the other one was in modelling, but nothing big time. They were playing at it, spending Daddy's money until something better came along. Not like little Tyler.' Greg Sen. grinned. 'Sharp as a knife, that kid. If he's as good as his dad, he's some operator.'

Wendy, head of housekeeping, was able to volunteer that she knew Levi from years back when she was training, and he was tough but fair. Tyler was the same, or so said an old friend of hers who'd worked in many of the Roth Hotels.

Ruby Jack, the hotel's bar manager, had worked in the New Orleans Roth.

'Tyler? Sure I know him.' He whistled in through his teeth. 'Bit of a hound for the ladies, our boy. Had two women on the go when I knew him and he was only eighteen.'

'Really?' Cleo was beginning to like Tyler Roth less and less. He sounded as if he was a smart aleck who thought his father's riches meant he could speed through life hurting people left, right and centre.

'They knew about each other, y'know,' Ruby added. 'The girls. Didn't mind, though.'

More bloody women who'd put up with anything for a rich man. Just like Paige. Didn't modern girls have any sense of personal value?

With so many people knowing the story of Roth because of the group's very public interest in growing the chain in Ireland, it didn't take much ingenuity to discover that when Tyler Roth came to Dublin to stay, he stayed in McArthur's. Where else? Cleo thought sourly. Well, she'd be ready for him. He'd undoubtedly have a room reserved well in advance and she'd make sure she was there when he arrived. What exactly she was going to do to wreak her revenge, she wasn't sure. But she'd work on it.

As it proved, she didn't have to wait long. Word was out that the Roths were interested in a landmark site outside Galway, and the land was being auctioned at the end of the week. Tyler and his team would be in McArthur's for five days. All Cleo needed was to swap shifts with someone.

Geena, a willowy Clare girl who spoke four languages and worked days on reception, had a note up on the notice board begging someone to swap shifts with her so she could have a long weekend with her boyfriend in Paris. That last bit wasn't in the note, of course. Management frowned upon shift-swapping and only in dire need were notes to be stuck up on the board. A family christening was Geena's official reason.

'I'll swap with you for that weekend,' offered Cleo. 'I need the money.'

'I'd love that,' Geena said regretfully, 'but it won't work. I'm back on the desk on Tuesday morning, so I can't do the day shift all week and nights too. Night people can never swap with day people. But it's really kind of you to offer.'

'No, I don't want you to cover my shifts,' Cleo insisted. 'I'm on time off at the weekend, so I can do your shifts, finish up on Monday evening and be back here on Tuesday night for my shift.'

'You'll be wrecked,' said Geena.

'I can manage it,' said Cleo. Getting even with Tyler Roth would be worth it.

Tyler Roth arrived in McArthur's on Friday evening and Cleo was at the reception desk, primed and ready. She wasn't sure if he'd recognise her. How could he? The incident in Carrickwell had been so fleeting and late at night.

Tyler was accompanied by another man. Did he ever travel on his own, Cleo wondered acidly, or did he always have a minder?

'Two reservations, name of McKenzie and Roth,' said the other man, who was nice-looking and tall, but too ordinary and pale beside the dark edginess of Tyler Roth.

Tyler wasn't looking at the reception desk or Cleo. He was on his mobile phone, not talking, just listening with a peculiar stillness, as if he was utterly focused on what the person at the other end was saying.

'Welcome to McArthur's,' Cleo said, doing her best to impersonate Sondra's sister Tamara's no-smiling-please-unless-you're-Brad-Pitt expression. 'I'll just check your reservations.'

She expertly flicked the touch-pad screen, found their names, gave Mr Larry McKenzie a card to fill in and checked him in on the screen. She left a second card for Tyler on the reception desk.

'I'll fill this in,' said Larry, grabbing it.

'*He* has to sign it,' Cleo said. Her grim Tamara-face slipped. She had to smile; it was second nature to her.

Larry gave her an admiring beam in return. That had not been part of the plan, Cleo thought. She knew she'd overdone it on the Irish colleen look as she was wearing her tiny gold claddagh earrings and the khaki eyeliner from Mac that brought out the green in her hazel eyes.

'Tyler,' called Larry, seeing that Tyler was putting his phone away.

Tyler Roth swung around smoothly on Italian leather shoes and as his dark eyes met Cleo's, she thought for a fraction of a second that he was trying to place her, then the moment was gone. He held out his hand to Larry for the pen, just a guy checking into a hotel for business. Why would he remember her? He'd insulted her in her home town in front of witnesses, that was all. Who'd remember that? Cleo burned at the injustice of men.

'Thanks.' His handwriting was heavy, with huge peaks and troughs, like a drawing of a mountain range. Cleo had watched a show where handwriting experts had analysed people's characters on the strength of their signatures. Heavy with extreme peaks meant egotistical, power-mad ingrates, didn't it?

He held on to the pen for a moment, as if about to put it automatically in his pocket, then seemed to realise it wasn't his and put it down. She snatched it back. Power mad was right.

'Thank you, Cleo,' he said, staring quite pointedly at her gold name tag. Cleo was suddenly conscious of the curve of her breasts under the badge.

'Thank you, Mr Roth. Welcome to McArthur's,' she said, trying to pull off the difficult trick of smiling and sending out icy-blizzard vibes at the same time.

'I'm sure we'll enjoy our stay here,' he said with a knowing look that made Cleo damn sure he remembered her after all. 'Have our bags sent up to our rooms, please,' he added.

Cleo somehow controlled the impulse to say, 'Oh, you want them in *your* rooms? Gee, glad you told me. I'd planned on sending them to the Four Seasons.' She was pretty sure such smart-assery was a firing offence.

'No problem, Mr Roth. Enjoy your stay. And you too, Mr McKenzie,' she added, switching off the blizzard effect and dazzling poor Larry McKenzie with a trademark Cleo-smile at the full one hundred watts.

If Mr McKenzie was surprised at this rapid change of temperature, he said nothing, although he did glance briefly at Tyler. He was probably used to women acting strangely around his boss, Cleo thought crossly, girls hoping a bit of the Roth magic – and money – might rub off on them. Well, not this woman. No way. Tyler had met his match here.

She had to wait until the evening before she saw him again. She was on duty with Eric, who was patiently sorting out an elderly guest who had lost her room key.

Tyler walked through the front door and automatically looked in Cleo's direction. She peered down at her screen instantly and had her hotel smile ready when he strode over to her.

'We meet again,' he said, dark eyes appraising. His accent was quite neutral, she noticed. Not obviously New York, but the softer accent of someone who'd grown up travelling all round the world and could slip into the dialects of other countries with ease. That article Paige had read out to her was right too: he did look ruthless. Like he always got his own way.

'Hello, Mr Roth. Is there anything I can do for you? Is your room satisfactory? Oh, sorry, your *suite*.' A little sarcasm never went amiss. 'Everybody loves the penthouse. So much space, big windows. Although it's a long way down to the ground.' Her smile was guileless.

'I'll have to make sure I don't drink too much and go out onto the balcony, then,' he said blandly.

Cleo's air of calm deserted her and her eyes hardened into emerald chips. He *had* remembered their first meeting.

'I knew it was you,' Tyler said, placing one elbow on the desk and leaning in far too closely to her, so she could see the dark shadow on his chin and smell his cologne. He was very disturbing up close. There was too much power and charisma in one package. Cleo moved back instinctively. She became aware that Eric, who had finished dealing with the elderly lady, was watching the little altercation with interest. 'I'd recognise those eyes anywhere,' Tyler went on. 'What mythical she-creature could kill a man with one look? The Hydra? Medusa?'

'Cleo,' joked Eric.

Cleo shot him a look that, if not guaranteed to kill, would certainly make the recipient need to lie down for a while. Eric suddenly became very interested in his computer screen.

'And your smile,' went on Tyler, ignoring Eric.

'What smile?' snapped Cleo, all pretence gone.

'The one you give when you're not aware anyone is watching you, when you're being friendly, instead of Über-bitch,' Tyler said silkily. 'Not the plastic one, the real deal. How long have you worked in McArthur's?' he asked. 'I've stayed here a lot recently, and I'd have noticed you. Definitely.'

'The whole hen party/lap dancing thing didn't work out,' she said smartly, determined to shock him. 'Not as much money in it as I'd have liked. And people, *men* actually, kept getting the wrong idea about me. It's funny, when you wear, say, a bunny girl costume, everyone thinks you are easy. They have no idea what sort of a person you really are, but they jump to conclusions. Does that sound familiar?'

What was irritating was that Tyler didn't appear put out by her acid remarks. She was conscious of him looking lazily at her, appraising, admiring.

She was also conscious of Eric listening avidly, and Greg Sen. watching the tableau with interest from the concierge's desk by the door.

Another guest arrived, thank heavens, and began to discuss a late check-out with Eric.

'Mr Roth, can I do something to help you?' Cleo asked, the perfect receptionist again.

'Have a drink with me?'

'We're not allowed to fraternise with the guests,' Cleo said sweetly. 'It's the same in the lap-dancing business. The management take a firm view on such matters.'

175

'So you *did* fraternise with some of the clients in the lap-dancing club?' Tyler asked innocently.

'Only the very sleazy ones,' she shot back. 'The ones who insulted me, in fact. I love men who insult me. It's really the way to a girl's heart, don't you know?'

'Ah, I get it,' he said.

'Good, because that's the only thing you'll be getting from me,' Cleo snapped.

'I may have jumped to the wrong conclusion back then,' Tyler said.

'*That's* why you're a multi-millionaire businessman, Mr Roth, is it? It's nothing to do with being born into a lucrative family business, it's your unerring ability to shoot first and ask questions afterwards? You know what they say about the word "assume"? It makes an *ass* out of *u* and *me*.'

Eric, still listening in, was open-mouthed – so was the guest he was dealing with – but Cleo no longer cared. 'If you hadn't made such a horrible assumption, you would have saved me the humiliation of being insulted by a stranger in my hometown with a fascinated crowd watching!'

'We've got quite a crowd watching here right now,' Tyler grinned, clearly enjoying himself hugely. 'Strike out drinks. Let's make it dinner. I'll take you to dinner and make it up to you. I'm really sorry.'

'You should have apologised then and there,' she said furiously. 'You made me look like a complete fool. I don't know whatever backwater you were dragged up in, but in Carrickwell, men don't hurl insults at women on the streets. A –' She broke off, not wanting the audience to hear a repeat performance of what he'd said. *Drunken hen night*, indeed. 'And I don't do dinner with strange men.'

'Breakfast? Do you take cream in your coffee?'

It was at that exact moment that Greg Sen. decided to meander over. His progress across the lobby looked aimless, but was actually as purposeful as a charter plane coming in to land.

'Oh, Greg,' said Cleo, the picture of charm itself, 'the very man I was looking for. Mr Roth has an unusual request, one that neither I nor the rest of the staff can help him with. He wants information on ...' she lowered her voice, 'a store for men with special needs.' She lowered her voice even more. 'For when a man wants to explore his feminine side. With clothes. Ladies' clothes.'

It was to Greg's credit that he didn't blink. Neither did Tyler for that matter.

'If you'd come over to the desk, Mr Roth, we'll see what we

can do,' said Greg expansively, as if they were off for a macho chat about the merits of Monte Cristo versus Romeo y Julietta cigars.

Tyler gave Cleo one last glance, which she returned with a truly triumphant smile, as if daring him to get her into trouble.

'It's a delicate matter,' Tyler said to Greg. 'I have a friend arriving and he would be interested in that kind of store.'

'A friend,' nodded Greg. 'Of course, of course. You'd be amazed at how we can sort out things for friends.'

Cleo's shift started at seven next morning. She was tired because her sleep had been haunted by disturbing images of herself and another body – male, muscled, lean, with cropped hair and dark, dark eyes – writhing in a bed. When she woke at four, she couldn't go back to sleep, and lay there until half-past five, when the alarm screeched at her to get up.

Trish was a lump on the other side of the bed, never stirring when Cleo threw the covers back. Cleo knew she'd have to get her own place soon. She couldn't go on sharing Trish's cramped room, although Trish said it was nice to have Cleo there. It was like being kids again on a sleepover, she said. They'd talked about getting a place for the two of them, but had decided they couldn't afford it yet.

Reception was busy, with lots of early check-outs. There were four staff members working on the desk and Tyler joined the queue in front of Cleo. After ten minutes where she was conscious of him looking at her tired face, there was only one person left before she'd have to deal with him.

Norah, the next receptionist in the line, sent her last guest off happily and was free. 'Can I help you?' she beamed at Tyler.

He shook his head and gave Norah an absolute killer smile, the type guaranteed to send ripples down into any woman's underwear, no matter what time of the morning it was. 'No thanks, I need to speak with Cleo.'

Norah swivelled slowly to Cleo with a wicked grin that said, 'Get you, babe!' On the pretence of reaching over for Cleo's stapler a second later, she whispered, 'Are you up to something with that fine man?'

Tyler was watching them both and smirking.

Cleo felt the heat rise from her chest right up to the roots of her hair. 'He's annoying me,' she hissed at Norah.

'He can annoy me any time he wants,' Norah whispered huskily, in a credible impersonation of Mae West.

'Yes, this looks about right,' said the harassed-looking man whom

Cleo was actually supposed to be dealing with. He signed the bill before rushing off.

Tyler moved smoothly in.

'Can I help you?' Cleo said. 'Checking out?'

'No,' he said. 'I've a query about something I asked for and haven't got yet. I'm a little surprised, I've got to say. A hotel of this calibre should see to all the guests' needs.'

'Oh, and what's the problem?' Cleo said, instantly professional, wondering where the hotel had failed.

'I wanted a bottle of champagne to share with a special someone and the mini-bar doesn't carry the brand I favour. Worse, the special someone from the hotel never arrived.' He smiled pointedly at Cleo. The insinuation was obvious.

Norah had a guest again, an elegantly dressed elderly gentleman with a set of matching hand-tooled leather luggage and a charming manner. He looked at Cleo and grinned.

Cleo felt a surge of irritation. 'Well,' she said, 'Sir could contact the bar about the champagne. We carry most brands here, and I'm sure that if we don't stock it, we can get it for you. However, generally the hotel doesn't provide dates for guests. The five-star rating doesn't cover that type of service, although perhaps it does in the Roth Hotels group.'

Norah stifled a giggle and the elderly gentleman laughed out loud at this. 'Looks like the lady's telling you off, son,' he said to Tyler.

'I keep telling him off but he just doesn't pick it up,' Cleo remarked. 'He's not too bright.'

'Can't blame a trier,' the guy added. 'And he looks bright enough.'

'She's playing hard to get,' Tyler said, ignoring Cleo, and turning to the other man. 'What is it about women?'

'My second wife did that,' the older man said thoughtfully. 'No, wait a minute, that was my third.'

'And what about the current Mrs . . .' Norah looked down at her screen to check before giving him a dazzling smile, '. . . Mrs Lewis?'

'There's no current Mrs Lewis,' Mr Lewis smiled. 'Four wives are enough for any man.'

'Four?'

'Four. Unlucky for some.'

'Thirteen is unlucky for some,' chipped in Norah hopefully. He was rather charming.

'For me, it was four,' Mr Lewis said drily. 'Good luck with her,' he nodded to Tyler. 'Take my advice and make sure you get her to sign a pre-nup before you marry her. No offence,' he added to Cleo.

Cleo exploded. 'I despise any woman who tries to take a man to the cleaners when they split up,' she said in outrage. 'I've always earned my own living and that wouldn't change just because I got a divorce. Anyway, it's hardly an issue here. I can't stand this man.' She glared at Tyler.

'She can't stand me,' Tyler agreed. 'I am the most irritating man she ever met, but that's a start, because I like sparks. What sort of excitement could you have with a woman if she was goofy about you? Cleo and I, we could have wild times together.'

The way he said 'wild times' made Cleo's pulse speed right up.

'Now that sounds like wife number two,' warned Mr Lewis. 'Sparks are kinda sexy but dangerous. Although,' he reflected, 'I still love her. She left me. I oughta phone her.'

'You do that,' said Tyler. He reached over the desk, which was easy because he was so tall, and he deliberately brushed his hand gently against Cleo's before moving back. He hadn't touched her since that awful night in Carrickwell when he'd picked her up off the ground, and Cleo felt the spark he'd been talking about shear through her. She jerked back.

'Dinner? Pick you up at seven? I know a great little place we can go to,' Tyler said, hooded dark eyes staring fiercely into hers.

'My shift ends at seven,' she gave in, determined not to lose her cool. 'And I don't go out in my work clothes. I'll pick you up here at half-eight, and I'll show you a great little place that I like. Yeah?'

'Masterful,' sighed Mr Lewis. 'Wife number four.'

'I like masterful,' grinned Tyler. 'It's fun taming it.' And he left, blowing Cleo a kiss as he went.

'It's only seven thirty a.m. and you've already got a date for the evening,' Norah sighed.

'She's got the looks,' Mr Lewis said, admiring Cleo. 'That guy's Tyler Roth. He's what my mother would have called "a catch".'

'I'm not out to catch him,' said Cleo, still smarting after the remark about the pre-nuptial agreement.

'That's plain to see,' Mr Lewis said. 'He's the sort of man wouldn't be interested in you if you were.'

If only he knew, Cleo thought. She didn't want a date with Mr Heir To The Roth Millions because of who he was: she wanted a date so she could humiliate him the way he'd humiliated her. Then she'd be happy.

'You'd swear you liked him the way you're worried about what to wear on this date,' Trish grumbled as she sat on the floor in their shared bedroom. The bed was covered with all Cleo's clothes, most of Trish's clothes, and some belonging to Diane, who also shared the house, and who had a real eye when it came to vintage stuff.

'Course I don't like him,' said Cleo. 'Don't be ridiculous. And it's not a date.' She turned sideways to try to see Diane's flippy black lace skirt in the mirror from another angle. Diane said she normally wore it with a pastel pink scoop-neck top, but Cleo wasn't sure if pink was her colour. And with her long legs, the skirt was shorter than it was on Diane and just skimmed her knees. 'I'm not sure about the skirt and is the top too low?' she asked, pulling at the neck and considering the effect her cleavage had on it.

'Too low? Too bloody high, if you ask me,' Trish said. 'You don't want to look like you've just got off the bus from Ballygobackwards.'

'I don't want to look like a total slapper either,' Cleo said, twisting some more at the mirror. 'That's what he thought the first time.'

'Oh, don't go on about it,' grumbled Trish. This was a minor bone of contention between them. Trish was the one who'd been so deliriously drunk that she had tarred her companions with the same brush. 'It wasn't my fault. I was only celebrating. And who cares anyway?'

'I care,' said Cleo. 'It's not the ideal message for women to be giving out to the world at large: that we get so plastered we fall down outside clubs and have blackouts.' And certainly not the message to give to handsome men that, under other circumstances, you'd like to impress.

'Men do it,' countered Trish, 'why not women?'

'If it had been anywhere else but in Carrickwell . . .' Cleo said. 'People talk and my family would be mortified to imagine I'd been sitting drunkenly in the gutter. To think of the times myself and Dad have helped people out of the hotel bar when they're plastered . . .'

'Have any of your precious family been on the phone discussing it with you?' asked Trish tartly.

'No.' None of Cleo's family had been on the phone at all. An even sorer point. 'Truce?' she added.

'Truce. Sorry. That was bitchy,' Trish said mournfully.

'Forget it. What about this?' Cleo twirled in the black lace skirt with a simple white shirt.

'Classy,' commented Trish. 'Honestly, Cleo, anybody watching would think you were crazy about this guy.'

'I don't like him,' Cleo insisted again.

'Then why are you going out with him?'

Cleo had asked herself the same question all day. 'It's about revenge.'

'You could have got that without going out with him,' Trish pointed out. 'Connect his room TV to the porn channel for hours on end so he gets the most embarrassing bill on the planet, put laxative into his breakfast, book him alarm calls every fifteen minutes from three a.m. – there are *endless* things you could have done,' she finished airily.

'You have an evil mind,' said Cleo in amazement.

'Thanks,' grinned Trish.

'That's all too sneaky.' Cleo didn't like sneakiness. 'When I get my own back, I want him to know I did.'

When she walked into McArthur's and saw Tyler sitting in the lobby, sleek dark head bent studiously over *Newsweek*, the taste for revenge momentarily weakened. He wore dark trousers, a fine knitted sweater that moulded his powerful shoulders, and was receiving admiring looks from the girls on reception. Cleo decided that it had been a bad idea to meet him here in gossip central: the fact that they were going out would be on the news next.

Tyler glanced up and looked genuinely pleased to see her, as if this was an ordinary date. Hell, thought Cleo. This lying stuff was harder than she'd thought.

'You look beautiful,' he said, getting to his feet. He leaned down and kissed her formally on the cheek.

In her borrowed outfit, with her hair flowing loose around her shoulders and her eyes made up in beguiling shades, Cleo knew she looked her best. 'Thank you,' she replied, as directed by all those magazine articles on graciously accepting compliments. Saying 'I borrowed the skirt and my hair's a bit woolly because I'm out of serum' would have sounded stupid.

'You look nice too,' Cleo said. She was a modern woman, after all, and didn't believe that compliments should be the preserve of the male. And he did look pretty good.

'Thanks,' he nodded, seeming pleased. 'What's the plan, Cleo?'

She was a bit taken aback by this because she'd anticipated a whole battle over what they'd do and had been quite looking forward to it. Maybe Tyler confined his ruthless persona to business matters.

'The plan is there's no plan,' she replied, although there was. She'd spent the whole day working it out, which had rendered her reasonably useless as a receptionist. 'I'm going to take you on a walk round the parts of Dublin the tourists don't see,' she said. 'Not that there's anything wrong with the tourist trail, but I don't want you to think that we're all about old knitted *geansais* and woolly hats.'

'What's a geansaí?' He hadn't heard it quite right.

'Gan,' she said, 'zee. It means jumper, sweater, jersey.'

'Can you teach me any other words?' he asked enthusiastically.

Cleo grinned. He'd definitely left the ruthless streak in his suite. 'Of course.'

They walked into the city, enjoying the warm early summer air, and talking non-stop. Walking made it easier to talk, Cleo found. If she wasn't looking at Tyler, she could be more normal, but when she stared up at his face, she found herself behaving strangely. Like some idiot girl who fancies a guy like crazy, she thought. How utterly embarrassing.

Finally, they arrived at the French restaurant Cleo had chosen. Both of them were starving, and ordered quickly. Cleo had scallops, Tyler had Dublin Bay prawns. A flock of girls in flirty dresses showing lots of leg sashayed past their table, and a couple of them eyed up Tyler very openly.

'How trashy,' said Cleo crossly.

Tyler did that arching thing with the eyebrows that irritated her so much. He seemed to like teasing her.

'Too much gold, too much flesh and too much bleach,' she snapped in explanation.

'You disapprove of too much flesh, then?' Tyler asked silkily. 'I guess it's a religious thing. You're Catholic, right? And you went to school in a convent and wouldn't dream of having sex before marriage, and confess your sins to a priest, right?'

As soon as scientists came up with eye lasers to blast people with a single glance, Cleo was getting one. 'For your information, Mr Roth, while I did go to a convent school . . .' he grinned evilly at this, 'I consider myself a Christian first and foremost. Some people describe it as being an à la carte Catholic: we pick what we want from the menu. The same way you're an à la carte Jew,' she added sweetly, nodding at his plate. 'If you were orthodox, you would not be eating that prawn.'

Tyler just smiled at her and speared another prawn, before biting into it with his very white teeth.

'My first boyfriend was Jewish,' she said by way of explanation. 'He was very interesting on Jewish customs.'

'Rebelling even then, huh? And the same for him, dating a *shiksa*?'

'He respected my cultural heritage just the same as I respected his,' snapped Cleo, enraged yet again.

'I respect your heritage, Cleo,' Tyler said equably. 'I'm just winding you up because it's such fun. You are so windable. Is that a word? You Irish are supposed to be the literary geniuses, you should know.'

'If Ireland's famous for literary geniuses, what's Manhattan famous for then?' she growled. 'Smartasses who ought to go home and mind their own business?'

'I remember the other thing Ireland's famed for – the friendliness,' Tyler added with great insincerity.

Cleo changed her mind: he could be ruthless and edgy when he wanted.

'That's the other great Irish schtick, isn't it?' Tyler went on. 'A hundred thousand welcomes. *Cead* míle fáilte.' He pronounced the Irish words perfectly. 'I love those Irish phrases. What's that other one . . . ? "Thanks be to God." That's cute. What's it in Gaelic?'

He was winding her up, Cleo told herself. '*Buíochas le Dia*,' she translated.

'Wonderful,' Tyler nodded in delight and if he hadn't been so irritating when he was being smart, she would think he looked adorable.

Even his ears suited him. Not those big jugs that stuck out of the side of some men's heads when they had cropped hairstyles. No. Tyler Roth's ears were neat, refined, sat close to the perfectly shaped skull and didn't detract from the chiselled masculinity of his jaw. God, why was she noticing these things?

'Irish phrases are so cute. Like the girls. No offence.' He held up his hands. 'I wouldn't care to offend you, Cleo, by implying anything with that comment. Gender equality is an important belief in Roth Hotels. One of our core beliefs.'

Cleo nodded. A fabulous idea had just occurred to her. 'I can see that equality is important to you,' she said gravely. 'Actually, I thought of another cute Irish phrase.'

'Really?'

'Really. You'll love it. It's very you. *Póg mo thon*.' Surely whoever had taught him his few Irish phrases wouldn't have taught him how to say 'kiss my backside'?

'What's that mean?' he asked.

'It means good luck,' said Cleo, smiling broadly. 'It's one of the older sayings, dates back to the er . . . Brian Boru years, I think.' A bit of historical flimflam would impress him. 'And because it's so old, it's considered pure Irish, rich and full of meaning. "May the glorious luck of the Irish and the blessing of God be upon you at all times" is the longer, probably more accurate translation.'

'It's a short phrase to say all that, isn't it?'

'Irish is a lyrical and unusual language,' Cleo pointed out. 'Simple words have many meanings.'

'Get you. Say it again so I can learn it,' he commanded.

Cleo had to bite the inside of her cheek to stop herself laughing.

'Pogue – a bit like the word rogue … mmo hoe-in, but say it quickly. Hoe-in. Ho-in.'

'Pog mo thoin,' he repeated. 'Gotcha.'

Yes, Cleo smiled inwardly. Gotcha. She couldn't wait to see him tell people to kiss his ass in Irish.

They talked about their jobs. Pride meant Cleo deliberately didn't tell him about the Willow or her rapid departure from Carrick-well. She was sure he'd know about her beloved hotel if he'd been sniffing around Carrickwell for land to buy, and somehow she didn't want him to know that she was one of the people who'd essentially run a beautiful hotel into the ground. For the same reason, she'd told him her surname was Malley. Malin wasn't a common name.

Tyler explained that he'd worked his way up through the family business.

'People think nepotism gets you everywhere,' he said. 'It gets your foot in the door, but you've got to work to get on. My dad believes in hard work for everyone and harder work for me. He says he used to push himself twice as hard as everyone else because the buck stopped with him, and that's what I do too.'

Cleo would have loved to have explained about her upbringing, but she didn't. Her parents were retired from a small business, she said, miserably aware she was deceiving him and disliking herself for it.

Tyler lived in Manhattan and it sounded like another world to Cleo.

'Where are you living?' he asked.

'With my friend Trish,' Cleo said before she'd had time to think about it. Staying with her best friend and sharing Trish's not precisely comfortable futon would not sound like the behaviour of a thrusting young hotel executive.

'An apartment in the city?' asked Tyler.

'Er, no, a house, a town house actually, with another friend of ours,' Cleo added. It wasn't entirely untrue. Trish did live in a house and there was a friend living with her. Another six in fact. Still, it wasn't as if Tyler was ever going to see it. 'We're outside the city, we prefer a more laid-back lifestyle, you know; the city's so busy.' City apartments were way beyond the gang's collective means.

'Right,' said Tyler, nodding in understanding.

The plan was to end the night in a pub, the Shepherd, where Trish and Cleo had spent so many evenings when they were in college. As arranged, Trish and some of the gang were there. As Cleo *hadn't* sent the emergency text message that meant 'Help, this

184

is a nightmare, phone me and get me out of here!', Trish was waiting, eyes on stalks to see what Tyler was like. He must have passed some invisible test if Cleo was still with him and there had been no involvement with security guards or the police.

'Hi, Cleo, long time no see!' chirped Trish across the bar as Tyler and Cleo arrived.

The whole bar craned their heads to look and there was a buzz of approval at the sight of such a handsome couple.

'I didn't know we were meeting your friends,' was all Tyler said as he followed her to the gang at the corner table.

'I didn't know they'd be here,' Cleo said, sure she was being unconvincing.

'What a surprise!' Trish went on, hamming it up like the third spear carrier in an amateur theatre production.

Settling down on the stool beside Trish, Cleo gave her a poke in the ribs to say shut up.

'Drink, anyone?' asked Tyler.

Miraculously, the whole group, eight of them, had just finished their drinks and would have another, thank you very much. Tyler didn't quail at the size of the order.

'That's two pints of Guinness, a Paddy, two Diet Cokes, a Heineken, an orange juice for you . . .' Diane, whose skirt Cleo was wearing, smiled, 'a gin and tonic . . .' Trish batted her eyelids, 'and a sparkling water for Cleo.'

As he went to the bar, Cleo glared at the rest of them. 'Have you lot no pride?' she demanded. 'He's my date, not the Allied Irish Bank!'

'Sorry,' several of them chorused.

'Yeah, sorry,' said Barry, owner of the treasured REM CDs.

'Didn't mean to be scroungey,' muttered Ron, who, Trish said, never put the loo seat down.

'Your date, is he?' murmured Trish. 'I thought he was the living incarnation of revenge being a dish best served cold.'

'Shudup,' hissed Cleo, but she was smiling. 'I'm working on it.'

'I think he's gorgeous,' said Trish's new friend, Carol. She was indeed model material. Slender as a reed, palely blonde and very Gwyneth Paltrow.

Cleo said nothing.

Tyler fitted into the group very well, mainly because he had the gift of being able to talk to anybody. Carol, in particular, was very chatty with him and to Cleo's intense irritation, Tyler chatted right back.

It was when Carol was offering to show him around – how *dare* she? – that Tyler said he'd try out his Irish phrases to see if he could remember them. Everyone applauded his *cead mille failte*, and his *go raibh maith agat*. But what really made them fall off their stools laughing was when he told Trish to *'pog mo thoin'*.

'Cleo, you brat, I bet you taught him that! What a nasty trick!' Carol said, patting Tyler's arm in a very intimate gesture.

'So it doesn't mean what you said it did,' Tyler said, unperturbed.

Cleo was puce with mortification at this proof of her nastiness.

'No!' shrieked Carol, still clinging, as she explained the true definition.

'Cleo likes teasing me,' Tyler said. 'Don't you?'

And he stared at her. Cleo felt her heart flip.

'He's nice, isn't he?' said Trish in surprise an hour later, as she, Cleo and the rest of the housemates sat on the Nightlink bus, nicknamed the Drinklink because people took it home after a night on the town. None of the housemates' funds ran to taxis, although Cleo had pretended to Tyler she was getting one. It would look so uncool to clamber onto the bus with the lads like a couple of school girls while he was hopping into a cab.

'He is lovely,' Cleo said, sitting back on the bus seat dreamily, ignoring the diesel fumes. More than lovely.

'Of course, there's no future in it,' Trish went on. 'He's an international, rich, playboy type with a wealthy daddy. He's probably got a million girls on the go,' she added. 'Those guys always do.'

'Yeah,' said Cleo, feeling downcast. She knew that someone like Tyler could easily have a girlfriend in every port but all evening he'd talked to her as though she was the only person in the universe, despite the horrible Carol's attempts to cling to him. He'd loved talking to everyone else in the group, sure, but he was one of those people who made you feel as if he was there for you alone. It was very flattering.

'It's just a laugh,' she said now to Trish, and then she realised she was lying. She had never really lied to Trish before. You weren't supposed to lie to best friends and they had been through so much together. But Trish would laugh at her if she told her that she no longer wanted to get some horrible revenge on Tyler Roth. She had changed her mind. Instead, she wanted to feel his arms around her, holding her close, and to feel his breath on her skin. How had this happened?

There was an envelope marked 'personal' for her at her place on reception the next morning. More of Tyler's extravagant scrawl. Funny how his handwriting didn't look so much like that of a tyrant any more. Forceful, Cleo would have said now, if asked to describe the writer of the short missive.

For a man of many words, Tyler was succinct in print: 'Second date? What would you like to do? Don't want to ride roughshod all over you.'

For a giddy moment, Cleo imagined Tyler Roth booted and spurred, ready to ride roughshod. Then she dragged herself back to the current century. Get a grip, Cleo!

'Mr Roth left that for you,' said Stan, one of Cleo's old friends from the night shift. 'But he has your name wrong on the envelope. He's written "Cleo Malley" not "Malin".'

'You didn't correct him?' asked Cleo anxiously.

'Nah,' said Stan, 'he was in a rush. Going into breakfast for a meeting with some woman, some babe I should say!' he added appreciatively.

'A *babe*?' said Cleo, in much the same way as Lady Bracknell enunciated the word '*handbag*'.

Stan, clearing up his things to make way for the day shift, nodded. 'Some guys have all the luck,' he muttered.

The thought of the babe bounced around in Cleo's brain for the next hour and a half. Whom exactly would Stan consider 'a babe'? Someone utterly stunning, or more of a girl-next-door type? That question haunted her.

But it was impossible to concentrate on checking out the man in Number 172, who insisted that he hadn't had anything from the mini-bar, even though housekeeping had logged him down as having consumed two whiskeys, three vodkas and a Toblerone when they had gone in at turn-down the night before. Cleo was working alongside Norah, Paige and a sweet Italian guy called Nero. She processed Mr Liar from Number 172, then turned to Paige, who was beside her.

'I'm just going to the loo, OK?' she whispered and fled. She did go to the loo, for a quick look at her flushed face, and then she went into the dining room where breakfast was being served. It was still only half-eight but the majority of the business clientele had either left or were finishing off their breakfast meetings. The people staying in McArthur's for fun were beginning to amble down for their breakfast, their relaxed dress and progress a sharp contrast to the business-suited men and women, who had places to go to, people to see and no time for another Danish pastry.

Cleo tried to look as if she was on official hotel business rather than spying on Tyler bloody Roth. She peered round the enormous dining room as if searching for a particular guest so she could deliver an important message. Then she spotted him. At a nice, intimate table, without his henchman, Larry McKenzie. It was just

Tyler and a woman who could indeed be described as a babe. Exquisitely groomed, dressed in black, she had the shiny mahogany hair that Cleo envied. All glossy and *'I don't need serum for my hair, thank you very much.'* Cleo turned in fury and flounced out of the restaurant. How dare he? That woman was hardly a breakfast meeting – she was breakfast!

'You feeling OK?' whispered Paige when she got back to the reception desk.

'I'm fine,' hissed Cleo.

Paige nodded sagely. 'You can tell me at break,' she said.

By the time Tyler appeared, later that afternoon, Cleo was a shimmering haze of bad temper. The Malin family would have known that when Cleo's eyes glittered and her normally smiling mouth set like concrete into a thin line, it was time to beware.

Tyler Roth, on the other hand, had no idea.

'Hi,' he said, leaning down on the reception desk and giving Cleo a sexily lazy look that last night would have melted her bones. Today, her bones were hard as reinforced steel.

'Hello,' she said frostily.

He suddenly caught on that something was amiss.

'Bad day?' he asked, arching one eyebrow.

Cleo thought of how he hadn't shrugged off Carol the night before, and how he'd breakfasted with an identikit glamour babe, albeit with different hair, this morning. He probably did have a girl in every city in the world.

'Oh, leave me alone,' she snapped.

'What's up with you, Cleo?' he said equably.

'I have an early business breakfast tomorrow,' she said, 'and I want to go home and fix my hair, my make-up and my nails so I'm perfect for it.'

Ah, he got it.

'Do you have spies all over the hotel?' he asked.

'Not spies – they're my friends, they tell me things. Like when a guy who is interested in me suddenly has a very cosy breakfast with another woman.'

'Right,' said Tyler, 'you mean gossip?'

'I do not mean gossip!' she snapped back.

'If I told you she was gay would that make a difference?' he asked.

'She's gay?' said Cleo. 'The girl you met is gay?' That did make a slight difference. It was unlikely that Tyler was interested in the babe romantically, if she was indeed gay, but then some men loved a challenge. 'Is she gay?' she demanded.

'No,' he admitted. 'I just thought I'd check if it made any difference.'

'You bastard,' she said. 'You are so annoying. Why did I go out with you last night?'

'Because you like me?' he said.

'No, I don't,' Cleo replied. 'I don't like people who go off and have breakfast with strange women and then laugh at me and pretend the strange woman is gay and –'

'Well,' he interrupted, 'if I said it was a business meeting, which it was, you wouldn't have believed me; you'd have thought I was trying to throw you off the scent. In fact, it was a business meeting. She just happens to be an extremely lovely woman.' He enjoyed saying it, Cleo was sure. 'A woman I do find extremely attractive,' Tyler went on.

Cleo controlled the urge to hit him.

'However,' Tyle continued, 'she's happily married and has no interest in me whatsoever – not that I've ever tried, in case you want to know. We talk business, that's all. You're the one who's so hot on career women. Don't you think it's possible for a woman to have a great career and look good? *You* do both.'

'Don't think you'll get round me by flattering me,' Cleo snapped, although she had to admit she was a bit gratified. It did all sound very plausible, but then maybe Tyler was the sort of guy who always had a plausible excuse for his behaviour.

Cleo decided that she wasn't going to be one of his conquests. 'I'm sorry,' she said formally, getting to her feet. 'You know this was a mistake. You and I, we come from different worlds. I must have been out of my mind to have dinner with you. Thank you for a nice evening, but goodbye.'

He reached out and grabbed her wrist gently, but firmly. 'Don't be like that,' he said, 'please.'

'Should I scream and demand the police be called because you're holding me against my will?' she said.

'You can go if you want,' he said softly, and his dark eyes raked over her face, 'but I wish you wouldn't. I want to get to know you, Cleo. Can't I do that? Maybe we do come from different places, but so what? Can't Manhattan and Carrickwell have a merger too?' It sounded so ridiculous that she had to laugh and she sat down on her seat again. She knew when she was beaten. 'OK, you win, you're a big eejit but you win.'

'What is this eejit thing everybody keeps saying?' Tyler said.

'Mmm,' said Cleo thoughtfully, 'it means wonderful, wise person . . .'

'Bullshit,' he laughed 'you're kidding me again, right, like with those Irish translations? You do not get me a second time, Miss Malley.'

Cleo winced at the fact that he still didn't know her real surname. She couldn't tell him now. She'd tell him later.

They went out again on Sunday evening, this time to the cinema, although Cleo found it hard to remember much about the film – she was so completely aware of sitting close to Tyler, holding his hand. It felt wonderful.

She knew it wasn't just a physical attraction: she liked him, she liked the way he laughed, liked the way he gently teased her, liked the way he was interested in her. It seemed a strange thing to admit, but she felt as if she'd known him for years. He might have a ruthless streak in business, but there was another side of Tyler Roth too. A side she loved seeing.

Tyler was due to fly to Galway on Monday morning for the property auction, and Cleo was miserably aware that their little romance was coming to an end. He'd go back to his world, she'd stay in hers, and his line of girlfriends in every city would claim him again.

Would she be the Dublin girlfriend? No, Cleo didn't want to be just another number in his phone. That wasn't enough. The more time she got to spend with him, the more she fell in love.

And she was in love with him. She was sure of that. She wouldn't have believed it possible to fall in love with someone so quickly if it hadn't happened to her.

After the cinema Tyler asked her to come back to his suite for a nightcap. Against her better judgement she agreed.

'I want to say goodbye properly,' he'd said.

'I hope you don't think that saying goodbye properly means bouncing up and down on the bed,' Cleo reprimanded him sternly to hide how miserable she was feeling.

'Hey, do I look like that sort of guy?' Tyler teased, as he hailed a taxi.

Cleo had never been in one of the hotel's penthouse suites. She'd seen many of the other bedrooms, but there were only four penthouse suites and on the day she'd had her orientation tour, they hadn't been included. Tyler's suite was every bit as grand and luxurious as she'd imagined. McArthur's Hotel prided itself on simple but classy interior décor. Your feet sank into the carpets, your body sank into the huge, velvety couches and she was pretty sure that the rest of you would sink deliciously into the linen sheets too.

'Nice room,' she said nonchalantly, as she walked around admiring the white roses in the simple, square vase on the low coffee table.

'Yeah, it's lovely,' Tyler said, 'really beautiful.'

And she liked him for that, for not being so used to richness and luxury that he thought it was normal. If only he'd seen the cramped bedroom she was sharing with Trish at the moment.

'What would you like to drink?' Tyler said, taking off his jacket and laying it on the back of a chair. He was wearing an open-necked shirt that revealed a tiny triangle of dark skin at the neck. Was there anything sexier than that little bit of a man? Cleo moistened her lips.

'Mmm, I'd love some tea actually. Camomile would be nice.' Camomile would help her sleep and she wasn't sure if she would when she got home because she was so wound up after the excitement of the day.

He sat on the edge of the armchair and picked up the phone to ring housekeeping.

He ordered two camomile teas, which was sweet, Cleo thought. Most guys hated it. Nat used to say it tasted like something you'd sweep up from the backyard, though he'd tried it to please Cleo. How different he and Tyler were, she reflected. Nat was a pleaser, a puppy dog of a person, while Tyler was aloof and aggressively leonine, and first impressions would suggest he wouldn't want to please anyone but himself. Yet here was this Alpha Male trying to please her. There was something incredibly attractive and seductive about that. And he'd be gone soon. Cleo felt herself sink a little on the inside.

'So,' he said, and sat down on one end of the couch. She was sitting on the other end. It was a big couch.

'So,' she said back, smiling at him.

'Do I look as though I bite?' he said, patting the space between them.

'You mean you don't?' Cleo said.

He grinned and slid up beside her. 'We're probably rushing this,' he said, 'but you know I'm flying to Galway tomorrow and off to New York the day after that . . .'

'Yes, I know,' she agreed gravely. 'You need to get to first base before you go.'

'It's not like that,' he said, and he actually looked offended. 'You're not that sort of girl, Cleo, and I'm not that sort of guy.'

'That's not what I've heard,' she said, suddenly serious. She didn't want to get hurt, not by Tyler. She didn't want to be the Nat person in this relationship: trusting and naïve, not able to see reality and mortally wounded when the blow came.

'Forget what you've heard,' Tyler said harshly. 'People talk about me, they'll talk about you, that doesn't mean they know anything. I don't mess around with women and I don't mess women around,' he said, and he looked so serious that Cleo had an urge to run her fingers along the side of his face to smooth away the lines.

'What are you thinking?' he said, leaning disturbingly close.

And she laughed. 'I was thinking the service in this hotel is outrageous because you ordered our tea at least five minutes ago and there's no sign of it.'

'There is definitely a job for a woman of your capabilities in Roth Hotels,' Tyler said.

'So that's why you've brought me up here?'

'No,' he said, and he moved infinitesimally closer. He put one arm around her and Cleo felt that heat of excitement again. They were so close now, she could feel the warmth of his body. 'That's not why I brought you up here,' he said, 'and if you believe it is, you must think this is the strangest job interview ever.'

She grinned. 'I thought you brought me up here because you liked me,' she said, 'and I came because I like you,' she added.

'I'm glad,' he said softly, and then his mouth was upon hers and their arms were around each other, his hands moving over her. It was like nothing she had ever known before – none of the fumblings with Laurent in Bristol, no kissing with any other boyfriend, nothing. This heat, this excitement was something new, something special, something entirely to do with Tyler. She moaned his name and pulled him closely to her as his mouth moved to the curve of her jaw, to the soft place under her earlobe, down her neck, touching her gently. And suddenly, Cleo knew that she wanted to rip all Tyler's clothes off, have him rip all her clothes off and to make wild love there and then. Have him touching her, caressing her, saying her name . . .

'We shouldn't,' he said, breathing heavily.

'I know,' she said, and at the same time his fingers were fumbling with the wrap ties on her cardigan and hers were undoing the buttons on his shirt.

'It's a mistake because it's too soon,' Tyler was saying, his hands tenderly skimming over her skin as if he couldn't get enough of her.

'I know, too soon, too soon . . .' Cleo added, her face buried in his hair, her fingers touching the plane of his muscled chest.

'We really ought to wait,' he said.

'Absolutely,' Cleo said, her hands feeling his heart pound in his chest.

The phone rang: a blistering shriek that Cleo had never realised the phones in McArthur's could make until that precious moment.

'Shit,' said Tyler, and he pulled away.

'Shit,' said Cleo, hurriedly pulling the front of her wrap top together.

He picked up the phone. 'Hi. Yeah, sure, no, no problem,' he said. 'It's only eleven here, so I guess it's what, five, four back home?'

He sat down at the desk, pulled a pad towards him and started to write, shooting an apologetic glance at Cleoand mouthing, 'It's urgent.'

She held a hand up to say no, it's fine, and got up and went into the bathroom to tidy herself up. Her mouth looked bruised and swollen in the mirror, her pupils were dilated and her hair was a wild tangled mess. Yes, she looked like she had just been kissing wildly on a couch.

She used Tyler's mouthwash and ran her fingers through her hair to try to tame it. There was no comb. Tyler's dark hair was so shorn he probably never used one. She peered into his toilet bag to see what sort of unguents and aftershave he used. It felt intimate, but they'd just been kissing after all, which meant that it was probably just this side of acceptable.

She came out. Tyler was still on the phone and he looked at her and rolled his eyes. 'Sorry,' he mouthed. He put a hand over the phone. 'Crisis at head office, got to deal with it.'

'That's OK,' she said.

Of course, the camomile tea would choose then to arrive and the person who delivered it would have to be a member of staff that Cleo knew. Xi, a beautiful Chinese girl, smiled in surprised confusion when Cleo opened the door.

'Hello,' Xi said.

'Hi,' said Cleo, feeling her face go hot. 'Thanks, Xi,' she said. 'Yeah, I'll take it, thanks.' She didn't have any money for a tip, but anyway wouldn't it be crass for a member of staff, who was improperly in a guest's hotel bedroom, to tip another member of staff? Who knew? Etiquette books didn't cover that situation.

She poured her tea, and some for Tyler, left it beside him and then ambled round the suite, looking at things. He had a travel chess set out on the coffee table amidst the papers and magazines and she wondered who his opponent was because he was mid-game. She sat down and flicked through the magazines. Under a society magazine she found a folder with architect's beautifully coloured pen and ink drawing on the front. It was sideways, so she turned it round to look at it. It was oddly familiar. And then she realised – it was the Willow Hotel. An architect's drawing of her home, but much improved and vastly bigger. Only the façade of the house was the same, though it was cleaned up: there was no wisteria climbing untidily all over the portico, no cracked stone urns outside the door. It looked beautiful.

Cleo sank back into the cushions and flicked through the loose pages in the folder. She didn't care whether Tyler saw her or not, although he appeared too preoccupied on the phone to notice. There were several aerial photos, along with architect's sketches and three-dimensional computer drawings of how the Willow would look when it was a grand Roth Hotel – for that was what was written in elegant script to one side of the drawing on the front – the Carrickwell Roth. Much bigger, much more imposing, much more beautiful than before. Her family home and her birthright, looking every bit as wonderful as she knew it could. Except this time, she wouldn't be involved.

Cleo's hands were shaking when she put the bits of paper back into the folder and replaced it on the coffee table, with the magazines on top. Tyler was in another world now, talking, writing and gesticulating on the phone. He hadn't touched his camomile tea. Bloody typical, he'd only said he wanted it so he'd get her into bed. She was sure of it. A liar and a corporate raider, Cleo thought angrily. The town house developer who had supposedly bought the Willow was obviously a front for Roth Hotels. Her family had betrayed her by selling up in the first place but Roth Hotels had betrayed them all with this underhand dealing. Cleo was sure her father would have kept the Willow running, no matter what, rather than sell to another hotel group. Was that how Roth bought their valuable sites – by pretending to be someone other than a vastly rich hotel group? Was the Galway land sale a front for another purchase, some other little hotel on the verge of breakdown with an owner who might sell to a local developer but never, ever to Roth Hotels?

Tyler put his hand over the receiver. 'Hang on, Cleo, won't be long. Us New Yorkers have no concept that the rest of the world is in different time zones,' he joked.

She didn't even look at him. She couldn't bear to, not now. Because she had liked Tyler Roth, really liked him.

Thank God she hadn't told him her name was really Malin. It would be too humiliating for him to find out that she was a part of the family who had owned the Willow and who had run it into the ground. She wouldn't give him that satisfaction. She took a long, steadying gulp of her camomile tea, gathered up her things, and walked to the door.

Tyler was so busy on the phone that he never noticed Cleo walk out of his life.

CHAPTER THIRTEEN

For a week after Alex had told her it was over, Daisy stayed at home doing her grocery shopping on the internet and nipping out to the corner shop every couple of days for things like chocolate.

She didn't bump into anyone she knew there: they wouldn't have recognised her, anyway. With a baseball hat pulled over unwashed hair and huddled into an old sweater of Alex's that still smelled of him, she was unrecognisable. He'd taken nearly all of his clothes when she'd been in Düsseldorf, lots of his possessions too. He'd left only the big things, like the TV they'd bought together and a few pictures. The apartment looked bleak without all the little things that had made it his home.

Sitting on her own in misery, Daisy didn't answer the phone, although she jumped every time it rang in case it was Alex. It never was. The machine got all the calls: from Mary to see how the 'flu' was, from Paula, from Daisy's old friend Fay, and once, from her mother, saying she was going on holiday to Prague this summer with Daisy's aunt, who was recuperating from an operation.

Her mother liked talking to the answering machine and had a far livelier chat with it than she ever had with Daisy. Answering machines never had their own opinions and just listened.

'I wasn't going to go because your Aunt Imogen thought she wasn't well enough but she is, so we're off. Brendan from next door is going to go in and check the post. See you when I get back. Hope all's well. Cheerio.'

Ensconced in her den on the couch with the duvet wrapped around herself and the crumbs of a bar of chocolate on the lamp table beside her, Daisy stared sorrowfully at the phone. Cheerio? What kind of a thing was that for a mother to say to her daughter? No 'I love you, sweetheart, and will miss you'. But then how could Nan Farrell miss her daughter when they rarely saw each other?

Daisy had planned to raise *her* baby with more warmth and

love. None of that children-should-be-seen-and-not-heard rubbish her mother's family liked. Daisy's child wouldn't have been sent off to the nursery to have tea away from her parents or shipped off to boarding school. That was what had turned her mother into the person she was.

Daisy's children would have been adored and cuddled. They'd have snuggled up on the couch with her and giggled their way through *Monsters, Inc.*

There was an emergency bar of caramel still in the cupboard. Daisy went to get it. Then she turned the TV up very loud. That way, she couldn't hear herself think.

After a week at home, in which there were strangely no calls from her and Alex's collective friends, Daisy emerged into the real world half a stone heavier and with a break-out of spots. She would have stayed in her cocoon for ever, but knew she couldn't. She had to go back to work and, who knew, it might feel less painful to be with other people? But how was she going to tell anyone?

In the end, she didn't have to say anything. When Daisy arrived at Georgia's Tiara at ten in the morning, Mary took one look at her and knew that whatever had kept Daisy out of work, it hadn't been flu.

'What happened?' Mary had been marking up the stock list with a biro. She put them down and came rushing over.

'Alex's in love with Louise and she's pregnant,' whispered Daisy. It was like telling her mother should have been.

'Louise?'

'His assistant in work. Is my life a cliché or what?'

Neither of them laughed.

'I don't know what to say, Daisy,' said Mary. 'No, I do. Let's close the shop and go to Mo's for a late breakfast.'

'Not all of us. I don't want to tell Paula,' begged Daisy, thinking that she couldn't possibly bear having Paula pity her.

'We'll say nothing,' Mary said. 'Tell her we're off for a chat and I don't want to leave her taking care of the shop on her own in her last week of work.'

'I'd forgotten she was going on maternity leave,' said Daisy dully. This week they'd planned to have a baby shower in Mary's house with all Paula's friends coming. Daisy didn't dare ask if it was still going ahead. She'd bought the present already: two exquisitely soft babygros, one in white and one in yellow velour. She'd ask Mary to give the gift to Paula. There was no way she could cope with going now.

Mary put an arm round her. 'I saw a book recently on how to

put a hex on an ex-boyfriend. Should we buy it and give it a go? I'm convinced that Zara in Mystical Fires has white witch para-phernalia at the back of the shop. She's bound to be able to put a hex on Alex.'

Daisy laughed in spite of herself, although she wasn't sure if it was at the thought of sweet Zara putting a hex on *anyone*, or at the image of Alex suffering. 'Why don't I cut out the middle man and simply go round and shoot him myself?'

Mo's Diner was only a decade old, yet seemed always to have been part of Carrickwell. The look was 'fifties American diner, with mini jukeboxes on the Formica tables, cherry-red banquettes in the booths and scores of pictures of Elvis, Mo's icon, on the walls. The waiters and waitresses dressed as if for an amateur dramatic version of *Grease*, with the girls in swirling skirts, ponytails and bobby socks, and the guys in drainpipes and shirts with sleeves carefully rolled up to bicep level like James Dean.

Mo himself was all-American, despite coming from County Clare and, after half a lifetime in Memphis, had come back to Ireland with a bit of Tennessee with him. His diner served grits, coffee, burgers and ice-cream sodas, and people had been known to fight over his blueberry muffins. A job in Mo's was prized and many a Carrickwell student had supplemented college by waiting tables at weekends.

The early morning breakfasters were gone and there was a lull at Mo's when Mary and Daisy slid into a booth at the back. 'Love Me Tender' was playing soulfully in the background.

Mary didn't say 'spill' the way she normally did when there was a bit of gossip to be heard. She waited until they'd ordered before placing both hands on the table and leaning forward, waiting for Daisy to start.

'Alex said we needed time apart just before I went to Düssel-dorf,' Daisy began.

'Time apart, pah!' hissed Mary. 'What was his excuse? Some-thing lame, I'm sure.'

Daisy sighed. 'We'd had an appointment with a fertility clinic and he said he needed time to think about it.'

'Oh ...' Mary looked astonished. 'I had no idea,' she said, stunned.

'I couldn't tell you, Mary. It was too painful to talk about. You have kids and Paula's pregnant, I didn't think you'd understand what I was feeling. I thought you'd say I was being overdramatic or –'

'I hope I wouldn't have said anything so hurtful,' Mary said

197

fervently. 'Having children doesn't mean I can't empathise with anyone who longs for them. Having my kids is the most wonderful thing that's ever happened to me,' she added simply. 'If I hadn't been able to have them, it would have been agony. I've always wanted children, so, no, I wouldn't have thought you were being overdramatic. I'm sorry you couldn't tell me what you were going through. I feel as if I've let you down.'

Daisy shrugged. 'You didn't let me down. My ovaries have or something else has. Who knows what? We've been trying to have a baby since I turned thirty – well, I've been trying since I turned thirty – and I decided to do something about it instead of simply buying pregnancy testing kits and crying when I wasn't pregnant. So I rang a few infertility clinics, made an appointment with one and when I told Alex, he wasn't keen – I *knew* he wasn't keen.'

Mary reached across and squeezed Daisy's hand.

'I thought it was simply that it was all too fast and he was scared,' Daisy went on. 'It is your basic male nightmare after all: masturbating into a cup, having someone analyse your sperm count – who wouldn't be scared? But we could have had a baby at the end of it and I'd have done anything for that.'

A very young waiter with embryonic sideburns delivered their coffee and muffins.

'And then?' prompted Mary when he was gone.

Daisy broke up her muffin with her fingers but didn't eat any of it. 'He said we needed a break.'

'And you said, why?'

'And I said why,' agreed Daisy. 'He needed time out or something, he said.'

'Liar.' Mary aimed a sugar lump at her coffee and lobbed it in.

'I believed him.'

'Why didn't you tell me? You went to Düsseldorf knowing this. Jesus, Daisy, you should have said. We could have cancelled Düsseldorf. How did you go and work with all this misery hanging over you?'

'If I hadn't gone,' pointed out Daisy, 'I wouldn't have rushed home from the airport to his office ready to tell him we didn't need to have a baby and that our love was enough and then I wouldn't have found out the truth.'

Mary winced.

Daisy kept breaking her muffin into smaller and smaller crumbs. 'Going away was the catalyst. I had this flash of inspiration in Germany that the whole infertility issue was worrying Alex and we should forget about it. What was a child compared to our love, right? A baby would ruin everything. Imagine Alex and the perfect apartment with baby sick and toddler toys everywhere! So I rushed to the bank to tell him this, literally straight from the plane, and he was there outside the bank with Louise. I mean, I could tell something was wrong straightaway because she ran away and he looked so shocked to see me. And then he told me. He does want children after all, except not with me. With Louise. I feel so stupid not to have known. It's official: I am an idiot.'

Mary ignored this. 'How long has it been going on?'

'Months – almost a year. I don't know which bit is worst: that he's gone or that he's with another woman who's having his child.' Daisy looked up. 'I think I'm still in shock, to be honest. It doesn't feel . . .' she touched her chest at heart level, '. . . real. I can't believe that it's happened, like it's happening to someone else and I'm hearing about it and empathising, but it's not me, not me and Alex.'

'He's happy about the baby with Louise, is he? It wasn't a fling? He's not staying with her because he feels he should? Because he can raise his child and be with you at the same time, you know. You'd have to learn to forgive him but you might be able to,' Mary said doubtfully.

'Oh, he's happy about it all right,' said Daisy in a low voice. 'I wasn't "the one", you see. Nobody who meets up in college stays together, apparently. We were always looking over our shoulders for the right one.'

Mary looked mystified.

'That's what Alex told me,' explained Daisy bitterly. 'I was looking for "the one" too, wasn't I? We were biding time. And it just so happened that he found his one before I found mine.' That was one of the most painful things about the whole mess, she realised. That she'd been utterly in love with Alex and he had felt differently. His words made a mockery of their love over the past years.

'Course you weren't looking for anyone else.'

'That's what I said, but he insisted I was wrong. Didn't I see what he was trying to tell me all along? Not getting married was the biggest hint you could give a person and he couldn't understand how I was so trusting and didn't cop on. If he'd wanted to be with me, he'd have married me. So I should have worked it all out and not been so shocked when he fell in love with Louise.'

'It's your fault, then? For not realising you were just biding your time with each other?'

'That sums it up, yes,' said Daisy. She tried a bit of squashed muffin. Delicious. Could muffins be the cure to a broken heart?

'Of all the low, lying scumbags I've heard of, Alex Kenny has got to be the worst,' Mary said furiously. 'At least Bart had the balls to say he was no longer in love with me, not deny he was ever in love with me in the first place!'

It was a small comfort that Mary sounded so shocked at Alex's callousness.

'What do you want to do?'

Daisy knew exactly what she wanted: Alex back. Mary wouldn't approve. 'I want it all the way it was before,' she said.

'It would never be the way it was before. Never. You could never forget what he's done and what he's said. Strike what I said earlier about taking him back: he doesn't deserve to be taken back.'

'But I would if he came back.'

'No you wouldn't. I know that I'm breaking the unbreakable rule of friendship by dissing your man,' Mary said, 'but Alex is a two-timing shit and he doesn't deserve you.'

'That doesn't stop me loving him,' Daisy said.

'Has he been in touch since?'

Daisy shook her head.

'He will, you know.'

A surge of hope lifted Daisy's heart. If only she could see Alex again, she could make it all right, couldn't she?

'He'll try and make it all up to you so he can sleep at night,' Mary said. 'You can't throw fourteen years down the plughole in one move. He'll want to fix it so he can tell all of your friends that you broke up amicably, that you were like brother and sister, really. That it's all fine, you'll always care for each other and be in each other's life, blah, blah, blah.'

Even though she knew she shouldn't, Daisy had held on to that thought tightly. Friends. If they could be friends, then she'd still have Alex and he'd be there sometimes, and it might be all right. The boulder crushing her heart would lighten if she knew he was still in her life. She could understand how women shared men, knowing about another woman and putting up with it because the man in question was worth it. Daisy would share Alex if that's what it took.

Because otherwise, he wouldn't be there, and his not being there would be like his being dead, only worse because he'd have chosen to be on the planet and not anywhere near her, ever.

'The world and his wife knows that staying friends isn't an option,' Mary advised quickly. 'If you want to get closure, you need a total break, and pretending it was all for the best is just avoiding painful issues.'

Since Mary had been going to therapy to get over her divorce, she was full of psycho-speak. 'Closure' was her favourite word, and she was keen to see everybody's side of the story. Apart from Alex's.

'Mary, I don't want it to be over,' Daisy said. 'I want to close my eyes and have it all back the way it was.'

'No you don't.' Mary was brisk. 'You want to go to his new home, hide prawns in the hems of Louise's curtains, and then have a torrid and very public romance with some twenty-four-year-old guy with a washboard stomach. And in the meantime, I've got some books to lend you. *Women Who Love Bastards* is brilliant. You'll love it.'

Mary was right, though it was another six weeks before Alex came back. Daisy saw him before he saw her. Hands full with her handbag, groceries and a bookshop bag with two more books on how to live through the pain but get better, she spotted him sitting in his car in one of the visitors' parking spaces outside their apartment. It was still *their* apartment to her, even six weeks after he'd left. Six weeks of no phone calls, no nothing. Six weeks in which Daisy had gone to hell and back.

And she'd come through it, sort of. By stumbling through every day and hoping that it would be better tomorrow.

Alex had come alone.

There was no sign of Louise in the passenger seat, so maybe this wasn't the visit where Alex suggested that they all try to be friends.

He finally saw Daisy as she stepped onto the tiled path that led up to the main front door.

'Hi, Daisy.' He stood behind her as she keyed the numbers into the security lock. She could smell his aftershave, some new cologne that wafted sexily around him, and she wanted to lean back into his embrace the way she would have before.

'Hi, Alex. How are you?' That didn't sound too needy, did it? If she made it obvious how much she'd longed to see him again, then he'd run. She had to play it cool.

Alex held the door open for her. 'Fine, I'm fine. You're looking well, Daisy.'

She'd put on some weight – the toll of all the late night forays into the fridge. People who said that wine and chocolate didn't go together had obviously never been dumped. She hated the fact that she couldn't fit in her thin clothes again, but Mary was always trying to buoy her up by saying she looked better with curves. 'The hourglass look is in,' Mary pointed out. 'Men love it.'

I only want Alex to love it, Daisy thought as the rounded body she'd hated all her adult life began to return.

At the lift door, she turned to him. 'What are you here for, Alex?'

'To see you, to talk,' he said.

The lift arrived and as she moved into it, Daisy banged her bookstore carrier bag against her shin. Feel the pain and get on with your life, she remembered. 'What do you want to talk about?' she asked firmly.

'Us, everything, how you are. That's all.' He hesitated. Alex had always been so definite. He wasn't the sort of person who hesitated. 'I care about you, Daisy. I hate to see you hurting.'

Score one for Mary. Daisy was grateful that at least she was prepared for this approach.

The lift hummed up to the fourth floor. Inside the apartment, he handed her an expensive green and gold gift bag.

'I brought you these,' he said.

Inside was a small bouquet of yellow roses and a bottle of wine. Hope surged inside her. Nobody would visit their ex-girlfriend with wine and roses if they weren't planning to get back with her and tell her leaving had been a mistake. It was a sign.

Mary had been wrong. Alex wanted Daisy back. She knew it.

'Would you like a glass of wine?' she asked, trying to hide her excitement.

'Yeah, that'd be great.' Alex prowled around the room, looking at the place without his things. There were so many bits and pieces they'd bought together over the years, that he had said it was impossible to imagine working out who owned what.

'We can work it out later,' he'd written in the note he'd left for Daisy while she was in Düsseldorf. 'I'd hate to fall out over splitting up the furniture.'

He'd taken his CDs and his books, and the big *Blues Brothers* movie poster that used to hang over the couch. He'd left the huge television with its intricate family of wires and matching pieces.

Daisy picked up the digital remote control and threw it to him now.

'The sports channel is getting withdrawal symptoms,' she said. 'Put it out of its misery and switch it on while I get the wine.'

There, that sounded suitably happy, didn't it? No pressure, cool and relaxed. Alex clearly thought so too from the big grin he gave her.

Outside the room, she rushed into their bedroom and tore off her black trouser suit. Humming to herself, she rifled through her underwear drawer and found an Italian coral bra and G-string set that was halfway between her skinny undies and her fat, suck-it-all-in ones.

With her suit trousers and silk tee back on, with the sexy fresh underwear underneath, she felt better, more in control. And it wouldn't look as if she'd done anything except brush her hair.

Because if she was wrong – dear Lord, let her not be wrong – and he didn't want her back, then she wouldn't have made a fool of herself.

She poured the wine, took a large gulp out of her glass, then refilled it and carried both glasses into the living room.

The television wasn't on the sports channel. It was set to one of the soaps that Daisy loved and Alex hated. Another sign.

Now that he was here, Alex didn't seem in any mood to talk about anything in particular. He sat back in the armchair he had habitually occupied, rested his wine glass on the arm of the chair just like normal, and chatted. How was the shop? Was business good? How was Mary?

Keen to see you disembowelled at dawn, Daisy thought. 'Fine.'

'I suppose she wants me roasting on a spit over burning coals,' Alex said.

Daisy laughed. 'Close enough,' she admitted.

'She's a good friend,' he said approvingly.

'You've never got on with Mary,' Daisy couldn't resist saying. Mary and Alex had existed in an uneasy truce from day one, which had always irritated Daisy. She had so much to be grateful to Mary Dillon for.

'Doesn't mean I can't see that she's good to you,' Alex said, unperturbed. 'She's tough as old boots, just not my sort of woman, that's all.'

Silence hung in the air. Mary wasn't his sort of woman but Louise, pretty, dark and pregnant, was.

Alex took another drink from his glass. 'And Paula, how is she?' Another clanger.

'She had her baby, a little girl.'

Born early to an ecstatic Paula after a mercifully easy labour, little Emma Marie was now a week old and weighed seven pounds one ounce. She had perfect little ears, Mary said.

'Oh, right.'

It felt so tense. Daisy's stomach was in a knot from wondering what was the right thing to say. She didn't want to sound desperate with longing or heaving with bitterness. And yet not so cool as to make him think that he couldn't come back. The door would be wide open if Alex wanted it so. How did you say that and stay calmly unruffled all at the same time?

Desperate for a topic that didn't have high explosive content, they cast around wildly for something to talk about.

The bank.

The bottle of wine and an entire jumbo packet of cheesy nachos were consumed over a long story about the bank, a story that never made a single mention of Louise.

Loosened up, thanks to half a bottle of wine and the empty calories of the nachos, Daisy thought about blithely introducing the subject of Louise and the baby. How's the pregnancy? When is she going for her next scan? Something like that. But she just couldn't.

She couldn't bring herself to be that forgiving.

'Do you have any more wine?' Alex was halfway out of his chair as he asked.

She nodded, eyes shining up at him. He knew where the wine was kept. This was his home, after all. While he located another bottle, Daisy went to the bathroom. Wine suited her, she decided, happy *in vino* with her reflection. Her hair was better behaved when she'd had a drink and her face never looked fat, just welcoming and with rounded cheeks. A rosy Madonna with a child. No, strike that.

She brushed her teeth, sprayed Eternity into the air, walked into the falling droplets, and slicked on strawberry lipgloss.

Alex was back in his seat with a full glass when she returned. 'I love this chair,' he said, stretching out his long legs.

'It's here for you anytime you want it,' Daisy said. She curled up on the corner of the couch close by him.

'I know.' Alex's hand reached out and rested on her thigh, so it seemed natural to lean her head over in his direction. 'You're an amazing woman, Daisy,' he sighed.

Warmth that had nothing to do with the wine swirled inside her.

'I miss you and our life. Everything's changed and it's hard to accept.' His eyes grew misty and he stared blankly at the wall over the bookcase where a wooden painted tribal mask hung. 'Do you remember that trip to Puerto Rico where we picked that up? And we had practically no money left and the guy in the stall said I was a lucky guy and he would buy you?'

'Yeah,' said Daisy. 'Remember the photos of us on the beach where I got sunburned because we fell asleep?'

'And you had one red cheek and one white one,' finished Alex. 'That was a great holiday. We didn't see that much, did we?'

It had been the first time they'd gone away anywhere outside Ireland as a couple, and they'd both been broke. They'd had a tiny white-walled bedroom in a small cheap hotel where the wine was plentiful, the sun danced on their balcony all day, and the bed had been soft enough to lie in for hours after they made love. They'd spent a lot of time making love on that holiday. Bare skin, the swell of Daisy's golden body in the white bikini Alex insisted on buying for her, the feeling of sunlight on their limbs made lovemaking seem like the only sensible way to spend the long, hot days.

'Do you remember the white . . .'

'. . . bikini.' She finished for him and smiled. 'I've still got it.'

'Bet it looks even better on you now,' he said, smiling too. And he meant it, she knew, because his dark eyes were full of love as they rested on her.

'Alex . . .' she began.

'I know, Daisy, I know,' he said, and then he was off the armchair and pulling her onto the floor beside him.

Their mouths found each other and Daisy could have cried at the familiar taste of his lips.

'Daisy,' he moaned again as he pulled off her T-shirt to reveal the Italian lace in all its glory. His lips brushed and sucked, devouring her flesh as his hands ran over her body. 'Your skin is so soft,' he murmured, fingers splaying out over the creamy silken flesh, with its delicate tracery of blue veins visible in the swell of her breasts.

And Daisy felt herself melt to liquid in the arms of the man who'd introduced her to both the concept of sex and the reality. Alex had been her first lover, her only lover, and he knew exactly which buttons to push to turn her on.

Somehow, they got out of their clothes, still clinging to each other, then, on the soft chenille of the cream rug, Alex was inside her and Daisy felt as if she was at home. Nestled in the protective circle of his arms, his scent in the air, his breath on her skin, she stretched against him ecstatically.

It wasn't about sex. It was about the comfort of his arms and when he came, quickly, calling her name the way he always had, Daisy cried. Salty tears pooled in her eyes and she did her best to brush them away, because she didn't want him to think she was sad. They weren't sad tears: they were tears of joy. She'd never thought she'd have this again, this luxury of Alex in her arms, loving her, and she held on to him tightly.

'I love you,' she murmured into the solidity of his shoulder. He rested his weight on her briefly and grunted as he moved off. Daisy didn't want him to move away, so she curled around him as he sank back onto the carpet.

This moment, this place on the floor, it was all perfect. She didn't want it to end.

Alex moved and looked at his watch anxiously. 'I better go,' he said. 'You know . . . it's hard to explain.'

Daisy nodded. He was right. He needed time to tell Louise that it was all over. It couldn't be easy, so he needed time. Now he was coming back to her and that was all that mattered.

'I understand,' she said.

'You're a woman in a million, Daisy,' he said affectionately.

With a swift kiss goodbye, he pulled his clothes back on and left. Languorously, Daisy got ready for bed, still on a high from their lovemaking. She put the feel-the-pain-and-get-on-with-it books at the bottom of the pile beside her bed. Then she picked up a glossy magazine and settled back to read. Everything would be fine.

The next morning, Mary noticed a spring in Daisy's step.

'You look good,' she said approvingly.

'I slept well,' said Daisy guiltily. It was true but that wasn't the reason she looked happy.

'What did you think about *Women Who Love Men Who Can't Love*? It's not bad, is it?'

'No,' said Daisy dreamily. 'Not bad at all.'

When another week had gone by and there had been no phone call from Alex, no email, no funny text message on her mobile phone to set up another date, Daisy finally panicked.

The yellow roses had died but, stubbornly, Daisy had pressed them all. She felt sick in the pit of her stomach every time she stared at the spot on the floor where she and Alex had made love. She'd been so happy then and now that bit of carpet was mocking her. The whole apartment was mocking her. She felt like moving out there and then just to get away from the memories.

But that would be stupid. She had to wait and see, didn't she? There was nobody she could ask for advice. Not Mary, that was for sure. And so many of their friends were just that: *their* friends. Not hers or his. But both. Shared friends. She had no idea who was on which side.

It would be so much easier if separating couples divided up their friends in the same way they divided up the CDs: '*You can have Gerry and Michelle, as long as I can have Sheryl and Ian.*' Then Daisy would know that she could phone Michelle for support, and not be afraid that Michelle would get off the phone and say 'That was *awful*. I hadn't the heart to tell her that Alex and Louise are coming out with us on Friday. Poor Daisy. Louise was worried about how she'd cope and Alex says she's a bit unstable . . .'

'Don't be such a wimp,' Daisy lambasted herself. 'You need to find out what's going on. Phone him, phone somebody.'

She left a message on his mobile phone: 'Alex, I need to speak to you. I was worried whether everything was OK. I thought after last week that . . .' Shit, what could she say now?

Quickly, she pressed the button that allowed her to erase her message and tried again.

'Alex, it's me. I wondered if you were OK. Could you phone me? We've still got things to talk about.' Simple but to the point, she thought. 'I keep thinking about that night on the living-room floor,' she added, almost as an afterthought. She wouldn't erase this one.

Daisy got the train into the city the next day so she didn't have to worry about parking. She'd been invited to the launch of a new range of costume jewellery, and Mary had urged her to go. Paula's replacement was with her in the shop and Daisy could do with a break, Mary said.

'I'll be back in the afternoon,' Daisy had said. 'It won't take long.'

'Take as long as you need.' Mary waved her off airily. 'You might meet a gorgeous man there.'

Daisy laughed. She didn't plan on looking for one.

There was an air of summer drifting about the streets of Dublin: people were shedding their winter clothes, and a few hardy souls were fashionably bare-legged at the jewellery launch.

The collection was good – definitely suitable for the shop, Daisy decided – and after a few glasses of champagne with a fashion stylist old friend of hers, Daisy was feeling no pain.

'How's Alex?' asked Zsa Zsa, the stylist.

'Well . . .' Daisy hummed and hawed. She'd been waiting for her mobile phone to ring all day. Surely he'd reply soon, although she'd had to switch it to silent for the actual show. 'We're on a bit of a break now.'

Zsa Zsa was taken aback briefly. 'Lots of fish in the sea,' she added. 'You can come fishing with me.'

'Yeah,' said Daisy, reaching into her handbag for her phone. Why was everyone trying to set her up with men? She was a one-man woman. Anyway, all relationships went through difficult times, didn't they?

'One missed call' read the phone display. Alex's number flashed up first when she scrolled into the missed calls menu. He hadn't left a message, so Daisy dialled his number. If he was in a meeting, so what.

'It's me,' she said, unnecessarily. His phone had a smiling photo of her that came up when she rang. Or it did have.

'Hold on a moment,' Alex said in his office voice.

She heard footsteps and imagined him walking out of wherever he was, away from people listening. That was good. He had something to say to her.

She sipped her champagne and smiled over at Zsa Zsa, who was talking animatedly to the person on her left. The place was still buzzing after the launch and Daisy felt a confidence from both the alcohol and the excitement of the day. She was good at buying for the shop, she had a good eye. And people were glad to see her. She wasn't a hopeless person, after all. And Alex would see that.

'Daisy, I couldn't talk. I was in a meeting.'

Once, Daisy would have apologised for dragging him out of the meeting, but she didn't this time. Her self-help books had been showing her that always being the one to say sorry had set a precedent in their relationship. She said sorry and he accepted it, no matter who had actually screwed up.

'I was worried when I hadn't heard from you,' she said, holding on to the stem of her glass and twirling it.

'Worried, why?'

'After the other night,' she prompted. 'Us,' she lowered her voice, 'making love.'

'What about it?'

Daisy felt the old melting sensation in her bones, as if she was dissolving in to a giant puddle of nothingness. 'What it meant, what you said,' she whispered. She got up and hurried to the lobby where it was quieter.

'I didn't say anything,' he snapped.

'You did, you said I was wonderful and –'

'You were. Forgiving – you were forgiving, Daisy, but that was all. We're not back together or anything. It was just sex.'

'You don't mean that,' she said, stunned.

'I do, Daisy. Jesus, don't do this every time. It's over and you've got to accept it.'

'But why did you make love to me?' she said it so softly.

'It just happened.' He sounded annoyed now. 'Sex happens. It doesn't have to mean anything. I'm with Louise now, Daisy. Don't go all weird on me.'

'But why did you do it?' she asked again. How could that have been just sex?

'You were there, it happened, so what? It won't happen again. I thought you knew. You said you understood,' he added almost plaintively.

'I understood nothing, except that we'd made love and you must have been going to come back to me. That's what I understood and then you didn't phone –'

'OK, Daisy,' interrupted one of the jewellery organisers. 'We're booking cabs to take people back to work . . .'

Daisy shook her head and held a hand up to show she couldn't talk.

'Listen,' said Alex, 'you've got to get a grip, Daisy. You and I are over. I thought we could see each other and be friends, but I guess I'm wrong. That night was a mistake – forget about it. I'm going to forget about it.'

'Because it might hurt Louise,' Daisy whispered.

'She doesn't need to know, and if you think you're going to cause trouble by telling her, then you're a bad bitch,' he hissed at her.

That was what finally made her see that he was serious. Alex never spoke to her like that. But he just had, which meant it was over. She was no longer anything to him. She was his past, someone he'd rather forget, someone he'd never be with again because it might come back to haunt him and Louise.

'I wouldn't do that . . .' she began, but she was talking to herself: Alex had hung up. Daisy felt that huge emptiness inside her. She was hollow, so hollow she could never feel warmth or life again. How could you live with that inside you, that vacuum?

Never to have Alex again, never to hold him close to her and feel his breath on her skin as he kissed her lightly? He no longer loved her and she still loved him. And no matter how hard she wanted to make him love her, she couldn't. She was powerless. She could see for ever and it looked bleak and lonely, stretching out in front of her.

Flashes of the night before came to Daisy as she lay in her bed the following morning, the dull pulse of pain beating in her head.

The party had started with cocktails at the Diamond Bar, a city centre venue close to where the jewellery show had been held. When it rolled on to nine o'clock and they'd been partying since the afternoon, some sensible person had suggested going out to dinner.

Buoyed up by at least six Martinis, each with the kick of a mule, Daisy had shrieked 'No!' at the top of her voice. Dinner would be boring and normal, and if she ate, she might start to sober up and the pain would kick in again. Sitting down to eat with people who weren't Alex, who would *never* be Alex, would ruin the evening.

The crowd – Daisy and Zsa Zsa; a grizzled, seen-it-all photographer named KC; a couple of session make-up artists; a cosmetic company PR named Ricardo; and an avant-garde interior designer – considered the options.

'Dinner would be fabulous,' pleaded Sita, one of the make-up artists, who'd been up since five that morning on a television advertising shoot and was now ravenous. 'You can't all be on diets.'

'But it might put a dent in the party atmosphere,' interrupted Zsa Zsa, who was keeping up with Daisy in the Martini stakes. 'And we've already eaten. See, six olives,' she added, waggling her last one on a silver cocktail stick. 'That's food. We're not all on diets.' An inspired idea hit her, like Michelangelo realising that ceilings were where it was at and that walls were passé.

'Forget dinner. Let's go to Pilgrimage instead and start the night early.' Pilgrimage was the latest club, so cool it didn't look like a club, had an unlisted phone number and had a door policy second only in entry requirements to the Freemasons. Naturally, it was always full and impossible to get into without having your name on the guest list at least two days earlier. Rock stars, record industry people and the fashion crowd were the only types who stood a chance of getting in without prior notice.

'Pilgrimage is such an incredible name,' sighed Zsa Zsa.

Everyone agreed.

Daisy gave her olive to Zsa Zsa. For the first time in weeks, she wasn't hungry. 'Let's put it to the vote,' she said, mentally hoping they'd go to the club, where she could have lots more lovely Martinis to numb the pain. Oblivion was what she craved.

Everyone voted for the club. Only Sita wanted to stop and eat.

'Pilgrimage it is,' cried Zsa Zsa happily, and waved for the bill before anyone could order any more Martinis.

From the comfort of her duvet, Daisy pieced together what happened next. The actual trip to the club was a bit hazy in her head, but she certainly remembered lounging around on very low nubian-brown leather seats, with clear liquids in Scandinavian shot glasses in front of them all. And the music ... she remembered how she'd whooped with joy when the DJ played Sister Sledge's 'We Are Family'. Daisy loved that song. She had a vision of herself twirling around in front of the others, not even on the dance floor, if she remembered correctly. And taking off her filmy cobweb Lainey Keogh cardigan because it was too hot, and hearing Ricardo tell her she had to put it back on because the management didn't feel that a bra, even one that was part of a lovely wild rose set courtesy of Elle Macpherson, was suitable as a top.

'It matches my knickers,' Daisy kept insisting sadly, because this was important. Women who cared about such details always kept their men, she was sure of it. It was the women who adopted a couldn't-care-less attitude to lingerie and things like cherishing their men who got dumped. Not ones who cherished to beat the band.

Daisy was *good* at cherishing. She had taken Alex's clothes to the dry-cleaners regularly without him ever having to mention it;

she remembered the toothpaste he liked and bought only that; she always folded his shirts when he went on business trips. And she kissed his neck, just like the magazine supplements mentioned. Men's Adam's apples were highly erogenous zones and kissing there could drive them wild with desire. She did all those things and look how it had turned out.

Ricardo had held her close, a warm, kind hug. He was a very tactile person and holding Daisy seemed to come naturally to him. He was taller than she was and slim, rather like Alex in some ways. Daisy fitted into the curve of his arms with her cardigan draped loosely around her and inhaled the scent of Ricardo's white linen shirt and vetiver cologne. Being held was so nice. Would nobody ever hold her again? The thought made her cry and she nuzzled closer to him, wondering if he liked her or not. He felt so good and she'd missed a man's arms.

Gently, Ricardo detached himself from Daisy's embrace and settled her down on her seat. As if he was dressing a mannequin, he managed to get her back into her cardigan and did up the buttons without once touching her skin.

'Don't you like me?' she asked, so drunk that she didn't care about the neediness dripping from her every pore. 'I'm thinner than I used to be five years ago, you know.' And she was. The mirror told her so, although the remnants of her self-esteem refused to believe it.

Ricardo sat down beside her and gazed into her bleary eyes with his pale ones. 'We're not compatible,' he said softly.

'You mean I'm not your type,' Daisy muttered. She was never anyone's type. She'd only ever been Alex's type.

His hands cradled her face with such kindness, like a parent holding a child's shining little face up for a bedtime kiss. 'No, but you're lovely,' he said, and she could see retreat in his eyes.

Of course, he was gay, she thought now with a burst of embarrassment, wanting to sink under the duvet and not emerge until everyone had forgotten how drunk she'd been.

She didn't really know Ricardo and could sort of remember Zsa Zsa telling her that, but, even so, she should have *known*, though Ricardo didn't wear his gayness on his sleeve.

A card – she'd send a card to apologise.

Another wave of memory made her flinch. KC, the photographer. Oh no, what had she done with him? Nobody was quite sure what KC stood for, although Mary Dillon, who'd once used him on a shoot for Georgia's Tiara, said it might be Kinda Cute, because he was sexy in an unshaved way. He wore a denim shirt that looked moulded to his body and smoked like a trooper, but this didn't detract from his appeal and if the Marlboro men were looking for a new, sexily dirty cowboy, he could be their poster boy.

He'd sat down beside Daisy at some point.

'Life's a bitch,' he'd said, lighting up a cigarette.

'You can't smoke in here.' Daisy was shocked, even through the Martini haze. It was illegal to smoke in clubs or restaurants, which was why the people who made giant outdoor ashtrays were doing such business. Zsa Zsa, who didn't smoke, said she often went outside the door with the smokers just for fun because you met such interesting people.

'So?' KC blew a smoke ring into the air.

Some long-dormant part of Daisy flared up. 'You're right,' she said. What had being a good girl ever done for her? 'Give me one,' she said defiantly. She'd never been a smoker, even though her mother had never been spotted without a cigarette dangling from one elegant hand.

She inhaled and felt the kick of the drug filtering into her body. It did work, she thought. It was relaxing, or was it all the Martinis?

'You're breaking the law,' said a grim voice. Daisy looked up to see a menacingly large doorman hovering over her and KC. 'I'll have to ask you to leave. We are very strict on our no-smoking policy.'

KC's eyes, already slitty with tiredness and smoke, narrowed down to boa constrictor slits. He dropped his half-smoked cigarette on the floor, ground it in with his cowboy boot and drained his drink.

Daisy, suddenly feeling like a wild girl saying 'eff off' to the headmistress, did the same.

'We're leaving anyway,' KC growled, and pulled her away with him.

Daisy shifted uncomfortably in her nest of pillows. She'd left with KC and there were a lot of blanks, but she dimly remembered taking him back home and sitting in front of the fire kissing and then . . . please no . . .

She opened her eyes, turned over in the bed but she was there alone.

'Thank you,' she said in relief. Whatever else had happened, at least she hadn't gone to bed with him. That would be unforgivable, stupid, utterly moronic, not to mention disloyal to Alex. How could she tell Alex about it? But she didn't have to. Alex wasn't a part of her life; he had no rights of jealousy.

As the shame of her behaviour the night before filtered back into her consciousness, Daisy cringed, trying to take comfort from the fact that at least she hadn't ended up in bed with KC, right?

But she must have been incredibly drunk. She was still wearing her very unsexy opaque black tights over her knickers. Too plastered to take her clothes off. Charming.

Gingerly, she got up, head pounding. Tea would help, she thought, stumbling a little. She reached for her dressing gown in its habitual place on the wardrobe door and then, she saw them. A pair of cowboy boots at the end of the bed, obviously abandoned the way their owner had stepped out of them. The detritus of a man's pockets lay scattered around on the floor beside the boots. Shame, remorse, regret and lots of other things from the Big Mistake section of the dictionary swept through Daisy.

She was still half-dressed, so clearly nothing of a sexual nature could have happened. But that was a small mercy compared to the embarrassment.

Two painkillers – damn, they were good; she must get another pack because they disappeared so quickly for some reason – and five minutes with the toothbrush later, Daisy felt closer to human. Then, she risked a look in the mirror. She didn't know what appalled her most: the smell of booze seeping out from her body or the bloated, grey state of her face. She felt so utterly ashamed. Tying her dressing gown more tightly around her, she padded out of the bedroom.

Dressed in jeans and a T-shirt, KC sat at her kitchen table watching the news channel and smoking. In the morning light of curtains not pulled the night before, he looked older and certainly less sexy. But not as bad as she did. He was drinking what looked suspiciously like a Bloody Mary, although Daisy couldn't imagine how any person could face alcohol after the amount they'd consumed the night before.

'Hey, Daisy.'

The two-word greeting made it worse.

Daisy cringed at the crude morning-after conversation. At least he knew her name. Surely that counted for something?

'Hey yourself,' she said, attempting to be blasé. 'How are you feeling this morning?' She'd never done this before, so she wasn't sure of the protocol.

'Rough. This helps.' He gestured to his glass before finishing the drink. 'Want one?'

'Tomato juice?'

One eyebrow raised infinitesimally. 'What do you think?'

'I'd be sick if I had a Bloody Mary,' Daisy said.

'It will help.' That was as close to being intimate as this conversation was going to be.

'No, really.' She made herself a cup of coffee, added lots of sugar, and drank it slowly. Her hands were shaking, she realised. Hangover hell.

'Sorry we didn't get to . . . y'know . . . last night,' KC said. 'I'm not in a rush anywhere now.' He stubbed out a cigarette in his makeshift ashtray – one of Daisy's antique market finds, a pretty bowl in blue and white mosaic – and lit another. The smell made her feel sick.

'Gotta go . . .' and she ran to the loo, making it just in time. She retched until her stomach hurt and only then was she able to stop. Crouched on the floor by the toilet bowl, nauseated in every way possible, Daisy's red-rimmed eyes stared around.

Two months ago, she and Alex had shared this bathroom, talking as they flossed their teeth, side-stepping to get to the mirrored cabinet over the sink. Alex's great trick was smacking her cheekily on the bottom as she climbed into the shower, saying, 'Hurry up, sexy. I need you.'

And she'd laugh back at him. 'Is that a promise or an idle threat?' she'd say. From her current vantage point, she could see how her housekeeping had become non-existent since Alex had left. There were dust bunnies clustered behind the sink pedestal, while the white wicker bin was jammed full and she hadn't had the energy to empty it. That would never have happened before. Daisy couldn't sit down at night until she'd cleaned up after dinner and every surface was shining. This mess wasn't her.

But what was her? She just didn't know. It was as if Alex had taken her identity with him when he'd left, she realised. Daisy was desperately trying to find herself but there was nothing to find. Without Alex, she was nothing.

'You all right?' roared a voice.

A nothing with a strange man in her apartment after a drunken night. A nothing who was a slut into the bargain – well, she could have been a slut but clearly had been too drunk. Although KC was offering to make all that up to her. The nausea came back at that thought, and she had to hang over the toilet bowl again. Her life was over, she thought in despair as she retched again. Nobody else cared, so why should she?

It took ten minutes for her to summon up the courage to tell KC he ought to leave, and another two hours to feel reasonable enough to leave the apartment for work. Daisy decided to walk, thinking the air might help her feel better. On the way, she stopped off in the newsagent's and bought cigarettes, although she didn't smoke, a big bar of chocolate, and a bottle of water.

'Hi,' she said cheerily to the girl behind the counter in Georgia's Tiara when she rolled in at the horrendously late hour of half-eleven.

Paula's replacement, Carla, was very young, very fashionista and very shocked. Daisy hadn't bothered with much in the way of make-up and her face was a funny grey colour. Worse, she was wearing the weirdest combination of clothes: a vintage-looking silk skirt in plummy colours, black tights, a man's big grey sweater and what looked like suede slippers.

'Er, Mary . . . ?' called Carla nervously.

Mary's blonde head peeked out from behind the office door. 'Holy Mother of God,' she said at the sight of Daisy. 'What happened?'

'Wish I knew.' Daisy still looked drunk. Now she plonked herself down on the edge of the window beside a mannequin dressed in a chic urban summer suit. 'It's over, Alex is totally finished with me. Finished, over, all gone!'

Mary grabbed a handful of notes from the till and thrust them at Carla. 'Two coffees from Mo's and a muffin. Lattes with extra shots of espresso.'

Carla fled. Daisy didn't appear to notice.

'What I don't understand, Mary, is how I didn't know.'

'Compartmentalising, my dear,' announced Mary. She flipped the shop sign to closed and sat down beside her friend. 'Men can put their lives in lots of little boxes, while they can't put their socks in the correct drawer. While we, who know which drawer to put all the laundry in, are incapable of keeping our lives separate. If we love someone, we love them and everyone knows.'

'I didn't think it was love with Louise, you see,' said Daisy. 'I sort of hoped it was a fling and he'd come back to me.'

Mary shot her a glance filled with sympathy. 'You shouldn't get your hopes up,' she said gently.

Daisy took a deep breath and confessed everything: about letting Alex have sex with her and then the awful incident with KC.

'Oh, Daisy, that's not the way to get over a man, pet,' said Mary, when Daisy had finished, trying to put an arm round her.

Daisy pushed it away. 'You can say that again,' she said tearfully. 'It's awful, bloody awful. I've never done anything like that in my life and now, one day after I know it's totally over, I've brought a strange man home and I don't remember any of it. I'm a mess.'

'You're not,' Mary said, trying to comfort her. 'You're a good friend, a talented person, look at all you've got. A financial interest in the shop! That has nothing to do with Alex. You earned it because you're clever and talented.'

'None of this matters,' Daisy said suddenly. 'What's the point? What's the point of all this,' she gestured around the shop at the racks of clothes, 'this rubbish?'

'It's not rubbish,' Mary said patiently. 'It's clothes, it's work.'

'It wasn't work for me. I thought it all meant something and if I wore the right things, then I'd fit into the world but I was wrong. Clothes mean nothing. Words mean nothing. *I have nothing*.' Her eyes stared up at Mary beseechingly.

'You do,' Mary said, wishing she could say the right thing. But what was the right thing exactly?

'I don't.' Daisy plucked at the packet of cigarettes with nervous fingers. She wanted to smoke them all, then drink so much her head spun, and eat her way through a fridge full of cake and biscuits and cream. 'I've spent my grown-up life with a man who no longer loves me or wants to be with me. I thought I was fine because he was with me, and without him I don't think I'm anyone. I'm empty – nothing – empty. The first thing I do when he dumps me is screw my life up.' She looked down at the skirt she was wearing, the pretty plum silk with its appliquéd flowers, and began to rip it systematically. 'See, it's like everything in the world: just rubbish, easily frayed rubbish.' Daisy tore and ripped so all she could hear was the sound of ripping fabric.

Mary did nothing. If it made Daisy happy to tear a perfectly good skirt apart, then she might as well do it. Mary had her own version of ripping clothes. When she and Bart had first separated, she'd got his collection of motorbike magazines and torn them to shreds. Every single one. She'd had to take a trip to the tip with bags full of shredded paper because the neighbours would know she'd lost her marbles if she left them outside the house for the binmen. Mary might have been on her own but she wasn't going to be pitied by the neighbours.

Poor Daisy was way beyond that point. She didn't care who pitied her. That was what was frightening. Because in all the years Mary had known Daisy, she'd always cared too much about what other people thought. Not caring was a sign that she was in deep distress.

'You should take time off,' Mary said carefully. 'If you want, that is. You might want to work like a mad woman, and if that's the case, go for it, we're behind you. But time off could help.'

Daisy raised bloodshot eyes to her friend. 'I'm going home,' she said.

'That's good,' said Mary with relief. 'I'll drop you back.'

'Not the apartment. To my old home, to my mother's. I don't want to sit in the apartment on my own. I don't want to go back there at all,' Daisy said. 'There's nothing there I want.'

She grabbed her handbag from behind the counter and left the shop, the overhanging bell twinkling sweetly as the door slammed.

Mary rushed out after her to see Daisy climbing clumsily into a cab. 'Blast!' yelled Mary as the cab whizzed off. It took ages to order a cab in Carrickwell and when you didn't want to see one, they appeared and whisked upset people off into the ether.

Mary ran back inside and picked up the phone. She had enough experience of dealing with men to know that Alex Kenny would not take a phone call at the office from his ex-girlfriend's boss, particularly a boss he'd never got on with. So she'd pretend to be his mother.

Unless Mrs Kenny had changed radically in the time since Mary had seen her, she still adored Daisy and was unlikely to have instantly welcomed Louise into the bosom of the Kenny family. Which meant that Louise was not likely to chat and realise I wasn't Mrs Kenny. Lying really was access all areas.

The faltering, sweet voice of 'Mrs Kenny' having an emergency got her through to Alex's direct line in thirty seconds flat.

'Mum . . .' said Alex, sounding as if he'd run to pick up the phone.

'It's Mary Dillon and don't hang up. There's a problem.'

'With Daisy?'

'No, with Julia Roberts and the Dalai Lama. *Of course* with Daisy,' snarled Mary. 'I know you've a wandering dick but I didn't think your brain was wandering too.' She cracked on before he could respond. 'Daisy is having some sort of breakdown and I'm worried about her. She just left here and she says she's going to stay with her mother, which, as even *you* know, is unusual. They never talk, so why would she go and visit her? And she wouldn't go back to the apartment to pick up any clothes. You have to talk to her, you have to do something.'

Silence. Then, 'What can I do?'

'Follow her, talk to her. Do something!' Mary was furious with him.

Her mother's car was sitting on the gravel drive outside the cottage, but there was no answer to the door when Daisy rang the bell. Her mother surely couldn't still be away, Daisy thought blindly. And then she thought of the phone messages on her machine – unanswered, naturally. One had been the usual breezy missive from her mother about a trip abroad, 'to help Imogen recover from the operation'. What operation? Daisy wasn't sure, and she cared less. Her mother ran to take care of her own siblings, and left her daughter on her own.

The taxi driver was looking at his watch. 'I've another job, love,' he roared out of the car window. 'An airport run. I can't miss it. Are you staying or coming back into town with me or not?'

Daisy was about to say that she didn't know when a head popped over the hedge.

It was Brendan, her mother's elderly neighbour, the man who had the keys when Nan Farrell was away. Daisy smiled tiredly at him. 'Brendan,' she said, finding the name in the recesses of her brain. 'Forgot my keys,' she said, knowing it would all be all right now.

When Brendan had been persuaded to go – he'd seemed very anxious at Daisy turning up unannounced, and kept saying that her mother had never mentioned it to him – Daisy shut the white painted door and leaned against it with relief. Peace and quiet, at last.

Unlike Daisy's first home, the terraced house in Carrickwell, the cottage had always been a quiet place to live. The centre of Carrickwell had buzzed, as had the small cul de sac Nan and Daisy had lived on. But the cottage was one of a line of six detached dwellings, farm cottages from another era, and they were more or less in the middle of a field in the countryside. Apart from the one at the end, which had been bought by a young couple, the residents of the other five were all past fifty, and the lane was quiet.

The cottage was small but postcard perfect, with a tiny drawing room complete with walls the same colour blue as the morning room in the mansion Nan had grown up in, and some of the silver from the mansion in the walnut cabinet. Watercolours painted by her mother hung on the walls. The kitchen, the room most used, was the cosiest and boasted a huge stove – sadly, not an Aga, Nan always said – and a yellow cushioned window seat where Daisy used to read when it was too cold to sit in her bedroom.

She went up the winding stairs to her bedroom, although it wasn't really hers any more. The coverlet she'd made with her sewing machine when she was sixteen was gone, as were all the things she'd left at home when she'd moved out. Her mother wasn't one for sentimental hoarding.

But the bed was the same. The bed she dreamed of a future on.

Daisy lay down on it, slipped off the slippers she'd worn into work, and fell into a dreamless sleep.

When she woke up, she made herself some tea and switched on her phone. There were several messages, most from Mary, who sounded increasingly worried but trying to hide it, and one from Alex.

'Mary rang me. She's worried about you. Says you've gone to see your mother ... I am sorry, Daisy.' There was a pause, as if Alex knew he'd said the wrong thing. 'Just phone me and tell me you're OK.'

Reassure you that I'm all right so you can go to sleep with Louise in peace and lie up against her belly and feel your baby kick, Daisy thought bitterly. The bitterness was the most awful bit. It choked her, rising up in her stomach and flooding into every part of her so that she couldn't so much as look up at the sun without feeling rage and bitterness against it for looking so golden when her world was so bleak.

She searched for something to drink, although she knew she was wasting her time. Her mother might have the odd bottle of sherry around for guests, but that would be it.

She'd have to drive to the small shop. Her mother never left her car at the airport, and the keys would be in the basket inside the door.

The shop nearest to the cottage sat on a tricky junction where the road went up to the old Delaney place, or down to Lough Enla. There were a few houses, a tiny chapel and a bright green establishment with 'Slattery's Grocery & Draper' shining in big letters over the door.

It looked exactly the same as it had when Daisy had lived down the road, and was the sort of shop where you could buy anything from olive oil to engine oil. The retail-trickery that meant supermarket shoppers were steered in the correct direction had totally bypassed Slattery's. The stock was piled on the shelves every which way: canned goods beside bleach, bin bags squashed against biscuits and a brightly coloured display of children's flipflops and sunglasses looking madly incongruous beside the week's special offer: litre bottles of Chilean pinot noir.

Daisy picked up a basket and put two litres of the Chilean wine in. What the hell, another one would be a good idea. She added a third litre, some bread, cheese and a pack of coleslaw, and a jumbo pack of chocolate biscuits.

'House warming,' she said by way of explanation to the teenage girl behind the till when she brought her suspiciously alcoholic basket to the checkout.

'Oh right,' said the girl, scanning the coleslaw.

'A few friends are coming from Dublin,' Daisy added, wondering why was she justifying herself.

The girl nodded.

'You've got to have a few drinks, don't you?' Daisy knew she must sound mad. She paid and said thank you a little too heartily.

That was a good impression to give people all right, she reflected as she left: a total nut who narrated her every move.

Back at the cottage, she sat down in the kitchen and got the stove going, sipping a glass of wine as she did so. There was a small, elderly TV and wall-to-wall opera CDs, so she found her favourite, *Tosca*, and flooded the room with music to match her melancholy.

She did think of making a sandwich, but by the fifth glass of wine, she decided not to bother. Why bother about anything any more?

CHAPTER FOURTEEN

The magazines hadn't changed in the doctor's surgery. Still the same dog-eared copies of *Hello!* and *GolfPro*. The people waiting didn't appear to have changed either, Mel decided: still mainly mothers hissing *'Don't!'* at their children. Today, one small boy, his bottom lip stuck out in misery, was trying to rip out the seal from the cover of *National Geographic* in order to make a collage with a Christmas fashion spread from a tattered copy of *Vogue*. His mother, a tired-looking woman in cords and a denim jacket, was trying to distract him with various toys.

Mel sat with Sarah beside her, and a sick Carrie on her lap – tonsillitis again, she reckoned – and decided that the main change in the whole place was herself. No longer Ms Career Babe who stood out like a sore thumb, she now fitted in perfectly in her faded jeans with frayed hems, thonged sandals, and simple white T-shirt. Her hair was longer than it used to be and her skin had a healthy glow from spending so much time out in the garden with the girls.

'I look like a hippie at a music festival from the Summer of Lurve,' she'd said the previous morning to Adrian, catching a glimpse of herself in the mirror as she was stepping into her jeans. 'Make love, not war, and don't worry about make-up or even hair-brushing.' She was struck by the thought that she looked younger than ever, with her freckled, happy face and blonde curls trailing round her ears. Her morning routine was embarrassingly quick. Wash face, brush teeth, shower, rub on a bit of moisturiser, and pull on jeans/blouse/T-shirt.

'It's sexy,' Adrian had said, sidling up to her with his damp towel still round his waist. 'Suits you. You look all relaxed and wild child. Like you were when I first met you. I like it.' His towel dropped.

'Adrian,' laughed Mel, leaning back into him. 'The girls will be up in a minute.' It was nearly seven.

'I'm up now,' he murmured into her hair.

'We don't have time, do we?' she said, feeling herself respond to his caresses.

'Let's give it a try,' he replied. 'We only need a few minutes.'

'Oh, foreplay too,' teased Mel, but she turned around and kissed him deeply, and they fell onto the bed.

Just as well it hadn't been this morning, she reflected now. After a sleepless night with Carrie, she certainly wouldn't have been in the mood for lovemaking.

'How are you feeling, love?' she asked Carrie, kissing the top of her daughter's head.

In response, Carrie wriggled out of her mother's arms and went to investigate the toy box. Sarah watched her in a superior manner for a moment, then joined her little sister on the floor.

'Gimme,' said Sarah, grabbing the *Mr Happy* book that Carrie had picked up.

'Mine.' Carrie whipped it right back. She was pretty good at standing up for herself.

'What's wrong with your little girl?' asked the woman in the denim jacket. Her toddler – Mr *National Geographic* Ripper – had finally found his mother's mobile phone to suck, which seemed to be keeping him from further destruction.

'Tonsillitis,' Mel sighed. 'We've been lucky lately; she hasn't had it for ages. But she was very bad last night. I'm terrified she'll have to have her tonsils out.'

'My daughter had them out,' said the other woman, clearly ready to chat. 'They can grow back, you know.'

'You're kidding!' A young woman sitting opposite them with a sleeping baby on her lap was astonished at this.

'It doesn't happen that often,' replied Ms Denim, 'but can you imagine going through it all only to have to do it again! My daughter had them out when she was five and she's fine now. It's so hard for them to understand, though, isn't it . . .' she trailed off, clearly remembering the trauma. 'I stayed with her overnight. I couldn't leave her; she cried every time I had to go to the loo. I told my husband that I didn't care if I had to sleep in a chair beside her bed, I was going to be with her. She was out the next day and back to normal straightaway. Kids are so resilient, aren't they?'

'Yes,' the younger woman agreed, holding tightly to her baby as if to protect it.

Mel shuddered at the thought of her tiny daughter having to go into hospital. She knew that wild horses wouldn't drag her away from Carrie's bedside. She remembered thinking of such an eventuality when she was working, and wondering how she'd cope because she'd have to take time off work. Now all she'd have to manage was her sick child – and not an irate Hilary as well.

'Tonsillitis,' agreed the doctor when she got in to see him. 'We should consider the option of taking them out. How many bouts has she had this year?'

'Four,' said Mel quickly.

'Right,' the doctor was engrossed in Carrie's medical notes. 'It's tough when they're up all night, isn't it, and you know you're doing everything you can, but they're still crying?'

The doctor was about her age, maybe older, and his hair was flecked with grey. He obviously had kids too, since he was so familiar with the personal side of having a small child sick at night. She found herself warming to him for the first time. She wondered how she could have thought him supercilious or condescending when he'd spoken to her mother about Mel dropping in to see him when she had time. Because she felt so guilty, she'd assumed that he was getting at her.

Guilt – what a wasted emotion. How many hours of her life had she frittered away feeling guilty about things over which she had no control?

At least she didn't have to feel guilty about the girls any more. What a relief.

By four that afternoon, relief was a long-forgotten emotion in the Redmond household. Carrie was hot and miserable, and Mel had to carry her on her hip all afternoon.

'Mummy, no,' she wailed every time Mel thought she was happier and tried to settle her on the couch in front of her favourite TV show. 'No, no, no, nooooo.'

'Hold me too!' demanded Sarah. She was wearing her Halloween fairy costume – she'd yelled so much to be allowed to that Mel had given in – and was now stamping her pink feet in rage, looking less like a fairy than a furious little hobgoblin. 'Me, me, me!!'

It was hard to stay calm, especially when you were dying for both a cup of tea and a pee. 'It's all right, Carrie,' Mel soothed, trying her best to sound serene. 'Mummy won't put you down. Mummy loves you. And you too, Sarah. Only you're a big girl and Carrie's sick, so Mummy has to hold Carrie. How about we all go out to the kitchen and, since you're so grown up, you can pour some milk for yourself and then we'll put *Nemo* on?'

Sarah's angelic little face grew angry at such blatant manipulation. 'No,' she wailed. 'Don't like *Nemo*!!! Hate *Nemo*!! Want to be up!' 'Up' meant in her mother's arms.

Mel crouched down on the floor with Carrie, and tried to hug Sarah in close too. Naturally, this plan was not popular. Carrie wanted to be hugged on her own. So did Sarah. The wails were ear-splitting, and in stereo.

'Let's put on *Shrek*,' said Mel in desperation. Adrian's brother, Eddie, had given Adrian the video as a present and, even though Mel was convinced the film was too old for them, the girls adored the bits they'd seen and were always demanding to see more.

'No,' roared Sarah, upping the decibel level and simultaneously hitting out at her little sister in an attempt to be the only person being cuddled by Mummy.

Calm thoughts, Mel told herself. Think calm thoughts.

TV and videos were out, so what next? She mentally ran through what she called her Bad Mother's Bribe List.

The electronic babysitter was normally the trump card, followed by chocolate. If chocolate failed, Mummy's Make-Up came next, followed by A Trip to Play on the Winnie-the-Pooh machine in the supermarket, with Daddy Will Be Very Upset to Hear His Girls Were Naughty as the last-ditch attempt at peace talks. It took two packs of chocolate buttons for Carrie and Sarah to begin to cheer up. Mel managed to boil the kettle and get as far as putting a teabag in a cup before realising that she would wet herself if she didn't visit the loo.

'Let's all go on a trip,' she said gaily, scooping Carrie up and taking Sarah by the hand.

'Don't wanna,' said Sarah, happy now where she was.

'We could have more chocolate buttons upstairs,' Mel begged, cursing the fact that they still hadn't summoned up the cash to put in a downstairs cloakroom.

Sarah shook her head.

'Mummy, sick,' moaned Carrie, holding one chubby little hand up to her head.

'We can play with Mummy's make-up,' said Mel in desperation.

Sarah got up and flew up the stairs, and even Carrie felt well enough to climb up herself.

'Lipstick is MINE!' Sarah shrieked as Mel followed.

'Mine!!' shrieked Carrie back, rounding the landing at high speed.

Carrie's tonsils were sounding better, at least, Mel thought wearily. And since she didn't use much lipstick these days because she wasn't working, it didn't matter if they destroyed every one she had, did it? Anything for a moment's peace.

When Adrian got home at seven, both children were calm and happy after a joyous afternoon painting each other with eye-shadow and blusher. The beige carpet in Mel and Adrian's room would never be the same, nor would Mel's make-up bag.

She'd nearly lost it when Carrie found the precious moisturiser Mel had bought on her pre-redundancy shopping spree and emptied at least half of the carefully rationed cream onto her teddy's woolly head.

'Carrie, I don't believe it! That's naughty, no!' Mel yelled. 'You can't have everything of Mummy's!'

Losing your temper didn't work, she realised, when both girls burst into tears at this crosspatch version of Mummy.

Mel had finally managed to get to the bathroom, and have a cup of the tea, as well as some of the children's supper and four chocolate biscuits. Being a full-time mother wasn't just bad for your nerves, it was bad for the waistline too.

'They've had their bath and they're fine,' she said tightly to Adrian, greeting him in the hall with a now-smiling Carrie on her hip. It was all she could do to speak without screaming that every nerve was stretched to breaking point and why hadn't he been able to get home earlier to help? Just because Adrian had suggested dinner out on Saturday night at the local Chinese restaurant, didn't mean he could evade all parental duties, oh no . . .

'Mama.' Carrie snuggled into Mel's neck and began sucking her thumb.

Not in front of the children, Mel remembered. She breathed deeply.

'Carrie's had her medicine and they're ready for bed. You can use a wipe to take off the make-up. Carrie wanted hers left on for a while longer.' She took the car keys from the hook in the hall. 'It has been a nightmare afternoon, Adrian, and I'm going out in the car,' she said, handing Carrie over to him. Carrie beamed at her father so he'd admire her silver eyeshadow and Aunt Sally-style red spots of blusher.

Adrian was startled. 'Is everything all right?' he asked anxiously, looking from the heavily made-up toddler to his white-faced wife.

'Fine,' said Mel briskly. If she didn't get out of the house soon, she'd explode. 'I just need some time on my own.' She reached for her handbag. 'It's been a tough day,' she added. Understatement of the year. 'I won't be long. I might go to Mo's for a coffee.'

She'd never done that before in all the years they'd lived in Carrickwell. Mo's Diner was where they went as a family at weekends, not at seven on a week night when bedtime loomed.

Adrian took it very well. 'We'll be fine,' he said. 'You go.'

Mel sat in the car on the drive for a good five minutes before she started up the engine. Then she drove down to the centre of Carrickwell, parked near Mo's Diner and went in.

As she stirred sugar into a creamy decaf latte, Mel suddenly realised that she hadn't spoken to Caroline in a very long time. Not since the big row that followed their January night out when Lorna had needled her about how her job meant she missed seeing Carrie and Sarah growing up. Caroline had been so upset the next day, and even though Mel had left a couple of messages for her, she'd never phoned back.

Today, for the first time, Mel really understood Caroline's point of view. Nobody gave the stay-at-home mum any awards. There was no bonus for doing all the cooking and cleaning, no pat on the back from the MD for endless washing, no awards ceremony for calm mothering in the face of sick children, nothing: just the expectation that it would all be done again the next day. No wonder mothers lost their rag.

Right now, Mel would have killed for a girlie night out where she could laugh with like-minded women, let her hair down and be someone else other than Mummy. When she'd been working, she hadn't understood. Now she did.

She fished her mobile phone out of her bag and dialled Caroline's number. 'Hiya,' she said warmly when her friend answered. 'I'm sorry I haven't been talking to you for so long and I'm sorry about the row.' No point beating about the bush. 'I gave up work to stay home with Sarah and Carrie and, as you know, that means I haven't had a moment to myself since.'

'You gave up work?' Caroline said, surprised. 'I thought you were welded to that job and would be buried with four land lines, two mobile phones, a lap top and a BlackBerry in your coffin.'

Mel laughed. She'd forgotten how black Caroline's humour could be. 'Nearly,' she said. 'Except the company wouldn't have allowed a lowly member of staff like me to have something as posh as a BlackBerry. Hand-held email devices are for the top echelons only. Listen, how do you fancy a night out – just you and me?'

'I can't do any nights out right now,' Caroline said, with a certain bitterness. 'Graham's working late a lot. What about lunch tomorrow? I can't go out as I've got a guy coming to give me a quote for painting the windows – they haven't been done for years. But you could come here . . .'

Mel hadn't been to Caroline's house for a very long time. 'I'd love that,' she said. 'And Carrie and Sarah too. If Carrie's better from her tonsillitis.'

'Of course. Poor Carrie.'

Caroline's house would not have featured in a homes and interiors magazine: there were too many scuffed skirting boards and grubby bits of wall where ten-year-old Ryan, eight-year-old Fionn and six-year-old Luka had been practising their football skills. The back garden was also testimony to a trio of footie-mad boys, as there was a scorched, dry patch on the lawn where they clearly played ball each day and most of the shrubs looked crushed. But the house oozed homeliness and love, from the wild flowers sitting in a jug on the sun-dappled windowsill to the smell of cooking that lingered in the kitchen where Caroline had been filling her freezer with homemade soups, lasagnes, and her speciality, vegetable and parmesan gratin. She'd also made a batch of fairy cakes topped with girlie pink icing with a Smartie on top of each.

Sarah, and Carrie – who was much better today – were enchanted with these.

'I went through a muffin-making phase,' Mel admitted, sitting down at the kitchen table while Caroline gave flowery plates with the little pink cakes to Mel's daughters. 'I grew out of it.'

'You do,' Caroline agreed. 'Muffin-making is like PMT – it comes in waves. When I feel the wave coming, I stock up and freeze most of it. The rest of the time, I go to the bakery down the road. Why would anyone want to bother making pastries when you can buy them cheaper? Anyway, I'm on a diet, so I don't buy them now. Saves money and calories.'

'I thought you baked all the time.'

'It made me feel better if people thought I did,' Caroline said. 'Otherwise, they want to know what you do all day. As in "How do you fill your day?" delivered in a condescending tone. If people think you're a wonderful cordon bleu, they tend to imagine you spend your time bashing the hell out of basil leaves with a pestle and mortar, and they respect that.'

Caroline sounded very miserable, Mel realised.

'We could have lunch in the garden,' Caroline said. 'I've made sandwiches and the girls can play with some of the boys' old toys.'

'Perfect.'

They sat on deck chairs at a weatherbeaten wooden table and talked, while Sarah and Carrie explored this new garden.

It wasn't long before Caroline came out with what was bothering her. It seemed that her marriage to Graham was going through a difficult patch.

'I've been experiencing my own little mid-life crisis,' Caroline explained. Her gym membership had been one of the first things to go when she'd given up work to stay home with the children, and no matter what anyone said about how good walking was for you, it was hard to summon up the energy to walk in the dark of winter. The weight had piled on.

'Everyone puts on a few pounds when they get older,' was all Graham had said when Caroline had told him she felt fat, frumpy and middle-aged.

'What sort of answer was that?' she asked Mel. 'It got to the point that we were talking like radios with transmission problems.' She talked but Graham didn't receive. She wanted to receive but Graham wasn't interested in talking.

'He used to tell me I looked wonderful years ago,' Caroline said sadly. 'Now I could wear my pyjamas all day and he wouldn't even notice.'

Mel remembered how Caroline used to look when they worked together: sleek and sexy, and admiring men eyed her as she walked through the office. She didn't look like that now, though she still looked good: her face was alive and intelligent, her figure curvier than before. But the spark in her eyes was gone.

'Graham said that women moaning about diets is so boring and didn't want to discuss it any more.'

Then Caroline had joined WeightWatchers. She'd lost twelve pounds but still had another stone to go to reach her target weight.

'The people at WeightWatchers were so thrilled for me but Graham didn't even notice,' she said, bitter again. 'He used to notice when I'd achieved something at work, but now, nothing I achieve is of value to him – nothing.'

Mel's heart ached for her friend. She searched around for the right thing to say. 'Remember when we had that row about Lorna,' she said ruefully, 'and you said that nobody recognised that being the CEO of the house was the hardest job in the world? You were right and I was wrong, Caroline. It is hard,' she admitted. 'Adrian supports me and says I'm brilliant all the time, but it's not quite as rewarding as someone saying thanks for a report at work or the feeling of satisfaction you get when you've completed a particular project. Everyone seems to think any human being with an IQ in double figures should be able to cook, clean and bring up children.

You're busy nurturing your children so they grow up into clever, well-adjusted adults, and you may think this is special, important work but nobody else does.'

'No, nobody values it.' Caroline's mouth was set in a grim line. She took one of the pink fairy cakes and ate the Smartie from the top. 'Nobody thinks mothering is anything much. *My* husband certainly doesn't, and unless I am seriously deranged and he's started wearing Obsession for women he's having an affair.'

Mel opened and closed her mouth like a fish, so stunned, she was unable to make a sound.

'I know the signs,' Caroline went on, taking another cake and removing the Smartie from the top. 'Not what the magazines tell you – is he wearing new underwear? does he shower more often? Though there's definitely the perfume. No, I can tell because I know Graham. It's the way he looks at me. We've been married twelve years and the train carrying unbridled lust left the platform a long time ago, but he looks at me in astonishment now, as if to say how am I married to this woman? How did I get to this place?'

'Caroline, I'm so sorry –' began Mel.

Caroline interrupted her. Now that she'd started this sorry story, she wanted to finish it. 'I can see him looking at me and wondering, how did she turn into this woman with the chain-store jeans and the scrubbed shiny face? I can see it written on his face. He married a go-getting advertising manager and boring Mummy is not what he thought he'd end up with.'

'Are you sure he's having an affair?' Mel asked. 'This could be a bad patch and you're feeling down and –'

'I'm ninety-nine per cent sure. I haven't caught him in bed with the next-door neighbour or anything, but he is. I know it. It's so obvious. He never buys clothes, Mel, and he's got several new ties lately, and all these overnight trips he's been on suddenly – they're fabricated. I phoned his office one day with a message for him and they said he was on a day off. He'd told me he had an urgent trip to London and would probably be away overnight.'

Mel sighed. That sounded conclusive.

'What do you want to do about it? Don't be passive, Caroline. If you've changed, so has he and he's got to take responsibility for that. When you got married, a cheating Graham wasn't what you thought you'd end up with,' Mel said spiritedly, turning the whole scenario on its head the way she used to do with problems in the office.

'Probably not,' said Caroline, 'but I can't afford to look at it that way. He's working and I'm at home. We couldn't survive without him. That limits my options.'

'Caroline, no it doesn't,' Mel insisted. 'You can't settle for second-best just because Graham pays the bills. You have a marriage, a partnership. Being a parent is something separate. You can be parents together and not be married. Getting out of your marriage is an option.'

'You can say that because you haven't wondered what would happen if you ever split up,' Caroline said harshly. 'This isn't Bel Air where they each end up with half of a ten-million-dollar fortune: the woman gets the ten-bedroom mansion for the kids and he gets the beach house. This is the real world and I don't want my children to suffer financially.'

'You can still walk out,' insisted Mel. 'You don't have to stay with him and suffer in silence.'

'In theory, yes. In practice, no.'

'You know what, Caroline.' Mel was exasperated. 'When I met you first, you were so tough and I admired you more than any other woman I worked with. You said what you thought, you didn't pussyfoot around like the rest of us. You were honest, upfront and you believed in yourself. Now you've forgotten all those things, as if being at home has beaten you down.'

'Being at home hasn't beaten me down –' Caroline said sadly – 'well, perhaps a teeny bit. Graham has; the kids have; life has. I feel as if Caroline is gone, buried deep beneath the cloak of Mummy.'

'Are you really sure he's having an affair?' Mel asked again. 'There could be a perfectly innocent explanation for everything,' she added. 'Well, there could. He might be depressed, have you thought of that? And,' Mel paused because this was dangerous territory, 'what about sex?'

She'd read that men having affairs often had wonderful sex with their wives to make up for the infidelity, instead of swearing off it altogether as the popular myth had it.

'Sex is not on my agenda and it's not on his either,' Caroline said flatly. 'We get into bed, normally at different times, we kiss chastely on the pillow, and he rolls over and reads his latest thriller and I read my catalogues. Thankfully I had my coil removed or it would have rusted.'

Mel felt an incredible rush of pity for her friend. 'I'm sorry. I feel as if I haven't been around much as a friend to you.'

'You couldn't stop Graham from having an affair,' Caroline pointed out. 'I half thought that if I clung on to my old life, I'd still be a bit the old me, the me he fell in love with. Meeting you occasionally made me feel that I could be.'

Mel thought of how she met her old colleague Vanessa for lunch, convincing herself that this link to her past life and Lorimar would

229

help make her current one more varied. It didn't. The two lives were different.

'Hanging round with people from our old jobs isn't what we should be doing,' she said decisively. 'We need to cut the cord. We need to find new ways to define ourselves, make ourselves feel better. But first, you've got to confront Graham. You owe it to yourself and the kids to see if you've got a marriage any more. You can't hide from this; you need to know for sure and then, if needs be, you can butt him out of your life. But you must be sure, Caroline. You could destroy things if you confront him and you're wrong.'

Caroline shuddered. 'Is him coming into my bed at night smelling of another woman's perfume any less destructive?'

'Point taken. Just don't do anything rash.'

'I haven't done anything rash in years,' Caroline said bitterly. 'Graham's affair has probably been going on for months now and I've said nothing. I've rolled over and played wifey. Hear no evil, see no evil, et cetera.'

'You need a holiday or some time on your own so you can think,' Mel said. 'A bit of quiet time where you don't have the boys pulling at you, so you can feel a bit like your old self. Then, you can see what you think.'

'There's no chance of me getting away on my own,' Caroline said. 'I'd love to, but me-time is low on the list of priorities here. Graham is "working" all hours, and we can't afford the sort of childcare involved in me slipping off for a week away. I wish.'

'Not even a long weekend?'

'No. The hour it takes to cut my hair is about as much me-time as I get.'

Mel had a thought. The spa voucher! She hadn't had a moment to use it and it was just as well: this was the perfect time for it.

'My leaving present from Lorimar was a two-person day session in Cloud's Hill, this new luxury spa at home. How about you and I booking ourselves in for a day of luxury? You can stay overnight with me that evening, and we'll hit the hot spots of Carrickwell afterwards when we're all painted and pampered. Graham can babysit and you can take the time out to review your options.'

Caroline's face brightened marginally, then it fell. 'What options?' she said.

'Well, there's the option to tell Graham to get his cheating ass out of your house and that you're consulting a lawyer. OK, you might not mean it but he doesn't know that and it would be good for him to get a shock. He needs to know that you're serious.'

'What if he says bye bye, he was just waiting for the right time to leave me anyway?' Caroline asked.

'Then you're not doing yourself any favours by staying with him if he doesn't want to be with you.'

'It'd be a nightmare,' Caroline shuddered.

'He started the nightmare, it's up to you to finish it,' Mel said. 'You have the right to find out if you still have a marriage, if he wants to try again, or if he's just waiting for you to find out because he can't bear to tell you.'

Caroline digested this information and ate another fairy cake. 'I wonder what she's like. Younger, thinner, probably doesn't wear Tesco's jeans.'

Dwelling on this was not good for Caroline, Mel realised. 'Let's chill out at Cloud's Hill and you can make somedecisions then.'

The girls were worn out as Mel drove back to Carrickwell that afternoon and fell asleep in their car seats, which gave Mel time to think. She thought about how sorry she was for Caroline, how lucky she was herself to have a loving husband, and how wrong she'd been to spend years envying Caroline for having it all. Being at home wasn't the easy ride Mel had once thought it was.

She enjoyed cooking better meals for her family than before and the house had never been so clean. In fact, it was easy to see how women could become obsessed with housework and forget there was life beyond Windolene. When that was all you saw all day, it became your focus. That and the children. There was such joy to be had in playing with Sarah and Carrie – dressing up, painting, moulding dough animals, doing endless jigsaw puzzles and playing with Barbies. Before, when she was working at Lorimar, Mel had avoided reading what the educationalists said about the merits of creative and imaginative play. Knowing she didn't have time for it all was another source of guilt. Now that she had time to do it, she was surprised to find it was hard work, not a matter of lying on the couch with a magazine and letting the kids get on with it by themselves. When you played, really played with small children, it absorbed all your attention. It was tiring.

Why is the sky blue?

What do elephants have in their trunks?

Do daddies have baby boys and mummies have baby girls?

You needed a full night's sleep, lots of energy and the patience of Job. Mel remembered resenting the enormous sum of money she and Adrian had paid out every month to Little Tigers. These days, she had more admiration for the nursery staff than ever before.

She loved doing it and yet she could see Caroline's point of view too: without wanting to sound selfish, she still wanted to be more than Mummy.

It was noisy on Saturday night in Carrickwell's busiest Chinese restaurant, the Dragon Palace. The sounds of talking and laughter, and the plain white china clinking and banging on the wooden tables meant Mel and Adrian had to raise their voices to be heard. Despite this they were really enjoying themselves. It was the sort of Saturday night they used to have years ago, before they had kids, and which Mel had thought she would never enjoy again. When she had been working, she had been too exhausted to go out to anything that wasn't a 'duty' event, and, anyway, she had been so anxious that her mother-in-law, Lynda, disapproved of her, that she had felt guilty asking her to babysit very often. Now she was a stay-at-home mum she felt more at ease with Lynda.

'You deserve to get out,' Lynda had said firmly when Mel had phoned her, 'you know I love babysitting.'

And somehow Mel had believed her. It was funny how her own insecurities had, in the past, made every syllable that Lynda uttered seem more loaded with meaning than it was.

'We haven't been out like this for years,' Adrian said happily. 'Not having to be on our best behaviour because it's work, not worrying about whether we should be at home with the kids, just relaxing!'

Mel was startled. She hadn't realised Adrian had sensed how she used to feel when they went out at weekends in the Lorimar days. Now it appeared as if he'd felt the same way too. Her guilt had been infectious.

'I'm sorry,' she said. 'I didn't mean to stress you out too. I felt as if I was betraying the girls by being out at the weekend when I should be spending every second with them.'

'I know. But it's fine now. You're not so hyper any more.'

'What do you mean, I'm not so hyper?' she demanded.

'I'm only kidding,' Adrian said. 'I'm teasing you.'

But there was probably a grain of truth in it, Mel knew. Blast it, she had to have the last sesame prawn toast, even though she'd promised herself that the way to maintain a good figure was not to eat everything on the plate, including the pattern. 'I'm not as hyper, you're right,' she said, munching.

'You're calmer, I'm calmer,' Adrian said. 'We're all calmer.'

'But we're broke,' Mel pointed out. 'Let's face it, the next time we get to go on holidays, the girls will probably want to bring their teenage boyfriends with them.'

'It's not that bad,' he argued. 'We're managing and we're happier.

It's sort of nice coming home each night and having you there.'

'You mean in an *I'm home, woman, get into the bedroom so I can ravish you* way,' Mel laughed.

'That is it exactly,' he grinned back at her. 'When I'm sitting in the traffic on the by-pass, getting home and ravishing you is the first thing on my mind, naturally, and possibly *then* sitting down and reading the newspaper and relaxing.'

'As long as you've got your priorities right,' Mel said gravely. 'Me first, relaxing afterwards.'

Their main courses arrived.

'We definitely should do this more often,' Adrian said.

'Stuff ourselves senseless, you mean?' Mel asked.

As usual, their eyes had been bigger than their stomachs and they had ordered far too much. The table groaned under the weight of the succulent sizzling dishes. 'No, go out together, on our own,' Adrian said.

Mel reached over and squeezed his hand. She'd told him about Caroline and Graham and he understood how upset she'd been by their marriage difficulties.

'Yeah, but that's the whole point of children,' Mel laughed. 'As soon as they come along they do their best to make sure that you never have any more, because you never have any romantic, intimate moments. They're the best contraceptive in the world.'

'I didn't say anything about making babies,' Adrian interrupted, 'but we could try some intimate moments later . . .'

And through the steam of pilau rice and sizzling beef, Mel smiled at her husband. 'Practice makes perfect,' she said.

CHAPTER FIFTEEN

When Cleo got off the train at Carrickwell, after two miserable days at Trish's, hiding from Tyler, she was relieved to see there was a taxi waiting. She instructed the driver to take her up to Cloud's Hill Spa, but as they drew near the turn-off to the Willow Hotel, she gave in to temptation and asked him to take a detour.

'You don't want to actually go into the hotel, you just want to sit in the driveway and look?' said the taxi driver, incredulous.

'I just want to see it, that's all,' said Cleo, irritated, wishing he'd mind his own business. She was feeling very irritated these days – well, for the past forty-eight hours, to be exact.

The morning after walking out on Tyler she had called in sick. She couldn't face going in to work and having him confront her, and though skiving off went against the grain, she had to do it.

Anyway she did feel sick – sick to her stomach, sick to her heart, sick to think that she had trusted Tyler and he had acquired her family home in an underhand way.

Even if he hadn't, how was she going to spend time with a man who was going to rip her lovely home apart and turn it into a great soulless corporate hotel? He'd probably have confidence-building talks with his staff about how appallingly the Willow used to be run and how it was going to be a model of modern hotel practice now that it was part of Roth Hotels. She just couldn't cope with that idea.

'He couldn't have known who you were. It's just a coincidence he's bought the Willow,' said Trish, when Cleo came home that night, distraught and wild-eyed over what she'd seen as Tyler's betrayal, 'and even assuming he *did* know – and I still don't know how he could have, seeing as you never told him your second name was Malin – what would he gain by going out with you?' she went on, reasonably. 'Your family have sold the place; it's not as if he is going to get any inside information from bonking your brains out in his suite.'

'I was not going into his suite to bonk his brains out,' Cleo said furiously. 'I was going in for a nightcap.'

'Yeah,' said Trish, 'and the cheque is in the post. Two of life's great lies. Nobody goes in for a nightcap. You must have been aware you were going to fall into bed with him.'

'I was not!' said Cleo. She was really getting angry now. Even her best friend refused to see her point of view.

'No, seriously, Cleo,' insisted Trish, 'what good would it do him to go out with you just because your family once owned the hotel that his family now owns?'

Cleo gave her best friend a stony look. 'You don't have to make it sound so like a business deal,' she said bitterly. 'It's about feelings and emotions and how I'd feel if I was involved with him, knowing what I do and –'

'Ah-ha,' said Trish, 'so you are really crazy about this guy and it's upset you that he doesn't know who you are? But you'd still be angry with him if he did.'

'Trish!' screamed Cleo, so loudly that Trish had to tell her to shush.

'You'll wake everyone up! You know the walls in this house are paper thin.'

'Sorry,' mumbled Cleo. 'I'm upset. It was all going so well and . . .'

'You don't trust him, that's all,' said Trish knowledgeably. 'If you trusted him it wouldn't matter who he was or who you were, or what Roth Hotels were doing to the Willow. But you don't because you think he was going to bonk you senseless and forget you and you'd be just another notch on the Roth bedpost. Isn't that it?' she demanded.

'What's with all this straight-talking all of a sudden?' demanded Cleo suspiciously.

'You're the one who tells me to say what I think,' Trish said, 'and I'm trying.'

'I meant say what you think to men,' Cleo said crossly, 'not to me. You're supposed to cheer me up and say the things I want to hear, like how he's a lying, cheating scumbag and he doesn't deserve me, et cetera, et cetera.'

'Fine.' Trish got into bed. 'He's a lying, cheating scumbag and he doesn't deserve you, et cetera, et cetera. Now can we go to sleep?'

The next day, Cleo decided that she wouldn't feel quite so bad if she went home to Carrickwell, except there was no home to go to. Her parents must have left the Willow by now.

And they haven't even told me where they've gone, she thought angrily. But if that was the way they wanted it, she wasn't going to bother them – or her brothers. She could be just as stubborn.

And then she remembered Leah at Cloud's Hill and how she'd said there was always a job for Cleo there. It would be nearly like being at home.

When she phoned Leah, she'd only got halfway into explaining before Leah interrupted her.

'Of course I meant what I said then,' Leah said. 'I never say what I don't mean. Not any more, anyway,' she added, somewhat mysteriously. 'We'd love to have you here. I've got just the job for you. Shall I meet you off the train or do you want to get a taxi?'

'I'll get a taxi,' Cleo had said, frantically wiping away the tears that had begun to fall when she'd heard Leah's gentle voice again.

The taxi driver obediently turned up the driveway of the Willow and parked. 'Is this all right for you?' he asked, in a long-suffering voice.

'Perfect, thank you,' said Cleo. She looked out of the side

window at her old home. It looked as though it had been empty for some time, it seemed so run down and overgrown. There were no guests now dragging their cases into the reception hall, there would be no sound of laughter or conversation echoing through the rooms, no steam rising in the kitchen, no yells from Jacqui, the chef, as the strawberry soufflé suddenly collapsed and she found out she was out of Dover sole just as table nine ordered four of them.

The once-loved old house looked miserable, sad and lonely, exactly the way Cleo felt.

'Some big developer has bought it,' the taxi driver informed her. 'Going to build town houses, they say. Don't know how they got their planning permission to rip down a lovely old place like that, but they're going to.'

Cleo wanted to correct him and say that, no, in fact, Roth Hotels had actually bought the property and it wasn't going to be town houses at all, but she didn't have the energy.

'Aren't you one of them, the Malins?' the taxi driver added, looking at Cleo curiously in his rear-view mirror.

'No,' she said, and it felt horribly as if she was telling the truth. She wasn't one of the Malins any more; her family had turned their backs on her. 'I stayed here once, that's all. I was interested to see what had happened to it.'

He nodded. 'Do you want to go on up to Cloud's Hill now?' he asked. 'Only the meter's running.'

'Of course, let's go,' Cleo said. There was no point sitting here looking at the past.

She wondered where her mum and dad were and what they were doing. It hurt her more than she could say that they hadn't been in touch again, hadn't sent so much as a text message after the first few angry phone calls where her mother had said that if only Cleo would say sorry, it would all be fine.

Except that Cleo hurt too much to say sorry. Her pride wouldn't let her.

Trish said they hadn't rung because it was up to her now to make the first move.

'The kid always apologises first,' Trish said. 'That's the rule of families. Don't ask me why, it just is.'

Now, as she thought about what Trish had said, Cleo was flooded with longing. She needed to see her family again and have everything the way it was before. But as she took a last, lingering look at the shabby façade of her old home, she knew finally and completely that it could never be that way again. The Willow had moved on, her family had moved on without her, and she would never get over the hurt and upset. The memory of that last row in the kitchen still burned deep inside.

First her family and now Tyler. What was the point in being honest, genuine and up front with people when all you got back was betrayal and misery? She was going to do what Trish had done and get on with her life on her own. What was it Leah had said on the phone to her the other day? 'It'll all work out in the end, even if it's not the way you'd planned or the end you'd planned.'

Between Leah's philosophising and Trish's rabbiting on about how you had to make your own life, Cleo was getting confused.

She was jolted out of her thoughts as the taxi drove into a pothole of enormous proportions.

'Jaysus,' said the driver as the car lurched out. 'Whoever's bought the hotel I hope they fix the bleeding road, that's all I can say.'

When the taxi finally dropped Cleo and her luggage off at Cloud's Hill Spa, she was aware of great peals of laughter coming from the terrace. Hauling the suitcase she had borrowed from Trish around the back, she found Leah and some of the spa guests sitting out on the terrace, drinking iced tea in the evening sun and chatting.

'Cleo, how lovely to see you,' said Leah, getting to her feet, a smile on her beautiful face. She walked over and enfolded Cleo in her arms.

Cleo was hit once more by that gorgeous scent of roses. It was so lovely being held by Leah, so like the way Mum used to hug her. She hadn't been hugged in a motherly way for ages. Since she'd left home, in fact. And now here she was, back in Carrickwell, and it was obvious her family didn't care about her. Leah didn't look surprised when Cleo burst into noisy sobs.

'Travelling is hell,' she said cheerily, giving a little goodbye wave to the rest of the guests and steering Cleo in the direction of the house. 'Leave your luggage here, darling; we'll pick it up later.'

'It's just it was so nice to come here and see you and feel welcome,' Cleo hiccuped as she walked, Leah's arm around her waist.

'Coming home can be very emotional,' Leah said sagely. 'When you feel as if a place is not your home any more, it's worse.'

'That's it exactly,' said Cleo, sobbing even harder. 'I made the taxi driver go by the Willow and it looks so lonely and sad, I can't bear it. And I don't know how they are or what's happened or anything.'

'Well, I may have news for you on that,' said Leah. 'Does your mom know a lady called Mrs Hanley?' she enquired.

'Yeah, Irene Hanley,' said Cleo, perking up.

'Irene Hanley should be working for the CIA,' Leah said, 'because she knows everything in this town. I don't mean she's a gossip, she just delivers the information to wherever she thinks it'll do the most good. I liked her a lot.'

'Me too,' said Cleo, snuffling. 'What did she say?'

'Your mom and dad have gone abroad for a holiday because they were upset by everything that has happened. Your mom was devastated that you wouldn't come home when she phoned you,' she added. 'She took it very badly, Mrs Hanley says.'

Cleo felt another bout of tears coming on. 'I was so hurt then, and she said I had to say sorry and it was like they were choosing Barney and Jason and Sondra over me. They wouldn't see that I'd been hurt and left out of all the decisions.'

'Everybody was hurt, I guess,' Leah went on. 'If she'd phoned you a few weeks later, you'd have cooled down, right?'

Cleo nodded.

'Your mom and dad were afraid that you wouldn't have anything to do with them any more, that they'd screwed up, so when they went away they asked Barney and Jason to talk to you. They were supposed to be the conduits.'

'Oh, Jason and Barney,' snapped Cleo, 'they couldn't spell the word "conduit", never mind be one.'

'That was also what Mrs Hanley thought,' agreed Leah. 'She's a smart woman.'

'My brothers have never got in touch,' said Cleo fiercely. It all made sense now. She knew her parents wouldn't go away without telling her where they had gone.

'Mrs Hanley heard, because her daughter knows Sondra's best friend quite well, that Barney and Jason thought it would do you good to be ignored for a while.'

'I bet Sondra had something to do with that!' Cleo said. 'She's never liked me. The other pair are too weak to make a decision on their own.'

And then she started crying again, because no matter who'd pushed her brothers, it was hard to imagine they'd try to hurt her so much.

Leah brought Cleo to one of the prettiest bedrooms in the old house, a flowery bower with rose-coloured curtains and a comforter that looked as if petals had been strewn upon it.

'Lovely,' sighed Cleo. 'Nobody does bedrooms like this any more. I always wanted one in the Willow and nobody really agreed; thought it might be too feminine and no man would ever want to stay in it, but . . .'

'I understand,' said Leah. 'Women sometimes need a few frills.'

'But I should be in staff quarters, shouldn't I?' Cleo added. After all, she was coming to work for Leah. Cloud's Hill was becoming so successful, Leah needed another receptionist and Cleo was looking forward to a nice, unstressful job for a while.

'Yes, we have a lovely room, but it's not quite ready for you,' Leah said. Which wasn't entirely true. The room was ready, but she felt that Cleo could do with a couple of days of pampering.

'Why don't you go to bed early?' she said, drawing the curtains. 'I'll get some dinner sent up to you, and you can have some time on your own.'

'That would be lovely,' said Cleo. Living in Trish's constantly busy house, there hadn't been much time on her own. And there was so much to think about.

'Thank you, Leah,' she said with heartfelt gratitude.

Leah gave Cleo one last hug. 'You're welcome,' she said. 'Everyone needs a little looking after occasionally.'

After two heavenly days in which Leah insisted that Cleo did not work, but tried practically every treatment in the place – so she could talk knowledgeably about them, as Leah put it – Cleo began to feel better. She certainly looked better, 'and that always cheers you up, doesn't it?' she said to Leah as they sat in the hot tub with Leah admiring Cleo's now beautifully manicured hands. 'I could get used to this doing nothing,' Cleo added, stretching voluptuously in the hot water.

'Could you?' said Leah. 'I wouldn't have thought so. If anyone had asked me to guess, I would have said that you were one of those energetic people who were always on the go.'

'You're right,' Cleo admitted, 'I am, but somehow this is what I feel like at the moment. Doing nothing is always nice when it's a break from doing something, especially when the something is stressing you out. Leah, you should be a motivational guru or something. You're amazing, the things you know.'

Leah smiled. 'I don't know anything more than anyone else,' she said. 'I just trust my instincts.'

'I tried that,' said Cleo bitterly. 'I trusted my instincts when it came to Tyler and that was a mistake.' For the first time since she'd come to Cloud's Hill, she felt emotionally strong enough to talk about the relationship, and she had filled in Leah on all the details. Even now, in the cool, clear light of this wonderful place, the memory still hurt.

'It wasn't a mistake,' said Leah.

'What do you mean?' Cleo asked.

'You liked him and it didn't work out quite how you wanted it to, that's all. There was no mistake there,' Leah said.

'I suppose.' Cleo was unsure. 'You're saying I had something to learn by it not working out with Tyler, is that it? I'm fed up of learning,' she said gloomily. 'Learning always hurts. Why can't you learn things and not get hurt? All I've learned lately is that your family get fed up with you, and men use you . . .' She knew that wasn't strictly true. Tyler hadn't used her, not really. And Nat, dear Nat, hadn't used her either. What a pity he wasn't her sort of man.

'Trusting your instincts means just that,' Leah said firmly. 'What have your instincts told you about your mom and dad?'

Cleo's eyes brimmed again. 'I couldn't believe they hadn't got in touch again,' she said, 'I just couldn't believe it.'

'See, your instincts were right. They *did* get in touch,' Leah said. 'The first time, you were too upset to accept the olive branch and the second time, your brothers didn't pass the message on.'

'Leah, this is all very difficult, thinking about this,' said Cleo. 'Can't we just sit here and blob?'

'Blob away,' Leah said, rising elegantly out of the water. 'I have to get out. I have a few things to do.'

Leah was very clever, Cleo reflected, to leave her there to stew in the hot tub and think. Even though she was sick of thinking. Her parents had got in touch – that was the wonderful thing – although it was painful to think that Barney and Jason were so full of bitterness that they hadn't passed the message on. Cleo felt a twinge of remorse that she hadn't rung her parents back long ago . . . She might phone her dad's mobile phone later, just to see. The thought made her feel happier. She was going to be brave and adult and heal the family rift.

But there was still one cloud – Tyler, and Roth Hotels buying the Willow. There was no easy way of resolving that situation. Even if Tyler arrived crawling and apologising, Cleo could have nothing more to do with him. He and Roth Hotels were the enemy: it would break her father's heart to know he'd sold the hotel to them.

No, Tyler could rot in hell. And he hadn't tried to get in touch with her, either. Her instinct had been totally wrong on that one, no matter what Leah said. Still, she sighed, as she got out of the tub and reached for her towel, she would never have to see him again, would she?

CHAPTER SIXTEEN

Since arriving at her mother's cottage a week ago, Daisy had barely ventured out of her cocoon. Her days had slipped into a routine that would not make it into any lifestyle 'n' diet book. In the mornings, she sat in front of the TV in her pyjamas, ate sugar-coated breakfast cereal and watched reruns of television shows she normally wouldn't dream of looking at. In the afternoons, she drove to the little shop at the crossroads and stocked up on food – chocolate, more breakfast cereal, pizzas – and whatever variety of wine was on special offer. In the evenings, she played her mother's opera CDs at full blast, wallowed in misery as endless heroines sang of lost loves, felt her waistband getting tighter, and drank her week's safe intake of alcohol in one fell swoop.

The next day, she repeated the cycle. She didn't return her phone calls, except for one to Mary to say she was fine and would be in soon. Both statements were patently untrue.

'I've been worried sick about you,' Mary said. 'I rang bloody Alex and told him to contact you. Did he?'

'He did.' Daisy didn't mention that Alex's phone call had been nothing but a single message left on her voice mail. She'd begun to think that if Alex could have dumped her by voice mail message, he would have.

'I gave him a piece of my mind, I can tell you,' Mary went on. 'The louse. He didn't know what to say to me.'

It gave Daisy a grim satisfaction to imagine Mary verbally ripping Alex to shreds. But it was a useless exercise. He was gone and nothing could change that.

'You need to come back to work, Daisy,' Mary said. 'Believe me, I know what it's like to have your heart broken, and hiding away doesn't cure it. Alex was just one part of your life – forget him and think of your future. It's not as if having a man is the be-all and end-all, now is it?'

When she was in cheering-up mode, Mary was a force to be reckoned with. But she was missing one vital concept, Daisy felt: the fact that Alex really had been everything to Daisy.

She tried to explain this. 'He gave me confidence. When I was with him, I liked myself and even when I wasn't with him, I could still like myself because he loved me.'

It sounded so stupid, no matter what way she put it. So full of naked self-dislike. How could someone like Mary, who was the ultimate in strong, confident businesswomen, understand what Daisy had been like before she'd met Alex? She'd been shy, scared and afraid of the world. He'd changed all that. Most importantly, he'd managed to make Daisy like herself.

'You can't . . . you shouldn't . . .' Mary seemed to be having trouble taking this information on board. 'Alex didn't make you who you are,' she managed finally. 'If it was all down to him, how did you cope when he wasn't with you? Answer me that! How did you travel to Paris, London, Düsseldorf, do your job so fabulously and have everybody adore you if Alex wasn't with you? *You did it because of you, not because of him!*'

The logic of this might have been obvious to Mary but not to Daisy. 'When he wasn't with me, I was happy because I knew he loved me,' Daisy said simply. 'Having Alex in my life said I was doing OK, somebody loved me. I didn't have a wedding ring or even an engagement ring to tell the world that, but it didn't matter because I knew I had Alex. I was content in myself. Then, when he was gone, it all fell apart. I didn't look much different but how I felt was the difference. I felt, sorry, I *feel* unloved, odd . . .'

'Being single doesn't mean that,' Mary insisted. 'Daisy, you can't say you have nothing and are nothing just because Alex is gone.'

'But that's what it feels like,' Daisy said bleakly. 'It's like waking up from this lovely dream to find out that I'm seventeen, fat and lonely again. Alex took me away from all that.'

'You took yourself away from it,' Mary insisted. 'Where are you phoning from? Your mother's?' she asked.

'No, she's back so I'm staying with friends,' Daisy said, hating lying but not wanting Mary to find her and make her come back to the real world.

'Why don't you come and stay with me?' Mary suggested.

'No, really,' said Daisy. She didn't want to be with anyone: she wanted to be on her own. 'I'll call soon, I promise.'

She put down the phone and walked aimlessly round the cottage. She'd eaten all the chocolate biscuits she'd bought the day before, there was nothing for dinner in the fridge and only one bottle of wine remained.

There was no point going near her mother's drinks cabinet. Nan Farrell took the odd gin and tonic and occasional sherry at parties, but that was it.

Daisy's dad had been the opposite, a hail-fellow-well-met type, ready to have a pint with anyone he met on the street. He hadn't made time for his family; he'd far preferred the company of strangers in the pub.

That was why Daisy was almost happy he lived abroad now. If he'd been around, she might have had to think about why her father had preferred other people to herself and her mum. She'd loved him for his humour and his light-heartedness, such a contrast to her mother's grim attitude to life. But he hadn't wanted to stay with either of them.

Men didn't stay around Nan and Daisy, it seemed.

Oh, she needed a drink. That might make the dull ache feel better. She'd just have one glass. But then one turned into two and somehow, the last bottle of wine was empty.

Shit. Just one more glass and she'd forget Alex, forget Louise, forget the beautiful baby ... warm velvety skin snuggled up against Daisy in the bed. She drifted into a waking dream of herself as a mother: her, Alex and the baby, a girl – she was sure her first child would be a girl. They were all lying in a big bed, not the bed in her apartment, but a family bed with fat pillows, cuddly baby toys and soft throws, and Alex looking adoringly at his wife and daughter.

The dream was perfect because Daisy finally had her own child – that's all she wanted. Was there something wrong with that? Was there something wrong with *her* that she couldn't have that? Because it was her fault, she knew now. Alex had been able to get Louise pregnant. So Daisy was the barren one, not him. Had she done a terrible thing in the past and was paying for it now with her infertility, her inability to hold on to any living thing, child or man?

Books and magazines told you you hadn't done something wrong not to deserve children, but she felt they were lying.

She remembered the anonymous woman in the IVF diary she'd been given on that awful day in the Avalon Clinic.

Is it my fault? I can't tell T because he says it's not, but I wonder. Is this punishment for not being a good enough daughter, sister, friend, wife? Infertility seems like a disease you bring on yourself. Sex with the wrong person, messed up tubes, not being whole. You feel you are to blame, no matter what anybody says.

Daisy's shimmering dream of motherhood faded. The IVF diary represented the end of her happiness. The day she'd started to read it had been the day Alex had said he wanted a trial separation.

How naïve had she been not to see what he really wanted. She hated herself for being so gullible and full of hope that day. Two dreams gone in a flash. She'd lost Alex and she was unable to have the baby she yearned for.

Pure despair washed over her and Daisy sobbed until her face was raw, the top of her pyjamas was wet, and her nose ran.

She must have dozed off briefly on the couch for when she woke up, half an hour had passed and evening had come. The sinking sun of a beautiful summer's evening shone in through the mullioned front window and in the distance, Daisy could hear the gentle lowing of cows making their stately procession to their milking parlour.

She still felt mildly drunk but she wanted another drink, something to blot it all out. And yet she couldn't drive to the shop to stock up. Buried inside her, a fragment of self-preservation remained. She never drove when she'd been drinking. She hadn't sunk that low, and besides, the shop wasn't far away: half a mile there along the winding lane and half a mile back. The exercise might help her sleep later and save her from the sweat-soaked wakenings in the middle of the night.

Daisy didn't bother scrubbing away the ravages of her tears, just pulled on a wide-brimmed hat of her mother's and some sunglasses before setting out. She walked along the laneway, still with that alcohol buzz inside her. Her mind raced, thinking, thinking. Just what she didn't want to do.

Supper – think about what she'd have for supper. Perhaps one of the shop's homecooked apple pies, with cream, and a large glass of red wine to wash it all down and take her away from it all.

She reached the crossroads, so set upon *not* thinking, that she walked straight out of the lane onto the busy main road. A car whisking past had to swerve with a great squeal of breaks to avoid her.

'Ohmigod!' gasped Daisy. Her hands flew to her chest.

The car screeched to a stop outside the shop, leaving black brake marks behind on the road. Shock rooted Daisy to one place and she stared dumbly at the car, unable to cry because she had no more tears left. The driver, a tall, dark-haired woman in blue jeans and a filmy rose-coloured shirt, got out and ran over to Daisy.

'Are you hurt?' she said.

'No. Yes. No,' gulped Daisy. 'I was walking to the shop, I didn't mean . . .'

'Shall I drive you home then?' the woman asked gently. 'Or do you need to see a doctor?'

'Home,' Daisy nodded. 'It's a short walk.'

'You shouldn't walk. You had a near miss.'

'I have to get shopping,' Daisy said suddenly. She needed food and, more importantly, wine.

'I'll go with you and drive you home,' the woman said firmly. 'Is there anyone at home with you?'

Daisy shook her head.

'It's Daisy, isn't it?' the woman said, staring intently at her.

For the first time, Daisy really looked at the woman. She did look familiar.

'I'm Leah Meyer, from Cloud's Hill,' the woman added. 'I met you when you came to the spa a couple of months ago. You work in the designer store in town, don't you? I nearly didn't see you because of that lethal bend. It's a miracle I didn't hit you.'

Daisy looked back at the crossroads and the sharp bend before it. She thought of herself lurching unthinking out into the road and how if Leah had been going faster, she'd now be lying on the asphalt unconscious.

'I'm sorry,' Daisy muttered, as her legs trembled. 'I have to sit down.'

Beside them was a tiny old-fashioned petrol station that boasted just one solitary pump that sold diesel. There was a wooden bench outside the sales booth and Daisy sank down onto it.

'Wait here,' commanded Leah. 'I'll get my car and drive you home.'

She was back in moments and helped Daisy into the car.

'Down the lane,' Daisy said, somewhat unnecessarily. 'It's the second cottage half a mile down.'

'What a lovely place,' Leah said in admiration as they stopped outside.

'My mother's,' Daisy explained, reaching into all her pockets to find the door key. 'I'm staying here for a few days while she's away.'

'Show me the kitchen, and I'll make you tea,' Leah said, once they were inside.

The rest of the cottage was tidy enough: Daisy had confined herself to cuddling up on the couch in the tiny living room, and each night she tidied up any glasses or plates that had been left on the coffee table.

But the kitchen told a different story. Under the cracked Belfast sink was where Nan Farrell kept things to be recycled, and out of habit, Daisy had put her wine bottles and carafes there, ready to be taken away when she left. There was a shameful number of bottles lined up, she realised, seeing the place with Leah's eyes.

'I've been meaning to get to the bottle bank, so the place is a mess.' Daisy gestured vaguely. She was about to make her excuse of a party but thought better of it.

'You're staying here on your own?'

Daisy nodded.

'You've had a shock,' Leah said decisively. 'It's probably not a good idea for you to be here on your own tonight. I'll take you to Cloud's Hill for the night.'

'I couldn't . . .' began Daisy.

'Hey,' Leah held her hands up. 'I'm being neighbourly and you'd be doing me a favour if you went along with it.'

'Well . . .'

'Great. I'll pack a bag for you.' With the speed of the mistral, Leah swept upstairs, collected up some things for Daisy, put them in a holdall she found on the floor, and came down again. 'You should check if there's anything else you want,' she said cheerfully, 'and I'll be waiting for you in the car.'

In her old bedroom, Daisy couldn't see anything else she wanted. Leah appeared to have packed everything up.

She might as well go with Leah. Why not?

The scent of roses woke Daisy up at dawn the following morning and, opening her eyes, she thought she'd died and gone to heaven in a blue petal boat. Above her were folds of duck-egg-blue muslin draped in a canopy. Pale blue pillows with tiny flowers scattered on the fabric and scalloped edges cushioned her, while a quilted coverlet of cream damask studded with cerulean embroidery knots covered her. Even the room itself was subtle blue, with walls painted the colour of the sky on a summer morning. Lifting her head, she could see the source of the rose smell: a bouquet of velvety crimson blooms in a beaten copper bowl beside the bed.

Daisy had no real idea where she was, but she felt safe. She sank back into the bed and slept again. For the first time in a week, her sleep was deep and good. When she awoke the second time, it was half-nine and she was ravenous.

Her clothes were still neatly folded in the bag where Leah had packed them. Daisy showered, washed her hair until it squeaked, then dressed quickly and left the room.

There were steps in the hall beside her bedroom door, so she went down them and found herself in a white corridor, stark as a monastery, with stone floors and no curtains on the long narrow windows. The servants' part of the old Delaney house, she guessed.

246

At the end of the corridor was a big kitchen with the same stone floor and white walls. It appeared to be the staff kitchen and there was a woman sitting at the scrubbed refectory table eating breakfast. She was a fresh-faced girl in the Cloud's Hill olive-green uniform and she seemed pleased to see Daisy.

'Hi Daisy, I'm Jane. Get yourself some coffee. I'll tell Leah you're up.'

'Thanks,' mumbled Daisy, feeling slightly disconcerted that this stranger knew who she was.

She was on her second cup of coffee, had eaten some fruit and toast and was talking with Jane when Leah arrived.

'Did you sleep well?' asked Leah, pouring some hot water into a mug.

'Yes, thank you. Very well. It's a lovely room.'

'The China Blue room is beautiful,' Leah agreed. She opened a drawer, took out a teabag and dunked it into the mug, instantly filling the air with the smell of raspberries.

'I like the Rose Pink room best,' said Jane.

'Cleo's in there,' Leah said. 'You'll like Cleo,' she added confidently. 'Come with me to my office for a chat.'

Leah's office was near the reception area, a small room filled with personality. Paintings, photographs and books lined the walls, while the small table between the two armchairs had yet more photos on it, along with a fragile white orchid. The desk was perfectly clear apart from an old-fashioned black phone.

Leah sat down on one of the chairs and Daisy sank onto the other, cradling her coffee.

'Were you trying to kill yourself?' asked Leah, slender fingers dunking the raspberry teabag by its string.

'What?' asked Daisy in genuine confusion.

'Yesterday. Were you trying to kill yourself or was it an accident?'

'An accident,' Daisy gasped. 'Why would you think otherwise?'

'Because of how much you'd obviously had to drink.'

Outraged, Daisy rushed in to argue with this suggestion. 'I just had some wine.'

'Rather a lot of wine,' Leah said gently. 'I saw the bottles. You've only been staying there a week. And unless your mother entertains a lot, you've gone through a lot of alcohol. A couple of bottles a day?'

It sounded so shameful that Daisy flushed. 'I was depressed and I wanted a pick-me-up.'

'Alcohol isn't a pick-me-up,' Leah stated. 'It's a depressant, and anyone who considers two bottles a day a reasonable amount, obviously has a problem with alcohol abuse.'

I don't have a problem, Daisy wanted to say, but she was shocked into silence, because the way Leah explained it, it all sounded so plausible.

'Where I come from, people don't drink like that,' Leah said. 'In LA, if someone has a cocktail at lunch, the rest of the table give them the AA service number. Here, well . . . it's one of the issues I have with Europe. You do drink and smoke to excess.'

'You mean like fat?' asked Daisy.

'That's an American issue,' Leah said. 'We eat too much, you drink too much and live dangerously. Neither is good.'

'I know lots of women who drink as much as me,' Daisy insisted.

'And that makes it right?'

Daisy felt put upon and angry suddenly. How dare this strange woman interrogate her about her drinking? Daisy had just suffered an appalling loss and this woman hadn't a clue how that felt.

'Who died and left you in charge?' she demanded with hostility.

Leah's serene face didn't change. 'Nobody,' she said. 'I'm running a holistic centre here. It'd be pretty dumb if I didn't know the facts about what you can and cannot put into your body. It's like a machine: if you care about it, you cherish it. If you don't care about it, you put the worst gas in and aren't surprised when the engine falls out.'

'I don't like my body,' Daisy blurted out and then stopped.

'That's obvious. But even if you want to give up on your own body and your own life,' Leah paused, 'you don't have to destroy anyone else's in the process. I drive pretty slow but what if someone had been rushing at that bend and they'd hit you?'

Daisy flushed red again. 'I know, I keep thinking about that,' she said.

'They could have been killed – not just you.'

Daisy wished Leah would stop. 'My partner left me,' she said, leaning forward and holding her face in her hands. 'He left me for another woman and she's pregnant. Now do you understand?'

She told Leah everything: about the years before Alex, how he'd rescued her, how she'd adored him, the hope of having a child, the fertility treatment and his leaving her. Given all that, Daisy felt she was perfectly entitled to do whatever she wanted – get drunk or throw herself off a bridge.

'So you'll make Alex sorry for hurting you by getting sclerosis of the liver or being hit by a car?' asked Leah.

'No . . .' It did sound stupid put that way. 'I wanted to feel less sad, that's all.'

'And punish him by hurting yourself?'

'Give me a break!'

'That's what you were doing.'

'I wasn't,' Daisy said defensively. 'People need to let off steam when they're hurt, that's all.'

'Letting off steam like that doesn't work,' Leah said.

'How do you know bloody everything, then? Are you the expert on emotional pain?' demanded Daisy, angry with herself for being so hopeless, and angry with Leah for knowing exactly which buttons to press. She'd just spilled her heart out and now it was being thrown back in her face.

Leah didn't answer at first. She drank some of her raspberry tea, sitting back in her armchair. Time stretched into two minutes, then maybe three, with no sound but for the noise of the phones on reception and someone saying, 'Hello, Cloud's Hill, can I help you?' in a cheery voice.

'Now that you mention it, I am an expert on pain,' Leah said softly, 'although it's not expertise I'd wanted. My son died, you see.'

Daisy felt herself stiffen. 'I didn't know you had a son,' she stammered, thinking of how she and Mary had assumed Leah was some wealthy divorcee with no ties and lots of money.

'I don't any more,' Leah said simply. 'I'm a mother with no one left to mother.'

For the first time in a long while, Daisy felt ashamed of how she'd behaved. Her hope of having a son or daughter seemed to have died but she hadn't had a *real* child who'd died. A living person you'd given birth to dying was much, much worse than the death of the dream of one.

It wasn't as if anybody had said she'd never have a child. There was still hope. She might meet Mr Fabulous and be deliriously happy and pregnant within a wet week. But Leah's son would always be dead. Always.

'What happened?' she asked softly.

'I don't like to talk about it,' Leah said.

'Sorry.'

'It's OK. What I meant to say was that I don't like talking about Jesse's death, but I do talk about it. Grief corrodes from the inside out and talking helps, they say.'

'I didn't mean to stir up memories . . .'

'Memories are things you think about from time to time,' said Leah. 'I think about Jesse every day. He's with me, not a memory.' She touched the amethyst crystals around her neck. 'He bought these for me on a holiday and I saved them and didn't wear them much until he died. They bring me peace.'

'How can you have peace?' Daisy asked in astonishment.

'A kind of peace,' Leah amended. 'The peace that comes from knowing you can't change things, no matter how many times you wake up in the night screaming. The peace of acceptance. You learn to live with it.' She smiled wryly. 'I guess the old clichés are the best.'

'I'm so sorry.'

'He would have been thirty-three this year. You'd have liked him, Daisy. He was tall, handsome – or I could be biased,' she smiled, 'but I thought he was handsome. He'd had lots of girlfriends, so he must have been. Funny, clever, kind, loved his dog. I sound like a besotted mom, don't I? He was perfect – to me, anyhow. He liked danger – that was his big flaw. Heli-skiing, abseiling, rock climbing in Utah, anything the insurance companies sucked in their breath at. Motorcycles,' she added finally. 'A motorcycle killed him.'

'How did you deal with it?' Daisy simply couldn't imagine how a person would manage after such a loss. She would self-destruct, she knew.

'I had to learn to rely on myself,' Leah said. 'I looked at me and didn't like what I saw. The only good thing in my life, apart from my husband, Sol, had been Jesse and he was gone. I wanted to end it all, but I didn't have the courage to take the pills. It was a scary place to be in.'

Daisy sat silently and listened.

'For the first couple of years I was just surviving,' Leah went on. 'My marriage broke up – it's not uncommon after a child's death, so everyone told me. Then I got involved with a group helping to raise awareness for people to carry donor cards. It's a big deal for some people. Most of us haven't thought about it. What to do with your organs when you die wouldn't have been a dinner party conversation in my home.

'Working for the charity was helpful and I felt I was adding something good to the world, but it wasn't enough. I was like . . .' she was searching for the correct way to describe it, 'a drug addict who was clean but was still a drug addict, if you get my point. They haven't dealt with all the stuff, they're just not actually abusing the drugs.'

Daisy nodded. She understood.

'That's what I was doing,' Leah continued. 'I appeared to be living – on the outside, anyhow – but I wasn't. I was dead inside and I hadn't dealt with any of it. It all seemed so wrong, you see,' she said. 'No mom should have to bury her child.'

'I'm so sorry,' Daisy said again helplessly. 'And I'm so ashamed,' she added. 'I thought the worst thing in the world was happening to me and it wasn't, it had happened to you.'

'Infertility is a grief too,' Leah said. 'You have to mourn and there isn't a quick fix. It's the same as when a woman has a miscarriage and people stupidly say, "Have another baby," as if a new one will make you forget the one who died. Parents will still mourn the tiny baby they've lost, like you still mourn the babies you haven't had yet. I understand that. But it's not over for you yet, Daisy. It's over with Alex, for sure, but nobody has told you that you can't bear children, and, if that is the case, nobody says you can't adopt or you can't foster. The only limitations are the ones you put on yourself. If you adopted a baby, would that child be any less yours?'

'No,' said Daisy. 'I hadn't thought about it really. I'd assumed we would go down the fertility treatment road first and see then. That was the first big step and everything would follow. And all the time the love of my life was cheating on me, getting someone else pregnant. Dumb, that's me.'

'You're not dumb,' Leah said firmly. 'When you're hurt, you feel stupid because you think you should have seen it coming. But if we knew everything that was going to happen to us we wouldn't get out of bed in the morning. All I'm saying is, open your mind and your heart to the possibilities.' Leah looked at her watch. 'I've got work to do, Daisy. In the meanwhile, there are some lovely people here today. You should join in with them this afternoon and have a couple of treatments, and a hot tub.'

'It didn't do me much good before,' Daisy said, thinking of the last time she'd been here and how, a few days later, she and Alex had gone to the fertility clinic, from where everything had gone rapidly downhill.

'You weren't ready before.'

Something pinged in Daisy's head but she couldn't quite think what it was.

'But I haven't booked in or anything.'

Leah smiled. 'We can always make room for someone who really needs it.'

CHAPTER SEVENTEEN

At eight in the morning of that same day, Mel had picked Caroline up from the train station in Carrickwell for their day of pampering at Cloud's Hill.

Adrian's mum, Lynda, was looking after the girls in the morning, and Mel's mum, Karen, was taking the afternoon shift. Graham's sister was picking up Caroline's boys after school.

'Diplomatic,' Adrian had pronounced when Mel explained the arrangements for Sarah and Carrie that morning.

'I fine-tuned my peace-keeping skills yesterday when Carrie and Sarah both inexplicably wanted to play with the same Teletubby. There was nearly war and I solved it.'

'How?'

'Took away Tinky Winky, switched the television on to *Dora the Explorer* and doled out milk and biscuits all round.'

'I'd run for president if I were you,' Adrian grinned. 'You'd get my vote.'

Mel was still smiling when she saw Caroline walking down the platform steps, carrying a small suitcase.

'Hi!' yelled Mel happily, then stopped.

Instead of looking thrilled with anticipation of the day of luxury ahead of her, Caroline looked weary and red-eyed, as if she'd been crying all the way from Dublin.

'What's happened?' Mel had visions of Graham and Caroline having had some great argument that would undo all the restorative power of the day ahead.

'Everything's fine, totally fine,' Caroline said in a bunged-up voice. 'Graham was perfectly happy that I was going to be away tonight. His sister's staying over to babysit and he said he might work late.' She gave a hollow laugh and her eyes brimmed. 'I'd love to know where he's going to be tonight. Some fantastic little restaurant, the same sort he used to bring me to, or an expensive hotel with . . . her. And his sister won't realise. He'll say he's taking clients out for a drink.'

'You don't know for sure that he's having an affair,' Mel said. It certainly sounded as if he was, but that didn't mean it was true.

'I know, but . . .'

'We'll talk in the car.' Mel put her arm around her friend and hugged her. Poor Caroline.

'I know I shouldn't be crying but I can't help it,' sobbed Caroline. 'I'm a mess, aren't I? I can't go into a swanky spa looking like this.'

'Nobody will notice,' Mel said, 'and if they do, say you've been having your blackheads squeezed in preparation for your face mask. That would bring tears to anyone's eyes.'

She wasn't sure how they got to Cloud's Hill because she was so busy trying to comfort Caroline that the drive was a blur. Now that she'd told *someone* how awful it all was, in between crying, Caroline talked non-stop about the mess of her life.

'I feel so useless,' she sobbed, 'as if it's my fault. I've changed, I know, but what can I do? The children do come first. Graham's old enough to look after himself and make a sandwich if he wants one, so I don't bother doing those things for him. But,' Caroline added, 'the irritating thing is that he wants all that. He wants to be mothered too, and I only have enough mothering in me for the children. He wants me to be Mum and Sex Goddess and the career woman I once was and I can't . . .'

'Of course you can't,' Mel said briskly. 'You've changed. I've changed since I've given up work to stay at home. It's an enormous adjustment, and you needed Graham to understand that.' She said a silent prayer of thanks that Adrian was the type of man who did understand. He'd taken her change of life in his stride. He loved *her*, not whatever role she had to play that day. It was true that if somebody truly loved you, you could be yourself with them. She'd never be able to tell Caroline this; it would sound so smug. But Mel didn't feel smug, just very lucky.

'Isn't this lovely?' she said cheerily as they parked outside Cloud's Hill.

It was fabulous: elegant, luxurious and somehow serene in its lofty position high up the mountain.

'Remember years ago when we used to save up and go for a load of sessions at the Beauty Sanctuary opposite the office?' Caroline said mistily.

In their early days of working together, partying and paying rent on their apartment had taken up much of their salaries, but they'd still managed to take time out for bikini and leg waxings, and deep cleansing facials.

'I loved that time,' Caroline added. 'I thought I had life all worked out.'

'You'll have life all worked out again,' Mel promised, and she really hoped so.

In the three days she'd been at Cloud's Hill, Cleo had felt herself relax. Only then had she realised how wound up like a spring she'd been when she'd got there. She'd gone for long walks around Cloud's Hill, enjoying climbing Mount Carraig and looking down at Carrickwell in the distance, and she'd enjoyed meeting the other members of staff.

They were all crazy about Leah.

Niall, who'd worked on the house as a brickie when it was being built, and was now the spa's handyman, had told Cleo that Mrs Meyer had given him the best bit of advice he'd ever been given. It seemed that his mother and his girlfriend, Liza, didn't get on with each other and Niall was torn between asking Liza to marry him while, at the same time, knowing that his mother would go mad if this happened. When there was such naked dislike on both sides, what hope could there be for the future?

Mrs Meyer had said that it seemed as if both women wanted to be the only woman in Niall's life. Which was unfair.

'She said I should get them both together and tell them I loved them both and couldn't cope with them being childish any longer, and it was up to them to get on because they were both important in my life,' Niall told Cleo with relish. 'It worked! I don't know how, but it did.'

'I know what you mean,' Cleo said, thinking of the long talks she'd had with Leah. She wasn't sure how Leah managed it, but she gently prodded you along until you came up with the solution to your problems – a solution you'd known all along. Cleo was beginning to figure out what she should do. She'd talk to Jason and Barney, and she'd phone her parents. She loved them and she'd been crazy to let this family feud stand in the way of that.

'You've got to come to Cloud's Hill – you'd love it,' she told Trish on the phone. 'I'd get you a discount. I've had the Indian head massage again and –'

'Never mind the Indian head massage,' said Trish. 'Tyler phoned the house looking for you.'

'What?' Cleo couldn't believe it. 'How did he get the number?'

'From the hotel, I guess. They have your private details on file and you can buy any information, if you really want to,' Trish said knowledgeably. 'Nobody's identity is safe, I've said it before. Once you're on a computer, anyone can hack in and find out everything about you.'

'Trish, you've got to stop reading crime novels,' Cleo sighed. 'What did Tyler say?' She felt a shiver of excitement that he'd tried to contact her. He did care! She wasn't just his Dublin stopover girl. Or was it that he hadn't got anywhere sexually with her and he couldn't bear to leave any girl unbonked?

'I didn't talk to him. Ron did,' Trish explained.

'Ron answered?' Cleo could imagine how Tyler would construe a man answering her home phone number.

'He met Ron in the Shepherd the first night you went out with him, so he sort of worked out that we all lived together.'

So much for the cool town-house-shared-with-a-girlfriend notion Cleo had pitched to him.

'And?'

'And Ron told him you'd hot-footed it off back to Carrickwell and you were all upset anyway, because some awful bastard had bought your family's hotel to rip it down and you had this great plan to throw yourself in front of the bulldozers and stop them.'

'He didn't!' Cleo hoped this was just Trish's idea of a joke.

'Afraid he did,' Trish said apologetically. 'Ron's not the brightest bulb in the pack. I gave out yards to him and said you'd never said you were going to throw yourself in front of the bulldozers, but he thought it was the type of thing you'd do.'

'And then what? What else did Tyler say?'

'He asked was that the Willow Hotel and Ron, like a big gobshite, said yes, and it had been sold out from under your nose.'

'I don't want to hear any more,' groaned Cleo. 'OK, I do. How did Tyler sound then?'

'Ron is not the sort of person who tunes into people's personal emotional frequency,' Trish pointed out. 'He thinks a woman saying "let's talk" is code for "I have a deep inner problem and I want you to turn off the football so I can wreck your head by sharing it with you".'

'True,' Cleo agreed. 'Did Tyler say he was coming to Carrickwell to see me?' She hoped he had.

'No. But Ron and Tyler are going to the Aussie Rules match next time Tyler's here.'

'Great. Just great. Male bonding at its most primal.'

Cleo was still mulling this over when two women walked in through the door and came over to her desk. This was her first morning working on reception and she was enjoying it all so far. People were so pleased to be here, anticipating a day of pure relaxation. Nobody had marched in, irate from late plane connections and traffic snarl-ups that had made them late for meetings.

'Hello,' she beamed. 'Welcome to Cloud's Hill. Can I help you?'

'Mel Redmond and Caroline Casey checking in,' said the smaller woman with the heart-shaped face and the huge blue eyes. She was very pretty and animated-looking, and her hair was the sort of funky blonde messy style that Cleo would have loved to try but knew her hair would rebel against.

The blonde woman's friend, who looked as if she'd just heard some dreadful news, leaned against the desk as if she might fall over without support. Cleo quickly found their reservations. 'If you'd sign in here . . .' she said to the blonde, who signed 'Mel Redmond'. 'You've twenty minutes before your first treatment. Would you like to go into the den and relax, and I'll get some coffee and pastries brought in for you?' she said kindly.

'Thanks,' said Mel gratefully.

'You're booked in for an aromatherapy facial first with Li-Chan, and Ms Casey is having the holistic body therapy with mineral clays.'

'Sounds wonderful,' said Mel.

'It is,' Cleo replied. 'And wait till you have the reflexology treatment. I had it yesterday and it's incredible. You'll float out of the room. And you've got a massage and a paraffin manicure then.'

Mel grinned. 'I have been so looking forward to this,' she sighed.

By five that evening, Leah was tired. She didn't have the energy she used to have, in the days when Jesse was a child.

She'd been thinking a lot about Jesse since she'd told Daisy about him. Not that he wasn't with her every day, in her thoughts and her heart. But that was the grown-up Jesse who'd died. Hearing Daisy talk of her longing for a baby reminded Leah of Jesse as a small child, and then as a gangly adolescent. She remembered those happy years when she, Sol and Jesse used to go skiing at Lake Tahoe. They'd be up early, out skiing all day, and come home at night exhausted and happy. They'd sit in the hot tub looking out at the lake, and talk.

Jesse had loved skiing. He'd had no fear.

'Momma, watch me!' he'd yell when he was six and already an expert skiier, brown eyes shining merrily as he turned on his skis and pushed himself off in the snow to perform manoeuvres that Leah wouldn't dare to try.

They used to stay in Leah's mother's cabin in Tahoe: a big, comfortable place that Vanna, her mother, hadn't been in for years because Vanna preferred the heat of LA, though she never let the sun get on her face.

Sun was so ageing. Vanna, a one-time B-movie star who'd become a daytime soap queen, had taught her daughter about how to protect her face from the sun. 'Your face is your fortune,' Vanna said, and she believed this with a religious fervour. 'Do whatever it takes to stay young because once this is gone,' she'd touch her face with its high cheekbones and now-fading beauty, 'it's all over.'

Leah might have become like her mother – obsessed with appearances and material things – if it hadn't been for Sol and Jesse.

Sol Meyer owned furniture stores and she'd met him when she was twenty-five.

'He's not in the business, you mean?' her mother had said horrified, when she'd heard Leah was seeing this man. 'The business' was the movie industry. Anyone outside it was a non-person.

'I'm not in the business, Vanna,' Leah had pointed out. 'And I love him.'

Her mother had waved one perfectly cared-for hand theatrically. 'See if I care. You'll be back.'

Leah hadn't been back. She and Sol got married, and a couple of years later Jesse had been born. They lived on the outskirts of Carmel. Jesse went to the local school, and Sol's business went from strength to strength.

They became rich but their life together was still pretty much the same: comfortable, companionable, good.

Jesse went to college to study aeronautical engineering. He was interested in the space programme and had been on the Mission Control tour in NASA Houston many times.

'Look up, Mom,' he'd say to her on clear nights as they stood on the deck outside the house. 'Look up at the stars. That's the world we've got to explore. Mankind has only touched a fraction of the universe. There's so much out there.'

Leah, who got weak on the highest escalator in department stores, thought of her beloved son going up into space and shuddered. But you had to let people live their own lives.

The phone call had come early in the morning, from Jesse's friend, Carl, in the hospital. Some kids in a stolen car had swerved in front of Jesse's motorcycle and he'd crashed into a wall.

The medical staff were wonderful to her and Sol.

Jesse was still technically alive. That was the crux of the matter. He was brain dead; he would never recover; he'd never be Jesse again, ever. The question was, would his parents let the doctors harvest his organs? It was a bewildering choice to be faced with. Your son is dead, now he can help other people. Corneal transplant, liver transplant, lungs, skin grafts – the list was endless. She later learned that hospital staff described motorcycles as 'donor cycles', because so many people became organ donors as a result of bike accidents.

Distraught with grief, she and Sol tried to think about what Jesse would want them to do. It was not something that families usually discussed.

It was Carl who had made sense of it all. Traumatised but refusing to go home, because Mrs and Mr Meyer had to have support, he mentioned the run Jesse had recently done for charity. 'It was a ten K for kids with cancer; he was really into it. My guess is he'd have liked to donate anything he could. Keep living on, you know, his spirit being alive in someone else . . .' Carl talked a bit like a born-again hippie, Jesse used to say fondly.

Leah and Sol agreed to donate as many of Jesse's organs as were viable. Carl hugged Leah, a bit like Jesse might have hugged her, and said, 'Way to go,' with tears in his voice.

Twelve people benefited from Jesse Meyer's death – which was a beginning for all of them, and it was a beginning for Leah too. Once Jesse was dead, she had to learn to live again herself, and she didn't know how. She didn't know who she was, what she was or where she was.

She and Sol inhabited different pain-filled worlds. Within a year, they'd split up, after twenty-six years of marriage. They couldn't cope with each other's pain, and every time Leah sat down to dinner with Sol, she thought of how Jesse should be there too, and she'd have to get up to cry.

She never thought she'd learn to live again. She tried all sorts of therapy, healing diets, retreats run by television evangelists, you name it. But finally a friend took her to a spa in Arizona, a remote, sun-baked place that looked like one of the last places God made: untouched by civilisation and exquisitely beautiful in its wildness. There, in the heat and the dust, in a place away from the trappings of her old life, Leah felt at peace.

Many different people came to Cloud's Hill, the old Indian name for the small, rocky patch of land, to recuperate after illnesses or emotional stress. The owner, an ageless American Indian woman named Sequoia, had many different types of clients: from the very rich who arrived on the private runway in Lear jets, to people who couldn't have afforded Cloud's Hill at all if Sequoia didn't run the place so that the rich essentially subsidised the non-paying guests. The first week Leah was there, she spent time with two East LA teenage girls battling their way back to health after coming off drugs, as well as going on walks with a New York comedian who'd turned to food addiction when his beloved mother had died. Cloud's Hill couldn't magic all their problems away, Sequoia told Leah, but it seemed to help.

'You're good with people,' Sequoia added. 'You're gentle, kind, and you know what pain is. You can't pull people out of the pit if you haven't been in there yourself. Would you consider staying on, to work?'

In the end, Leah remained in Cloud's Hill for two years. She learned that helping other people helped her and she learned that she had a gift for helping others. Her pain would never go away and, if she'd had an addictive personality, like Daisy and so many of the people she'd met at Cloud's Hill over those two years, she'd have turned to pills or booze or food. She could understand the need to block out pain, but it was still there when you woke up again in the morning. You needed to find another way to deal with it.

One day, she told Sequoia that she'd love to set up her own spa in another healing place.

It had taken her a long time to find the spot with the right sense of healing and tranquillity. The old Delaney house on Mount Carraig had been perfect. And in the end, the name had been obvious: Cloud's Hill.

'Cloud's Hill in Arizona and Cloud's Hill in Ireland,' she'd said to Sequoia. 'Can I use the name?'

'Of course. The two places can be like twin stars in the sky, lighting the way,' Sequoia answered.

Leah remembered Jesse love of the stars and what lay beyond them, and thought Sequoia had got it exactly right.

There was a knock on her office door.

'Leah,' said Cleo, 'are you going down to the hot tub?'

'Yes. I asked Daisy if she wanted to come with us.'

'Good,' said Cleo, who'd met Daisy for the first time the night before at dinner. 'There are a couple more guests who aren't finished yet, Mel Redmond and Caroline Casey. They're going to the tub as well. I just met Mel in the changing room.'

'See you there in five,' Leah replied.

The hot tub room in Cloud's Hill faced southwest, so that when the evening sun was sinking gently down towards the horizon, it shone in through the huge sliding doors. The doors were open, letting the drowsy heat of the evening mingle with the warm damp air from the hot tub.

Mel slipped into the water feeling wonderful. She wasn't so sure about Caroline, though. They'd both had a wonderful day with lots of treatments, but Caroline's spirits were still low.

At lunch, Mel had felt wearied by this and felt like challenging her to cheer up. But then she saw Caroline was spinning her wedding ring round and round her ring finger absently, and she'd felt a bitch for being impatient. Caroline wanted to save her marriage and didn't want to leap to conclusions: that was the brave thing to do, Mel knew.

Now Caroline sat opposite her in the hot tub, lying back with her head resting on the edge of the tub, her eyes closed.

There was one other woman in there with them. She was younger than Mel, voluptuous and sexy, with the creamy pale skin of a natural redhead, and strawberry-blonde curls piled out of the way on top of her head.

She'd given Mel and Caroline a shy smile when they'd come in, and had leaned back and closed her eyes too.

Closing your eyes was a handy way of not talking to anybody at such close quarters.

'Juice, anybody?' It was the tall girl who'd been on reception that morning, carrying a tray of jugs and glasses. Mel thought her name was Cleo.

'I've got orange, mango and,' Cleo grinned, 'for those of us in need of some excitement in our lives, passionfruit juice!'

The other three laughed.

'It's the only passion I'm likely to get these days,' Cleo went on, setting the tray down.

'I don't believe that for a minute,' said Mel wryly. 'I bet I'm the oldest one here. You young ones should be having loads of passion.' She included the redhead in this sweeping statement.

'You couldn't be the oldest,' Cleo said in amazement. Mel looked as if she was in her mid-thirties at the latest. Everything about her suggested someone who didn't intend to get old before her time.

'I am,' said Mel. 'Forty and counting. You're what . . . twenty-four?'

'Is it that obvious?' laughed Cleo. 'I'm trying to look more mature for work. I've a hotel management degree and looking a bit older helps.'

'It's the only job where it does, then,' said Caroline. 'Can I have some passion juice, please?'

'Me too,' said Daisy. 'You're wrong about the passion,' she said to Mel. 'This is the only passion I'm likely to get, so give me a big glass, Cleo.'

The juice poured, Cleo got into the tub and the four of them lay back in comfortable silence.

'I had no idea a hot tub could be so relaxing,' Caroline said finally. 'I could never see the attraction before but it's soothing, isn't it?'

'I know just what you mean,' Daisy said. 'The first time I was here, Leah said this tub was special and was the Hot Tub of Truth. Or was it Honesty?'

'No, Truth, I think she told me,' said Cleo.

'The water makes you tell the truth?' Caroline laughed. 'This tub must have heard some secrets then. I don't think it would be interested in mine.'

'You have to say what you'd like most in the world,' Daisy explained. 'You're supposed to be truthful.' She thought then of the white lie she'd told when she was here with Mary and Paula. She'd said she'd like to be able to eat as much chocolate as she wanted.

'Remember Truth or Dare when you were a teenager?' Cleo asked.

'I hated that,' Mel shuddered. 'People tried to trick you into revealing things about yourself. You had no control over it.'

'I never played it,' Daisy said. Fat girls weren't asked to play anything sexually charged like that. She touched the roll of her stomach under the water. She was getting bigger all the time. She'd put on pounds and pounds. She needed a whole new wardrobe.

'Oh, Daisy, you must have,' said Cleo.

Daisy shook her head.

'We used to play a version of Truth or Dare years ago, Mel,' Caroline said. 'Mel and I worked together in an office,' she told the other two, 'and we had some wild times. We're boring and settled down now. I've got three kids and I'm a full-time mother.' She looked defiantly at Cleo and Daisy, as if daring them to say anything negative about staying home with the kids.

'I recently gave up work to stay home too,' Mel said hastily, noticing that Caroline hadn't mentioned that she was married. 'I'm married with two little girls, Sarah and Carrie.'

She didn't allow herself to say, 'I used to work for Lorimar.' That sort of validation was in the past. Who she had been wasn't important. What mattered was who she was now. She didn't need a job to define her.

'That must be wonderful, staying at home to raise your children,' Daisy said enviously. 'I'd love children but . . .' She stopped, having been about to say something oblique like 'it hasn't happened'. Why lie? Where had lying got her? 'My boyfriend and I split up recently, just when we were about to have fertility treatment because I wasn't getting pregnant, so the whole baby business is off the agenda right now,' she said shakily.

'Poor you,' said Mel in sympathy.

'What happened?' Caroline seemed to have forgotten her own problems for the first time that day.

'He said we needed a break.'

'Ah yes, I've heard that one before,' said Cleo vehemently.

'Typical bloody man,' added Caroline.

Daisy shrugged and slid further under until her shoulders were beneath the water. 'I thought he was scared of the treatment, but it turned out he was in love with someone else, someone he worked with. And she was pregnant. *Is* pregnant.'

Caroline gasped.

'That's terrible,' Mel said.

'It's awful.' Cleo was white-faced. 'I had no idea, Daisy. At dinner last night, Leah said you'd come here for a bit of recuperation, but I hadn't a clue it was something that bad. What a betrayal!'

She thought that her family briskly turning their backs on her had been the ultimate betrayal – it hadn't been. It had been a family row and there was a way back from it. *She* was the one who'd decided that her family had to capitulate or they didn't love her. Imagine if they'd really pushed her coldly out of their lives, the way Daisy's boyfriend had done.

'What are you going to do?' Cleo asked. 'Is he staying with this other woman or what?'

Daisy nodded. 'He loves her.'

'I'm so sorry,' Mel said sympathetically. 'That must be so difficult for you.' Daisy was so pretty: very sexy in a voluptuous way, and vulnerable too. Mel didn't think there were many women who could manage to look sexy in a hot tub with their hair all tied up, but Daisy somehow managed it.

'You wouldn't want him back anyway,' Cleo declared.

A few days ago, Daisy knew that was exactly what she'd wanted. 'Before I came here, I would have taken him back,' she admitted. 'Under any circumstances.' It was good to say it out loud, to remind herself how hopelessly addicted to Alex she'd been.

'You *couldn't* have him back,' Cleo said passionately. No way could she settle for second-best. Love should be a hundred per cent pure or there was no point to it. 'What about the other woman and the baby? They'd always be there.'

'I stupidly thought she could go off somewhere, though he'd be involved with the baby because it would be the right thing to do,' Daisy said. 'But we'd have our own baby, so he'd still be mine. We would have our little family and that would make everything better again.'

'And you'd never look at him in the middle of the night as he slept, and wonder what the smile on his face was for?' demanded Cleo. 'I would.'

Mel had wanted to ask the same question but felt it was too

personal, especially with Caroline sitting across from her, on the verge of tears.

'He'd be with me,' Daisy said, as if that was enough. 'That was what I used to think,' she added. 'I know it won't work now. It's obviously my fault we couldn't have a baby. Alex has just proved that. But anyway, we can't go back to the way it was before. If Alex wanted to try again, we probably could, but he doesn't, so that's that.' That pinging in her head was there again, telling her something. But what?

'You think you could have tried again if he wanted to?' Caroline asked shakily.

'Maybe. Who knows?' Daisy said.

'It's just that . . .' Caroline reached behind her on the tiles for her towel so she could wipe her eyes dry. 'I think my husband is having an affair and I don't know what to do about it.'

Mel held her breath.

'You think?' said Cleo, leaning forward. 'I'd confront him and demand the truth. If he was, he'd be out on the street like a shot with his entire wardrobe flung out after him! And I'd take his wallet before I threw him out so he had no money and would have to scrounge off his friends. Let him see what it would be like to be humiliated!'

Mel burst out laughing. She couldn't help it. Cleo was hilarious and so fierily passionate in her beliefs.

'Sorry, Cleo,' Mel said. 'That's a brilliant plan but it mightn't be that easy. What if . . .' She looked at Caroline and thought how different they all were. Cleo, youthful and impetuous, would throw her man out on the street, while Caroline wanted to do her best to keep the marriage together at any cost, for her children. 'What if you had kids and you still loved him?'

'It would depend on whether he loved you enough,' Daisy said thoughtfully. 'If he wanted to try again, and you did too, you could. Your relationship would be different and it would take a long time to trust him again, but you could do it.' She realised that if Alex had come back to her, so much about their relationship would have had to change for things to work out. If she'd remained the passive, lesser partner, then they'd have been back to square one instantly: Alex in charge and her eager to please him, because she was so desperate to be loved.

'I don't know if Graham loves me any more or wants to be married,' Caroline said softly.

'Ask him!' It seemed so clear to Cleo. 'Don't waste time, just do it.'

'You're absolutely right,' Caroline said. 'I will. Tomorrow, as soon as I get home.' She looked at Mel for confirmation that this was a good idea.

Mel nodded sympathetically. 'You owe it to yourself to find out, Caroline,' she said. 'It's not going to go away if you ignore it. I know you want to do what's right for the children, but ignoring it isn't the right thing for them either.' She decided to go ahead and speak her mind and hope it wouldn't offend her friend. 'Children are so sensitive, they'll notice if the marriage is in trouble, Caroline. So you owe it to them to find out the truth, and to yourself. You're a brilliant mother and I admire you so much . . .' She'd said enough, too much probably.

Caroline bit her lip but she nodded bravely at Mel and mouthed, 'Thanks.'

'Don't do anything you don't want to just because I said it,' said Cleo, suddenly contrite at seeing how upset Caroline was. 'I'm very all-or-nothing, and lately, I keep making the wrong choices. In the past few months, I've had a huge row with my family and walked out on the only man who's ever made my heart go jump, because at the time, they appeared to be the right things to do. Cleo, the Super Heroine! Flattens relationships in a single bound!'

'It can't be that bad,' Mel said, glad they'd changed topics.

'It is,' Cleo sighed. 'You see, I met this wonderful man,' she began, and told them the story. 'I thought Tyler had lied to me, and my friend Trish kept asking me why he'd bother lying? She's queen of the conspiracy theory, so if she thought he was being honest, I should have listened to her. But I was so angry when I saw Roth Hotels' plans for the Willow and I just ran out on him.'

'You haven't talked to him since?' Daisy said.

Cleo shook her head. 'I never gave him my mobile number because we saw each other every day and he could get me on reception, and I had his suite number, so, no. I ruined it, anyway. He'd hardly be interested now. That's the past,' she said firmly. 'I'm not looking back.'

'What about your family?' asked Daisy.

'I'm going to phone them,' Cleo said. 'But first I need to talk to my brothers. Just to clear the air.'

Caroline nodded. 'Clear the air, that's what I've got to do.' She looked at Mel tearfully. 'That's what you're saying, Mel?'

'Caroline, it's got to be your decision and you've got to feel happy with it,' Mel said carefully. 'You have to think it over and decide it's right for you. I'm not the expert, you know. Look how long it took me to make the biggest decision of my life.'

'You made the right one,' Caroline said. 'You're much happier now.'

'What happened?' asked Cleo. She had to know – these women had seen so much in their lives.

'I was a working mother is what happened and it all got too much for me,' Mel said wryly. 'I worked in publicity in Lorimar, the health insurance company, and I loved it. But it got so much harder once I'd had Carrie and Sarah. Every day was a slog and it was so difficult to do it all. I had ideas about the sort of mother I wanted to be and how I wanted my career to go, and they weren't compatible. This is boring for you two, you don't want to hear this,' she added.

'We do,' insisted Daisy.

'Yes, go on,' urged Cleo.

'Lots of companies aren't ready for working mothers,' Mel went on. 'They don't see that job-sharing or flexitime can help everyone. All they see is that working mothers leave on the dot of five and have to take days off when their kids are sick and the people in suits think their eye isn't on the ball. What the company wants are "team players", and that means being at your desk later than everyone else, being able to go to the pub with the boss, and pretending you don't have a life to get back to, and of course, you'll stay late for another meeting tomorrow, because the company is your life. Which is total rubbish. We all have lives outside work – working women are just more honest about the fact.' Mel was getting into her stride now. 'What makes it worse are the ball-busting corporate women who think that being as much like a man as possible is the only way forward in the business world, and they look down on every other woman who doesn't want to be like them. My boss was like that, so there was no point accusing her of sexism. How could a woman be sexist to another woman, people would say.'

'I never knew it was like that,' said Cleo. 'I thought there were laws to protect women at work.' She sat up in the hot tub, quite worked up over this injustice. 'Women are just as good as men at everything,' she said fiercely. 'We don't need to prove it any more. We've done the feminist bit. Nobody should have to chain themselves to the railings any more like a suffragette to win their rights.'

Mel sighed. 'My mum's generation had to prove that they were as good as men. Now the battle is to point out that we're just as good as men, but we're different because we give birth to the children. The majority of people looking after kids are women and nobody's making it easy for them.'

'I never thought of it all that way.' Daisy had imagined having a baby would be part of a happy fantasy life where there were no problems and she could carry the baby into work in a sling if necessary. 'I'm a partner in a clothes shop, Georgia's Tiara,' she said. 'I suppose I could manage childcare better than most because I part-own the business.'

'But if you weren't part-owner and you worked in the shop,' Mel said, 'what then? Would your average boss be more understanding if you had to take days off to take your baby to the hospital, say, for an operation?'

'I don't know.'

'Mel, are you happier now that you've left your job?' asked Cleo. She couldn't imagine not having her career and yet she'd always assumed she'd bring up her kids in the Willow, the way she'd been brought up. That wouldn't be an option now.

Mel thought for a moment. 'I don't have to indulge the children with quality time, which means you try to cram a whole day into an hour, and still feel guilty, while your child goes to bed tired, wondering why Mummy is so hyper,' she said. 'When I was working in Lorimar, I'd come home at night, try and play with the kids, and then lie there in bed later, shattered, and still feeling I was getting it wrong. So yes,' she grinned, 'I am happier. But it's not always easy. When I was at work, I was guilty. Now that I'm home I feel guilty when I snap at Sarah and Carrie. There's no free time, not even a trip to the loo.' She smiled. 'And I feel guilty that I should have tried harder to make it work in the office, because having only one salary is very tough financially, so the girls might miss out that way. Guilt still rules.'

'But,' went on Cleo, because she wanted to have all the facts, 'if you could have combined work and the children in a way that you were happy with, would you like to have kept doing your old job?'

It was the sixty-four-thousand-dollar question.

There was still something missing from her life, Mel had to admit. Yes, she and Adrian were happy, they had time for each other, their conversations weren't limited to the familiar *hello, how was your day, there's a pizza in the fridge*. And the girls were blossoming. But . . . Mel thought she knew what the missing ingredient was: balance.

She didn't want to get on the hamster wheel again, like at Lorimar. But she did want to go back to work and this time she wanted it to be on her own terms. 'I want to be a hands-on mother and have some sort of career. Lots of people do it – it's got to be possible. I couldn't work out how.'

'But like you said to Daisy, if you were your own boss, then you could work and be with the kids,' Cleo said triumphantly. 'You could work hours that suited you, and you'd understand that women need flexibility in work to do their jobs properly.'

'Why don't you do it?' Caroline said eagerly. 'You could run a company from home and staff it with other people who want part-time flexible work.'

'Yes,' Cleo was eager. 'That's the way forward.'

'And you could still make muffins if the mood hit you,' Caroline pointed out.

'You're missing one thing, girls: what sort of company would I set up?'

'Oh,' Cleo waved this problem away, 'we'll come up with something.'

'How about I try and get some part-time work first,' Mel suggested, 'and see if I can combine work and motherhood before I begin my fight to become an entrepreneur?'

'That's a better idea,' said Daisy wisely. 'And we can meet up every month and discuss how you're getting on.'

'How we're all getting on,' Caroline added, 'with all our plans.'

'I think I'll work on my plans tomorrow,' Daisy said. 'This evening, I just want to relax.'

The pinging in Daisy's head suddenly made sense. 'I keep thinking of something and I couldn't quite remember it, but now I can!' she said, thrilled. 'When the student is ready, the master will appear. I heard it ages ago and thought it meant I was ready to have a baby, but I think it means I'm ready to change my life. I know, I'm going to move apartment. I keep thinking about it because the whole place reminds me of Alex, and I was scared. Not any more. I'm ready! Bring on the changes.'

The others raised their now nearly empty glasses of juice.

'To being ready,' Mel said.

Leah was out in the garden, sitting on the small curved wooden seat just under the window. When the big windows were flung back, and the only outside noise was the droning of insects in the evening sun, you could hear a lot of what went on inside. She had come out to collect flowers earlier, and when she'd heard the women talking, she'd decided to stay outside and forgo her evening hot tub. They were doing pretty well without her.

CHAPTER EIGHTEEN

'*You are strong, confident, beautiful, wise* . . . You're talking to the mirror, you big idiot. And look at that pimple.' Daisy sighed.

This idea of making positive affirmations to yourself in the mirror every morning sounded great in theory. In practice, it made Daisy feel a bit ridiculous and gave her the perfect opportunity to study her make-upless self close up. How had she never noticed her pores before? They were huge. Crater-like.

Giving up wine and drinking lots of water had not had the desired effect on her skin. Her kidneys and liver were undoubtedly breathing a sigh of relief that Daisy's bottle opener was retired, but her bladder was in shock at the floods of water passing through and all the impurities were making a break for it through the skin on her forehead. She'd just battled off three huge pimples there, with a lesser outbreak on her chin, and now another giant one was shining through just in the middle of her forehead. This clean living was making her look terrible, she thought. And she was still overweight. She'd swapped a bottle of wine a night for a box of chocolates. It was a week after she'd returned home to Carrickwell after her visit to Cloud's Hill, and, despite the pimples and the increased chocolate intake, Daisy was feeling better. She'd bought some new clothes to go with her new figure and she'd been checking out apartments and houses for sale around Carrickwell, because she was determined to move out of the home she'd shared with Alex.

There were a couple of lovely apartments in the centre of Carrickwell that sounded perfect, but even though Daisy had told the estate agent she wasn't really interested in houses, she'd found her mind kept returning to the For Sale sign she'd seen on a cottage on her way back from Cloud's Hill.

Leah rang almost every morning before Daisy went to work.

'I'm still sad,' she told Leah on the phone. 'But I can cope with it. I know I can do it, and the pain isn't going to go away, but I have faith in myself. Does that sound stupid?' she asked anxiously.

'Not at all. You're doing wonderfully, Daisy. You're facing up to all the awful parts of your life, and that's empowering. Before, you tried to blot out what you felt; now you're like a boxer, saying, "Hit me with what you've got!"'

'It's hitting me,' Daisy said wryly. 'You wouldn't believe the number of adverts on the telly last night for nappies. Gurgling babies everywhere. It'd break your heart. Then, there was a film on about a mother whose daughter was kidnapped, and I cried non-stop for the first half an hour because I felt like my baby had been taken away too.'

'I understand,' Leah said gently. 'When Jesse died, I got the feeling that the population of twenty-three-year-old men in California had quadrupled. They were everywhere: pumping my gas, giving me change at the store, walking along the sidewalk looking happy, healthy and alive. It was like they were reminding me of what I'd lost. And I thought: why didn't one of *them* die and not my son?'

'Leah,' said Daisy. 'I shouldn't whine to you. You've gone through far too much to have to listen to me moaning. I'm sorry.'

'When you confide in me about how you feel, you're helping me,' Leah said simply. 'I can't talk to most people about what it was like when Jesse died. But when you talk to me about Alex and the sadness you feel about having your baby dream snatched away, I know I can talk back to you. We help each other.'

'I'm not going to wallow any more,' Daisy promised. 'When I couldn't cope with that film last night, I switched over to the news and they had a report about children in Africa orphaned by HIV/AIDS. That's a wake-up call. I'm sobbing into my chocolate box and there are these beautiful kids with the saddest eyes you've ever seen who've got nobody left to love them and who've had to watch their mums and dads die. I thought I might get involved in charity work to raise funds for those kids,' she added. 'It seems selfish to moan about yourself all the time, doesn't it?'

In her office at Cloud's Hill, Leah smiled. 'I admire you so much, Daisy,' she said.

'Admire me?' squeaked Daisy, thrilled.

'You've such a kind, tender heart. You will be a wonderful mum one day, you know that. Even if your child isn't biologically yours, you'll still be its mum.'

Daisy was too choked to reply for a moment. 'I hope so, Leah,' she said finally.

Now that she was feeling better, Daisy was back at work. The summer sale was winding down in Georgia's Tiara and there was a lot of sorting-out of clothes every day and marking things down. It was hard work keeping track of it all, as well as getting the latest autumn/winter stock out on the rails. Clothes, shoes and accessories that Daisy had bought in February were arriving all the time and had to be unpacked, accounted for and priced.

They were working on a shipment of beautiful French knits when Daisy idly mentioned to Mary that she'd decided to move house.

'Why?' demanded Mary, astonished. 'You've got a beautiful apartment; you'd want to be mad to get rid of it!'

'It reminds me all the time of Alex,' Daisy explained. She went on calmly opening the wrappers on the knits, lots of subtle-coloured cardigans and camisoles with velvet trims. Daisy had adored them when she'd first set eyes on them in Paris in January, and she was delighted to see that they still appealed to her. It was so easy to buy stacks of something that looked wonderful when you first saw it, and then hate when it actually arrived in the shop.

'Bullshit,' said Mary succinctly. 'My house reminds me of Bart and I'm not getting rid of it.'

'That's different,' Daisy laughed. Mary could always make her see the funny side of things. 'You've got the kids. Alex and I don't have anything to bind us together; we haven't even talked about the flat.'

'I hope you're going to come to some fabulous financial agreement with the help of a complete shark of a lawyer,' Mary interrupted. 'I'll give you the name of my guy – he's brilliant. Still owes me a ride in that Porsche I paid for,' she added.

'I don't want a shark,' Daisy said. 'I want to let go and move on.' Since she'd left Cloud's Hill, she'd thought of nothing else. She'd spent too long locked in the past, grateful to Alex for rescuing her.

'Letting go and moving on does not mean turning into a complete idiot who throws away a valuable asset,' Mary pointed out. 'You are sitting on a piece of real estate that's worth a lot of money and you want to have something after fourteen years with Alex.'

'Oh, you can't say he left me nothing,' Daisy deadpanned. 'I have got a massive inferiority complex, after all.'

Mary grinned. 'I don't think that the courts would consider that an asset.'

'Besides, I suppose I had that long before I met Alex,' Daisy added honestly. 'I want my half of the money for the apartment, that's all, Mary. No more.'

'Where would you move? Not out of Carrickwell?' said Mary in alarm.

'There's a cottage for sale near Leah's. And my mum's,' Daisy added. 'I've driven past it a few times and I've decided to see it on Saturday afternoon. I've never thought of a cottage before, but that was because Alex was an apartment person. I thought I was too, but I'm not, actually. Funny, I've lived in apartments all my grown-up life and now I think that I prefer houses.'

Carla, who'd taken over from Paula in the shop, stuck her head in the stockroom.

'Just sold tons off the sale rail,' she said delightedly. She held up a pair of denims with embroidered hems. 'But nobody's gone near these for days. Should we drop the price?'

'I suppose so. I'll fix the labels,' sighed Daisy, taking the denims so Carla could go back to the shop floor. 'I hate the sale. It's constant recrimination for all the articles I bought that were wrong. I thought people would want cute jeans like these.'

'They did,' Mary pointed out, 'they just didn't want that pair, size ten.'

'I fitted into a size ten once,' Daisy began.

'Oh, don't start,' warned Mary.

'No, I won't,' said Daisy. 'I'm going to go and lose the weight.'

'Why?' asked Mary. 'So you can be thin once again and Alex will come back to you?'

'No,' said Daisy, 'so I can be thin and beautiful, and when I go off to the shows next month I can find a fabulous new man to romance.'

'If that's what you're doing, I want to come with you!' said Mary, pleased to see her friend getting some of her sparkle back. They both knew that Daisy was joking, because she was a long way from wanting romance, but laughing about it was a step in the right direction.

Daisy smiled. 'No way, Mary, you're not coming. I travel alone. Cleo tells me that mysterious men are far more likely to chat women up when they're travelling alone. She says she sees it in hotels all the time. Groups of women are threatening, but single women aren't. Although, you have to watch out for strange men, obviously. She laboured that point, actually. Do I look like the sort of woman who'd attract strange men?'

'I'm saying nothing,' remarked Mary. 'Don't forget to buy some clothes when you're off eyeballing mysterious men, will you? We have a shop to run.'

The cottage was a mile away from Cloud's Hill, on a winding part of the road, and had a long stone wall topped by a hedge facing the road. Daisy wasn't sure what to expect because she knew that estate agent-speak translated reality by way of wildly optimistic descriptions.

'An opportunity to purchase a unique old cottage with unusual features,' could easily mean she was going to view a house that was hideously ugly with rising damp, a heating system straight out of Dickens and a close-up view of a pylon.

She drove in the tiny gate of The Anchor – the name would have to go for a start; there was no sea for miles – and sighed with pleasure.

The Anchor looked idyllically cottagey on the outside with a sloping roof, a sea-blue door and a tumble of wild flowers in the garden. Unless the name was a hint that there were plumbing issues, it was so far, so good. It had diamond-paned windows like her mother's house, and looked as if it had been designed by the same hand. The estate agent was waiting with the key.

Inside, the nautical reference became apparent as the owner was clearly ship mad. There were ships in bottles, out of bottles, and maritime bits and bobs hanging from every inch of the low ceiling. The walls were in need of decoration and the carpet in the hall, living room and tiny dining room could probably qualify for antique status, but the house had enormous character.

'The kitchen's not that big,' the estate agent said cheerily, flattening himself against the wall so they'd both fit into it, 'but you could extend. And look at the view.'

The back of the house looked out over the valley with Carrick-well visible in the distance, and the swathe of the mountains surrounding it.

Daisy imagined adding on a sun room and sitting out there, gazing down at the town the way she had from the safety of Leah's hot tub room.

She felt comfortable here, at home, safe.

Paula's baby's christening was the following Sunday. Despite feeling that she'd made so much progress in the past couple of weeks, in her heart, Daisy wasn't looking forward to it. Little Emma was thriving and her besotted mother wanted everyone and their granny to come to the party in her home afterwards. Daisy was terrified of descending into black gloom again at the sight of the baby. Gurgling infants in nappy adverts were one thing: a real, live baby would be something else.

'You've got to come,' Paula insisted on the phone to Daisy. 'I know it's been so hard since you split up with Alex, but please, Daisy, it would be terrible if you didn't come.'

Daisy was very glad that Paula had no idea about the fertility treatment she'd hoped to have. Paula wouldn't have pushed her to come to the christening if she had known.

'That's why I tried to keep it quiet,' Daisy told Mary the next day in work, 'because I didn't want people pitying us because we didn't have children. Sorry,' she corrected herself, 'I didn't want people pitying *me*. Obviously Alex didn't give a damn either way.'

'Fertility treatment is a big deal for men,' Mary said thoughtfully. 'It scares them.'

'Are you on his side now?' demanded Daisy.

'No,' Mary said, 'I'm not. But therapy does teach you how to look at both sides of the story.'

'Mary, I preferred you when you were being an evil bitch and you were threatening to make a wax dummy of Alex, stick pins in it and put a hex on him!'

Mary did her best to look serene. 'I have moved on to a better place,' she intoned grandly, 'and being negative is so ageing. I was reading an article in *Vogue* the other day and they were saying that negativity drags your face down and gives you more lines. I would have stopped being a bitch years ago if I had known that.'

It was Daisy's turn to laugh. 'I think we both need a session in Leah's hot tub – that will soothe away all the lines and it might work on my pimple outbreak.'

'Oh, yes,' moaned Mary. 'Maybe we can get a couple of treatments before the christening. I could do with a bit of work. One of those hot stone massages.'

'A detoxifying facial –' decided Daisy – 'that would be perfect. It would help me to face all Paula's lovely relatives, who'll keep commiserating with me for not being with Alex any more and patting me every time we pass baby Emma and saying things like, "Don't worry, it will be you soon". I don't know if I can cope with that!'

'They won't,' Mary insisted. 'Now they'll just think you're a sad and twisted single woman who hates men and they'll leave you alone. Simple.'

'That sounds so much better,' Daisy agreed.

'Did you go to view the cottage yesterday afternoon?'

Daisy nodded, her face animated. 'It's beautiful. I'm going to put an offer in but I need to talk to Alex about putting the flat on the market. I hate contacting him, though.'

'You'll need a lawyer to sell the apartment, so get one and ask him or her to send Alex a letter saying you want to sell as quickly as possible. That way, you don't have to talk to him ever again.'

Daisy nodded, but she felt that Mary was avoiding the issue here: Daisy would have to see Alex again at some point, if only to finish it all in her mind. There were things she had to say to him and when she was strong enough to say them, she was determined to do it. She wasn't sure when that was going to be, though. A person could only be brave a little bit at a time.

Baby Emma didn't have Enrico's huge ears or a squashed little face. She was perfect. She had Paula's big blue eyes, her father's café au lait skin, and wrapped in her cream christening shawl, she looked like a sleeping cherub.

'Go on, you hold her,' said Paula, thrusting out the little bundle to Daisy. 'She's so good, she'll go to anyone and she practically never cries.'

'Isn't she beautiful?' cooed Mary.

'Yes,' agreed Daisy, and somehow she found herself holding Emma, who hadn't woken up when the Holy Water had been poured on her head, or when she had been handed freely around between grannies and godparents, but who opened her tiny eyelids now. She looked up at Daisy with wise baby eyes and the rosebud mouth curled up at the corners.

'Oh, she smiled, did you see that?' said Daisy excitedly, feeling a lump in her throat.

'I know,' crooned Paula, waggling a finger at her beautiful daughter. 'She keeps smiling at me too. Everyone else says she's not smiling and that she's got wind, but I know that she's smiling at me because she knows I'm her mummy. And she knows that you're going to be her friend, Auntie Daisy.'

'Her eyelashes are so long,' Daisy said, lost in contemplation of the tiny little girl. 'I've never seen anything like them, and her hair is so dark.'

'She *is* beautiful,' agreed the besotted mother. 'Enrico's mother says she looks just like he did when he was a baby, apparently. Without the ears.'

They all laughed.

'Do you want to hold her?' Daisy said to Mary, still cradling the baby close to her.

'No,' said Mary, 'she's happy with you. You're a natural at it.'

'Yeah, isn't she?' agreed Paula.

Mary and Daisy exchanged a glance over the baby's head. A glance that said Daisy had been right to come after all. Holding the baby felt wonderful. Daisy didn't feel bereft, as she'd expected to – just peaceful and hopeful. Her day would surely come. She was so glad she hadn't stayed at home and missed the christening. It wasn't easy being generous and kind-hearted when that heart was breaking, but it was worth it in the end.

Paula's mother, a vision in purple silk with matching feathers in her hair, appeared, hands held out for her beloved first grand-child. 'Oh, isn't she lovely,' she cooed, 'and she really suits you, Daisy. Oh, you'll be next.'

Daisy gently kissed the baby's forehead and handed her over to her grandmother. 'Well, I'd love to be next, Mrs O'Shea,' she said, 'but Alex and I split up a few months ago so it looks like I won't be joining the motherhood club for quite a while now.'

Mrs O'Shea refused to be put off by this lack of a man. 'Nonsense,' she said, happy on two glasses of cava. 'You're a gorgeous thing. I was only saying to Paula the other day that nobody wears clothes like you, and the bit of weight suits you. There'll be men queuing out the door any day soon. I never did like that Alex fellow anyway,' she added.

'Mum!' said Paula admonishingly.

'Well, I didn't,' said Mrs O'Shea. 'Speak as you find, that's what I do. He wasn't good enough for our Daisy and she'll find someone who *will* be good enough for her, you mark my words.' Mrs O'Shea carefully took the baby from Daisy's arms.

'Thanks, Mrs O'Shea,' said Daisy cheerfully.

'Now my brother-in-law's cousin's son,' said Mrs O'Shea, warming to the theme, 'is a very handsome young man and he's got over the divorce and they have no children. That'd be a perfect set-up for you. He has his own business and everything.'

Mary, Paula and Daisy laughed.

'I'm off men for a while,' Daisy said politely.

'Ah, now,' said Mrs O'Shea, knowingly, 'you'd want to dip your foot back in the water, my dear. It'd be good for you.' And off she went with her granddaughter.

'Sorry,' said Paula. 'I hope Mum didn't put her foot in it . . .'

'No, she didn't,' said Daisy. 'She said nothing wrong at all. She was dead right: Alex wasn't good enough for me.'

Mary sighed. 'Hallelujah! You're preaching to the converted,' she said. 'We're glad you've finally seen sense.'

'Hello, Daisy,' said another voice, and Daisy turned around to see Mel Redmond, one little girl on her hip, another, older child holding on to her hand.

'Hi, Mel,' said Daisy with pleasure. 'What are you doing here?'

'Enrico works with my husband, Adrian,' Mel explained. 'Carrickwell is a small place, isn't it?' She kissed Paula. 'Congrat-ulations, I've just seen the baby. She is beautiful.'

Mel kissed Daisy too. 'How are you holding up?' she whispered, knowing this must be tough for Daisy.

Daisy gave her a firm smile. 'Great,' she said.

Faced with another mother, Paula was keen to talk mother-talk about sleeping schedules, feeding and how you couldn't die of sleep deprivation, though it felt like it.

Mel kept glancing anxiously at Daisy because this motherly conversation couldn't be cheering her up, but Daisy shot her a brave smile in return and mouthed, 'It's OK.'

Daisy crouched down to talk to the little girl at Mel's side. 'Hello,' she said, 'I'm Daisy. What's your name?'

'Sarah,' said the child, staring at Daisy with a grave little face. 'I like your necklace.'

Daisy looked down. She was wearing a pendant she'd bought years ago on a trip abroad. 'It's amber,' she said. 'That's a special type of stone made by resin which comes from trees being squashed over millions and millions of years and then it ends up like this, all shiny, golden and a bit see-through.'

'Millions of years?' said the little girl curiously. 'Like when there were dinosaurs?'

'Exactly,' agreed Daisy. 'Here, try it on and see how it looks on you.' She unhooked the pendant and put it around the little girl's neck.

Sarah tried to look down at herself.

'We ought to find a mirror,' said Daisy. 'We're going to check out the pendant in a mirror,' she said to Mel, standing up.

'Great,' said Mel. 'I'm afraid Sarah's been a bit bored.'

Daisy took Sarah's hand. 'Well, she's not going to be bored now,' she said. 'Come on, let's find a mirror. I bet Auntie Paula has a big one somewhere so she can admire herself in the morning! Do you admire yourself in the morning when you get dressed?'

'Yes,' said Sarah thoughtfully, her tiny hand curled up in Daisy's. 'Mummy says you work in the shop with Paula, with pretty clothes. I like clothes.'

'I'm afraid we only do grown-ups' clothes,' Daisy said, with regret. 'But maybe we should have some children's clothes too, for very pretty girls like you.'

'That would be nice,' said Sarah appreciatively. 'I like you.'

It turned out to be a good day after all. Daisy had thought she'd stay half an hour and leave. Yet somehow, at half-seven in the evening, she, Mary, Mel and a few others were among the last in Paula and Enrico's house. Baby Emma had been adored and minded all day, which had given her mother a rest, so Paula was happy. Mrs O'Shea had spent a lot of the day coming up with names for the find-Daisy-a-man list and had amused everyone greatly by listing the qualities of these prospective suitors.

'Tim, that guy with the small farm, sounds the best of the lot,' Daisy said when she, Paula, Mary and Mel were flopped out in the conservatory of Paula's tiny house. 'But the guy who's into vinyl records and has three thousand catalogued by name ... I don't know, sounds a bit obsessional.'

Mel laughed. 'That reminds me of a friend of mine from Lorimar – Vanessa. She's a single parent and wow, but her mother was intent on finding her a man. You wouldn't believe some of the guys she came up with! All sons of her friends and strangely single. Vanessa used to say she had enough trouble with the one man in her life, Conal. He's thirteen now.'

'Oh, they're a handful at that age,' said Mary knowingly.

Daisy sat back and tuned out, thinking that a couple of weeks ago she wouldn't have been able to cope with this conversation. She would have felt so excluded – the only woman in a group of four who wasn't a mother, who couldn't join in, who wasn't part of the secret sisterhood of being a parent. It would have hurt. It still hurt, of course, but not as much. She was coming to terms with her childlessness. It didn't have to be for ever.

Daisy knew she couldn't blame Alex for everything. She couldn't blame him because she wasn't pregnant and Louise was. She could deal with all that herself. In her longing for a baby, she'd mistakenly thought a child was a Band-Aid that would make everything better. She was wiser now.

She tuned back into the conversation. Mel and Mary were talking about consumerism and how children wanted things they saw on the TV every day. 'The adverts on the kids' channel are unbelievable,' Mel was saying. 'No wonder the Christmas lists are longer than *Gone With the Wind*. There are so many new products every day. I mean, how do you say no when all their friends are getting them? We've had to cut back financially because I'm not working any more and yet so many of Sarah's friends seem to get everything they want. We can't compete with that and I don't want to! It's wrong for children to have every single thing they want. That isn't the way I was brought up.'

Paula looked anxious. 'I worry about that too,' she said. 'I'd hate Emma to be spoiled.'

Mary grinned. 'She's only a few weeks old. They say you can't spoil a baby, although you can spoil them when they get older, that's for sure.'

'I know, but how do you know if you are spoiling them and if you're not spoiling them?' went on Paula.

'That's the big problem,' said Mel. 'There's no right and wrong way to do it, and you're always convinced you're doing it wrong.'

It was funny, Daisy reflected, she'd assumed that all mothers had this instant, instinctive knowledge and knew everything, and yet they didn't, and they worried about what they did and they didn't know. That was comforting. It seemed nobody had all the answers.

She got home to find a message on her answering machine from Claudia, one of the few friends she'd shared with Alex who'd kept in contact. Most of the others had clearly chosen Alex and Louise, instead of Daisy and Whoever. That had hurt. She thought of the times she and Alex had spent with those other couples – many nights out and even weekends away – and all the time they'd been his friends and not hers.

Claudia was one of the exceptions. Her husband, Andrew, had known Alex from school, so they went way back. But Claudia hadn't let this affect her friendship with Daisy and had kept in touch.

After such a sociable day, Daisy felt like more chat, so she phoned Claudia back.

Claudia was her usual voluble self, telling Daisy the trials and tribulations of work, and wasn't it great that Michelle and Gerry were finally getting married?

'Are you going to come to their wedding?' Claudia asked Daisy gently. 'You can come with Andrew and me, you know. You shouldn't let the fact that you and Alex have split up stop you seeing old friends getting married.'

'I haven't been invited,' Daisy said quietly. 'I didn't even know they were getting married.'

'Shit, I didn't mean to put my foot in it,' Claudia groaned. 'I assumed you'd be asked. You and Michelle were always so close . . .'

'Not that close, it seems.' Daisy didn't want to sound bitter, but it was hard not to.

'Perhaps you didn't get your invitation yet,' said Claudia lamely. 'Although it's in a week and you would have, wouldn't you?'

'We've dressed so many wedding parties this summer,' Daisy said lightly, 'that I'm totally weddinged out, Claudia. You can tell me all about it afterwards.'

Was it technically stalking if you went to a wedding you weren't invited to just so you could look at your ex and his new girlfriend? That question haunted Daisy all week. She was overcome with the desire to see Alex and Louise together, to get a mental picture of them as a couple in her head, and then she'd be able to move on.

But was it strange behaviour? Yes, it was stalking, she decided the night before Michelle and Gerry's wedding.She may as well buy a bunny and boil up some waternow. She wouldn't go.

The next day Daisy unobtrusively joined the congregation at twenty past three, twenty minutes after the ceremony was due to have started. Michelle was clearly determined to be fashionably late, Daisy thought, as she moved cautiously up the side of the church. Normally at weddings, she enjoyed noticing the clothes other people were wearing and she tried to catch her friends' eyes, smiling at this person or that. Today, she didn't want to be noticed and she tried not to look at either the clothes, the jewels or the hats.

She slid into a seat two-thirds of the way up the side aisle and kept her head down, hoping that people would think that she was a very devout person who had just dropped in on a Friday afternoon to discover a huge, glamorous wedding in progress. Of course they might think, in her big and unseasonable raincoat and her large-brimmed cream canvas hat, that she was one of those loony women who walked around pushing shopping trolleys and waving rosary beads. But either way, they wouldn't notice her. People did their best not to notice those sort of women.

There was a buzz coming from the church, the buzz of people squealing 'Hello, lovely to see you, love the hat, the dress . . .' whatever. At the top of the church, Daisy could see Gerry, standing looking slightly nervous, with the best man, who must be his brother.

She carefully scanned further back on the groom's side of the church and then she spotted Alex. He was easy to see because he was so much taller than everybody else, although Daisy would have noticed him in a crowd of a million. Her heart felt that sudden ache at the sight of him. He was wearing the grey suit that they had bought together in Paul Smith, the one he hadn't wanted to buy, the one he said made him look too edgy, like a fashion victim. And now he was wearing it and he looked great.

Then she saw Louise, and whatever ache had surfaced in her heart for Alex was multiplied by ten at the sight of Louise, because she looked radiant. Not for her the pregnant-woman-in-a-circus-tent look. No. Louise looked like an advert for a pregnancy clothes shop, a designer one. Her long hair was lustrous and dark, caught up in the sort of careless knot that Daisy had never quite managed to achieve herself. Her dress was a stunning crimson wrap that highlighted her swollen belly. Diane Von Furstenberg, Daisy was sure.

She looked like a fertility goddess or an exotic beauty who'd have poems dedicated to her and artists fighting to paint her. She looked ripely pregnant and utterly happy. Despite all the weight she'd put on, Daisy felt like a shrivelled-up old prune by comparison. Louise had it all. Everything. She had Alex, and soon she'd have a baby. Daisy had nothing and no one, and it was probably all her own fault.

The bridal march started and Daisy watched as Louise clutched Alex's sleeve excitedly. The gossiping crowd got to their feet as one and turned back to look at the bride. From her vantage point, Daisy couldn't see her, but she was pretty sure that Michelle, who was endlessly stylish, would not have gone for the big meringue effect. As she waited for Michelle to come into view, Daisy watched the congregation watching the bride walk down the aisle, violins playing romantically in the background. There was no big gap around Louise or Alex, a space signalling anybody disapproved of their relationship and how he had dumped Daisy. No, nobody seemed to have noticed the fact that Daisy wasn't there at all. Daisy and Louise were interchangeable. One girlfriend was much like another, except that the new one was pregnant and the old one hadn't been able to get pregnant.

The grief rose again inside her. She might never have a child, never. The pain of it was physical. She had to get out of here. She moved towards the side aisle, and in that instant, somebody from the congregation swivelled in her direction. Oh God, it was Alex's friend Jem . . . Jemmie . . . something like that. He had seen her. In an agony of embarrassment, Daisy looked for the first place she could hide. Maybe he hadn't really seen her, maybe all he had seen was a big woman in a raincoat and a stupid hat pulled low. The pew was right beside one of the church's confessional boxes and she ducked inside, pulling the door shut after her. The scent of elderly velvet curtains and lovingly applied wood polish assailed her nostrils. It was a smell she hadn't smelled for a very long time.

'Oh God,' groaned Daisy out loud, feeling safe. 'Hope he didn't see me. Why do these things always happen to me?'

'Sorry? Could you speak up?' said a wheezy old voice.

'Oh God,' she muttered again under her breath.

The grille between the two parts of the confessional box slid open and a frail white-haired old priest, who had obviously been seeking refuge there to say his prayers, peered at her. 'I'm afraid confession's over,' he said kindly.

'Oh, yeah, that's fine, I didn't come in here for that,' stammered Daisy.

'But if you are in need, my dear . . .' the priest went on.

Daisy knew she must look dreadful, with her miserable face and eyes brimming with tears. 'Well, I am sort of in need, but not necessarily in need of confession,' Daisy said. No, that sounded wrong. 'I mean I haven't been to confession for ages, although . . .'

'You thought you might try to come back to the Church?' volunteered the priest, sweetly.

'That wasn't it either, really,' Daisy said, reaching into her pocket to see if there was a long-lost tissue shrivelled up there. She pulled out a scrap of kitchen towel. It would do.

'We listen too, you know,' said the priest. 'You can have a talk, if there is something troubling you. We don't dispatch people to say ten decades of the Rosary any more. We've moved on.'

Daisy knelt down on the soft kneeler, worn by countless knees. 'A talk would be nice,' she said politely, wiping her eyes and her nose with the kitchen roll. It would seem rude to rush off since she'd disturbed him, and it was quite nice talking to someone who didn't know the facts either way. 'I've made a bit of a mess of things, Father,' she said.

'That's what life's all about,' he said. 'But you can get back on the right path you know, just hand it over to God.'

That sounded very simple to Daisy. Simple and a bit unrealistic. Handing it over to God. Where had God been when Alex had run off with Louise, leaving Daisy in the lurch?

'I've never found that worked,' she said apologetically.

'You didn't have faith in it,' he said earnestly. 'Faith is the key. God will take care of things in His own time. We don't know what He has planned for us, you see.' It was a bit like the one about the master appearing when the student is ready, she thought with a shock. Buddhism and Catholicism were conspiring together to put her in a spiritual place where she went with the flow. What the heck, she thought. Some of them must be right. She might just give it a try.

'Thank you, Father,' she said, getting up. 'It was lovely talking to you and I'm sorry I disturbed you.'

'You can always come back if you want us,' he said. 'We're always here. The church is always open.'

'Yes, thanks,' said Daisy automatically.

'No,' he said again and, looking through the grille, Daisy realised that he was very old because his bald skull was a fragile shell with a couple of tufts of white hair at his ears. 'We're *always* here. Lots of things and lots of people go away, but God doesn't.'

When Daisy peered out into the church again, she could see the entire congregation was engrossed in the wedding ceremony, which meant that she could sneak down the back of the church and out. Once out of the church, she raced down the drive to her car and sped off before she met any late guests rushing in.

She was glad she'd gone. A moment ago she thought she had been stupid because she had nearly been caught, but now, since meeting that lovely old man, it seemed like the right thing to do. She had seen Alex and Louise, looking gloriously happy and together, with all their old friends, and the world hadn't changed, and thunder clouds hadn't rolled over the church. Life had moved on for everyone except Daisy, and she had to accept it, no matter how painful. There was no going back, only moving forward.

Three days after the wedding, Louise gave birth to a baby boy. Claudia phoned Daisy to tell her.

'I didn't want you to hear it by accident. There's nothing worse than everyone not telling you the important news.'

From her apartment window, Daisy could see the River Tullow below where a couple of canoeists were paddling downstream. They wore bright yellow waterproofs, and didn't look very experienced as they kept bumping into each other. They were laughing – carefree and happy.

'Thanks, Claudia,' Daisy said, turning away from the river and the view of Carrickwell. 'Thanks for telling me. What's the baby called?' She didn't need to torture herself with this, but she had to know.

'Daragh.'

'Daragh.' Daisy said the name aloud. It was a good name, strong and memorable. Daragh was a person now, not just the catalyst for breaking up her and Alex. It would be easier to think of Daragh as a person who was also caught in the middle of this. It wasn't his fault Daisy had suffered because of his conception.

'How are you?' Claudia asked awkwardly.

'Not too bad,' Daisy said. And that was the truth. She'd been expecting to hear that Louise had the baby sometime. So she was as ready for it as she could be. Leah's daily phone calls and Daisy's own determination to be brave had helped. She had a future, she had hope. If Leah could be positive after all she'd been through, then Daisy wouldn't be much of a human being if she couldn't hold her head high, stick her chin out and get on with her life.

Daragh had a new life stretching before him too. Daisy would not be a bitch and send bad karma into the world by feeling angry at this child's birth. The sweet elderly priest and the Buddhist master would approve of this sentiment, she thought.

'I've nearly bought a new home,' she told Claudia now. 'It's a cottage out near where my mother lives. It's small, sweet and it's lovely. Needs redecorating, but I love a project. I'm going to make it all feminine and olde worlde. Alex was so into the whole modern, minimalist look and, you know, that's not me.'

'I never thought it was,' said Claudia. 'Your apartment was like a show house.'

'Alex was always straightening things on the coffee table,' Daisy admitted. 'All the magazines had to be at exact right angles to the edge of the table or he'd get irritated.'

'Oh *yes*,' said Claudia. 'It drove me nuts to watch him. It was obsessive compulsive disorder or something.' She laughed again.

It was fun to be able to laugh about Alex and not want to die at the mention of his name, Daisy reflected. That was definitely progress.

'I'm going off on another buying trip as well – to Milan at the end of the month for spring/summer next year.'

'That sounds wonderful,' sighed Claudia, who was bored by her job.

'I hope so,' Daisy said. 'I've only been to Milan once before and it's incredible. I'm really looking forward to it. Then I'm going to the Paris and London prêt shows.'

'Do you fancy going out some night next week?' Claudia asked. 'Nothing coupley,' she added hastily.

'I can cope with couples, actually,' Daisy said, 'just as long as they're not Alex and Louise.'

'Oh, of course not,' gasped Claudia. 'I wouldn't dream of it. No, this is just a few old friends of mine and Andrew's. We thought you'd like it.'

'As long as you're not setting me up with anyone,' Daisy said.

'Well . . .' said Claudia, 'there is this guy who works with Andrew and he's really nice. He's had a bit of a bad run, but you'd love him, he's so sweet.'

'Claudia,' warned Daisy, 'do not try and set me up with guys, please. I'd love to come out with you, but as long as this sweet colleague of Andrew's realises that I am not in the market place, right?'

'Right,' said Claudia, 'it's just that we thought it would be nice for you to be dating again.'

Daisy thought how she'd missed Alex's arms around her, the presence of another human being in her life, someone to cuddle up to in bed, someone to open jars of pasta sauce when they seemed welded shut. It was the little things you noticed most.

Yet wanting another presence in her life was not a good enough reason to throw herself back into the man-market again. What was it Leah had said the other day: *'You've got to heal yourself, Daisy. There's no point relying on anybody else to do it. Otherwise you're putting a dressing over a big wound and it'll never get better.'*

'Claudia, I'm enjoying being single,' she said firmly. 'I can do what I want, when I want. I can decorate my new home in floral and frilly things and all sorts of stuff that Alex would have hated. I can be me. And that's what I need right now. Not a guy. So thanks, but no thanks.'

'Wow,' said Claudia. 'I really admire you, Daisy, the way you've turned everything around and dealt with it all. I don't know if I'd have been able to do it if Andrew had left me and gone off with someone else.'

'Well, he wouldn't have, would he?' Daisy said quietly. 'Andrew loves you. That was the problem: Alex didn't really love me. I was his stop-gap until he found The One.'

'He didn't say that, did he?' asked Claudia, disgusted.

'Yes. It seems Louise is The One and I was the Will Do For Now one.' It still hurt, but not quite as much. You could get over the pain, Daisy had discovered, you just had to get up every morning and keep going until it was time to go to sleep.

'But you'll come out with us then, next week?' Claudia asked.

'Of course,' Daisy said, 'just no blind dates.'

Daisy dropped into Cloud's Hill on her way back from another viewing of the cottage the following day.

Leah was out walking and wasn't expected back, but Cleo was thrilled to see Daisy. She'd looked so sad and untogether when they'd met first, but now Daisy had a glow about her. She was beautifully dressed too. Initially, Daisy had seemed to wear nothing but huge baggy tracksuits that did nothing for her. Now she looked both fashionable and miles more self-confident in a honey-gold sweater and faded denims with a silky scarf wrapped round her neck, her strawberry-blonde hair tumbling around her shoulders. Proof that Cloud's Hill and Leah could work magic, Cleo thought.

She probably looked a lot different too, she reflected. She felt so much happier now that she'd come to terms with everything that had gone wrong. Unhappiness left its mark on your face. Now when Cleo looked into the mirror, she saw a woman who didn't have the weight of the world on her slim shoulders.

'Can I cadge a lift into Carrickwell with you?' she asked Daisy. 'I'm biting the bullet and going to see my brother Barney. He always had Tuesday afternoons off, so I'm going to drop in unannounced so he won't have time to concoct a story about why he and Jason left me to stew in my own juice. The brats.'

The drive was not long enough for all the filling-in the two women had to do, but finally, both of them were up to date with each other's stories.

'When are you going to move into the cottage?' Cleo asked as they drove through the town.

'A couple of weeks, I hope. Keep your fingers crossed that nothing goes wrong.'

Daisy parked at the end of the road where Sondra and Barney lived. 'Are you sure you don't want me to go in with you?' she asked. 'I don't mind. It's nice to have a friend along when you're doing something scary.' She knew that Cleo had mixed emotions about visiting her brother and his wife for the first time in months.

Daisy thought Cleo was being very brave. She was naturally furious at how her brothers had conspired to keep her away from her making up with her parents, but Daisy could see she was nervous about her reception too.

'I know a lot of it's my fault for being childish,' Cleo said, 'but Barney and Jason are just as bad. I hope they didn't not get in touch because they were being childish too. You know, like when we were kids and we fought, Barney could go ages without speaking to me. I never lasted more than fifteen minutes. I'm a bit scared that it's more than that, though – that Barney and Jason really don't want me in their lives any more.'

What if everything was different and the family she'd grown up with had been irreparably hurt by the rift? A squabble that had escalated she could handle: a family rift with no end in sight would break her heart now that she'd decided to make things up to them all.

'I don't mind coming in too, honestly,' Daisy said again.

'Thanks but I ought to do it on my own,' Cleo said gratefully. 'It's fine. Barney doesn't bite. Sondra sort of does but I can handle her, more or less. That was the problem all along, me not knowing how to deal with her and thinking that Mum and Dad liked her better than me. Very childish,' Cleo sighed, thinking of herself, Sondra and the stand-up rows they used to have. In one way, it was a miracle the Malin family hadn't had a huge falling-out years ago. Only Harry's determination never to have arguments had kept things on an even keel – but perhaps that argument-free atmosphere had been artificial, Cleo reflected. If there had been normal rows, then the air would have been cleared.

'I wish there were lessons at school on adulthood,' Daisy said thoughtfully. 'Instead of Geography and Home Economics, we could have had Parents: A Guide, or Train Your Boyfriend in Three Months.'

'Clever idea,' agreed Cleo. 'How about How to Speak Other People's Languages – so you understand what they're saying and don't end up with constant misunderstandings?'

'Would that be a two-year syllabus?' asked Daisy in amusement.

Cleo shook her head. 'At least a twenty-year course.'

'Put me down for the whole course,' Daisy said. 'I cannot speak man-speak at all.'

'Bluntness works,' said Cleo firmly. 'Tell them what you think and let them deal with it.'

'I'm not much good at saying what I think to men,' Daisy muttered. 'And neither are they. Alex would say one thing and he'd mean another entirely. He was never honest. Even at the very end, he couldn't be honest. In female-speak, having sex means something. It's this glorious fusion of two people who want to be as close as humanly possible and make a commitment that's precious and intimate. In male-speak, sex means: *I've left you and have another girlfriend with a baby on the way but hey, we're alone. Nobody will have to know, so, why don't we have sex?* Or maybe that was just Alex.'

Cleo laughed so much, her hastily applied mascara began to run.

'It's true,' Daisy went on. 'Isn't that what men are always rabbiting on about – that women say one thing and mean another? *They're* worse.'

'You've got a point,' Cleo said, thinking of Trish and her latest man disaster involving a guy named Lucas who'd dumped her by text after six *'You are incredible, Trish. I've never met anyone like you in my life!'* dates. 'For two whole weeks, he sent fifteen text messages a night, and then suddenly, he's gone. Has his phone been stolen? Has he severed a limb? No, he was busy. "Like 2 end it. Sorry," he texted. Two hundred and ten text messages professing huge interest, and then he's sorry but it's over. He hid behind messages. Why bother? What's wrong with picking up the phone and saying sorry, but no thanks?' Cleo demanded, rage at people like Tyler bloody Roth spilling out onto the whole of the male race.

She'd been brutally honest with Nat about their relationship and it had been incredibly painful for him, but she'd had the courage to do it. Not like awful Lucas, who'd been dating poor Trish.

But she'd walked out on Tyler without saying goodbye . . . That was different, Cleo told herself firmly.

'I'm going to be so truthful in future, I'm going to be a pain,' Daisy insisted. 'I'm going to say what I think all the time.'

'Won't that be a problem in the shop?' asked Cleo. 'If a woman tries on a horrible outfit, do you have to say it's nice so you won't offend her?'

'I'd never lie to make a sale,' Daisy said horrified. 'That's how we have customers who come back again and again. If they look

286

hideous in something, I'll tell them or Mary will. Mary's good at it, actually,' she reflected. 'She can get them out of the hideous outfit and into a fabulous one in about thirty seconds flat. And she whisks the bad one out of the dressing room and gets someone to hide it.'

'I'll have to come in some day and try on clothes, but only if you promise to be honest with me.'

'Unflinchingly,' Daisy agreed.

'And I don't have much money,' Cleo added.

'Staff discount,' Daisy said. 'Shop owner's prerogative.'

Cleo gave Daisy a quick hug before she got out of the car. 'You're coming to that yogalates class on Thursday, right? Now I'm staff at Cloud's Hill, I've got to plug the classes. And it's great.'

'I don't know,' said Daisy. 'I was never very good at sports at school. I don't want to be the only one there who can't wrap their leg round the back of their head. Classes can be so humiliating when you're bigger,' she admitted. 'Plus, I'm so unfit and will be all stiff for ages afterwards.'

'There's no contortionism involved,' Cleo promised. 'It's an easy-peasy class. Now Ashtanga – that's one where you can't walk for a week afterwards. But you'll love this. Honest.'

Sondra and Barney lived on a small street near the cathedral, one of the better preserved redbrick terraces in Carrickwell. It was at the end of the terrace, a slightly larger detached redbrick house, bought, Cleo knew, from a generous injection of funds from her parents.

Just as well she wasn't bitter about money, she thought, as she opened the black gate and walked up the path. Her brothers had both got huge payouts over the years from the hotel and she hadn't. It would be easy to feel outraged and put upon by this unfair division of the family spoils but she never had. Money caused so many arguments. There was one well-known Carrickwell family who'd split into two outraged factions over money left in a will, with the ones who felt they'd been neglected loudly telling everyone how their relatives had conned them out of their inheritance. The other side ostentatiously crossed the street whenever they spotted any of the other gang. Cleo had always thought they were mad to fall out over a few pounds in an old woman's will.

She wouldn't make the same mistake because she had every intention of making her own fortune by running her own hotel. Unfortunately, the hotel she'd be running couldn't be the Willow and she'd probably feel sorry all her life for that. You couldn't grow up in a place, love it with every ounce of your being, and not feel devastated when it was taken away.

But she wouldn't let resentment hold her back. What had Leah said? '*Every obstacle is a learning opportunity.*' Cleo had been so struck by this that she'd written it down. Leah was always saying things that deserved to be written down.

And Leah was dead right. Cleo had learned a lot in the past few months, and she'd use that knowledge to build up her own hotel. It would be hers and hers alone, so that nobody could take it away from her. Ever.

She rang the doorbell, noticing that the front of the house could do with some work. Neither her brother nor sister-in-law seemed to realise that heather bushes could actually die and that their withered remains did not enhance any doorstep.

No answer. Cleo almost regretted not phoning ahead but she hadn't wanted to give Barney the chance to wriggle out of seeing her. She rang again, thinking that she'd go to Jason's office next. Her brothers were going to tell her exactly what sort of stupid game they were playing. Then she saw a shape through the opaque glass of the door. The shape shuffled closer, the door opened, and a woman said 'Yes?' in irritated tones.

It was Sondra, except that Cleo found it hard to equate her normally polished sister-in-law with this tired-looking, vastly pregnant woman. Sondra's once-shimmering blonde mane now sported two inches of brown regrowth and she didn't have the usual inch of slap applied.

It was hard to know which of them was more surprised at the sight of the other.

'Cleo!' Sondra gasped.

'Sondra, hi,' replied Cleo. 'Er . . . how's the pregnancy going?'

'Aw, as you can see,' Sondra said, 'it's not what I expected. Radiant, healthy skin and thicker hair . . . they're lying! I'm sick and hot and my back's gone. Come in,' she growled, turning and shuffling gingerly back down the hall, leaving Cleo to shut the front door. 'Water retention as well. My grandmother's ankles are thinner than mine now. I can't even sit down long enough in the salon to get my hair done. Look at my roots! And – what are you doing here?' she asked abruptly.

'I came to see you and Barney.' They'd reached the kitchen. It was ages since Cleo had been in this house. She remembered her first visit when the whole family had gone to admire the newly-marrieds' lovely home, and Cleo had felt grim as she looked at the large flat-screen television and the expensive stereo system, knowing that these were funded by the family business. At the time she'd said something smart about how it was a very expensive house for two people starting out in life.

'Would you prefer your brother to live in a hovel?' her mother had demanded hotly.

Cleo felt ashamed of what she'd said now. It had been bitchy.

The kitchen had improved a lot since those early days and Cleo was surprised to find it looked quite cosy with lots of feminine touches. Pretty cushions on the pine kitchen chairs, china ornaments of ballerinas on a walnut whatnot in one corner, and lots of other very un-Sondra-ish touches, Cleo thought. There were even frilled red checked curtains billowing at the windows.

'Will I make you tea?' Cleo asked, seeing as Sondra had made her way to an armchair piled high with cushions and was settling herself in.

'The pot's in the dishwasher and the teabags are in the cupboard by the sink,' Sondra ordered.

Some things didn't change.

Sondra put her feet up on a stool, took charge of the remote control and redirected her gaze towards the small television on the counter. Ricki Lake was on, exhorting an audience of irate women to say what they thought about an unattractive man who'd just described his devastated wife as 'a big fat woman' live on TV. Cleo wondered where Ricki got her guests. How dumb would a man have to be to go in front of a hostile, mainly female, television audience and say that?

'Idiot,' muttered Sondra. 'Can you believe this stuff? Ricki will soon sort him out. It's not as if he's an oil painting. I love Ricki. Yesterday she had this woman on who was going out with four men at the same time. It was amazing . . .'

Cleo made a pot of tea while Sondra talked. She knew how Sondra liked her tea: she'd made enough cups for her in the kitchen in the Willow. She found butter shortbread biscuits in a tin and put them on a plate. The whole kitchen was remarkably tidy, she realised. Sondra obviously wasn't the undomesticated creature Cleo had assumed she was. Either that, or Barney was tidying up, and as Cleo knew her brother was allergic to housework, this seemed unlikely. Tea made, she carried it to the table and pulled up a stool beside her sister-in-law.

'Being pregnant's not agreeing with you, then?' she said.

'No. I have to pee every twenty minutes, I can't eat anything or I get heartburn and look at my face with red veins, I'm an eyesore!'

Cleo had to laugh. She'd never seen this side of Sondra before. 'You're not,' she said.

'Mm, easy for you to say,' Sondra grumbled.

The man on the Ricki Lake show was taking a battering from

all comers, and the two women sat in companionable silence, watching the show, drinking their tea and eating biscuits. Sondra ate six.

Cleo reflected that if *she'd* eaten six in the old days, Sondra would have made some spiky remark about the connection between biscuits and unlovable love handles. And Cleo would have declared that she'd prefer love handles than spindly flanks like a greyhound. They'd been as bad as each other, she realised. Had she demonised Sondra – or had Sondra demonised her?

They chatted in the ad breaks. Tamara of the no-smiling-receptionist fame was back working in the beauty salon.

'She's happier there. She never really took to the hotel business.' Cleo held her tongue.

Jason had a new girlfriend. Liz. 'Sweet,' Sondra pronounced her. 'Not interested in her looks.' Once, that would have been the ultimate Sondra put-down. 'She wouldn't fit into my pregnancy jeans, never mind my normal ones.' Sondra looked miserably down at herself. 'Suppose I'll never fit into my normal ones again.' She sighed. 'Liz is good for Jason. She gets him out of the house. You know what he was like for sitting in on his own at night playing computer games. She gets him out all the time. He was mad to buy a new car too and Liz said that just because he'd made a bit of money from the hotel, there was no need to go mad. She's very sensible . . .' Sondra paused at the taboo subject. The Willow.

'That's why I'm here,' Cleo said easily.

'To give out stink to us all again?'

'No. To build bridges. Although before the bridge gets built, I'd love to know why Barney and Jason didn't bother getting in touch with me the way Mum and Dad asked them to?' Even in front of this new, improved Sondra, Cleo couldn't help but add a little bite to her voice.

'It's your own fault, Cleo,' said Sondra wearily. 'You make them feel so stupid, you know. You go on about how you know what's right for the hotel and they're a pair of idiots who know nothing. It's hurtful and I don't think you understand that.'

'What do you mean?'

Sondra reached for another biscuit. 'Ah, come on, now. You're always banging on about what you learned in college and your degree. Your father never stops singing your praises: "Cleo this", and "Cleo that". Of course that's going to have an effect on your brothers. Neither of them went to college. Barney has a complex about it, you know. He says our baby's going to third-level education no matter what.'

'I don't bang on about my degree,' said Cleo, wounded. 'And I'd never try to make Jason and Barney feel stupid. They used to laugh at me for working so hard at school!' she protested.

She remembered as a child when the three siblings were doing homework, Barney and Jason had always struggled with theirs. Cleo got top marks at everything and had kept some treasured copy books as mementoes. Her brothers hadn't been able to wait to leave school before ceremonially burning their books in the hotel incinerator.

It was because of them, in a way, that Cleo knew she'd never felt that women were in any way lesser than men. She was younger than Barney and Jason, yet much smarter. She'd never dwelled on how this must have made her brothers feel.

'Did they really resent me going to college and getting a degree?' she asked.

'A bit, to be honest,' Sondra said, shifting uncomfortably on her nest of pillows.

'Do you want help?' Cleo asked uncertainly.

Sondra nodded. 'I can't stay in the same position for long. If I sit forward, can you rearrange the pillows?'

Cleo did her best, then gently helped her sister-in-law to sit back. It was the most sisterly gesture she'd ever made for Sondra.

'I was afraid the boys didn't get in touch because of the money,' Cleo said finally. 'That they'd want my share . . .'

'As if your father would let that happen!' Cleo saw a flash of the old Sondra. 'Your share is still there.'

'But why didn't they get in touch with me when Mum and Dad asked them to?'

'They were angry and they both thought it would do you good to cool your heels for a while. And then so much time had passed, they didn't have the courage to phone. They thought they'd left it too long. But they'll be glad you're here now. Barney hates rows. Just don't do your old "I'm right and you're wrong" thing when you see him, Cleo. You have to respect people's feelings.'

'Pot, kettle and black!' retorted Cleo.

'Hello, stranger.'

Cleo turned to see Barney standing in the kitchen doorway, carrying several grocery bags. He looked exactly the same as ever: a bit rumpled, his face with its mischievous expression that hadn't changed since he was a kid, but there were definitely a few more lines around his eyes. The row had affected them all, she thought in surprise. Funny how she'd thought she was the only one hurting.

'Took you long enough to come back,' he grumbled. 'Another few weeks and you'd have been an aunt and you wouldn't have known.'

'I know, sorry.' All Cleo's plans for a grand argument went out the window at the sight of Barney. She thought of how her big brothers had been intimidated by her intelligence and she felt a rush of love for them both. 'You're not going to win any awards for staying in touch either, you know,' she said fondly, going over and hugging him, shopping bags and all.

'Have you rung Mum and Dad yet?'

Cleo shook her head.

'Well . . .' said Barney, 'you could always not mention that me and Jason didn't meet up with you to talk you round, and not say we didn't . . . ?'

'You mean Mum will kill you both if she finds out?'

'That's about the size of it.'

'I'll phone them,' said Sondra decisively.

She picked up the phone and had dialled before Cleo could begin to feel anxious. She waited for Sondra to say hi, but there was no reply so Sondra left a message. 'Hi, Sheila. Give us a call when you get this?'

Jason and his new girlfriend, Liz, were invited up for dinner.

'You have to cook the chicken, Cleo,' instructed Sondra. 'I can't and Barney can only do cremations or raw food experiments. My heartburn's bad enough as it is.'

Cleo made her speciality: spatchcocked chicken in barbecue sauce. She'd cooked it one night for dinner in Trish's and all the men in the house had adored it and wanted seconds.

'The way to a man's heart, that,' sighed Ron.

'No, the way to a man's heart is through his ribs,' joked Trish.

'This is great,' said Liz enthusiastically as they all tucked into the meal round Sondra and Barney's kitchen table.

Cleo could see what Sondra meant about Liz: she was lovely, gentle and sweet, and attractively voluptuous.

'Yeah, great,' said Sondra, eating happily for two.

Barney and Jason ate like two men who'd just finished a twenty-four-hour fast. Staying with tradition, they said nothing complimentary about the food.

'Jason,' hissed Liz, 'tell your sister how good it is! Where are your manners?'

'It's very good, sis,' mumbled Jason between mouthfuls.

Cleo grinned at Liz. She was definitely the sort of woman Jason needed.

Liz and Sondra encouraged the two men to do the washing up and Cleo said she'd join them.

'But you cooked everything,' protested Liz. 'Sit down.'

'I don't mind,' said Cleo, thinking it would give her a chance to talk to her brothers.

Alone in the kitchen with Jason and Barney, Cleo washed, Barney dried laboriously and Jason put away with a great clattering of dishes.

'I'd hate this row to linger for ever,' she said tentatively.

'Chill out, sis,' said Jason. 'It's all cool.'

'Yeah, it's fine,' Barney added. 'You've got some temper, though, Cleo.'

'Tell me about it!' said Jason. 'I still have a mark on my shin from your Tiny Tears doll. Remember you whacked me with it when I tried to take it off you at your fourth birthday party?'

Putting away the dishes was abandoned while Jason rolled up his trouser leg to show said mark.

'I've still got a dodgy collarbone from that time you persuaded me to slide down the front banisters,' Cleo retorted. She didn't know if a collarbone could be dodgy eighteen years after healing, but she didn't want this comparison of scars to be one-sided. 'You said I'd be in your gang if I slid down and I was barely five,' she added. 'Mum nearly killed you for egging me on.'

'We wouldn't let you in our gang afterwards anyway,' said Barney. 'Sorry. We were horrors.'

'And you called me Cross-patch Cleo,' she said, thinking of how she'd hated the name, hated feeling left out of her brothers' games.

'You broke my ant farm over that,' Jason laughed. 'There were ants everywhere for months. You've always had a temper, Cleo. Nothing's changed! Barney, what was it Dad said when we sold the hotel? If Cleo knew the Roths had bought the hotel, she'd rage like a tornado. What?' he said to Barney, who was giving him the evil eye. 'I only said –'

'You knew Roth Hotels had bought the Willow?' asked Cleo in a strange voice, feeling as though the world were turning upside down.

'Don't go mad!' begged Barney. 'They put in a fantastic offer and the bank were hounding Dad for money ... there was no option. We knew you'd hate it, but we all hated it. Why should you hate it more than the rest of us? It was our home too.'

Cleo couldn't speak.

'What does it matter who you sell to when you're selling?' Barney asked. 'It wouldn't be any easier to walk past and see a load of town houses there rather than a posh hotel, would it? Either way, it wouldn't be in our family.'

Sondra appeared at the door, alerted by the raised voices. 'You're not arguing again?' she demanded.

Cleo shook her head. 'The Malin family arguments are over,' she said. 'The boys are filling me in on the details about the Roths.'

'They'll make a fortune out of the Willow, I shouldn't wonder,' said Sondra gloomily. 'Probably revamp it and make it all modern.'

And Cleo, who'd seen the sketches for the elegant restoration project, could say nothing. She felt such a fool. She'd walked out on Tyler and walked out on her family because her temper had got the better of her. And in both cases, it had been a mistake. Would she ever learn?

They had coffee and talked until half-nine, when Cleo said she really had better call a taxi as she was on reception early next morning at Cloud's Hill.

'We'll drop you there,' said Jason.

Cleo was getting her things when the phone rang. 'It's Mum,' said Barney, looking at the caller ID. 'You take it, Cleo.'

Cleo's mouth went dry. 'Hi, Mum,' she said shakily.

'Cleo, love, is Sondra having the baby? Is there something wrong?'

'No, no,' said Cleo, and thought how once that would have annoyed her because she'd take it to mean that Sondra was more important than she was and had to be enquired about first. Now she was able to see that a heavily pregnant family member would take precedence in most phone conversations. Imagine when the baby was born. Just as well they'd sorted out the whole family pecking order thing before that.

'Sondra is fine. I'm here with the boys, and Liz, and we all wanted to talk to you.'

'You're sure Sondra's all right? You're not breaking it to me gently?' asked her mother suspiciously. 'It's been such a difficult pregnancy . . .'

'Promise. Sondra's fine.'

'Hiya, Sheila,' roared Sondra from her spot in the big armchair. 'Still here, still pregnant.'

'Thank God for that! Cleo, I missed you. We both missed you.'

Cleo's eyes stung with tears. 'Me too, Mum. I'm sorry. I was upset and –'

'Harry, come here, it's Cleo on the phone!' There was no mistaking the joy in her mother's voice.

There was the noise of the phone being grabbed by someone else.

'Cleo, we love you!' said her father, sounding choked.

'Me too, Dad,' repeated Cleo. 'I love you both and I'm so, so sorry but I loved the hotel and I didn't realise how bad things were.'

'I should have told you,' Harry said. 'I couldn't do it. I knew it would break your heart and then we had to do the deal quickly or lose it and, I could hardly phone you up in Bristol and tell you the news. Especially about . . .' he hesitated.

'Roth Hotels. I know, Dad,' Cleo said quietly. 'Barney's right. He said it didn't matter who we sold it to once we had to sell it. I'm sure Roth Hotels will do a fine job of it.'

A sigh on the other end of the phone told her of her father's relief. 'They will too, love. The small hotelier is never going to like the big one, but I have to say, the Roth Hotels are a credit to them. Now, when are you coming to France to see us? We've got a lovely villa in the Ardèche and we have it for another two weeks. It's not big or in any way grand, but there are two spare rooms and one of them is yours if you want it.'

'Oh, Dad,' said Cleo. 'I've got a new job but as soon as I can organise a few days off, I'm there!'

After a few minutes talking to her dad – he was fascinated to hear about her time in McArthur's and would have talked for ages about Cloud's Hill – Mum came back on the line.

'Seriously, Cleo,' she said, 'I was very upset for lots of reasons. I know you're headstrong, but I thought we had a better relation-ship than that. Not to phone or write or anything, even when Barney and Jason talked to you.'

Cleo didn't have to think before speaking: her father would kill the boys if he knew what had happened. She might tell her mother some other time but not just yet. Let the family settle back into the way it was before first. 'Sorry, Mum,' she said contritely. 'I've no excuse. Cross-patch Cleo, that's me.'

'No it isn't,' her mother said affectionately. 'We love you, you know. You're the best feather in my wing and it's always going to be hard on you because you take everything so personally.'

'I know, Mum. I'm learning, though. Promise.'

'And you'll come out to see us soon?'

Cleo knew that Leah would be thrilled to hear that she'd been in touch with her family again. She had two days off next week, so if she worked a couple of extra shifts, she could maybe take a long weekend . . . 'I'll be there in a week,' she said. 'And I can't wait to see you both.'

Jason punched his sister lightly on the arm when she got off the phone. 'Thanks for not saying anything about us not getting in touch, sis,' he said. 'Dad would have killed us if he'd known. Should have let you in our gang after all.'

'As long as you let me in it now,' Cleo said, cuffing him back.

* * *

Jason and Liz drove her back to Cloud's Hill as night was falling.

'Wow, this is some place,' said Jason as they arrived at the house. There was a big black car parked where Leah usually parked, Cleo noticed, but didn't think any more about it. Leah must have guests and told them to park in her slot.

'Yes, it is a beautiful place, isn't it?' she said to Jason, seeing Cloud's Hill afresh with his eyes. 'I love working here, although it's still hard to be here, working in Carrickwell, and not in the Willow.'

Liz leaned back and gave her an encouraging pat on the arm.

'It was lovely to meet you, Liz,' Cleo said warmly.

She got out of the car and so did Jason.

'Nice to see you, sis,' he said gruffly.

'Oh, come here,' Cleo said, and grabbed him into a bear hug.

'Missed you,' Jason said in a muffled voice.

'I missed you too; I missed all of you.' Cleo stood back and smiled affectionately at her brother. 'Take care of yourself, and Liz: she's good for you.'

'You mind yourself too,' Jason said.

In the near darkness, neither of them noticed the man sitting in the strange car in Leah's parking slot, a man with close-cropped hair, who watched the whole exchange with interest.

'Bye.' Cleo waved them off down the drive, then went into Cloud's Hill. It had been such an emotional day and she was worn out.

CHAPTER NINETEEN

It was a glorious late summer day as Mel brought Sarah and Carrie to the park for their afternoon walk. Sarah launched herself through the gates, her skinny little arms waving with delight. The park was in full late-summer bloom, the footpaths dusty, the grass going yellow in places, and wild flowers sending seeds spindling off on the breeze for next year.

'Oh, look, Mummy, fairy flowers.'

Sarah liked to call flowers different names and she thought that daisies, of which there were millions rampant at the front gates of Abraham Park, should belong to the fairies. Dandelions were for elves, because she didn't like either elves or dandelions. And dog roses, like the ones that twined themselves round the railings of the tiny pavilion with the peeling paint, belonged to God because she'd never been able to say God when she was younger and said dog instead.

Now she beamed up at her mother, and rushed off the path into the grass where a crop of daisies drifted.

'Fawies,' said Carrie adoringly. 'Fawies.'

The two sisters giggled and threw themselves onto the grass by the playing field, on a mission to pick as many daisies as possible. A black mongrel, which they'd often seen before, galumphed into the middle of the girls' game, whirling excitedly, tail wagging at high speed, pink tongue lolling.

'You're squishing me!' yelled Sarah, but she hugged him all the same.

Then he bounced up to Mel, pushing his velvety nose into the bag that contained the girls' drinks and the goodies.

Mel patted the dog and gave him a bit of biscuit. 'Come on, girls, let's go to the playground.'

Carrie and Sarah ran ahead of her, the dog bouncing between them. They both petted him proudly from time to time, pleased he'd chosen to come with them for their walk.

When the foursome reached the playground, the girls raced in the small gate.

'You've got to stay outside,' Mel told the dog.

'Oh, Mum, please,' begged Sarah. 'We love him.'

'Dogs aren't allowed in here,' Mel said. 'He'll wait for us.'

They could get a dog now, she thought idly. Sarah had always wanted one and now Mel was at home all day and she'd love a dog too. It would have been impossible to have one before . . . And then the thought struck her: everything had changed since she'd stopped work. She was having fun.

Her life had been exhausting for so long that it had made being a mother hard. It shouldn't have been, of course. She'd been over-whelmed by the way she loved Carrie and Sarah when they were born. But there had been no time to enjoy them, because she had to be back at work so quickly, back on top of things, back 'giving one hundred and ten per cent!' as Hilary used to cry. Nobody had ever corrected her maths. Having children had stopped being the great joy of Mel's life and had become a kind of endurance test. Her life was a race against the clock. If she took such and such a route to work, she could save five minutes and if she cooked ten dinners at the weekend and froze them she might save fifteen minutes each night.

These last few months had felt like the first time since Sarah had been born that Mel had time to enjoy life.

She sat down on the bench in the children's playground and watched her daughters play. When Sarah's friends were around, she pretended not to play with her little sister, but on their own, like today, with only each other, they instinctively stuck together.

'Sarah, push, PUSH!' shrieked Carrie, sitting on the baby swing.

Sarah obediently pushed, sending Carrie soaring up on her swing, whooping with glee and wriggling her fat toddler legs happily.

'Sarah, move darling, the swing's coming,' warned Mel, and Sarah skipped out of the way smartly.

Children saw the magic in their lives that adults missed. Like the ladybird Sarah had noticed on the kitchen tiles that morning, and had reverently carried outside to leave on a bush.

'Look, Mummy,' she'd said, and Mel had come, had left the washing up to see, because the breakfast bowls could be rinsed at any time, and this moment was special.

After the swings, Mel, Carrie and Sarah met up with their canine friend and walked slowly past the line of sycamores, over the wooden bridge under which ran a trickle of a stream, and past the tennis courts where the 'thwack, thwack' of balls could be heard.

Sarah liked watching people play tennis and pressed her nose up against the green wire fence.

'Can we have a go, Mummy?'

'We'll get racquets soon,' Mel promised. She was dragging her heels over this because she'd seen how hard Sarah could whack a ball on the swingball at a friend's house.

'You said that yesterday,' grumbled Sarah.

'Tomorrow, I promise,' Mel said. 'Don't I keep mypromises?'

Sarah stuck her chin out as if to say no.

'Don't I?' demanded Mel, grabbing Sarah and tickling her.

'Yes!' squealed Sarah. 'Yes! Yes! Stop, Mummy!'

At the benches on the north side of the playing fields, they met Bernie and her children, one little boy and an older girl of perhaps six with a perpetually snotty nose. Bernie was sitting on a bench listlessly watching the children squabbling. She did not look full of the joys of summer and Mel knew part of the reason.

Mel had only stopped working a couple of months ago. Not going into work every day still had the feel of a holiday to her, like stolen time that would all end when she had to go back to the office. The contrast between her new life and her old one was what made it enjoyable. Bernie, however, had often hinted she was fed up to the teeth of her enforced non-office time.

The children were used to each other from playgroup. Carrie and Bernie's little boy, Stevie, were the same age and gravitated towards each other in a careful toddler way, while Sarah and Jaye instantly ran off a few yards away from the grown-ups to talk in secret. Mel hoped that Sarah wouldn't pick up Jaye's permanent cold.

'How's it going?' asked Mel, sitting down beside Bernie.

'All right,' said Bernie listlessly. 'Tired, you know.'

'Is that all?' asked Mel. 'Is there anything wrong?'

Not so long ago, she wouldn't have dreamed of such an intimacy with someone she'd only known for a short time. But she felt she knew the women in the playgroup now. It wasn't that they didn't have their private lives and secrets – of course they did – but when they talked they did so with great honesty. Motherhood had brought them all to the same place and gave them a bond.

'Mother-in-law hell,' said Bernie bitterly. 'I just wish that woman would respect me for once in her bloody life. I married her son, I'm raising her five grandchildren and she still won't give me one bit of credit for anything I do.'

'What did she do this time?' Mel had heard about Bernie's mother-in-law before, a woman for whom no chauvinistic cliché was too much.

'She was over last night for dinner and when she arrives, she talks to Mick as if his most important role in life is being her son. I don't matter, the kids don't even matter, and she adores them. No, Mick is the one. Mick, her darling baby. It's so rude!' Bernie growled.

'She wants to sit beside him, hear about his week, watch sport with him, and I'm like muggins trawling away in the kitchen, trying to cook a three-course meal, with Stevie at the cooking cupboard when my back is turned, and at least an entire bag of wholemeal flour all over the kitchen floor. And then,' Bernie got into her stride and she looked animated for the first time, 'after cooking the dinner by myself, I get a lecture on nutrition. Nutrition? This from a woman who thinks that children should drink low-fat milk too in case they turn into plump kids. And who then brings over a big packet of marshmallows every time she visits. I don't know how I didn't kill her. And do you know the worst?'

'He didn't back you up?' Mel had figured it out.

'Precisely. All I want is a bit of support, or recognition, or *something* to say I'm doing all right, thank you.'

Mel tried to think of the right things to say, but Bernie was so despondent, it was hard. Short of telling her mother-in-law and her husband to get the hell out of her house and make each other miserable, Mel didn't know what was to be done.

'I shouldn't be doing your head in with all this stuff,' said Bernie miserably.

'You've got to talk to someone,' Mel said, 'or you'd go totally nuts.'

'Thanks. Are you going to the coffee morning in Viv's on Friday? It's for the local hospice.'

'Sorry, I'm going into the city to meet an old friend from work,' Mel apologised. She fished around in her pocket for some coins. 'Give that from me. And,' she wrote her number on a scrap of paper, 'phone if you need another moan.'

The girls were tired and, once home, they flopped down on the couch while Mel began to get dinner.

Mel thought of Daisy, Cleo and Caroline urging her to set up her own business so she could work part time and from home. Nobody had come up with any actual business description, but Mel had an idea for one now. The At Home Mother Support Group. What a pity it wasn't a viable business option, because there were certainly plenty of women who needed it. Like Bernie and Caroline.

When Mel had dropped Caroline at Carrickwell train station the day after their spa break, she'd hugged her friend and said: 'Whatever happens tonight, if you need me, just phone and I'll come.'

'You're a good friend,' Caroline had said, hugging Mel back. She didn't cry, which she would have done the day before. Today, she was stronger, more together. Mel hoped so, anyway.

She spent the day waiting for the phone to ring, but nine o'clock passed and there was no call from Caroline. Mel couldn't phone her now. She knew how she hated hearing the phone ring at night when the kids were in bed and she was slumped in front of the telly; she didn't like doing it to other people.

At eight the next morning, the phone in the kitchen rang and Mel leaped to grab it.

'Mel, it's me. It's over.'

Mel's hand went to her chest. 'Over?' she repeated. 'He's left you?'

'No, the affair is over,' said Caroline. 'Really over. Oh, Mel, he cried. And I cried. And he said he'd never meant it and then he was so, so guilty. He didn't know what to do, he was afraid I'd find out.'

Carrie and Sarah were eating their breakfast, Sarah glued to the cereal packet, Carrie making a line of Cheerios into a pattern on the table. They were happy. Mel pulled a kitchen chair over to the phone and sat down.

'Who, why, where, when and for how long?' she asked.

'Someone from the company,' Caroline answered. 'She's moved.'

'Really?' asked Mel suspiciously.

'He told me who it was,' Caroline said, 'and I know she's left the company. She's married too and she's scared her husband will find out. It started last Christmas at the staff do and was a one-off until May, when they were working late. He says he's never felt so guilty in his life and he was terrified of losing me and the kids.'

Mel felt another ripple of suspicion, but said nothing.

'The odd thing is, she's not good-looking or anything,' Caroline added. 'That's what I don't understand. She's mousy if anything, although good at her job. It's easier that I know what she looks like because I'm not having to imagine her as someone gorgeous. I mean, *I'm* better looking and I'm not exactly up to Miss World standards right now.'

Mel thought she could understand how Caroline felt better that her rival hadn't been a stunning woman. That would have made it even harder to forgive because Caroline would never have been able to stop comparing herself to the other woman. But she did seem to be letting Graham off lightly.

'Did you give him an ultimatum?' she asked.

'He said it's over and I know he's telling me the truth,' Caroline answered. 'We're going for marriage counselling – I suggested it and you know Graham would run a mile before he'd talk about feelings, but he said yes straightaway. He wants us to stay together.'

'And what do you want?'

'That's what I want too.'

'I'm glad,' Mel said genuinely. 'Just remember, I'm here if you need me.'

She hung up and said a prayer that it would work out for Caroline and Graham. She admired Caroline so much for trying to make her marriage work. If Adrian had cheated, Mel didn't know if she'd have it in her to be so forgiving so the family could stay together.

Vanessa wanted to know if Kami, Mel's replacement, could join them for their swanky lunch in the Café de Montmartre.

'She'd really like to meet you, Mel,' Vanessa said.

Mel's antennae twitched. 'Why?' she asked.

'I've told her about you, that's all.'

Kami looked very young, although Vanessa had said she was in her mid-twenties. Her face was just as serene as Vanessa had said, and Mel could imagine Hilary getting furiously annoyed when she tried to remonstrate with Kami and was greeted with that calmly expressionless countenance.

'Hilary can't quite cope with Kami,' Vanessa said gleefully as they looked at the menus.

Kami shrugged birdlike shoulders. 'Why lose your temper?' she said. 'Hilary is the one who gets upset when things go wrong, not me. I'm here to do my job well. If it doesn't go well, we'll try harder tomorrow. I can do nothing more than my best.'

Mel laughed. 'So that's how I should have dealt with Hilary for all those years. She rarely raised her voice with me, but when she was angry I felt it was all my fault and it was up to me to fix it. I ought to have smiled at her and said, "We'll try harder tomorrow".'

'It annoys her,' Kami added, 'but that is not my problem. I am not responsible for her moods. The website shut down last week and there were lots of stories about it. Some angry subscriber phoned all the newspapers and we looked stupid. What can you do?'

It was comforting to know that all was not going perfectly in the publicity department without her, Mel thought. She liked the fact that Kami was honest about this.

'That's why Hilary can't cope with her,' Vanessa said, when Kami had gone to the ladies'. 'Kami is totally, utterly honest. She sees no point in lying. As Hilary is fifty per cent façade, she can't deal with this!'

It was an enjoyable lunch as they gossiped about people and work.

'You're brave to give up your career,' Kami said suddenly to Mel. 'It must have been hard for you. In China, women who work have their family to rely on, but it is harder here. You have to rely on yourself.'

'My mother was wonderful at stepping into the breach,' Mel said, 'but that wasn't the big problem. I felt that I should be looking after Carrie and Sarah all the time, not other people.'

'I don't think I'd give my job up, even if I could afford to,' Vanessa said. 'Your kids are small, but Conal's growing up so quickly. He'll be fourteen next January. In a couple of years, I'll be his boring old mother and he won't want to set eyes on me. I've gone past the hard phase.'

'Childcare is better in some countries,' Kami volunteered, 'and it is easier for women.'

'But I bet the women feel just as guilty when they miss sports

302

day because they've got an important meeting at work,' Mel pointed out. 'No matter how happy your kids were, there would always be a gremlin at the back of your mind, wondering if you were doing the right thing. I still don't know if I've done the right thing.'

'My sister still lives in China and she works in a hospital,' said Kami. 'When she comes home, she has to do homework for hours with her son. Children in China spend hours doing homework and their mothers do it with them. It is the system.' She shrugged again.

'Perhaps it's not too bad here after all,' Mel said.

'Right, that's the end of the politics tutorial. Are we ordering dessert or what?' asked Vanessa.

Mel turned and gave their waiter a polite smile. He looked past her. Blast it! Was she never going to attract a waiter's attention again? Mel thought crossly. Just because she wasn't wearing a suit . . . She looked sideways at the mirrored wall of the Café de Montmartre and saw herself reflected in many square panels. Her hair was shoulder-length and wavy, blonde again since she'd had her roots done. Her cream linen shift and aquamarine cardigan were decidedly not business wear but then she wasn't racing back to a business meeting or a tough talk with the boss like the rest of the people here. She was going to meander down the street, admiring shoe shops and boutiques, then she'd buy a present for her girls – something small, don't blow the budget – and go home to ask them how they'd got on at the birthday party her mother was taking them to. Then, they could play in the garden, she'd share a cup of tea with her mother, and cook a leisurely dinner for her family. Probably chicken again, because she'd got fed up with the made-from-scratch lasagnes and shepherd's pies, but still. It was perfect, really.

Raising her head, she glared regally at the waiter in that universal restaurant language that said 'I will not wait one second longer'.

'Madame?' He was at her side, charming up close.

She gave him her most dazzling smile. 'We're ready to order dessert,' she said.

On the way home, Mel stopped off at the butcher's and bought a really good piece of lamb. Adrian loved lamb and it would be nice to have a special Friday night meal together. She had something to tell him.

Her mother and the girls were in the garden when she arrived. Screams and yells of laughter could be heard, and Mel felt herself relax the way she always did when she came home to find everything all right. There was always that tiny niggling fear that something terrible would happen simply because she was out.

As she stood in the hall, Mel found herself really looking at her home. It looked different now. In the past three months, she'd done so much with it. The windows still weren't clean, but Mel felt you couldn't spend your whole life doing housework. Things were tidy, not in a hysterical, we-have-no-time-so-order-is-paramount sort of way, but in an organised, homely way. The freezer wasn't its old no-go area, full of supermarket ready meals and, buried down the bottom, the odd homemade shepherd's pie. Mel would have made the pie out of guilt over not giving her family proper food and then forgotten about it because the supermarket stuff was nicer. Now she didn't feel a moment's guilt if the family had supermarket frozen food for dinner.

She'd started to paint the woodwork in the hall one day, with the girls 'helping'. It had been great fun when she'd given them their own tiny brushes, some emulsion, and a section to paint, although she'd stopped the experiment halfway through when it became apparent that small children excelled in getting more paint on the floor than on the woodwork.

Mel compared that day to the Lorimar days of DIY, where she and Adrian would be grumpy at having to waste precious weekend time doing something as boring as painting. Tempers would be frayed and nobody would be speaking by nightfall. The woodwork was still only half done, but she wasn't worried. There was lots of time to finish it.

She put the shopping away and went into the garden.

'Hello, Sarah, Carrie. Hi, Mum,' she said, kissing everyone hello. 'How's everyone?'

When he got home from work at half-seven that evening, Adrian took an intrigued look at the tidied-up dining room, the white tablecloth, the place mats and the best napkins.

'Napkins?' he said. 'What's the occasion? No, let me guess. You're having an operation to turn you into a man but you want to tell me in style?'

'Close but no cigar, Sherlock.'

'You and the milkman are eloping and you had trouble writing the Dear John letter, so you're going to dump me over meatballs?'

'How did you guess?' Mel deadpanned. 'But it's the postman and not the milkman. You can lie on the mail bags in the back of the van and it's really quite comfy, although the blue pen off the registered letters keeps staining my clothes.'

'That's a relief. I could never have borne it if it had been the milkman.' Adrian put down his briefcase, unknotted his tie and sat down at the table.

She put the homemade tomato and fennel bread in front of him.

'The girls are asleep. They had a fabulous day. We went to the park in the morning and this afternoon, my mother took them to Tabitha's birthday party, which was wildly over the top, apparently, with face painting – a proper face painter at that – and a clown.'

Adrian looked startled. 'At a private kid's party?'

'Bling, bling,' Mel said. 'There was even a cake shaped like a princess, and Mum and I spent ages explaining to Sarah that not everybody gets a princess cake and a face painter, a clown and a doll's house for their fifth birthday.'

'What'll Tabitha get when she's twenty-one?'

'The whole of AC Milan and a Porsche, I shouldn't wonder. Now, dinner will be served shortly.'

'And you'll tell me in your own good time what this is about?' he said, gesturing at the flowers and the beautifully laid table.

Mel leaned over and kissed him, a long lingering kiss. 'In my own good time,' she agreed.

'Keep that up and I may put my foot down about sharing you with the postman,' Adrian said, pulling her close and slipping both hands round her waist. 'We could skip the main course, go upstairs and have dessert,' he added hopefully. One hand had slipped lower, onto the curve of her buttocks.

'Not when I have spent the evening cooking you cannot,' Mel said firmly, giving him another kiss. 'Dessert will be later. Nigella Lawson's slow-roasted lamb with Moroccan salad first.'

'I take it all back,' Adrian said, shaking out his napkin. 'Let's eat first and have dessert later. Nigella's lamb should not be wasted.'

'What gives?' he asked later, when they had nearly finished the lamb and were both so full that the notion of a romp in bed as the last course would definitely have to wait a while.

'I'd like to go back to work,' said Mel.

'I thought you might,' Adrian said.

'Did you really?' She was surprised, but only for a minute. He knew her so well; they'd been together for so long.

'I thought you might need something else,' he said, 'that's all. Not that this,' he gestured around the room where Carrie and Sarah's toys were tidied into white wicker baskets, 'isn't enough for you, but you've worked all your life. It's got to be hard to give that up. The kudos and the fun,' he added intuitively.

'But I want to do it differently this time,' she said.

'Differently how?'

'Differently part time. That would work.'

'What would you do?'

'I don't know, maybe something like I did before. Maybe working in the supermarket. I simply want to go back for a few hours every week because I like working. Working makes the fun time more fun and it would be good to feel I was earning my own money again.'

'It's our money,' Adrian protested. 'I don't expect you to account for every penny you spend.'

'Yes, but it is different when I'm not actually earning any,' Mel tried to explain. 'It's not that you make me feel any less like a grown-up because you're earning the money, it's me that feels it. How did you know I'd want to go back to work?' she asked suddenly. 'Did you think I wasn't happy? Because I was. I am.'

'I know you, don't forget,' Adrian pointed out. 'I know that you want to be with the children, but I also know you love the challenge of work.'

'Make no mistake, children are a hell of a challenge,' countered Mel.

'That's not what I meant. You like the challenge of doing something else every day.'

'But it's hard to have that and to have children,' Mel sighed. 'It was hard before. I thought I could be superwoman. I thought I could do the same job I did before I had the girls, and you know what? I couldn't. Not that I wasn't as clever or as committed or as ambitious, because I was torn in different directions. Having children changes you.'

'And I loved the way it changed you,' Adrian said gently.

'Do you?' She was struck by how much she loved him. He was her soul mate, he understood her and wanted what was best for her. She thought of Caroline and the way things were being patched up with Graham, and wondered ifCaroline would ever feel that Graham was her soul mate.

'I want,' she said, 'to be able to take care of our children and be there for them and not be missing for the doctor's appointments and have to rush off in the morning when they're sick. If Carrie's tonsils have to come out, I don't want someone else to be with her in hospital – I want it to be me. That's the freedom I need in a job.' She sighed. 'Where do you get a job where your boss understands that you're a mother first?'

'Start up your own business?'

Mel's eyes gleamed. 'You're the fourth person to say that to me,' she said. 'There might just be something in that idea.'

'Fourth? So I'm the last to know,' teased Adrian. 'Who else did you tell? The postman?'

Mel leaned back in her chair and put her bare feet on Adrian's lap. He gently stroked her toes, and began to massage the soles of her feet.

'Keep doing that and I'll tell you,' she sighed.

'We could have an early night and tidy up in the morning,' Adrian said.

Mel swung her legs down, jumped up and took his hand. 'Let's live dangerously.' Her eye caught the remains of the lamb on the table. There was quite a lot left and it had been an expensive cut of meat. 'Actually, I'll just put this in tin foil,' she said, letting go of Adrian's hand. 'There's loads left over and . . .'

Adrian burst out laughing.

'What?' she demanded, but she was laughing too. 'You love lamb and you could have this cold for lunch tomorrow.'

'I'm laughing at you, Mrs Beaton,' he said, and he began to tidy up with her. 'You're right. Waste not, want not.'

'We can't afford to throw money away,' Mel said seriously, briskly gathering up dishes and plates. 'Until I get some sort of part-time work, we have to economise.'

'What if I told you that I'd got a raise?' Adrian asked archly.

Mel instantly stopped tidying. 'What?'

'I've been promoted,' he said. 'That was my big bit of news and I was going to save it for later, after I'd had my wicked way with you,' he teased. 'We'd both hoped getting my Masters would have a knock-on effect at work, and it has. I've moved up a pay scale and I'm now part of the senior management team. They told me today.'

'Adrian!' Mel flung herself into his arms. 'I'm so proud of you.'

'Couldn't have done it without your support,' he murmured, his face buried in her hair.

'Yes you could,' she said.

'No.' He held her very tightly. 'I couldn't. We make a good team.' Then he kissed her and Mel felt a surge of excitement that made tidying up fade into insignificance.

'You're right,' she said firmly, picking up the lamb. 'This is going in the fridge and the rest can wait until tomorrow. We've more important things to do.'

CHAPTER TWENTY

Daisy looked around the big living room of her old apartment, empty now except for lots of boxes and plenty of dust. No matter how hard you tried to clean, there was always dust under furniture and in corners, she thought. She was sad to be leaving. This had been her home for six years. It was like a living diary, a part of her life. Would she forget those years when she walked out the door? Would it be like losing a diary, because everything here meant something? A coffee stain on the carpet in her bedroom, from the time they'd bought the new coffee machine and she handed Alex a cup and it nearly scalded him, so he dropped it. The special shoe section in her wardrobe that she had had fitted and that Alex had laughed at, calling her the Imelda to beat all Imeldas. The cottage barely had wardrobes, never mind adorable cubbyholes especially made for high-heeled shoes, but there was plenty of time to get all sorts of wardrobes built. She'd bought it at a good price, so there would still be money left over from her half of the sale of this place.

'Those stairs would kill you,' said a weary voice.

The removal men were back in the apartment. They had just brought the bed down to the van and they hadn't been able to use the lift because it wouldn't fit in.

'I think we'll have to have tea, love,' said the chief removal guy.

'Go ahead,' said Daisy cheerfully. 'I'm just having a last look around, then I'm going off to the new house. Can I leave you here with the keys? The estate agent will be around to pick them up at four.'

She walked out with her head held high, got into her car and checked the messages on her mobile phone. There were seven messages. Everyone knew it was moving day.

Mary said she was dropping by the new house later with a lasagne. 'Full fat, sweetie. Just because you want to be on a diet, I don't.'

Daisy had decided she had to lose weight and was determined to visit the local diet club soon. Just not yet.

Claudia had rung saying they were all still going out the following evening but they were starting off a bit later, eight instead of half-seven, was that all right? 'Casual really,' Claudia had said, 'just dinner in a pizza place. Andrew promises not to set you up with anyone.'

Paula rang to wish her luck. 'You've got to come and see me and Emma,' she said plaintively. 'We haven't seen you for ages. Emma's getting huge now. She wants to see her auntie.'

Daisy smiled at that message. She'd love to see Emma again. Recently, she felt as if she'd passed some sort of mental test. She could see women with pushchairs on the street and watch nappy commercials on the television, all without wanting to break down into tears. It wasn't that her longing for a baby was any less, it was just that she was able to put it on a mental back burner. Nobody had said she would never have children. It was still there, a possibility, waiting in the future. Since she'd never had any tests, she didn't know if her not having a baby was a fluke or something that needed work, but without proof she refused to believe that it couldn't happen.

First, she had to mourn the children that she and Alex would have had. Bizarrely enough, the birth of Daragh had helped her do that. Funny how a baby brought closure to the whole thing. Mary would approve, being big on closure.

Daisy's old friend Zsa Zsa had phoned to say she had been going out with the most divine man for the past month and he had lots of fabulous friends. 'Now you're footloose and fancy free – by the way, did that thing with KC ever work out? – you could join us double dating, whatever.'

Oh, no way, thought Daisy, with a shudder. She didn't want to be reminded of KC and the horrible dark days just after Alex had dumped her. No, thank you very much, she had moved on. She was not that craven, blithering idiot any more. Hanging around with the party crowd would put her back there.

Leah's message started with whale music. Amid the high-pitched squeals and coos, Leah left a message to say she was thinking of Daisy and would love to see her soon.

'Hope you like the music,' Leah said in her low voice. 'It took me ages to find it. Someone really doesn't want us to listen to happy whales.'

And Daisy had laughed heartily at that one. Trust Leah to come up with something totally different, to make her laugh.

The final message was from her mother.

'Hello, Daisy. Wanted to catch up. Myself and your Aunt Imogen have been away, as you know, but we're back now and mmm ...' Long pause.

Daisy could imagine her mother trying to work out what to say next. Strange that her mother's normal ability to talk happily on the answering machine seemed to have deserted her.

'I know that you were staying here for a while. Brendan told me, and thanks for keeping it all so nicely. Well, that's all. Hope you're well, Denise.'

Daisy hated it when her mother called her Denise. 'Why don't you tell her that?' said a little voice inside Daisy's head. Good point. She'd never told her mother that she didn't like her given name and preferred to be called Daisy, the name her father had given her when she'd been a baby and picked up daisies from the garden and tried to eat them.

What was it Leah had said? *'You're to tell other people what you think and what you feel, they can't guess.'*

'Do give me a ring,' her mother said. 'Goodbye.'

For the first time in years Nan Farrell's cold, crisp tones didn't upset Daisy. It was just the way her mother spoke. She couldn't help it, she'd been brought up that way, to be a lady and to know the correct way to greet an archbishop or a countess. Her mother's world ran on tracks made up of etiquette and *the way things had always been done*. She'd sooner run down the road stark naked than say something deeply personal to her only daughter. She couldn't help it, Daisy knew, any more than Daisy could help being naïve and trusting and easily hurt.

Wow, more closure, she thought to herself, startled.

She rang Mary back immediately. 'You can bring full-fat lasagne, as long as you bring cheesecake,' she told Mary, who laughed throatily.

'Now that sounds like the old Daisy,' Mary said. 'Will I bring a couple of bottles of wine too?'

'Maybe not,' Daisy said gently. 'I think I was sinking into the wine far too often when Alex left. It's not good for me,' she said. Not drinking wasn't easy. She'd got into the habit of it and a drink dulled the edges so nicely, but Daisy knew she'd been teetering on the edge of problem drinking and she didn't want to fall in.

'Oh, join the club!' said Mary. 'It's so easy to fall into the trap of the forgotten woman, sitting at home, with her litre bottle. So that's not a mistake I make, I just eat chocolate instead and digestive biscuits.'

'That sounds like a brilliant idea,' said Daisy, 'and there is no limit on how many units of digestive biscuits you can have in a day.'

'Precisely,' Mary agreed. 'And after seventeen digestive biscuits, you never want to ring up your ex and tell him just what a piece of shit he really is! See you at about six and I'll help you with the unpacking.' And she hung up.

Daisy was just about to drive off when she remembered one box of things she had wanted to carry with her in the car. It contained the kettle, teabags, milk, all the essentials for when she got to the new place. Her retinue of helpers – Mary, Cleo and Leah – had insisted that they wouldn't do a thing unless there was tea involved. She had to run up the stairs, because the removal men had obviously hijacked the lift yet again. At the door of the apartment, she pushed it open quickly, expecting to see nobody there. The movers were all gathered around by the lift discussing the best way to bring Daisy's favourite armchair down. But there was someone in the apartment. He was standing near the window, holding a big box close to his chest and looking down to the street as he must have done many times before. It was Alex.

'Oh, you startled me!' she said.

'I didn't mean to frighten you. I thought you were gone. I waited until I saw you go to your car,' Alex said warily.

How sad, Daisy thought, that the man she'd lived with and loved with had waited for her to leave the building before he'd had the courage to come in. So much for her theory that they could be friends.

'I just wanted to get the rest of my stuff. The lawyer said you'd leave it all boxed up and ready, and I was going to get it later but –'

'It's all right, Alex,' she said. 'You're entitled to pick up your stuff.' She could see him visibly relax. 'What did you think I was going to do?' Daisy asked, with a rare flash of irritation. 'Scream blue murder and wave a carving knife around?'

Alex looked so surprised at this flash of humour that she laughed out loud. 'I'm sorry,' she said, 'I couldn't resist it.' He still looked shocked. 'It's a joke, Alex. Remember jokes?'

'Yes, sorry, of course. Just this is all a bit difficult,' he said.

'I think it's probably more difficult for me than it is for you,' Daisy pointed out testily.

'I know, I know,' he said. 'I'm sorry, Daisy, I'm so, so sorry. I never wanted it to end up this way, please believe me. If I could turn the clock back, I would, but I can't.'

She would have killed to hear him say those words a month ago, but now she felt oddly unmoved by them. He was sorry, and that was good. It meant that their relationship *had* meant something to him, that he cared enough to feel regret over hurting her. Yet there was something hollow about the apology of someone who had been so cruel to her.

Daisy would never forget the words he'd said to her: she wasn't *the one*; that he'd been biding time from when they'd left college, waiting for the right person to come along.

Suddenly, she wanted to be cruel to him. He had no idea how low she'd sunk when he'd left her and she needed him to suffer for that. Words spun around in her head. Maybe she would ask him if he still thought she was an evil bitch who'd wreck his relationship with Louise by telling her about them having sex together on this very floor?

And then she felt ashamed of herself. He'd hurt her so much, he'd never comprehend how much, but the pain wouldn't get any better if she ranted and raved at him.

At least now she had memories of their time together. She could be proud of how she'd behaved towards him.

'You're right,' she said calmly. 'You can't turn the clock back. I just wish you'd been honest with me from the start. You let me go on thinking we could have a baby, when all along you wanted to leave me. That was terrible, Alex.'

He leaned against the window, the box still clutched to his chest. 'I know. I am sorry. I didn't have the balls to tell you, and you were so excited . . .'

'Don't blame me for the fact that you weren't being honest with me,' Daisy said, fighting very hard to keep calm. 'Take responsibility for what you did. You lied to me and the longer you went on lying, the harder it was for me.'

'I was afraid,' he said, looking at the floor. 'I didn't know how to tell you.'

'That's something we've both learned, then,' she said, feeling a sudden charge of power. 'Tell the truth, even when it hurts.'

'You've changed,' he remarked.

'I've had to. My life has changed. All the things I believed in are gone, that's a big adjustment.'

There was silence except for the talking of the removal men outside.

'How's Daragh?' she asked.

The surprise was written all over Alex's face. Surprise and grudging admiration.

She held herself a little taller. 'And Louise?'

'They're great,' he stammered. 'You . . . you're being so good about this, Daisy.'

Daisy thought of her collection of wine bottles, how she'd wanted to destroy herself because of how hurt she was, of the tears she'd cried.

'I want to be able to sleep at night, Alex,' she said. 'If I wish all sorts of disasters on you, I won't. For my own peace of mind, I have to try to forgive you.'

'My mother still hasn't forgiven me,' he said.

'What, not even now that you've given her a grandchild?' Daisy asked, and that hurt, because she wanted to be the one to give Alex's mum a grandchild; she had dreamed of it often enough. 'She wrote to me,' Daisy remembered, 'a lovely letter, telling me how sorry she was and how she was furious with you and how she hoped we'd always be friends. She left her mobile number at the bottom and asked me to ring her. I haven't,' said Daisy, 'not yet. I mean I will, but just not now.'

'She might get off my back if you were to ring her,' Alex said, and for a second he was like the old, selfish Alex, thinking only of himself.

'So if I ring your mother and tell her I'm fine really, then she won't give you so much grief for your behaviour?' asked Daisy.

Alex winced. 'OK, OK. I shouldn't have said that,' he said. 'I am sorry, Daisy.'

Daisy knew it was time to go. It was Alex's turn to be left behind. She picked up her small tea box.

'Bye, Alex. I don't suppose we'll see each other again. Take care.'

'You too . . .' He moved towards her and then stopped. 'You're being amazing about this, Daisy. Really amazing.'

Daisy smiled. 'I suppose I am,' she said, and left.

She walked with a spring in her step until she reached the safety of her car, when her legs suddenly felt shaky. She'd done it, she'd said the things she wanted to say to Alex. She hadn't lost her temper because she didn't want to waste any emotion on Alex Kenny any more. He was the past, part of her old life and she was moving into a new one.

Nan Farrell was surprised to see Daisy on her doorstep the next morning, bright and early.

'Denise!' said her mother. 'Lovely to see you,' she added, years of good manners coming to the fore.

'Thought I'd drop in, Mother,' said Daisy, determined not to be fazed by her mother's use of her real name. They'd have that conversation later.

'Drop in?' said her mother. 'How can you drop in from Carrick-well? I don't understand.'

'I have some news for you, Mum,' said Daisy, still determined to maintain the cheery front. 'I've moved. I'm living just down the road actually.'

It was some relief that her mother didn't look too horrified at this news.

'That's lovely, dear,' said Nan. 'It's so beautiful round here. The people are very welcoming.'

If Daisy was surprised, she didn't let on. She wouldn't have thought her mother was the sort of person who cared if the people in an area were welcoming or not, but then again, maybe she didn't know her mother that well. Her mother certainly didn't know her.

'Where exactly have you and Alexander moved to?'

'That's something else I have to tell you,' Daisy said. 'Alex and I aren't together any more.'

It was just strange that she was only telling her mother now, months after the event. Other women would have informed their mothers instantly, by speed-dial before the first tear could fall.

'We split up,' Daisy said.

'Gosh,' said her mother. There was a pause, while she waited for details.

Daisy tried not to flinch. 'Alex became involved with somebody else and she got pregnant. He's a father now.' She said it as cheerfully as she could, but no matter how far she had come along in the personal growth department, it was still hard news to deliver.

'I'm sorry to hear that, Daisy. Very sorry.'

And it sounded as if her mother meant it. Certainly calling her 'Daisy', and not 'Denise', was an olive branch.

'When did this happen?' Nan Farrell asked.

'A few months ago.' For a millisecond Daisy toyed with the idea of not telling her mother all the facts, and then changed her mind. She was going to be utterly honest and see if they could put their relationship on a better footing. If her mother wasn't interested and was her normal cool, removed self, then at least Daisy could comfort herself with knowing she'd tried. 'We were trying to have a baby at the time. I thought Alex wanted it too. That certainly added pressure on the relationship,' she said, 'although it wasn't the only reason.' She had to admit that, even to herself. 'I hoped we could have treatment to make me pregnant, then he fell in love with his assistant at work and she got pregnant. That's it – what can I say?'

'I'd like to have a few words with that young man,' said her mother angrily.

Daisy felt a dart of surprise. Her mother angry on her behalf?

'How dare he? To drag your name through the mud like that,

it's outrageous. If your grandfather was alive Alexander Kenny wouldn't have tried such a trick.'

Daisy's grandfather had been a local landowner and a powerful man. Doubtless he'd have made Alex marry Daisy long ago by pure force of his personality. But what would have been the point? She and Alex would have ended up married and not in love with each other instead of just living together and not in love with each other.

'Thanks,' she said to her mother, and Nan Farrell looked slightly surprised.

'Goodness. For what?' she said.

'Oh, just for saying that, for backing me up,' Daisy said.

'What else would you expect me to do?' demanded Nan. 'Poor Imogen will be so upset,' her mother went on. 'She's only getting over the operation and now this.'

'Aunt Imogen will be fine,' said Daisy comfortingly. 'If she could survive Lillian getting a divorce, she can survive anything.'

The big drama in the family a few years ago had been Aunt Imogen's daughter, Lillian's, marriage falling apart.

'You're right, I dare say,' said Nan. 'It's just that things are changing. We never had divorces or anything like that in the family.'

It was easier, Daisy had just figured out, to talk to her mother and try to tease her gently out of her fears. That's what she hadn't done right before, Daisy realised. She had been too anxious for her mother's approval, too anxious for everyone's approval. If her mother had said one cross word, Daisy had quailed.

'I'll phone Imogen and tell her if you like?' Daisy said.

'Maybe you'd go and see her,' Nan brightened. 'She'd love to see you, now that she's back on her feet. I think she's lonely. We could go together – that would be fun. Imogen and I were talking the other day about how we've got to stick together. Neither of us is getting any younger and we're all the family we've got left.'

'You've got me,' said Daisy.

'Well, of course I have you,' said her mother brusquely. 'I meant family from when I grew up, people who remember the old times and the way things used to be. You don't remember it, Daisy. It was all different when you were born. Times have changed.'

Her mother looked so sad that Daisy felt a sudden burst of love for her, love and pity. Her mother had tried to live in the past, relying on past glories to help her through her life. 'Poor Mother.' She said it aloud.

And she did something else she'd rarely done before: she reached out and hugged her mother.

Nan didn't sink into the embrace but then she wasn't that sort of person. Instead, Daisy was sure there was a slight unbending of her spine.

'Chin up,' Nan said briskly, pulling back. 'Never let them see you cry, that's the family motto.'

'I think we need a new family motto,' Daisy murmured under her breath.

Daisy sat in the very last row of the chairs set out in the room and looked at the other dieters who'd come to the Wednesday night meeting of the Carrickwell branch of Born To Be Slim.

They were all shapes and sizes, some glowing with pride at their new slim selves, others glowering with misery at not being slim. The ones who'd got through the awful business of being weighed chatted with each another, bandying comments about losing two pounds, losing only three ounces, how soon the wedding was going to be, the joy of fitting into a size fourteen and how they'd *kill for some real butter*.

Daisy could no longer get into a size sixteen. The shame of it. She'd tried everything: clearing the kitchen of goodies; saying 'I will not buy any chocolate' when she walked past the newsagent's; buying bags and bags of salad and low-fat salad dressing that tasted faintly of sugar-laced polystyrene. Nothing worked. Which was why she was here, parading her shame among some forty other women, and a couple of men.

The BTBS leaflet that she'd picked up in the health food shop (that detoxing and slimming herbal drink had been completely useless after all), promised that they could help anyone lose weight. 'All you need is to want to be thin,' the literature promised.

Well, Daisy certainly wanted that. If wanting was enough to make it happen, she felt thinner already. But then she'd wanted Alex back and he hadn't come back, so wanting was clearly not enough.

The woman in charge of the Carrickwell branch of Born To Be Slim looked vaguely familiar. Her hair was short but Daisy had a sudden mental image of it long, swished back with a confident flick of the head. Ballet classes. They'd been to ballet together.

The years she'd stomped around Ms De Fressange's studio in her ballet shoes were years Daisy had hoped to forget. She'd always felt too plump and too self-conscious to glide like a gazelle and in the studio's Christmas ballet productions, Daisy had always been confined to second swan at the back of the *corps de ballet*. But her mother had insisted. 'Ballet is so good for the posture, Denise.'

Daisy instinctively pulled herself up straighter now. Yvette had been one of the studio's ballet stars and she didn't appear to have changed. Still slim, poised and probably capable of a couple of *grands jetés* without looking like a baby elephant on ice. Daisy knew that Yvette must have been fat once or else she wouldn't have been running a slimmers' class, but there was no fat visible now. Why weren't the class leaders made to wear before and after photos? Then everyone wouldn't feel so intimidated.

Meekly, Daisy took her place in line in front of Yvette where the weigh-in torture was going on, and hoped that Yvette wouldn't remember her.

'Daisy! It's great to see you. And you look fabulous. Well, a few pounds you could do without, but don't mind that. We'll soon get it off and turn you into a new woman.'

For a thin person, Yvette had a big embrace, and her enthusiasm took Daisy by surprise.

'Hello, Yvette,' she mumbled in deep embarrassment.

'It's so nice to see you, really,' Yvette went on, briskly taking Daisy's weight and writing it down. 'Now, height. That's so we can work out your goal weight.'

Chatting blithely to get past the horrific statistics was obviously the secret to Yvette's success with her class. In a flash, Daisy was clutching a piece of paper with her shameful weight written on it, along with the weight she was hoping to reach. There was a difference of two and a half stones between the two figures, and even then she wouldn't be as thin as she'd been for the past few years.

A woman who'd just been weighed sat down beside her and smiled shyly at Daisy.

'Hi!' Daisy introduced herself.

'I'm Cyn,' said the woman. Cyn was huge. Not just fat but in the obesity danger zone. Daisy thanked her lucky stars that she wasn't that size. Yet Cyn had a lovely face and big eyes that sparkled with vitality. And she had such a sweet smile, though to see it, you had to get past the fat. Daisy realised that if she'd seen Cyn in the street, she'd only have noticed her huge bulk, not that there was a lovely person underneath. That was just the way people had looked at her years ago.

Suddenly Daisy felt horrendously ashamed of herself. She'd done just what she never wanted other people to do to her: to judge a book by its cover.

While Yvette talked about good foods, bad foods and foods that were so evil and calorific they should come wrapped in skull-and-crossbones paper, Cyn and Daisy talked.

'I'm here to get thin once and for all,' said Cyn, who was twenty-five and wanted with all her heart to be a nurse but couldn't due to her bulk. 'I am going to give it one last shot and then, it's stomach stapling time. I've been this size since I was a teenager. All my family are big, but they don't mind. What are you doing here?'

'Same.'

'Why?'

Daisy faltered. She couldn't say 'because I'm fat', because compared to Cyn, she wasn't, she didn't need to be there. The truth hit with sudden clarity. 'I'm heavier than I'd like to be,' she said lamely.

'You're a sprite,' laughed Cyn. 'You don't need this.'

Cyn had been coming for two weeks and had lost eight pounds.

'It's been so hard,' she whispered. 'I longed for white bread and cream cheese. Longed for it. I would have killed for some but I knew that if I started, I'd never stop.'

'Chocolate,' Daisy whispered back.

'Oh, don't!'

They chatted through the class, then Daisy asked Cyn if she'd like to have a coffee in Mo's Diner.

Cyn hesitated. 'I don't go out much at night,' she said, and she looked shy again, the way she had at first.

'Just one coffee, black, no sugar,' Daisy said. And if anyone made a single comment about Cyn's size, Daisy would kill them.

She could see herself in Cyn: hiding from who she really was. Cyn needed to lose weight, but she needed so much more besides. Daisy had spent years thinking that if she was thin, her life would be better. And it hadn't been. She'd lost the weight but the neuroses had grown fatter and healthier than ever.

They sat in the back booth in Mo's. Cyn had to sit sideways because she couldn't really fit her stomach under the table.

'It's lovely to be out,' she said, eyes shining brightly, looking around.

'I don't think I'm going to go back to the class,' Daisy began. 'I've spent years panicking about my weight and thinking if I was thin it would all be better, and that's wrong. It seems so obvious to me now!' she laughed. She'd been thin for years and yet Alex had left her. Her state of mind was what mattered – not what she weighed. The diet class had been a mistake, she knew that now. And that realisation felt wonderful, like several pounds being miraculously lifted from her body. Peace of mind was the ideal diet aid, Daisy thought happily.

'But who'll I talk to if you're not coming any more?' asked Cyn anxiously.

'I didn't say we wouldn't be friends,' Daisy reassured Cyn.

'Honestly?'

'Honestly. There's someone I think you should meet,' Daisy added. 'Leah Meyer, she runs Cloud's Hill Spa.'

'I don't know about that,' said Cyn, pulling her cardigan around her as if to hide herself even further. 'I don't do spas and gyms and that type of thing.'

Daisy reached out and took Cyn's hand. She had tiny hands and dainty little fingers and they clung to Daisy's. 'Cloud's Hill isn't about the gym and dieting,' she said gently. 'It's . . .' she searched for the word, 'it's a bit magical. If I tell you how it helped me, would you come and visit it?'

Cyn's eyes met Daisy's. She nodded. 'Nobody will laugh at me?'

'No,' said Daisy. 'They'll love you.'

'But what would I do there?'

Daisy thought about what Cloud's Hill had done for her. She felt like a different person now. She saw the world clearly; she wasn't the frightened, anxious teenager looking out from behind the big barrier of her own insecurities. She'd had to survive a lot, Leah had reminded her. She was a survivor and she had a future.

How could she explain all this to Cyn?

'You'll meet people who'll make you see your life differently,' Daisy said. 'You'll stop being scared, you'll learn to like yourself.'

Cyn looked frankly disbelieving at this.

'You will. I have,' Daisy said cheerfully, 'and a few months ago, I wouldn't have thought that was possible.' But it is, I promise.

CHAPTER TWENTY-ONE

Cleo's bag was packed, Leah was driving her to the train station the following morning, and she had to be at the airport by ten for her flight to France. Her mother said they couldn't wait to see her.

'And you need a break, love,' Sheila Malin fussed. 'You've been doing far too much, by the sound of it.'

'I'm so looking forward to it, Mum,' Cleo said. 'I've missed you both.'

A few days away sounded lovely, Trish said, and muttered about how she'd love a weekend away and now that her other plans had fallen through, she'd nothing planned.

'What other plans?' asked Cleo.

'Carol mentioned she and some friends were going to Tunisia in September but when I asked her about it the other day, she said she'd changed her mind. She's so unreliable.'

Cleo, who remembered the time she'd met Carol and had to endure watching her flirt with Tyler, was proud that she didn't make any of the smart remarks she could have made.

'We could go away somewhere at the end of the year,' Cleo suggested. 'Or,' she decided she'd tell Trish what had been on her mind for the past few days, 'we could go abroad for a month's holiday. I was thinking of Australia. I know you'd love to go and we deserve it.'

'Oh, wow!' squealed Trish excitedly. 'Wow! But like, what about your mum and dad's plans for the French B & B? Won't you be helping them out?'

Cleo's parents had discussed the idea of starting a B & B in France, but Cleo had decided that she'd be intruding on their retirement if she joined in. After years of being at everyone's beck and call, Mum and Dad wanted time on their own. And now Cleo must move on too. She'd grown up.

'Could you get the leave from Cloud's Hill?' Trish added. 'I'll have to beg to get a month off here, but I've holidays due.'

'I can,' Cleo said. 'It's not as if I'm tied down in any way, so why not?'

And if she wasn't around the Willow for the next month her heart might have healed a little. That way, she'd cope better when she got back and had to watch her old home being turned into a Roth Hotel, while she forever remembered what might have been with Tyler.

'Fantastic!' squealed Trish. 'I'll come down and celebrate. A month's holiday. Yahoo! You phone Eileen and I'll locate my party dress! The floordrobe's getting worse and I can't find a thing!'

A night out partying with Trish and Eileen the day before she flew to France had not been on Cleo's list of must-do things, but it might be good for her, she decided. All she'd planned was a quiet night in her room.

Eileen was delighted to hear that Trish was coming to town to party.

'Haven't seen her for weeks,' Eileen said. 'Bet I know what we're celebrating too! You're a dark horse, Cleo Malin.'

'What do you mean?' asked Cleo.

'Six foot something of all man?' teased Eileen. 'You know.'

'No,' insisted Cleo. 'What are you on about?'

'Tyler Roth is in town,' Eileen said in exasperation.

'Tyler? You saw him?'

'You didn't know? I thought he was here to see you and we were all going out to be introduced to him properly, minus the whole falling-over-in-the-street with the crowd of drunks watching.'

'I wish,' said Cleo before she could help it.

'You haven't seen him?'

'The combination of me storming out of his suite, and Ron telling him that I was outraged at some dastardly hotel group buying the Willow means that I am probably not his favourite person in the whole world,' Cleo said morosely.

'But he went looking for you?' Eileen said simply.

'And he could have found me and he didn't,' Cleo replied. That was the painful truth. Tyler had tracked her down to Trish's house and had discovered she was a Malin of Carrickwell. So it wouldn't have been too hard to find her in person. Except he hadn't bothered.

'You should find him then,' Eileen said matter of factly.

'I . . . but . . .' Cleo faltered. She'd never thought of that, but she couldn't. Men went after women and told them they loved them. That was how it was done. She'd read about it often enough. 'It's up to him,' she muttered.

'Why?'

'Because it is!'

'Because it is in all those daft books you read where the guy leaps onto his white charger and finds the maiden, who faints at his feet,' Eileen raged. 'Give me strength, Cleo! You're the independent woman who has twice as much brain, drive and ambition as any man, so why go all girlie and act like a daft bodice-ripping heroine when it comes to something you really want?'

Cleo was shocked into silence. Eileen was normally such a laid-back person. What had brought this on?

'Find him and tell him you're crazy about him. What's difficult about that?'

Put that way, it wasn't difficult at all. But what if his eyes hardened when he looked at her and he told her she'd had her chance? Cleo thought she could deal with thinking Tyler despised her if she didn't have to actually witness it.

'But where . . . ?'

'At the Willow, you big moron,' snapped Eileen. 'Or if he's not there, they might know where he is. Or ask in Mo's. Carrickwell's not that big. I promise you, Cleo, I am not going out with you tonight unless you've made an effort to talk to Tyler. Don't be a wimp. What's the worst that can happen?'

'He could be disgusted with me, or say I never gave him a chance and jumped to conclusions, and make me feel an inch high,' Cleo muttered.

'So what? Tell him it's his loss, walk away, then you, me and Trish can dance all night and find other gorgeous men. What have you got to lose?'

Cleo's shift ended at four and she'd arranged to meet Eileen and Trish in Eileen's flat at eight. That gave her time to finalise her holiday packing, return some phone calls and dress up for going out. But she did none of that. She asked Leah if she could borrow one of the spa's vans and as soon as she had finished work, she ran out the front door of Cloud's Hill, still in her olive-green uniform.

The gates to the Willow Hotel had a padlock chain but the padlock was unlocked, so Cleo was able to prise open the gates a little bit. In her family's time, the gates were never shut, but now they were so stiff that she couldn't open them enough to drive the van in.

She began to walk up the drive in her high-heeled work shoes, a disastrous move since the potholes were worse than ever. Beside the hotel, a prefabricated site office had been set up and there were several diggers onsite, a sign that work had started. Cleo felt another twinge of rage that her beloved home was being torn apart. A couple of men in luminous yellow safety jackets and matching hard hats were standing with their backs to her beside the office and Cleo was able to slip in the front door of the house without them seeing her.

Inside, her old home was neglected and dusty, and Cleo realised to her horror that the two-hundred-year-old marble fireplace had been ripped out of the hall. How could they? she thought, shocked. If this was what Roth Hotels was all about, then the Willow would be destroyed. What would be put here instead – some hideous reproduction edifice with gold inlays and a couple of china leopards on either side to finish it off?

The stair carpet had been removed and the brass stair rods were flung any which way on the stairs. It was difficult to see that the best of the gracious old building was being incorporated into the new hotel, only that maybe the Willow wouldn't even be standing soon. The more Cleo looked around, the angrier she became. This house mightn't be in her family any more, but she'd have her say one last time.

She marched outside to the site office in a temper.

The two workmen were still standing beside it talking.

'What the hell has been happening here?' Cleo yelled. 'This is a beautiful old house and you people are ripping it to shreds! Have you any idea how valuable that fireplace is?'

'Hey, don't tell us,' one of the workmen said, holding up his hands in surrender. 'Talk to the boss.' He looked towards the cabin door.

'Show me the boss and I'll talk to him,' Cleo snapped. 'I'd like to know if you've got planning permission to destroy this place.'

A third man appeared at the door. He was tall, wearing jeans and a T-shirt under his yellow safety jacket. His hair was cropped short, his dark eyes were narrowed and the expression on his handsome face was ice cold. It was Tyler.

'You're with the planning department now?' he said acidly. 'You do move around, Ms *Malin*.'

Cleo raised her chin an inch. 'Hello, Tyler,' she said.

The two workmen moved fractionally forward with interest. Tyler said nothing but swiftly exchanged a look with each of them.

'Er, yes . . .' one muttered.

'Work to do . . .'

'See ya.'

They hurried off.

'You wanted to come and see what the horrible Roths were doing to your precious home?' He sounded so angry, that Cleo was taken aback.

'Well, yeah. I wanted to see what had happened,' she said.

'Happy now? Are we destroying it to your satisfaction?'

Hard – that's how he sounded, she realised with horror. Not like the Tyler she remembered, the man with the wry sense of humour and the wicked glint in his eye.

'Destroying it is the word,' she said.

'Actually, we've hired an architect who specialises in old properties to make sure the restoration is historically accurate and that we don't damage anything. We've taken out valuable pieces, like the fireplace, for safekeeping. Destroying this old house is exactly what we're not doing. And you lied to me,' he said.

Stunned by his coldness, Cleo retorted: 'And you were so truthful with me! You never mentioned anything about buying a hotel in Carrickwell, and you'd met me in the town. Didn't it occur to you to say something?' If he was going to be hard and cold, then she would be too. And if this was the real Tyler Roth, then she'd done the right thing by walking out on him.

'Not mentioning important facts was very fashionable at the time,' he snapped back. 'I didn't think I needed to bore you with my business plans. I thought you were a beautiful, sexy girl from a country town, not a Trojan horse.'

Cleo could feel the blood roar in her head. She wanted to tell him that she lied about her surname because she didn't want him pitying her or her family for what they'd lost. But she wouldn't lower herself to explain why now. Not to this cold, arrogant pig.

'You've big plans for the Willow, I know,' she said. 'Oh, sorry, the Carrickwell Roth. Another notch on your bedpost or your empire or whatever. Although your bedpost and your empire probably merge. Lots of willing girls on the payroll in your hotels, I'm sure.'

'A different one every night,' he said sarcastically. 'You saw the plans the night it was your turn,' he added. 'Is that why you ran away?'

'I saw them,' she said quietly, remembering her shock at the sight of a new, improved Willow. It had all looked so different and big and glossy. 'I suppose you'll have confidence-building meetings when the new Roth opens, and talk about how you found this useless little country hotel that had been run into the ground by the Malins, and then you came along and turned it into the jewel in the Roths' new European empire.'

He looked at her curiously. 'Is that what you think? That I'd buy a small hotel and make fun of the people who'd spent thirty years trying to make it a success?'

'Isn't that the plan?' she asked bitterly, seeing her father's sad face in those last months when the hotel was losing money. 'Make it fabulous and laugh at us?'

'Oh, forget it, Cleo,' he said, and the anger was gone. 'Stop playing games. I'm tired. I've been travelling a lot. I got in last night and in the two weeks since I was last here, I've been on six planes and have more jet lag than I can cope with. I can't cope with you too, Cleo. Go home,' he added wearily.

'This is my home!' she yelled.

'Not any more. Go back to Cloud's Hill. I came to find you there a couple of weeks ago and when I did, it became clear I'd made a huge mistake. You're not who I thought you were, and I don't mean because of your name. You didn't waste much time after walking out on me, did you?'

Cleo couldn't think what he meant, though her mind whirled.

'I don't know what you're talking about. I came to see you to tell you the truth. About why I left.'

'Don't bother,' he said flatly. 'I don't want to know.'

He walked back towards the house, leaving Cleo standing impotently watching him.

How dare he? Furious, she began stumbling her way down the drive, angry with herself for having listened to Eileen and come here at all, and three times angrier with Tyler for treating her like that. What had she ever seen in him? And what did he mean, she wasn't who he thought she was? He was talking in riddles.

Two weeks ago he'd been here – she was hurt that he hadn't tried to find her. That's what a real man would do: drive at high speed up to Cloud's Hill and sweep her up in his sleek dark car ... Cloud's Hill – what did he mean when he said he had come to see her? She certainly hadn't seen him. Then she remembered. Two weeks ago Jason and Liz had dropped her home after dinner in Sondra and Barney's house. And outside Cloud's Hill, she and Jason had hugged each other. Cleo could remember how nice it had been to feel her brother's arms around her, and how she'd waved him and Liz as they drove away, and there had been a strange car on the forecourt. Could it have been Tyler's?

Tyler thought Jason was her lover! No wonder he was so mad. He had come to Cloud's Hill and he'd seen her hugging another man, and had rushed off in a rage. That must have been how it happened, she thought joyously. He didn't hate her after all! Quite the opposite.

But how could he believe she'd be interested in anyone else? Idiot. He should have trusted her and if he was any sort of man, he'd rush back down here and tell her it didn't matter and he loved her and they could sort it out ...

Cleo stopped. She was doing it again, living in the fantasy of the past, like Eileen had said. Tyler wasn't a knight on a white horse, he was a man who'd been crazy about her and who now assumed that she had no time for him any more because she was seeing another man.

Only one person could sort this out, and it wasn't him. If anyone had to be a knight on a charger, it had to be Cleo.

She swivelled on her heels and marched fiercely back between the potholes and into the house, her heels making a racket on the grainy parquet of the hall.

'Tyler,' she said, 'I want to talk to you.'

He was sitting on the bottom step of the big staircase and he looked bone-weary. 'Talk away.'

Momentarily disadvantaged because she was now looking down on him like some giant Valkyrie, Cleo marched over and took a deep breath.

'I walked out on you in your suite because I got upset when I saw what you were going to do with my home. But I should have given you a chance to explain. I came here to tell you that and that I am sorry.'

'And that's why you came?' he asked softly.

His face was unreadable but Cleo knew pretty much what he'd say next. Forget it, Cleo, or something like it.

'Yes,' she said proudly. 'I screwed up and I'm not ashamed to admit it. I was crazy about you but I guess I'll have to get over you.' Her courage began to go at that point. He was saying nothing; there was no warmth in his eyes. It was hopeless, she should never have come back. He didn't care about her or whether she'd been hugging her brother or another man. 'And you don't know what you're missing, Tyler Roth, because I'm honest and upfront and we could have had a wonderful love, but you didn't have the courage to ask me how I felt about you. I'd have told you I loved you and that the man I was hugging two weeks ago outside Cloud's Hill was my brother Jason. But you've missed the boat, Mr Roth. Goodbye.' She mentally added the words, 'So there!'

Turning with a flourish, her heel caught on a loose bit of parquet and she felt herself fall backwards until two firm arms caught her.

'Do you make a habit of falling into men's arms?' Tyler asked softly.

Cleo caught her breath and then lost it again, because of the way he was looking at her, with a kind of wild joy. She was still caught against him and his mouth was inches away from hers, almost moving as if to kiss her, like the romantic hero of her beloved Rodriguez books . . .

'What the hell?' she said suddenly, and she reached up, pulled his head close and kissed him.

'I didn't want you to get into this without knowing that I'm not your average girl,' Cleo said when they came up for air.

Tyler smiled at her lazily, a smile that sent a shiver through Cleo's entire body. 'I never thought you were.'

EPILOGUE

Four months later.

Far below, Mel could see Carrickwell spread out in the dark winter evening like a velvet cloak covered with twinkling fairy lights. Fairy lights made her think of all her unfinished Christmas tasks: tasks she should be completing instead of lounging in the comfort of the Cloud's Hill hot tub with Caroline, Leah and Cyn, sipping café mochas and chatting.

Outside, there was snow on Mount Carraig and a December bite to the air, but even with the sliding doors opened, the hot tub room was gloriously warm.

'I should feel very guilty to be lying here,' Mel said, stretching one leg out luxuriously in the water. 'It's only a week to Christmas. I ought to be rushing round the shops buying Santa presents, and panicking about emergency gifts for everyone.'

'Me too,' said Cyn. 'I went shopping last week and in the end, I didn't buy a thing for anyone else, which is awful. Just more clothes for me.' Her eyes shone and she looked so happy and alive, that everyone smiled at her pure pleasure. 'Did you know you could buy silk bras with bows holding the two sides together? I got two. Imagine, me with two silk, bow-tied bras! I never thought I'd see the day.'

The other three laughed.

Mel thought that the change in Cyn was incredible. The first time they'd met, she'd found it hard to see how even Leah could rescue the scared, lonely woman buried in self-loathing. Her weight hadn't been Cyn's big problem: it was the fact that she thought she deserved nothing better.

But Leah, with her genius when it came to troubled people, had somehow managed to make Cyn believe in herself and give her hope. Cyn would never be a sylph, but she was no longer dangerously obese. She was healthy enough to go to the gym, and, most importantly, she was enjoying her life.

So much had changed in all their lives, Mel reflected, and it was down to Leah.

'Daisy said she was thinking of selling lingerie in Georgia's Tiara,' Caroline revealed. 'Which would be lovely. She buys such beautiful, feminine clothes, I'd love to see what sort of lingerie she'd pick. And all the local men would be thrilled because they could just go into the shop, mutter that they needed a Christmas gift, Daisy could hand them a pretty box, and that would be it.'

'Is that what Graham's doing for Christmas?' teased Mel gently. Cyn wasn't the only one who sparkled with life these days. Caroline and Graham had managed to come through the agony of infidelity stronger than ever.

If Mel hadn't seen the pain it had put her friend through, she'd have almost said that Graham's affair had strengthened their marriage. It was so easy for people to fall into the trap of taking each other for granted, but being aware of what he could lose had clearly given Graham a shock.

'We've moved on,' Caroline had explained earlier that afternoon as they swam laps in the pool. 'It's different now. I'm different and so's Graham, but there's more respect for each other. Does that make sense? We both know we have to work at our marriage, but it's worth it.'

Now Caroline laughed and said: 'Graham is not the sort of guy to walk into a woman's clothes shop and buy any sort of lingerie, believe me. Is Adrian?'

Mel thought with affection about her husband. He'd walk through fire for her, and was enough of a new man not to blush at the notion of buying lingerie. He knew what she liked and he knew what size she was: the problem was money. Even though she was now working part time, they still couldn't afford luxuries.

They were saving to convert their hopeless oil central heating to gas, so bow-tied bras were low on their list of priorities. And Carrie's Christmas list for Santa was now nearly as long as her sister's. Santa would need several sleighs and extra nuts for the reindeers to bring everything Sarah wanted from the North Pole.

Mel had finally tracked down all the Santa presents and everyone else would have to make do with lesser gifts as a result. Well, it was a time for children, wasn't it?

'Adrian wouldn't mind going into a shop to buy underwear, but between paying for Santa, and saving for the new heating system, we're trying to economise,' she said truthfully. If Leah hadn't insisted on Mel coming to Cloud's Hill for a free day of pampering with Caroline, she wouldn't be here either. Working three mornings a week audio typing in Carrickwell Secretarial Services wasn't a big money-spinner, although Mel felt a thrill of excitement at the wonderful plan Leah had come up with for the New Year.

In Leah's usual gentle way, she'd taken Mel into her study earlier that day and explained how she was going to need more staff in January when Cleo left. First, Cleo was going off for her month in Australia with her friend Trish.

'Tyler still can't quite believe she's going away without him,' Leah reflected with amusement. 'He's used to getting his own way. Cleo is good for him.'

Mel grinned at the idea of the handsome Tyler, whom she still hadn't met, up against the iron determination of Cleo Malin.

After her holiday, Cleo was going to the Manhattan Roth to enter their trainee hotel manager programme.

'Tyler convinced her to apply for it, but she insisted that he didn't do one thing to help and she used the name Malley on her application form,' Leah said. 'She said she wanted to get the trainee position fair and square, and she did. Which brings me to my staffing problems. I know you only want to work part time, and I know you've no experience of reception, but I think you're just what we want here. Would you consider doing a few hours here every week? You'd be such a welcome addition to Cloud's Hill, Mel. Do think about it.'

Mel had said she'd think about it, but she merely wanted to tell Adrian. Working in Cloud's Hill was a no-brainer. Mel would love it.

'It's a pity Daisy's not here,' Cyn said, finishing her café mocha. 'I do miss her. I hate going to the gym on my own. But she and her mum got a fabulous deal for two weeks in Morocco.'

'Her aunt's gone with them, hasn't she?' asked Mel.

Cyn nodded. 'They've never gone away together – can you believe that? Her mother wants to go on a painting holiday in Italy this summer, and she's trying to convince Daisy to go. She says there are lots of nice unattached men on painting trips.'

'I thought Daisy wanted to go to Peru on an adventure holiday,' Mel said, surprised. 'That's what she told me last time we met.'

Daisy had entered into singledom with gusto, and she astonished Mel with her energy for new pursuits. In the past few months, Daisy had tried scuba diving ('not for me. I should have realised I don't like putting my head under the shower,' she'd said ruefully), salsa dancing ('fantastic!') and hiking. Salsa dancing appealed to her sense of rhythm and fashion, while hiking was so wonderfully physical that Daisy adored it.

'You ache in places where you didn't know you had places,' she said, 'but it's so satisfying. I love it. Actually, I've got some brochures for adventure holidays where you can walk along the Inca Trail to Machu Picchu,' she told Mel. 'I'd love it and people of all ages do it. You've got to be careful – it's so high, you can develop altitude sickness, but there's no telling who'll get it, so an old dear like myself can do the trail.'

'If you're an old dear at thirty-five, I'm in need of a Zimmer frame,' Mel had teased her.

'Perhaps she's going to do both,' Leah said, 'Peru and the painting holiday. It's wonderful to see her so happy.'

The others nodded. Despite her successful career, there was still something vulnerable about Daisy, and the people who loved her wanted to protect her.

Mel looked at the time. Nearly six. She had to go soon because her mum was taking care of the girls and Mel had promised to be back by six thirty.

There was just one more thing she wanted to mention to Leah. Now that she was going to work in Cloud's Hill, she could come up with plans. 'Leah, I had this great idea,' Mel said slowly. 'You know when you told us about the Cloud's Hill in America and the charity work they do? Well, we could do that here. I read about this woman with two autistic children and how she gets some respite care during the year so she can have a holiday, but she says she's too shattered to actually go anywhere. I thought –'

'Mel, now you're scaring me!' Leah interrupted. 'I read that article. It's in one of the new magazines Cleo got for the chill room. I only saw it yesterday and I had just the same thought.'

'Those parents could come here,' Mel said.

'Exactly,' Leah said. 'Is that a yes for you joining the team, then?'

Mel laughed. 'Yes,' she said. 'But I've got to stop making decisions without telling Adrian first.'

They talked enthusiastically about the new idea, then lapsed into silence again.

Leah stared out at the landscape and thought how much joy the Carrickwell Cloud's Hill had given her. She touched the crystal necklace around her neck. It was her talisman, another reminder of her beloved Jesse. He'd have loved this place, she thought: loved Carrickwell's sense of peace and healing. Christmas was a bittersweet time for her. She loved the festivities, but ached inside at the thought of all she'd lost. She missed her son so much.

Yet Jesse was with her, in her heart always and forever. She hoped that if he could see her now, he was proud of his mother.